KU-526-352

Michael Cordy worked for ten years in marketing. His first novel, *The Miracle Strain*, also published by Corgi, was sold in over twenty-five countries and the film rights were bought by Disney for more than $1.5 million. He lives in London with his wife, Jenny.

Also by Michael Cordy

THE MIRACLE STRAIN

and published by Corgi Books

CRIME ZERO

Michael Cordy

CORGI BOOKS

CRIME ZERO
A CORGI BOOK : 0 552 14604 8

Originally published in Great Britain by Bantam Press,
a division of Transworld Publishers

PRINTING HISTORY
Bantam Press edition published 1999
Corgi edition published 2000

3 5 7 9 10 8 6 4 2

Set in 10½/12pt Garamond by Falcon Oast Graphic Art

Corgi Books are published by Transworld Publishers,
61–63 Uxbridge Road, London W5 5SA,
a division of The Random House Group Ltd,
in Australia by Random House Australia (Pty) Ltd,
20 Alfred Street, Milsons Point, Sydney, NSW 2061, Australia,
in New Zealand by Random House New Zealand Ltd,
18 Poland Road, Glenfield, Auckland 10, New Zealand
and in South Africa by Random House (Pty) Ltd,
Endulini, 5a Jubilee Road, Parktown 2193, South Africa.

Reproduced, printed and bound in Great Britain by
Cox & Wyman Ltd, Reading, Berks.

For my mother and father,
Betty and John Cordy

Acknowledgements

My greatest debt is to my wife, Jenny, who has always been my true partner in crime. From the start she helped research the plot and characters, developing the good ideas and editing out the bad. Even at the end, when disaster struck and I thought I'd lost the entire completed typescript, she alone kept calm and recovered the computer file.

The other major thank-you is to my editor at Transworld, Bill Scott-Kerr, who invested an unusual amount of time, effort and patience to vastly improve the story.

To research *Crime Zero* the following sources were invaluable: *A Mind to Crime* by Anne Moir and David Jessel, *On Aggression* by Konrad Lorenz, *Virus X* by Dr Frank Ryan, and *In the Blood* by Steve Jones. For providing first-hand scientific advice I am grateful to Susan Robinson and Sejal Patel, both of whom used their respective Ph.D.s to weed out and modify my more fanciful inventions. I thank Betty Cordy for reading numerous versions of the book and for providing me with consistent feedback and encouragement. I also thank Bill Reinka, Simon Hoggart and Richard Cordy for their contributions.

Last, but certainly not least, I thank my excellent agent, Patrick Walsh.

'Certainly there is one gene which is shared by most criminals – and its complete DNA sequence is known. It is the single small gene, carried on the Y chromosome, which makes its carriers male. Most criminals are men: the criminality gene has been found! Needless to say, no one suggests that geneticists should do anything about it.'

STEVE JONES, PROFESSOR OF GENETICS, UNIVERSITY COLLEGE LONDON

PROLOGUE

San Quentin State Penitentiary, California.
Wednesday, 29 October 2008. 3.11 a.m.

It wasn't his pain that denied him sleep. It wasn't his fear that filmed his skin in clammy sweat and made him rise from drenched sheets to piss for the tenth time that night. And it wasn't his suffering that urged him to take his own life after seven years on death row.

It was *their* pain that made him do these things; their fear, their suffering.

Something had changed deep within him. He didn't know what it was or why it had happened; only that it was somehow fundamental, irrevocable.

Karl Axelman had taken many lives in his fifty-six years, but he had never once considered taking his own. He had always been untroubled by his past, savouring his conquests, using his photographic memory to summon up some exquisite detail of the girls he had raped, tortured and murdered for his pleasure. But now their faces came unbidden, tormenting him day and night. For the first time in his life he could hear their pain, smell their fear and understand their suffering.

Returning to the bed in his five feet by ten feet cell in San Quentin's East Block he stared up through the bars at the faulty lamp in the corridor outside. But he found no comfort in the light. The beacon only exacerbated his distress, intensifying the gloom that surrounded him.

Sitting up, he looked around the cell that was his universe: the stainless-steel basin and toilet in the corner; the shelf above the sheet-metal bed, stacked high with neatly ordered newspapers. He turned to check his pillow again. Strands of grey flecked the yellowed linen. His thick hair, although silvered with age, had always symbolized his strength, but now it fell in clumps from his scalp. His handsome face, once bait for his prey, was pitted with weeping acne more acute than any teenager's. Yet as he clasped his clammy palms together, and his pounding heart drowned out the sounds of despair from the neighbouring cells, he ignored these physical indignities.

He was aware only of dry-mouthed, heart-palpitating anxiety – an emotion he had never experienced before. Unwanted images of vulnerable flesh intruded on his mind, arousing the familiar desire to control and humiliate. Yet even as his erection hardened his whole body crawled with revulsion. And the acid bile of guilt rose in his throat.

Reaching up to the narrow shelf above his bed, Axelman's hands shook as he selected a copy of the *San Francisco Examiner*. Except for a shoebox at one end, the shelf was bowed beneath the weight of crisply folded newspapers. Knowing what was happening in the outside world had always given Axelman a sense of control, allowing him to imagine he was influencing events. But no more.

Carefully unfolding the paper, he ignored the warmongering headlines about Iraq and the latest polls on the first ever female presidential candidate running for office in a week's time. These issues no longer concerned him. He would be gone by then. There was only one question to resolve.

He turned to page three of the paper and studied the flash photograph of a man carrying a naked girl wrapped in his jacket out of a cemetery late at night. The headline read, FBI MINDHUNTER SAVES VICTIM NUMBER FOUR. Axelman stared at the man. Then he reached for the shoebox containing all the personal belongings he was allowed to keep with him. The old colour photograph was on the top of the letters and other paraphernalia. Squinting in the flickering light, he compared the faded photograph with the newspaper picture, as he had done countless times before. Finally he reread the text in the article, noting once again the age and the surname.

Axelman sighed. He was sure he was right. But even if he was wrong he would still confess all the details to this FBI agent for the first time. He had once savoured frustrating the police and prolonging the mourning and pain of the relatives by keeping the location of the bodies to himself. But now their pain was his pain and he could no longer keep the information secret. This man could do something with the knowledge.

Listening for the footsteps of approaching

guards, Axelman carefully replaced the photo and newspaper. He then knelt on the floor and lifted one corner of the bed. Slipping two long fingers into the hollow base of the tubular leg, he extracted a large steel biker's belt buckle from the chewing gum wedging it in place. The pin had been removed, leaving a squared-off figure of eight about two inches wide and three inches long.

The buckle had cost him six packs of cigarettes eighteen months ago; the con who'd sold it to him had smiled while pocketing the Marlboro. With no pin it was useless and harmless, but over time he had chamfered one bevelled outer edge against the concrete floor, the iron bed and even the bars of his cell, filing the end into a crude but keen blade. At first, sharpening the buckle was something to do – a small act of rebellion – but now it had taken on a new significance.

Sitting on the bed he passed his thumb over the nicked edge of the blade and drew blood. His atrophied testicles involuntarily retreated into his body, and for a moment Axelman wished he could wait for the executioner. Release would be so much easier if administered by a different hand. But this wasn't just about release; it was about punishment. He himself must remove the source of his dark urges.

Rocking back and forth on the edge of the bed Axelman didn't bother to lie down. Sleep wouldn't come and if it did he would gain no sanctuary there. He touched the buckle-blade again, reassured by its presence. Soon it would be dawn and later he would unburden his soul to the FBI agent. He could do no more to find peace. After that he would play out the final act. And then, redemption or no redemption, the torture would end.

PART 1

PROJECT CONSCIENCE

1

His head aches and he wants to go home, but he still waits in the cemetery under cover of the short fir tree. The damp bark smells as strong as any perfume. It is 1.57 a.m. The two San Francisco Police Department officers left an hour ago. After three days of staking out the area they and their replacements have been recalled to follow up other leads. The police say they will return in the morning but he knows they have lost the faith. Fourteen-year-old Tammy Lewis is missing and they are concerned that she will end up like the other three. Special Agent Luke Decker should leave too; he has only adviser status here and other cases are piling up on his desk at Quantico.

But Decker can't go yet. He knows deep in his gut that the killer will return here at night and bring the girl with him – perhaps even alive.

The night air is cool on his face and above him, through the branches of the fir, a crescent moon gazes down. Seventeen miles from San Francisco and nine miles from Oakland, the Gates of Heaven Catholic cemetery is still. Nothing moves and even nearby Interstate 80 is silent.

He retrieves a pair of night-vision glasses from his coat and rereads the inscription on the head-stone twenty yards away:

SALLY ANNE JENNINGS
TAKEN 3 AUGUST 2008
AGED 15 YEARS
You were taken from us too soon.
But we shall meet again
in a better place.

Decker grinds his jaw, remembering the crime-scene photos of Sally Anne's violated body. The killer's most recent victim must also be his last.

Car tyres on gravel break the silence. He turns to his right and sees a Domino's pizza van pull into the cemetery's deserted car lot. Sweat breaks out on his forehead. Decker knows the psychological profile of the killer because he wrote it. And the pizza van fits. His heart is beating fast now, but he feels no triumph about being right again. No excitement at the chase. Just weary sorrow and a vague disquiet that he should know the mind of a killer so well.

A sudden scream from the van rips through the night. It is short and quickly muffled, but Decker crumples inside, feeling her pain and terror himself. He reaches for his cell phone and calls the incident number.

He whispers urgently that the unsub is here. He needs back-up.

A sleepy detective snaps awake. 'Two squad cars will be there in ten minutes - max,' he promises.

The van's rear doors open and a muscular young

man with red hair wearing a black T-shirt drags something white out of the back and drops it on the gravel. Decker realizes that ten minutes will not be soon enough. The silent white bundle is moving, and even before he puts the night-vision glasses to his eyes Decker knows it's a naked girl. Tammy Lewis is gagged and bound, her eyes round with terror. The young man is strong; he lifts her easily over his shoulder and carries her towards the cemetery.

Decker reaches for his gun and releases the safety. He has won the FBI shooting competition at Quantico with the SIG semi-automatic every year for the last five years, but he dislikes using the gun for real. It means he's failed. But he has no choice now. If he does nothing the man will carry Tammy Lewis to Sally Anne's grave, where he will lay her down, torture and rape her. Then, when he is satisfied, he will kill her and defile her body. Decker knows this with a gut-wrenching certainty as absolute as if he's already witnessed the crime.

He waits for the man to lay Tammy down on the grave and start to untie her ankles before coming up behind him. Decker is ten feet away when he sees a knife flash in the man's hand.

'FBI!' he shouts. His voice sounds alien in the stillness of the night. 'Drop the knife, put your hands up and back away from her.'

Crouching over his victim the red-haired man looks over his shoulder, his long face surprised and uncertain. He hesitates.

'Now!' orders Decker. But the man doesn't drop the knife. He turns and raises it high into the air. The curved blade mirrors the white sickle of the moon as a bellow of rage cuts through the darkness. Then, in one furious movement, he brings it scything down towards the girl with the force of a guillotine . . .

'The defence calls Dr Kathryn Kerr.'

It was her name that jolted Luke Decker from the events in the graveyard nine weeks before and back to the warm stuffy chamber of the San Francisco appeal court. Above the judge's bench the clock showed 10.07 and the calendar below it the date: Wednesday, 29 October 2008. The hushed oak-panelled courtroom carried every sound, but when the woman's name was called Decker couldn't believe he'd heard it right.

What the hell was Kathy Kerr doing here?

Reorienting himself, Decker blinked his green eyes and ran a hand though his cropped blond hair. Shifting in his chair he looked around the panelled court. The judge, a bald man with a permanent pained frown, sat at the front of the chamber with both the prosecution and defence teams facing him on either side. Decker sat with the prosecution behind the District Attorney. This wasn't a full trial and there were few people in the public gallery behind him, except some junior press. No relatives of the dead girls had come, but Decker gained some satisfaction from noting that Tammy Lewis's family wouldn't have been among them. At least she had been saved.

Turning to his right, the first person he noticed was Wayne Tice, sitting beside his defence attorney. The killer's right arm was still in a sling from where Decker had shot him in the shoulder.

22

Tice caught his eye and flashed his crooked teeth in a cold, unrepentant smile. Luke ignored him. The man had been found guilty and condemned to death almost a month ago. This hearing was an attempt by his defence team to gain Tice leniency and a chance for rehabilitation. As the FBI forensic psychologist responsible for catching Tice, Special Agent Decker had been asked by the DA to comment on his psychological state and ensure that the man wasn't allowed back on the streets.

Now it appeared that Kathy Kerr, the woman he had last seen almost ten years ago, was here to help Tice.

He watched the woman take her seat and be sworn in. Decker couldn't help staring at her, although she seemed oblivious to his presence. She was slimmer and her glasses were gone, no doubt replaced by contacts, and her navy suit was smarter than the jeans and T-shirt she'd favoured in their Harvard days.

'Please state your name, occupation and qualifications,' requested Tice's attorney, Ricardo Latona.

The witness unconsciously raised a hand and attempted to run it through her dark hair before remembering it was tied back in a French plait. A flash of memory intruded on Decker's thoughts. No doubt she had tried to restrain her cascade of unruly curls in order to look authoritative. Decker guessed that many people still underestimated the formidable intellect behind the packaging of open smile, Celtic fair skin, freckles and pale-blue eyes.

'My name is Dr Kathryn Kerr and I am a research fellow in behavioural genetics at Stanford University.

I have a degree in microbiology from Cambridge University in England and a Ph.D. in behavioural genetics from Harvard.'

Her voice had lost none of its soft Edinburgh burr. In many ways Kathy Kerr had hardly changed and Decker wondered whether she would think the same of his appearance. The woman he had known all those years ago still seemed at once vulnerable and wild – both of which were only half true. He couldn't help wondering whether she used her maiden name professionally or because she was still unmarried.

'Dr Kerr, could you briefly outline the nature of your work, please?' requested the attorney.

'I specialize in the genetic science of criminal and anti-social behaviour. Apart from teaching at the university, most of my research work at Stanford is funded by the biotech company ViroVector Solutions and the Federal Bureau of Investigation.'

Decker raised an eyebrow. He didn't know she'd returned from England, let alone that she was working with his people at the Bureau. He wondered how long she'd been at Stanford.

'I realize that many aspects of your work with the FBI will be confidential,' said Latona, 'but isn't it true that one aspect of your research involves identifying the genetic risk factors for criminal behaviour?'

'Yes.'

Her eyes met Luke's for the first time. He tried to read her gaze but for once his famed powers of perception failed him. Although he had no idea that she was part of the Bureau project to explore the

24

genetic roots of crime, he had heard of it. Everyone had. After all, nature not nurture was the new religion at the FBI. Criminals were born not made, so the senior hierarchy believed, particularly Madeline Naylor, the first female director in the Bureau's long and illustrious history.

Decker had always disagreed with this philosophy. In his experience criminals – and their victims – were shaped by their backgrounds. At thirty-five, Decker was one of the youngest-ever heads of the behavioural sciences division at the FBI's training academy in Quantico, Virginia. His unit was once the glamour division of the Bureau; Hollywood films had been based on its exploits. It specialized in helping police forces target suspects for serial killings, bombings or other apparently motiveless crimes by developing psychological profiles of possible offenders based on the methodology of the crime.

Under the new regime, however, the behavioural sciences division had become ghettoized. Physiology not psychology was where all the money went now. The criminal brain was far more interesting than the criminal mind. PET brain scans, adrenalin levels, skin conductivity, theta activity and serotonin neurotransmitters were seen as the future of crime control – crowned, of course, by the promises of genetic science.

The new ideology had prompted Decker to tender his resignation last month and accept the offer of a professorship at Berkeley to teach criminal psychology. He had done his time on the front line – ten years in the minds of the sickest killers had taken its toll – he could achieve more now by training and inspiring a new generation of mindhunters. His mother's sudden death eighteen months before had also made him realize that he hadn't seen enough of her or his grandfather in the last ten years. He had been living out of a tiny apartment in Washington DC, travelling the country and failing to put down roots. It was time for him to settle back here on the West Coast, where his grandfather still lived, and sort out his life rather than trying to save everybody else's.

McCloud, the deputy director of the FBI, had refused his resignation, asking him to reconsider. But with every day that Decker stayed, the more he knew he had to go. He had already picked his successor. So after finishing off this case, and interviewing Karl Axelman in San Quentin this afternoon, he would return to Quantico and tell McCloud his decision was final.

'Thank you for agreeing to come here today, Dr Kerr,' said the defence lawyer with a smile. Ricardo Latona was a squat man with thinning dark hair. He turned to the judge. 'The reason we requested this hearing and the reason we asked Dr Kerr to give evidence today is that we believe a new approach to crime is long overdue.

'It is now apparent from all the research that biology is a central factor in crime, interacting with social, cultural and economic influences. This knowledge raises key questions. If someone is biologically predisposed to crime, should he be punished or helped? If he is sick, do we *dare* to treat him? Or do we feel that treatment somehow excuses "criminality" and robs us of the need to punish? Is society civilized enough to equate

26

justice with the merciful treatment of a disease, or must it always be linked to punishment?'

Decker watched Latona pause and turn to Tice, a man who had abducted and murdered three girls, and would have murdered a fourth if Decker hadn't prevented him. 'Wayne Tice has done wrong,' said Latona in his soothing, reasonable voice. 'No-one denies that, and he has been convicted of terrible crimes. But we intend to show that they were the result of genetically inherited biochemical factors beyond his control, for which a just, humane society would seek medical treatment, not the death penalty.'

Decker groaned. He was no advocate of the death penalty, so long as dangerous people were kept off the street. But the idea that genes determined violent behaviour was abhorrent to him and totally at odds with his work over the past fifteen years. Criminals already had enough excuses to avoid taking responsibility for their actions, without blaming their choice of parents too.

'Dr Kerr, would you please outline the key scientific evidence which demonstrates that biology is a central factor in violent behaviour and crime.'

Kathy Kerr cleared her throat and paused for a moment. 'Let me start with a few facts. First, biology is only *one* of several interrelated factors – including cultural, social and economic influences – that lie at the root of violent crime. But the more we have learnt over recent years the more important we now understand it to be. Second, the biggest biological factor is gender. The world over, it is *men* who commit over ninety per cent of all violent crimes.'

Decker thought back to their Harvard days, nine years ago. His criminal psychology Ph.D. on using patterns of behaviour to diagnose an offender's state of mind and determine his likelihood of re-offending, rather than relying solely on the patient's own opinion, had been much praised. But Kathy Kerr's Ph.D. paper on behavioural genetics entitled 'Why men commit ninety per cent of all violent crime' had been so ground-breaking that it had been published in *Nature*, one of the world's two most prestigious science journals. He hadn't agreed with it, but he'd had to concede it was brilliant.

Kathy continued, warming to her subject. 'The male brain is different from the female brain, and understanding these differences is pivotal to understanding the small subset of criminally violent males. A chemical mixture of neuro-transmitters and hormones drives the brain. Let me deal with neurotransmitters first. These are the chemical messengers controlling the flow of electrical messages in the network of nerve cells that allow the complex neural networks of the brain to communicate with each other. They influence and facilitate the thoughts of our mind and the actions of our bodies.

'Now, there are four key neurotransmitters. Three of them – dopamine, adrenalin and epinephrine - are very similar. They fuel the brain, stimulating many of our emotional and physical impulses such as the "fight or flight" reflex. The fourth is serotonin; this is the vital brake that inhibits and modifies our waking behaviour. Its specific function is to link the impulsive limbic part of the brain with the more civilized cortex. Put simply, without serotonin we would have no conscience or inhibitions.

'While neurotransmitters are responsible for the instigation of specific actions, hormones influence the broad pattern of behaviour, although the interaction between them is complex. Again put simply, the higher the level of androgens, particularly testosterone, the higher a man's aggression and the lower his empathy with the pain or feelings of others.'

Nodding, Latona stepped in. 'So overall the male brain is more specifically wired and fuelled for aggression, impulsiveness and crime than the female brain. But this doesn't mean that all men are violent criminals . . .'

'Of course not,' said Kathy with a wry smile. 'Violent criminals are the small minority of men well outside the norm for whom these natural differences have become amplified, exaggerated. There exists a range of physiological tests on which they can be reliably assessed versus the norm. For example, we can measure levels of MAO in the blood, an enzyme which acts as a marker for the neurotransmitter serotonin. And we can monitor levels of brain activity with PET scans and electroencephalograms—'

'OK,' interrupted Latona, 'so violent criminals are physiologically different. But how exactly does genetics fit into this picture?'

'The recent invention of the Genescope has enabled scientists to read an organism's entire sequence of genetic instructions. By conducting aggression studies on primates, my team and I have identified seventeen key genes that code for the production of critical hormones and neurotransmitters in male primates – including humans.

'These interdependent genes effectively determine man's aggressive behaviour. And depending on how each gene's promoter – or volume control – is set, we can tell how loudly that gene will express its instructions. For example, we can predict dangerously low levels of serotonin or high levels of testosterone by studying the calibration of these genes. What we discovered was that although everyone's gene settings change in reaction to particular stimuli, almost every individual has different base settings. If you see these seventeen key genes as cards, then every man is dealt a slightly different hand.'

'Is it true that although this work was done originally on apes it is now relevant to humans?' Latona asked.

'Yes, much of my recent work confirms these findings in men.'

'So a man's genes determine if he's going to become a criminal or not?'

'To an extent. But I stress what I said earlier: environmental, social and cultural factors also have an influence. However, the crucial point is that humans are different from animals because they possess consciousness. This means that they are aware of the consequences of their actions. So regardless of any genetic predisposition, free will still plays a significant part in the choices humans make. But certainly some men, regardless of other influences, will find it more difficult than others to behave as society expects them to. The genes they inherited from their parents give them little choice.'

Decker smiled. She sounded convincing. But then she'd always been a good teacher, with a flair for simplifying the most complex problem. As far as she was concerned the world was one big puzzle that, if she thought about it hard enough and long enough, could be broken down into its component parts to find the one overarching rule that explained everything. To her the whole was never greater than the sum of its parts. And that had been their problem. To him the whole was everything. He could never understand how humanity could be reduced to a line of programming. In the short time Kathy Kerr and Decker had been lovers during that last summer at Harvard they had spent most of their time in heated argument. The only area where they hadn't been incompatible was in bed. He thought of the five or six half-serious relationships he'd had in the last nine years and quickly realized that, despite or perhaps because of the friction, none shone as vividly in his memory as those few summer months with her.

'You're aware of Wayne Tice's family history, aren't you, Dr Kerr?' asked the lawyer, pulling out a large board and placing it on an easel by the judge. The network of names and lines on the board formed a simple family tree.

'Yes. That's why I agreed to be involved in this case.'

As the lawyer turned to the chart, Luke knew what was coming. He too had studied Tice's family and shook his head as Latona explained that the spidery lines leading to boldly typed names revealed how four generations of Tice men had, with two individual exceptions, been drawn to crime. All were famed for their tempers and aggressive drive. 'Think twice before you marry a Tice' was a watchword in their hometown.

The chart infuriated Decker. What did Tice have to complain about? He still had both parents and he had a brother. Apart from his mother being domineering and his successful brother making him feel inadequate, Tice had had it better than most. Decker would have given anything to have a whole family and to have known his father.

Fluent in Russian, Captain Richard Decker had been an interrogator with the US Navy at the height of the Cold War. As a child Decker had often fantasized about his father using his psychological skills to prise a piece of information vital to the safety of the free world from some recalcitrant Red admiral. Decker's mother used to reassure him that his own uncanny and unsettling ability to see into the minds of others must have been inherited from his brilliant father. But of course the Russians hadn't killed Captain Richard Decker; some street punk in San Francisco had. That was one of the reasons Decker had joined the Bureau – to fight the war on the streets.

Turning back to Kathy, the lawyer asked, 'Dr Kerr, you have applied your battery of tests to my client – and his immediate living family.'

'That's correct. I conducted a gene scan on Wayne Tice and a series of ancillary tests, checking serotonin, testosterone and adrenalin levels. I also gave him a PET scan to probe brain activity on his frontal lobe. Tice's readings put him in the top five per cent in terms of propensity to violence. His male relations also have dangerous readings, although not nearly as high.'

'So would it be fair to say that he and most of the menfolk in his family, through no fault of their own, carry a gene calibration that makes them predisposed to aggressive behaviour and crime?'

'Yes, but—'

'But, broadly speaking,' interrupted the lawyer, keen not to let nuances of interpretation cloud his crucial point, 'isn't it the case that Wayne Tice dances to the beat of a more violent drum?'

'Yes,' said Kathy cautiously.

Latona smiled and turned to the judge. 'So, your Honour, Wayne Tice was born with a particular set of genes, calibrated in such a way that he had to commit murder.'

'That's not what I said,' protested Kathy. 'I am talking about predisposition. No more, no less. Ultimately a person decides—'

'Excuse me, your Honour,' the lawyer deftly corrected himself, before the frowning judge could intervene. 'He was *predisposed* to commit violent crime. But the point is this: how can Wayne Tice be punished for his actions? He should be counselled, not executed. He was only doing what he was born to do.'

Latona paused and turned back to Kathy Kerr.

'How can we put a young man to death for simply doing what came naturally?'

2

After giving evidence to Latona and then the
District Attorney, Kathy Kerr retook her seat. Glad
her session was over, she began to relax. Unless
she was teaching she always felt uncomfortable
speaking in public, especially in court, where any
words could be twisted to suit a purpose. After
Latona had finished with her the DA had given her
a tough time, but she'd expected that. Latona had
angered her, though, trying to use her evidence to
shift all responsibility for the horrific murders from
Tice. She had only agreed to testify because Tice
was a classic case; and he would make an excellent
research subject, assuming that ViroVector
received the expected FDA approval to begin
Project Conscience Phase Two efficacy trials.
Kathy didn't support the notion that Tice's genes
allowed him to shirk all responsibility for his
actions.

There was one other reason she had felt uncomfortable giving her testimony. She had known
that Luke Decker was going to be here.

Watching the tall FBI agent take her place on the
witness stand she was surprised at how much he'd

34

changed. His appearance was similar: the lean physique a little broader perhaps, the blond hair shorter and the face more defined, but those penetrating green eyes had lost none of their sensitive intelligence. It was his bearing that was different. He had more presence somehow; his gait was more confident, as if the hunted younger man she had once known had now become the hunter.

Like most of America she'd seen the press coverage of Decker carrying Tammy Lewis from the graveyard near Oakland, his face a mask of rage. She'd recognized that look from years ago when his night terrors used to wake her at three in the morning.

Back then, of course, they had been lovers. She'd known Luke Decker was different from that first time she'd walked into him in the Harvard library, knocking his pile of books all over the floor. Each book had been about the darker side of humanity, from biographies of Jeffrey Dahmer and Ted Bundy to textbooks on the criminal mind. But as she'd apologized he'd just laughed and piled his books up under his chin, making a joke about how heavy a bit of night-time reading could be.

Even then she had discouraged men's advances, refusing to be distracted from her work, but she could still taste the disappointment when those soft green eyes had examined her, smiled again and moved on. Decker had made no attempt to exploit the occasion, so she'd had to stammer something about helping him carry his books – the least she could do after knocking them over.

'If you like.' He'd shrugged with a casualness that had both frustrated and delighted her.

35

They couldn't agree on anything they discussed, but within two weeks they made love, and for those precious, magical moments they were in total accord. After that they had become inseparable, but he'd always seemed to retain some small part of himself. Kathy felt she only caught a true glimpse of his soul during those terrifying nights when he would sit bolt upright in bed, drenched in sweat, his eyes wide open. He would start speaking to some invisible presence directly in front of him, his voice angry: 'You wanted control, didn't you? That was why you did it. You didn't actually want them dead. You only wanted slaves who would do whatever you wanted without ruining the fantasy. That's right,' he'd conclude, having solved some puzzle troubling his subconscious. Then he would lie down again. At first she'd tried to soothe him, until she realized that he'd remained asleep throughout. In the mornings he would remember nothing, except resolving something that had been worrying him. It took her weeks to realize that he had an ability to understand man's baser desires which went beyond normal experience. And that this ability haunted him.

His mother told him his intuition came from his father, but Kathy knew Decker felt it was more than just intuition. He was scared that somehow he was tainted.

While still at Harvard he would follow national cases and write in with advice to the relevant police authorities or even the FBI. She'd always felt he was driven by some inner force, trying to exorcize something deep within himself –

something she couldn't reach, let alone soothe.

She could handle the arguments and the fact that they couldn't agree on anything, especially their views on the roots of crime. It was his reserve she found the hardest to take. He could never relax and just be. He always seemed to be on the defensive, always on guard against himself. And as independent as she was, she needed at least one thing from their relationship: to be needed.

But now, as Luke answered the District Attorney's questions, she found herself asking what might have been, if the timing had been different.

When she'd returned to the States from Cambridge she often heard of him through her dealings with the FBI. But on the few occasions when she made a half-hearted attempt to contact him he had always been unavailable. In fact, he seemed to be forever in transit around the country, helping solve crimes or teaching local police forces profiling techniques. Despite the new regime's reliance on hard science and biology, time and time again Special Agent Luke Decker had proved himself indispensable in solving the more intractable cases. She'd heard that his colleagues, no mean mindhunters themselves, called him 'Luke the Spook', a tribute to his ability. She only hoped that by hunting down the demons in others, Luke had found some respite from those warring inside himself.

'I don't know whether Tice should be executed or not,' she suddenly heard Decker say. His voice wasn't raised, but from his tone she could tell he was angry. 'That isn't my province. My only concern is that he isn't allowed out on the streets again – ever.' For all his faults and distrust of the genetic revolution, Decker had one quality that she admired above all others: an almost naïve integrity.

But when Latona took his turn to question him, the defence lawyer soon realized that Decker was no patsy.

'Surely after hearing Dr Kerr's evidence you must concede that Tice needs help? That he's genetically programmed to do what he did?'

Decker smiled, a wide disarming smile that seemed to say, Surely you don't expect any reasonable human being to believe that. Then he turned to Kathy. 'Dr Kerr and I disagree on the relative importance of genetic predetermination. Genes may well be a factor, but they are only that: one in a series of factors. And they certainly aren't an excuse. But yes, I believe your client does need help. However, I'm also convinced he will always remain dangerous whatever treatment he may or may not receive. Let me tell you something about how he came to be the way he is.' At that moment Decker turned to Tice. Decker was still smiling, and his smile was genuinely compassionate. For the first time in the glare of the court's attention Tice looked self-conscious, his cocky, defiant grin frozen on his face.

'Wayne Tice is now twenty-one, and until his arrest he lived at home with his parents. His elder brother, Jerry, is a successful manager for a major insurance company. Jerry attended UCLA and had a string of girlfriends. He has recently married and has a beautiful wife. Both parents doted on Jerry, whereas they told Wayne not to expect too much

38

from life. His mother continually reminded him that he wasn't as smart or as good-looking as his brother.'

Still looking at Tice, Decker began to address him directly, sounding as if he was Tice's best friend and confidant. There was no judgement or censure in his voice. 'Your first overtures with girls weren't happy, were they, Wayne? They couldn't look beyond your crooked teeth, freckles and ginger hair, could they?'

Latona interrupted, his voice betraying a sudden slip in his slick composure. 'Excuse me, Special Agent Decker, but I don't believe that manipulative questioning of the defendant—'

Decker's eyes remained locked with Tice's, oblivious to Latona, to everything except his connection with the killer. He continued to talk, 'And you felt shy. You wanted them to like you, but they were unkind. They laughed at you, didn't they?'

Tice looked uncertain now.

'Your Honour, this line of leading interrogation is outrageous,' said Latona.

The judge paused, looking from Tice to Decker as he considered. 'This isn't a trial, Counsel. This is a hearing, and I want to hear where this goes.'

Decker continued. 'So every day you went to the gym to get stronger and stronger. How much can you press now? One-fifty, one-sixty?'

'Two hundred,' said Tice without thinking.

Decker raised an eyebrow in surprise. 'That's more than me and I'm about three inches taller than you. That's pretty impressive.'

Tice smiled.

'You do martial arts too, don't you, Wayne? Karate, isn't it?'

'Yeah.'

'What belt?'

'Black.'

Again Decker looked impressed and this time he smiled the smile of a proud elder brother. 'Only ever got to brown myself.'

Kathy saw Latona start to object, but the judge waved him down, watching the exchange. 'Must have really made you mad to have achieved all that and still be regarded as a loser by your mother,' said Decker. 'I would have been pissed.'

Tice said nothing; he just stared at Decker as if he was the first guy in the whole goddamn world to understand his shitty life.

'But you loved your mother and couldn't hit out at her. So you thought you'd teach one of the girls a lesson – one of the pretty girls who'd laughed at you. One day a young girl about the same age as the ones who used to diss you at high school came into the pizza parlour, and although she was real nice, you knew she was mocking you. She didn't even realize that you'd grown up, that you'd improved. You could now press two hundred and had a black belt at karate. But she was still giving you the brush-off, like you were some geek at school.'

Tice looked white, his eyes wide.

'Am I right?'

Tice didn't actually nod but Kathy could tell he wanted to.

'Killing her and the second girl felt good, didn't it? You got what you wanted: the control. You taught them that you weren't some loser. You

40

taught them respect and then you killed them. But the third girl was different, Wayne, you covered her head when you killed her. You felt bad about Sally Anne Jennings, didn't you? She liked you. Came to visit you at the pizza parlour and talked to you – really talked to you, like you were a regular guy. Am I right?'

Kathy saw Tice's Adam's apple bob in his throat, then he gave a definite nod.

'But you killed her anyway. Mistaking her kindness for something else, you made a pass at her, and when she got scared you killed her. You felt bad about it, so you covered her face, tried to depersonalize her. But you still felt bad about it afterwards, couldn't get her out of your head. You thought she was judging you. So when the next girl came along – Tammy Lewis – you decided to take her to Sally Anne's grave. You wanted to show Sally Anne that she didn't have any hold over you.' Decker shook his head. It was a gesture of sadness. 'But I was waiting for you. If it's any consolation, Wayne, it wouldn't have worked. You'd still have felt bad about killing Sally Anne, however many girls you raped and killed on her gravestone. In fact it would have got worse.'

Tice sat slumped in his chair, shaking his head. He looked as stunned as the rest of the silent courtroom.

Then Decker turned quickly to the judge and gestured at the chart of Tice's family tree. 'This isn't about genetics. In fact, Tice's own brother is in many ways a model citizen. This is about a man who's programming came from the screwed-up signals of sex, violence, inadequacy and love he

41

received from his family and his peer group. Tice, like all of us, is a creation of his past. But ultimately he *chose* to do what he did and the responsibility rests with him. Tice is a very dangerous man. He has acquired a taste for controlling women that he can't win through normal mating rituals. And the risk that he will revert to this behaviour in the future is very high. It's not in his genes, it's there in his head.'

Kathy could tell from the look on the judge's face that any chance of Tice's original sentence being changed had gone. And not long after Decker retook his seat, the judge's stern voice confirmed her fear, announcing that Tice's appeal had failed and that he was to return to death row pending execution. Kathy shook her head. She didn't agree with the death penalty any more than any other kind of killing. All her adult life had been focused on one aim: developing a way to modify the genes that predetermined senseless violence, to make it a thing of the past, an eradicated plague like smallpox. And Tice would have been a good subject for her trials if the Food and Drug Administration approval on Project Conscience came through as expected. Dr Alice Prince, her sponsor at ViroVector, was confident.

Turning, she watched Luke rise, shake hands with the DA and then walk towards her. She stood, uncertain what to do. Suddenly nervous, she remembered how they had last parted. Him seeing her off at Logan airport, both of them making vague promises to stay in touch, both recognizing the end. A kiss goodbye and then not a word exchanged between them for nine years.

'Kathy, what a surprise. And I do mean surprise.'

There was a fleeting pause before he extended his hand in greeting.

'I know,' she said with a smile as she took his hand in hers. Up close he looked tired. 'I guess I had a small advantage. I knew you'd be here. Although a courtroom's not exactly the place I thought we'd meet again,' she said. 'Certainly not on opposing sides in a murder case.'

Decker smiled. 'I thought we were always on opposing sides.'

'Perhaps,' she said, feeling the old abrasive itch return. 'Anyway, you won today. Another villain safely tucked away on death row.'

Decker's eyes flashed for a second, as if he were about to meet her challenge. Then he shrugged in that deceptively casual way of his. 'You're looking good, Kathy. What are you doing in the States? I thought you were in England.'

'I was for almost a year, but then I got a grant from ViroVector to come to Stanford University and continue my work.'

'So you've been back in the States eight years?' He frowned.

'I've tried to contact you a few times,' she said quickly. 'But you were never around when I called and, well, it didn't seem right just to leave a message somehow . . .' she trailed off.

'Yes, I've been busy – far too busy. So what brought you back? What about that brilliant offer from Cambridge? The one that made you go back to the UK in the first place.'

'Excellent academically, but this was better for practical reasons. You know, all the normal stuff:

43

unlimited funds, access to the resources of a lead-ing biotech company, learning from the great Alice Prince, plus, of course, the co-operation of your crowd, the FBI. I've been working with Director Naylor, and access to the FBI DNA database alone was enough to convince me.' She felt like she was showing off, but she couldn't help it. 'Perhaps we could go for a drink or something?' she said, not knowing what else to say. 'We could catch up.'

'I'd like that,' Decker said, checking his watch. 'Damn it! But not now. I've got to interview a killer on death row in less than an hour.'

Kathy smiled. 'I haven't heard that excuse before.'

Decker grinned, and in an instant his face changed and he was the younger man she'd known at Harvard. 'I'm sorry, that didn't come out right. Believe me, I'd much rather have a drink with you. But I can't. I can't do tonight, either, I'm afraid. I'm seeing my grandfather. And I'm due back in Washington tomorrow.' He reached into his jacket pocket and pulled out a card, then he scribbled something on the back. 'Look, I'll be around San Francisco more often in the future. This is my grandfather's address; it's the old family house in the Marina District. Give me a call and we'll catch up when I'm next over. For all I know you're married with kids by now.'

Kathy paused to look into his eyes, but they were giving nothing away. 'I've been far too busy to get married, Luke,' she said simply. In fact she'd had only three relationships worth talking about in the last nine years – all of which had been at best forgettable. She wasn't short of offers, just offers from people she liked. And apart from the occasional dinner date, usually with men who turned out to have less charm than the contents of a Petri dish, she'd been single and celibate for the last thirteen months and three weeks – not that she was counting. Reaching into her jacket she handed Decker her card. 'Anyway, here's where you can contact me when you're next over.'

'Thanks,' he said. But as soon as they'd both pocketed each other's cards she knew they probably wouldn't meet again for at least another nine years. There was simply no reason to. And it surprised her how sad this made her feel.

She shook his hand. 'Goodbye, Luke. I hope your killer on death row tells you what you want to know.'

3

Baghdad, Iraq. The same day. 5.13 p.m.

Salah Khatib could barely see for the sweat pouring off his brow. But his condition had little to do with the heat of the windowless chamber beneath the barracks of Baghdad's Al Taji Camp.

'What are you waiting for? Shoot them!' hissed the captain, his face inches from Private Khatib's ear, his breath hot on his cheek.

Khatib locked his elbow and aimed the heavy pistol at the nearest of the four men kneeling on the floor in front of him, but still he couldn't prevent his hand from shaking.

The four men in uniforms like his own had been caught trying to desert two nights ago. The rumours of the advance south to retake the province of Kuwait had excited most of his fellow soldiers. After all, they were the Northern Corps armoured division of the elite Republican Guard; it would be their invincible tanks that led the assault. But these four cowards had chosen to desert; not from some conscripted troop, but from the well-fed, well-trained Tenth Brigade. These dogs deserved to die. Bullets were a kindness to their shame.

He even knew two of the men and hated them. They had made his life hell when he'd first joined. But now, given the opportunity to kill them, he couldn't pull the trigger.

And he couldn't understand why.

Khatib loved the army and wanted nothing more than to obey its orders. He had joined two years ago and had never been more content. A twenty-one-year-old mechanic from the back streets of Tikrit, he had been caught in a failed gang robbery, but because of his gift with machines he had been given the choice of gaol or the army. The armoured division had given him a sense of direction and belonging he'd never felt before. Only a week ago he had received the full batch of vaccinations for going to war. He was destined to be a hero. So why couldn't he obey his captain's order?

Two of the men were looking up at him now, as if aware that something was wrong.

'Shoot them!' seethed the captain, his lips almost touching Khatib's ear.

'Sir, we can shoot them,' whispered Ali Keram, one of the five other soldiers standing at the back of the chamber.

'No,' said the captain, his face red with rage. He pulled a revolver from his holster and pushed it into Khatib's temple. 'I gave an order to Private Khatib and he will obey it. If you don't follow my orders I will shoot you dead. Now do your duty.'

Using the sleeve of his tunic Khatib rubbed the sweat from his face, the rough fabric scratching the pustules and acne that had broken out on his cheeks. Black flecks stuck to his sleeve. His hair had started falling out four days ago. He tried to clear his mind, but it was impossible. Last night he'd seen hallucinations of people he and his old gang had robbed in the past. They'd come to him in his bunk back at the barracks, taunting him, admonishing him for his petty sins. And now he felt so torn and confused he didn't know what was happening to him. Over the last few days he had been beset by surges of raging aggression, followed by sloughs of guilt-ridden depression. He had tried to disguise his mood swings but now he didn't even want to go to war. He could even understand why these dogs had deserted.

Standing there in the gloomy underground chamber, staring at the soiled walls, levelling his pistol at the men, he was unable to pull the trigger. As the snout of the captain's revolver ground into Khatib's temple he felt such mental torment that he found himself closing his eyes and pushing his head against the officer's revolver, willing him to fire. He was terrified of dying, but at that moment it seemed like an escape.

Slumping his shoulders, Salah Khatib dropped his gun onto the stone floor.

He didn't hear the captain's order to the other soldiers or see them step forward, he only heard the shots reverberate deafeningly around the confined space. Opening his eyes he saw the deserters jerk to the ground, a pool of red spreading from their bodies adding to the marks that already soiled the stone floor.

It was with a sense of relieved detachment that Khatib heard the shot fired from the captain's pistol before the bullet ploughed into his brain.

San Quentin State Penitentiary, California.
The same day. 3.19 p.m.

Diving over the Golden Gate Bridge from the court-house, Luke Decker turned off the car radio. He was sick of hearing about the Iraq crisis and next week's presidential election. Pamela Weiss already had his vote; a woman couldn't make more of a mess of things than her male predecessors. He adjusted his Ray-Bans and glanced out across the bay. The sky was a clear, pale blue and the darker sea below was bejewelled with reflections from the afternoon sun and the small armada of yachts and boats. The scene reminded Decker of his child-hood, when his mother and grandfather used to take him up Coit Tower to look out across the Pacific. As a child he would stare out into the blue and imagine the heroic father he never knew wav-ing from the bridge of a mighty warship, returning home from some secret and glorious mission.

Decker had been brought up in the bay area and had roots here. He may have neglected them, particularly his grandfather and the few old friends he still had from his college days at Berkeley, before he left for Harvard and the all-consuming FBI, but they still existed. He was convinced that he was doing the right thing leaving the grey, oppressive Bureau and returning here to teach at Berkeley. Perhaps he would follow up his surprise meeting with Kathy Kerr. Yeah right. All he needed now was Kathy Kerr back in his life, just when he was getting himself together – round-the-clock arguments and his world turned upside down.

Leaving the bridge and passing through Marin

County he glanced at the open files on the passenger seat of his rented Ford. A man's face stared out at him from a colour photograph on the top of a pile of documents. The face was handsome, with high cheekbones, green eyes and lightly tanned skin. His thick silver hair was cut short and neatly styled. He looked like a powerful politician, eminent doctor, or charismatic captain of industry.

But Karl Axelman was none of these things.

He was a killer who made Wayne Tice look like a choirboy.

Dubbed the Collector by the media, Axelman was still the only serial killer in American legal history to have been convicted and condemned to death without any trace of the bodies being found. A successful construction-site foreman for thirty years, Axelman was arrested seven years ago for the murders of at least twelve teenage girls over a period spanning decades.

Twelve neatly labelled boxes, each giving the girl's full name, physical statistics, date and place of abduction, were discovered in a concealed chamber built into a wall of his house in San José. Each box contained the clothing the girls had last worn, their personal effects and an audiotape. On the tape Axelman could be heard giving each victim a minute to explain why she should be spared. All were forbidden to hesitate, repeat themselves or cry while pleading for their lives. It would seem that all failed. None were seen again.

Decker hadn't been directly involved in the case, but he'd read the files and formed his own impression. Now in his mid-fifties, Axelman was still a master of control. He had been a highly organized killer who'd honed his technique over the years. His profile showed that he'd probably offended for most of his life, starting with indecent assaults, graduating to violent rapes and finally murders. The twelve teenage girls had been abducted over a twenty-year period, at roughly eighteen-month intervals. This told Decker that each abduction had been planned in meticulous detail, with the stalking and anticipation giving Axelman as much excitement as the actual act itself. The fact that the bodies had never been found meant Axelman had stored them somewhere he could revisit again and again, thus enabling him to stave off his need to kill for long intervals.

Karl Axelman would have gone undetected if, seven years ago, his Cherokee Jeep hadn't been involved in a collision on the Bay Bridge. The California Highway Patrol had found a tape playing in the car of one of the girls pleading for her life. Stacked alongside The Carpenters and Leonard Cohen, Axelman evidently listened to the tape for pleasure as he drove from his home to the construction site he was working on. Decker guessed it was one more trophy, along with the boxed belongings of each victim, which allowed him to relive his crimes and delay the need to kill again until he was fully sated.

After his arrest the FBI had searched his house and found the twelve boxes. Decker's FBI colleagues in forensics couldn't have amassed a better mountain of evidence confirming Axelman's guilt, but, despite every inducement,

51

threat and deal, Karl Axelman never told them where the bodies were. 'Don't worry,' he'd said with a chilling smile, 'their bodies are fine. And they'll stay that way.'

Even after being sentenced to death he had shown no remorse or inclination to reveal any details about how they had died, or what he had done with their bodies. Agents on at least three occasions in the past had interviewed him with no success.

So, as the yellow walls of San Quentin penitentiary came into view, Decker had few illusions about his chances. But this could be the Bureau's last opportunity. Somehow over the last seven years Axelman had managed to postpone his date with the chamber, successfully appealing and being granted a stay of execution on several occasions. Luke checked the file. His date with destiny was now scheduled for tomorrow, Thursday, 30 October. It was at least fifty-fifty he'd wriggle out of it again.

Parking his car in the visitors' lot Decker considered how Axelman had asked for him by name, probably because of his involvement in the Tice murders. It occasionally happened that way after a high-profile case. He took off his suit jacket and tie and rolled up his sleeves. The last thing he wanted to look like when interviewing a con on death row was a stiff G-Man. Gathering his files together he put them in his case and locked them in the trunk of the car. Then he collected his pad, pen and tape recorder and walked towards the imposing entrance of the prison.

* * *

The recent security changes meant that San Quentin, like most state penitentiaries, had increased the number of guards. Decker had been here often in the past and recognized most of the men on the gate when he handed in his gun and showed his badge. No-one bothered to ask him what he was there for; they just waved him through the metal detector and X-ray scanner. One guard, called Clarence Pitt, a tall black guy in a neatly pressed uniform, escorted him into the inner prison more out of habit than necessity. Decker knew exactly where he was going. He had requested the private visiting room he always used when interviewing cons.

'Watch the game, Decker?' Clarence Pitt asked as they walked past the adjustment centre where death-row inmates were placed when they first arrived. He looked perplexed, like something unjust and unfathomable had come to pass. 'The Forty-niners got creamed *again*.'

Decker laughed. As a kid he'd been an ardent fan. 'What do you expect? When was the last time they won anything?'

Pitt shook his head and frowned. He looked genuinely upset. 'You always gotta have hope,' he said and then fell into silence.

'Ain't that the truth,' mumbled Decker, looking around him. He'd never got over his hatred of these places, never got used to his deep discomfort whenever he visited them. There was a pervasive smell which tainted every prison he'd visited across the States, a bitter blend of institutional disinfectant, stale air, sweat and despair. He looked down and studied his shoes as they neared the north segment of the prison, where the green chimney of the gas chamber rose to belch its poisonous fumes into the sky. Decker's spirits lifted for a moment when he considered that this would be his last ever visit to death row.

Eventually they reached the private visitor room and Clarence Pitt stood aside from the closed steel door. 'He's waiting inside with his attorney. You know the drill. I'll be outside if you need me.'

'Thanks, Clarence.' In his mind he went over his strategy and the key points he wanted to cover with Axelman. Taking a deep breath, he ensured that he felt calm and in control, then he opened the door.

Not much surprised him any more. But the sight of Karl Axelman sitting manacled to the stainless-steel table in the middle of the room shocked him so much that he broke one of his cardinal rules and allowed it to show on his face. What astonished him even more was the equally obvious shock on Axelman's face.

Decker immediately turned to Axelman's attorney to regain his composure. The lawyer introduced himself as Tad Rosenblum. He was a round man with a cherubic face and curly brown hair, greying at the temples.

'Special Agent Decker, I want to make it perfectly clear that my client has agreed to speak to you against my instructions. His execution date is scheduled for tomorrow and an appeal is currently lodged with the governor. My client is in an extreme state of agitation verging on the irrational. If I feel that speaking to you makes his condition deteriorate any further I will overrule Mr Axelman and immediately stop this interview. Is that clear?'

Decker nodded slowly. He didn't bother to make it clear to Mr Rosenblum that his client had asked to see him, not the other way round. Or that if Decker felt Axelman was wasting his time, then *he* would stop the interview. 'Mr Rosenblum, I was under the impression your client wanted to see me alone.'

Rosenblum frowned and Decker could see the lawyer's jaw muscles twitch. 'I shall be outside.'

Now that Decker felt calmer he turned back to Axelman, keeping his face devoid of expression. But it was difficult. Axelman no longer looked like his photograph. His thick, groomed hair had fallen out in clumps, exposing pink scalp beneath. His skin was pitted with acne and he clearly hadn't slept in an age. The man's eyes were bloodshot and puffy with dark shadows beneath them. But what unnerved Decker the most was the way Axelman stared at him. He seemed mesmerized, studying Decker like some rare antique whose authenticity was in doubt.

Decker sat at the table facing the convicted killer. 'Karl, my name is Luke Decker. I run the behavioural sciences unit at the FBI training academy in Quantico, Virginia. You asked to speak with me.'

Axelman said nothing, he just continued staring at him. Rosenblum was right. He didn't look rational. This wasn't the man Decker had read about. Axelman was supposed to be an iceman, an arrogant control freak who would pretend to tell him where the victims were buried and then, at the last minute, give Decker nothing and laugh in his face. That's what Decker was prepared for. But this man looked on the verge of a breakdown. Could the imminence of his execution be getting to him this time? Or was this an even more elaborate mind-fuck? If so, then it was a good one.

Decker smiled at the man, as if he were a patient rather than a criminal. He kept his voice friendly and matter of fact. 'Karl, is there anything you want to tell me? Anything you want to talk to me about?'

For a second Decker thought Axelman was going to say something. He leaned forward, and Decker instinctively copied his body language and leaned forward too. But then Axelman shook his head and let out a low moan. He seemed to be fighting some battle in his head. 'I can't tell you,' he whispered suddenly, holding his head in his hands.

Decker frowned. A battle was raging in his head too. His experience told him the man was screwing with him – doing what he'd done to three other agents before him – but Decker could also see the man was patently troubled, physically and mentally. 'Why can't you tell me?' Decker asked reasonably.

'I can't,' Axelman shouted suddenly. 'I thought I could. But I fuckin' can't. Not face to face.' His body began to shake and he seemed about to crush his head in his hands, as if trying to make it disappear. From being unable to stop staring at Decker, Axelman now couldn't meet his eye.

Decker rose slowly from the table. He had seen manipulative killers feign madness before, and many had done it brilliantly, but usually he could tell. This was different. He kept his voice calm and matter of fact. 'If you have nothing to tell me, I may as well leave.'

Axelman stood and pulled at his manacles, reaching for him. 'No,' he shouted in panic.

'Then talk to me. There's no point in me staying if you won't say anything.'

'I can't,' Axelman screamed at him, so loud that Decker heard the scrabble of the door being unlocked behind him. The man was demented, or putting on a very good display. Either way, Decker wasn't too disappointed that Axelman's protective lawyer was coming in to end the interview.

But his instinct told him to try one last time. Moving to the door, he saw the handle being turned from the outside. 'I'm going now, Karl,' he said calmly. 'Just explain one thing before I go. Why couldn't you tell me? What's the problem here?'

Axelman slumped back into his chair, defeated. As he did so he said something so quiet and so out-landish that Decker assumed he had misheard it.

Decker turned and stepped towards the murderer. 'What? What was that?'

Axelman sat statue-still, his shoulders slumped, his head bowed. A droplet of sweat dripped off the tip of his nose onto the table. Behind him Decker could hear the door opening, but before Rosenblum could enter Decker grabbed the handle and pushed against the door with his body weight to keep it closed.

Then Axelman repeated what he had said.

Although the killer only whispered the four words, Decker heard each one as clearly as if it had been shouted in his ear.

'I am your father.'

4

ViroVector Solutions, Palo Alto, California.
The same day. 3.47 p.m.

Dr Alice Prince was more preoccupied than usual.
Adjusting her eyeglasses she brushed back her
grey-streaked black hair. Her lab coat had been buttoned incorrectly, making it appear as if her right
shoulder was drooping. And as she wandered
through ViroVector's vast, domed reception and
nodded at numerous members of her staff, a few of
them stopped to tell their boss that her jacket was
crooked. They all did so with a respectful and
affectionate smile, as if this wasn't the first time.
She gave each one a small smile and a thank-you
and then moved on, leaving her buttons
untouched. She had more important things on her
mind. The project she had been working on for
years was finally coming to fruition. And now the
theory was about to become a reality, she could
see all the small things that might unravel. In
particular, she was trying to remember exactly
when Karl Axelman was meant to die.

Now fifty-one, Alice Prince had founded ViroVector Solutions in 1987, two days before her thirtieth birthday. Twenty-one years later her brain-child was the world's third largest biotech company and the most influential on the West Coast. With headquarters just south of Palo Alto, between San Francisco and San José, its sprawling campus comprised the huge crystal dome, three separate 100-yard production sheds, a helicopter landing pad, a sports complex and a parking lot. Bordering a science park and the Bellevue Golf and Country Club, the perimeter was protected by a lightweight steel fence, linked to a series of sensitive scanners and alarms. The crystal dome, like the rest of the campus, was a so-called smart building, designed by the celebrated British archi-technologist Sir Simon Canning. It resembled a visiting spaceship, particularly at night, when the interior lights illuminated the glass structure. But everyone at ViroVector called it the iceberg, because the visible part of the building, which housed the commercial offices, administrative departments and the supercomputer TITANIA, was a tiny part of the overall structure. The majority of it was underground, where the extensive warren of biocontainment laboratories was located.

It was to the underground laboratories that Dr Alice Prince was heading. Going through one of three doors leading off the dome's reception foyer, she walked down a long corridor, past a white door on her left. *Authorized Entry Only* was stamped above the acronym TITANIA. As she passed, the temperature in the corridor dropped slightly. The

Cold Room housed ViroVector's vast protein-based biocomputer. TITANIA, an acronym for Total Information Technology and Neural Intelligence Analogue, was the artificially intelligent brain that controlled and co-ordinated all the smart buildings and most of ViroVector's corporate functions, from data capture and manipulation to production scheduling, project management, payroll and security.

At the end of the corridor Alice stopped before a yellow door marked with a large biohazard symbol. When Alice placed her palm on the door's sensor, it was TITANIA who recognized her DNA profile and ratified her gold clearance to the biolab complex. Through the door was a small vestibule with a computer terminal and a printer. Two lab-coated female technicians greeted her and she smiled back. She wished she had a better memory for names because she recognized their faces. From here she walked to another door, which again required TITANIA to check her identity before hissing open to reveal a transit station containing lockers and shower cubicles. She undressed, took a quick shower and then dressed in surgical greens and safety goggles. Then she walked to one of two elevators, again marked with biohazard symbols.

Inside the elevator there was only one button. Pressing it, the doors closed and the high-speed cabin descended fifty feet underground to the main complex. As the doors opened the safety goggles shielded her eyes from the ultra-violet light in the screening corridor outside. The light was used to break down viruses. At the end of the corridor was an entry area, which gave access to the underground system of five concentric circles forming ViroVector's biosafety laboratory complex.

The structure was built to exacting federal standards and could withstand an earthquake or a direct hit from any known warhead. This was intended less to protect the inhabitants, than to ensure nothing inside escaped. The concentric-circle design was based on a Russian model. Each glass-walled airtight circle was kept at an increasingly lower air pressure towards the centre, so that any breach in the reinforced glass walls would suck air into, and not out of, the structure.

Each circle represented a staging post, reflecting the four classified levels of virus. Level-one viruses, such as influenza, were stored and researched in the outer circle. Level-two and -three viruses, including HIV and Hepatitis, were in two circles closer to the centre and required increased protective clothing and vaccinations. Level-four viruses, so called hot agents such as ebola and marburg, with up to a 90-per-cent mortality rate, were housed in the penultimate area and required full biological suits. In the few institutions authorized to house these highly infectious agents, including the United States Army Research Institute of Infectious Diseases (USAMRIID) at Fort Detrick in Maryland and the Center for Disease Control in Atlanta, there was no more dangerous area than the biosafety level-four lab – the so-called Hot Zone.

But at ViroVector there was one more level of peril. The central circle was a level-five facility.

61

Ahead was an airtight door. *Biosafety Level One* was printed on the glass in ten-inch-high red letters. Again she placed her palm over the DNA sensor and stepped through when the door opened. Walking down a glass corridor she could see the level-one laboratory facilities to her left and right. They were busy but not over-populated with white-coated virologists. Much of her viral work was now automated. In one corner on the right were the huge stainless-steel refrigerators that housed ViroVector's library of bacteriophage samples. Alice Prince was particularly proud of her phage collection.

ViroVector owned the largest selection of phage specimens known to man. These quasi-viruses fed on bacteria such as *Mycobacterium*, *Staphylococcus* and *Enterococcus*. Each was bacterium specific, feeding off a particular strain, mutating with it so the bacterium could never develop immunity, like it could to antibiotics. In the mid-nineties, at a time when the power of bacteriophage technology was discredited by the giant drug companies still trying to sell their increasingly ineffective antibiotics, Alice Prince had seen an opportunity.

Her company had bought access to the vast phage library in the Tibilisi Institute in Georgia, collected during the Soviet Communist era of central control. Replicating and enlarging the collection, ViroVector now had a phage virus to kill most known bacteria. And since the year 2000 many Western hospitals, plagued by antibiotic-immune superbugs such as Methicillin-resistant *Staphylococcus aureus*, and Vancomycin-resistant

Enterococcus, had been forced to use her company's products to sterilize their wards and operating rooms. Now airports and many train stations and seaports used ViroVector's bacteriophage air-purifiers as viral customs officers in their embarkation and disembarkation tunnels to reduce the risk of deadly bacteria moving around the world with their human hosts. The bacteriophage business had become ViroVector's major income, funding much of its growth.

Looking straight ahead, Alice made her way through the sealed doors leading to biosafety level two and three. These labs were smaller and many of the personnel wore masks. Leaving level three, she found herself in a decontamination and preparation area, equipped with chemical decon showers, scrub stations and another row of lockers. Alice walked to her locker and pulled out a blue Chemturion biohazard suit with *Alice Prince* printed on the back. Checking it for tears she suited up and made her way to the biosafety-level-four door. Keeping her head still she allowed the retina scanner to confirm her identity through the glass of her visor and then walked into a buffer chamber. Once the first door had closed the next opened and she was admitted to a glass corridor that passed through level four. She was now in the hot core of the biolab complex. To her right was a door to the level-four labs, and through the glass she could see scientists wearing similar suits to her own. To her left was another elevator door; this led down two more levels to the extensively equipped biosafety-level-four hospital and the morgue below that. Both were rarely used, but every eventuality had to be covered.

Dr Prince carried on to the heart of the biolab complex, to the door with *Biosafety Level Five* stamped on it in red. Standing for her retina to be scanned one final time she waited for the door to open, allowing her access to what most scientists at ViroVector ironically called the Womb.

The Womb was one of the most perilous places on earth. Gleaming apparatus sat atop otherwise uncluttered worktops, and in one corner stood a six-foot-tall Genescope – the black swan-like instrument which could decode an organism's entire genome from one body cell. The room looked harmless enough, with its non-slip white floor tiles, spotless stainless-steel tables, freezers and walls of reinforced glass. But despite the reassuring cleanliness and hi-tech equipment, man did not reign here. The virus did. One pinprick in Prince's protective clothing could mean a short visit down to the biosafetly-level-four hospital before being transferred even lower to the morgue.

However, immediately she entered the Womb and heard the door hiss closed behind her Prince felt safer than when she was in the outside world. Usually she had an assistant with her, but today she wanted privacy, so she had the room to herself. This place was classified as biosafety level five because nature was not only studied in here, it was tampered with. And when playing God there was always the risk of creating an even more deadly strain.

It was in the Womb that Prince and her team genetically engineered viruses and created new ones. Viruses are basically non-thinking capsules of genetic material wrapped in protein, which exist to seek out hosts in order to reproduce themselves. When a virus finds a host with receptive cells it enters one of those cells and, like a cuckoo taking over a sparrow's nest, it usurps the genetic code already there, replacing it with its own. Then, when the cell containing the new viral DNA divides and replicates, the virus copies itself. Thus the virus spreads throughout the body.

This property made it ideal for delivering gene therapy – the technology of spreading modified genes throughout a human patient's damaged cells. By scooping out a virus's own genetic material, Prince and her team could render it harmless. They could then insert new therapeutic DNA into the virus and create a vector to target a diseased cancer cell or cystic-fibrosis cell and reprogramme its damaged genes. Creating viral vectors was at the very heart of ViroVector's work. Alice Prince founded her company by specializing in turning lethal viral killers into genetically engineered 'magic bullets' to deliver some of the most spectacular cures in modern medicine. With viral vectors she could change a human's genes, correcting the genetic inheritance they had received at birth.

ViroVector had become successful by focusing on viral DNA. They rarely developed the therapeutic human genes, just the viral vector to target and deliver them to the patient. Prince and her team knew more about viruses than any organization on earth. Even the CDC in Atlanta and USAMRIID frequently consulted them for advice, and personnel were often exchanged between the different institutions to foster learning.

Alice Prince felt at peace here in this temple to science, insulated from the stresses and worries of the outside world. When she put a lethal filovirus under the electron microscope and lost herself in its threadlike beauty she could almost forget about losing her only daughter, Libby, ten years ago, and the husband who had deserted her. Gazing at her glass library of viruses she felt safe and in control, each vial a precious and powerful balm.

The vials in the refrigerator in front of her were slotted into trays, and each carried a small white computer-generated label with a barcode down one side. *Ebola Filovirus (V. 3)* was typed on one vial, *HIV Retrovirus Hybrid* on another, *Adenovirus Five – Gene-Therapy Vector for Sickle Cell Anaemia* on yet another.

At the bottom of the refrigerator a black rack contained twenty shorter, stubbier vials. Each of these bore a label displaying a Pentagon-approved code. All contained viral vectors, genetically engineered to counter known biological weapons. *Bioshield # Seven* immunized against anthrax and *Bioshield # Thirteen* against most known rheovirus pathogens. ViroVector sold these vaccines to many of the world powers – friend and foe alike. Classified as medicines they could bypass even the most stringent sanctions.

Running a gloved hand over the vials, the tinkling sound was like the music of endless possibilities to her. Here in the Womb she could fundamentally change things: turn the bad into good and create order out of chaos for the random world outside.

With a small sigh she shifted her attention to the

job in hand. Turning, she walked to a small black safe in the corner beside the Genescope. *LENICA 101* was written in big red letters across the front. Bending, she punched in the code on the electronic keypad and the door opened. Inside the refrigerated interior was a tray of five vials, each the size of a large cigar. Two of them were red glass and three were green. The red vials were labelled, *Conscience Vector (V. 1.0)* and *Conscience Vector (V. 1.9)*. The three green vials bore the legends, *Crime Zero (Phase One – telomeres test)*, *Crime Zero (Phase Two – controlled trial)* and *Crime Zero (Phase Three)*.

Putting the tray on a work surface next to one of the three computer terminals, she turned the red vials round in their slots so their barcodes were exposed. Then she took a computer wand from next to the monitor and scanned the barcodes of *Conscience Vector (V. 1.0)* and *Conscience Vector (V. 1.9)*. As she did so she watched the monitor to her left, checking the differences between the two vectors. She pressed 'Print' so a hard copy would appear on the ground-level printer above. The differences between version 1.0 and 1.9 were negligible, certainly not significant enough to merit troubling the Food and Drug Administration. She only hoped Dr Kathy Kerr would agree.

She then turned to the green vials. These were even more important than the Project Conscience vectors. Kathy Kerr knew nothing about them. First she scanned *Crime Zero (Phase One – telomeres test)*. When she looked at the computer monitor and watched the project summary spreadsheet appear, she noted the six names with San

Quentin typed above them. The five younger men had recent dates beside them – all different – plus a file number, referring to the autopsy findings. The same five had a tick in the far-right column of the spreadsheet. So far all had met TITANIA's predicted timings. Only the sixth remained undated and unticked – Karl Axelman.

Alice Prince took a deep breath. She could see from the projected date in the left-hand column that Axelman was due any time now. TITANIA had already brought forward the Phase Two shipments to Iraq to meet the looming crisis. This was on the understanding that Phase One would be fine. They couldn't possibly go to Phase Three if either One or Two were compromised. To compound her concern there was also the call she had received from the orphanage in Cartamena. It was probably only a scare, and she would hear back any moment, but it still made her nervous. Project Conscience was going to be difficult enough. Perhaps Crime Zero was too ambitious, too risky, whatever Madeline Naylor said.

A sudden beep made her heart lurch and she instinctively checked her suit for tears. Then, realizing it was only the signal for the door opening, she breathed a sigh of relief and vowed to have the tone changed: it was too similar to the biosuit alarms. Turning round she heard the hiss of the airtight seals and watched the lab door to her left open slowly. She had expressly instructed her senior staff with silver-level access to the Womb that she wanted the place to herself for the next hour.

Flustered, she switched off the computer and

reached for the tray of coloured vials. But before she could move them a blue suit entered the Womb. When it turned, Alice saw Kathy Kerr's excited face smiling through the visor. Kerr glanced at the tray for a moment, before Alice awkwardly stepped in front of it.

'Alice, I've just heard the news. Isn't it great?' Kathy said. Alice smiled but said nothing, letting her carry on regardless. 'The FDA have approved all the Conscience safety tests for Version Nine. Now, at last, we can go ahead with the efficacy trials on criminals. Isn't it brilliant?'

Alice Prince nodded. 'Yes, yes, it's great,' she said quickly, turning to put the tray back in the safe. The last person she wanted seeing the vials was Kathy. She scolded herself for not including Kerr in her request for privacy. Kathy had silver-level clearance, but was based down the road at Stanford University. 'Look, Kathy, I'm busy now. And I really had planned on being alone.'

Kathy's smile faded. She looked embarrassed. 'Oh, I'm sorry, Alice. I didn't realize.'

Alice closed the safe, heard the lock click and then turned to Kathy. 'That's OK. It's good news. Madeline Naylor's coming tomorrow. We'll celebrate then. OK?'

Kathy looked at her, obviously disappointed that she wasn't more excited. 'OK, Alice. See you tomorrow,' she said quietly and left.

As soon as the door closed behind her, the speakerphone beeped. 'Dr Prince, I have a call from Director Naylor for you,' said a voice from the speaker by the door. 'It's on a secure line.'

'Thank you,' she said.

'Alice, are you there? Can we speak?' boomed the director of the FBI. Alice could just imagine Madeline Naylor sitting in her office on the fifth floor of the Hoover Building in Washington. Her professionally manicured Chanel-Rouge-Noir nails drumming on her desk. It still amused Alice to think that the skinny twelve-year-old girl with shocking white hair and dark eyes she'd known at school was now running the most powerful law-enforcement agency in the world.

'Yes, I'm alone, Madeline. You still coming over?'

'Of course.'

'Have you got my e-mail? We've got FDA approval to go ahead with Conscience.'

'About goddamn time. Pamela was getting more than a little nervous, as you know. She's got a TV debate tonight and wants to tee up the Conscience policy announcement for this Friday. Still, better late than never.'

Friday was only two days away. In less than forty-eight hours the first stage of their strategy would go public. Just enough time for the American voters and media to get excited, without giving Pamela's Republican opponents an opportunity to rally before the election next Tuesday.

'I'm still worried about Crime Zero, though,' said Alice. 'The Bioshield vaccine's been dispatched early to Iraq because of the escalating crisis, but we have a potential issue at the orphanage, and the San Quentin experiment is looking tight. Perhaps we—'

'Stop worrying, Alice. That's why I'm calling. I've got news as well.'

'Yes?'

'San Quentin. It's happened. Just as TITANIA predicted.' Madeline's voice softened. 'Relax about Crime Zero, Ali. Cartamena will prove to be a false alarm. The FDA Conscience approval was the big one. Well done. I'm due in a meeting about now, but I'll be over in a few hours.'

'See you later,' said Alice as the speaker went dead. Perhaps Madeline was right; she usually was. Gaining FDA approval to begin Project-Conscience-Phase-Two trials was vital before Pamela Weiss went ahead with her pre-election announcement. And it looked as though it would be increasingly crucial to the election itself, given the latest opinion polls, which showed a strong Republican lead. But as for the FDA approval to embark on efficacy trials, that was academic. Under the auspices of Project Conscience, Alice Prince and Madeline Naylor had been secretly testing behaviour-modifying gene therapy on unsuspecting convicts for over eight years now.

5

Cartamena Orphanage for Young Boys, Mexico City.
The same day. 5.23 p.m.

Dr Victoria Valdez looked down at the small boy lying on the gurney and released a sigh. Fernando was only thirteen, one of her favourites. Brave and cocky, with a skinny body and huge dark eyes, he had a gift for soccer and for making her laugh. He was far too young to have suffered a brain haemorrhage. She looked around the small, spotless clinic attached to the orphanage. His death was especially poignant because it was so rare for a child to die here.

The Cartamena Orphanage for Young Boys, thirty miles south of Mexico City, was fortunate. A large proportion of its costs and all its medical expenses were funded by a little-known charitable trust in the US called Fresh Start. The funding and resources had been provided for some nine years on the understanding that there would be no publicity. Valdez knew Fresh Start was a front for ViroVector Solutions in California, but if a large company wanted to help young children without claiming the credit she wasn't about to complain.

The great Dr Alice Prince even visited from time to time, selecting certain children for her personal attention. And if the children ever had any serious problems outside Dr Valdez's experience and training then Alice Prince and her company would provide specialist care. Valdez thought that she and the orphanage had much to be grateful for. The boys here were better cared for than in any other institution she knew. In the last nine years she had known of only seven fatalities, which was remarkable here in Mexico, and those had been just as sudden and unexplained as Fernando's death. Some of his hair had fallen out recently, but that could have been vitamin deficiency, and the acne on his face was normal for a boy of his age. When he'd gone to sleep last night he had been fine, but today he was dead.

As a matter of procedure she'd immediately called Fresh Start: they had asked to be notified of all deaths. Eventually she was put through to Dr Alice Prince herself. Victoria told her the boy had died of a suspected brain haemorrhage. At first she'd been touched by Dr Prince's apparently genuine concern, but had been surprised to be asked only one question: had Fernando reached puberty?

Nonplussed, Victoria could guess the answer, but had said she would check after putting the phone down. The orphanage cared only for boys until the age of puberty and then sent them either to other homes or found them jobs. The rules were strict and Fresh Start insisted on them, but Victoria

73

still thought Dr Prince's question was strange. The boy was dead. What did it matter whether he could still stay at the orphanage?

Looking down at the naked corpse she shook her head again. Walking to the wall, she picked up the handset and dialled the number Dr Prince had given her.

'Yes,' she said in reply to the American's question, 'but only just.'

Valdez frowned when she heard the sigh of relief. The response hardly seemed appropriate.

Marina District, San Francisco, California. The same day. 6.47 p.m.

Luke Decker felt calmer when he pulled up outside his grandfather's tall Victorian house in the Marina District. He had spent the last few hours driving aimlessly round the city. He'd almost called in on one of his old buddies from Berkeley – a journalist called Hank Butcher who lived in Sausalito – just to take his mind off things.

He was still reeling from Axelman's claim. What the hell was he playing at? Decker had tried to challenge him afterwards, but he'd begun screaming again and had frozen up, so Rosenblum had stopped the interview.

Obviously it couldn't be true. Axelman was either demented or playing stupid mind games. Killing time before *his* killing time. But however much Decker tried to dismiss what he'd been told, the notion still stirred something deep and disturbing within him.

Eighteen months ago, when his mother had died, he had been working simultaneously on six particularly gruesome cases. He had been in Buffalo, New York when his grandfather, Matty Rheiman, had called to give him the news. Apparently his mother had died quickly, but her last words had been, 'I want to see my son before I die.' It was only when he'd touched her cold face in the mortuary the next day that he'd realized how late he was. Decker had been so busy he hadn't made time to see her for almost nine months. He still wore the guilt like a cold vest. His grandfather, a mild man, had reproached him at the time.

'What's with you, Luke? Your mother needed you and yet you never visited. It's like you *prefer* to spend time chasing after killers.'

His grandfather had immediately apologized, but his words had struck home. The idea that he might *enjoy* inhabiting the minds of murderers terrified Decker. The notion that he empathized with the evil in others because he possessed it too was abhorrent. Combined with overwork and guilt, this thought had contributed to a breakdown. It had taken being institutionalized and more sessions than he cared to remember with the gentle Dr Sarah Quirke at the Sanctuary to soothe his frazzled brain. Until then Decker had always believed there was a mental firewall between his own mind and the inflamed minds he hunted, that the evil he pursued in others was somehow separate from him.

When he was younger he'd challenged his mother about his fascination with the darker side of humanity. But she had quickly reassured him, telling him that he was perfectly normal, and that his father was just like him. That was why Captain Richard Decker was such a good interrogator, his mother used to say. He knew the questions to ask the enemy because he could think like them.

But what if Richard Decker hadn't been his father? What if his inherited gift for understanding the darker side in others came from a more sinister source?

Even though he tried to dismiss these thoughts, they remained. He kept thinking of Wayne Tice and his family tree, and remembering how he'd scoffed at Kathy's theory of inherited evil.

Getting out of the car, Decker approached the house. He wondered whether he should have phoned ahead to let Matty know he was coming, but there was something almost childlike in his grandfather's enjoyment at seeing him when he least expected it. He seemed delighted that Decker had taken to dropping by since his mother's death, as if this house were still his home, rather than some hotel where he needed to make reservations in advance. As he neared the front door he heard the sweetest sound coming from the music room upstairs. Decker could picture his grandfather standing there, his violin on his shoulder, his gnarled fingers shaped by years curling round the instrument. The large windows would be wide open, and a breeze would be blowing in from the bay, as if summoned by his playing.

Opening the front door, which was rarely locked, Decker entered the spacious hallway. Rhoda, the live-in housekeeper who looked after Matty, greeted him from the lounge. She was a large woman with an even larger smile and she'd been with Matty ever since his wife died twelve years ago.

'Luke, what a great surprise,' she said, coming over to give him a hug. 'He's upstairs,' she whispered, with a conspiratorial wink. 'Come, give me your things.'

'Thanks, Rhoda. Good to see you.' Decker handed over his old tote bag and walked upstairs to the middle floor. The mahogany banisters had just been polished and the smell took Decker back to his childhood. His mother and maternal grandparents had brought him up in this house. He had spent half his life here, and whenever he entered the front door it felt like coming home. On the middle landing he walked into the spacious music room. A piano stood in the corner, alongside an empty violin case. Luke's own battered saxophone leant against a tall bookcase, which was filled with tapes, compact discs and sadly antiquated vinyl.

Photographs of his grandfather sat on top of the piano, next to an ancient metronome. Most of the pictures were taken at Davies Hall, where, despite offers from the best orchestras in the world, he had played with his beloved San Francisco Symphony orchestra for most of his illustrious career. Other photographs showed Matty at the Hollywood Bowl; in London's Royal Albert Hall with Yehudi Menuhin and, of course, the famous one of him embracing Isaac Stern on stage at Carnegie Hall. Beside them, slightly by itself, was a picture of a tall blond man and a petite dark woman: Richard and Rachel Decker, Luke's parents. The man was in naval uniform and his hair was cut short, like Decker's.

Just as Luke had imagined, his grandfather stood by the large window facing out across the bay, violin tucked under his chin and his guide dog, Brutus, at his feet. He was shrunken and stooped, with only wisps of hair on his head, but Matty Rheiman still played as if his very survival depended on it. And there was a time in his life when it had.

Matty had spent his early teenage years during the Second World War at the Buchenwald concentration camp, where most of his family had been led to the gas chambers. He had been blinded in the camp's experimental hospital by Nazi doctors injecting blue dye into his brown irises, trying to change his eye colour and turn a Jew into an Aryan. Only his prodigious gift for the violin had saved him. The commandant's wife, Frau Ilse Koch, wanted a talented violinist to entertain guests at their villa in the camp. The fact that the scrawny Matty was barely a teenager only made him a greater curiosity.

'Hello, Gramps,' Decker said, walking over to embrace him. As he put his arm around Matty's frail shoulders he was reminded of his age – eighty-one in December.

The sound of music was replaced by a deep laugh as his grandfather turned, levelling his blind brilliant-blue eyes on Decker and smiling. 'Hello, Luke.' He placed his precious violin down carefully on top of the piano. 'Brutus, look who's here,' he said as he returned Decker's embrace. Luke felt a warm wet tongue graze his hand as Brutus raised himself up on two legs and began barking his greeting.

'Come, come, Luke. Sit down,' said his grandfather, ushering him to the nearby sofa. 'How long are you staying this time?'

Decker heard the pleasure in Matty's voice and was stricken by the brevity of his visit. 'Just the night, then I must get back to Quantico. But I'm thinking of moving back here, you know, Gramps.'

'Really?' Matty said in a way that meant, I think I've heard this before. 'What, they've finally had enough of you in Virginia?'

'No, I'm thinking of leaving the Bureau altogether.' Decker told him about his offer from Berkeley and how he wanted to come back here to settle down and get his life in order.

'Well, that sounds like a good plan to me. And about time too,' said Matty with a surprised grin. 'You could stay here. It's your home, after all.'

Decker smiled. He suddenly had a compelling urge to ask him about Axelman's claim, to hear him laugh at it. But before he could say anything the doorbell rang.

Matty's eyes lit up. 'That'll be Jocy. He's coming round for a violin lesson. Hey, we could all play together, Luke.'

'Joey Barzini?' groaned Decker. 'Come on, Gramps, you're not still schmoozing with that old hood.' Decker wanted to talk to his grandfather about Axelman, and instead he was giving a music lesson to a man reputed to head up one of the most powerful Mafia families on the West Coast. Decker knew about Barzini. His business – real estate and lots of it – was ostensibly legit and he'd famously donated $1 million a year to the San Francisco Symphony orchestra for the last decade or so.

However, it was widely recognized by the great and the good that Barzini was still far from respectable.

But Matty had never cared much for the great and the good, and over the last few years the sixty-year-old Mafia man and the eighty-year-old concert violinist had become unlikely friends. Perhaps that was why Matty felt so relaxed about leaving his door and windows unlocked? Nobody with half a brain cell would burgle the home of a pal of Joey Barzini's.

'Why do you still see him, Gramps? And why do you invite him here? I don't like you dealing with crooks.'

Matty frowned. 'Because he's my friend and because he comes to visit. And just because he's from a criminal family doesn't mean he's a crook. '

Decker couldn't argue with that.

'Matty, how are you?' a rich voice called from the stairs.

'I'm fine, Joey. Come on up.'

Decker shook his head. 'Have a good lesson, Gramps,' he said. 'I'm going for a drink.'

'Luke, don't go.'

Luke rested a hand on his shoulder. 'Gramps, I came to see you, not Joey Barzini. Don't worry, I'll be back later.' He turned to leave. Decker wasn't really angry about his grandfather consorting with Barzini. He wasn't even angry about not being able to talk about Axelman. In fact, he was rather relieved he could leave that particular sleeping dog undisturbed. If he was honest, he was angry with himself for being unable to shrug off Axelman's stupid words.

On the stairs he passed a huge man in a suit – the violin case he held looked like a toy in his hands. He had blue-black hair and the darkest eyes Decker had ever seen. Decker knew Barzini was about sixty, but the man looked little more than forty-five.

They acknowledged each other with a cautious smile, never having met face to face before. 'Your grandfather's a remarkable man,' was all Barzini said.

'That I know,' said Decker. 'Enjoy your lesson.'

Outside, Decker breathed in the evening air and walked to his car. He was free now to catch up with Kathy Kerr, but he quickly dismissed the thought. He would call Hank Butcher, or whoever was around, and have a few cold beers. He'd feel better after that.

He didn't see the white BMW pull up outside Matty's house as he pulled away from the kerb and drove downtown. And he certainly didn't see Axelman's lawyer, Tad Rosenblum, climb out and knock on his grandfather's front door. In his right hand he held an envelope, addressed in a spidery handwritten scrawl to Special Agent Luke Decker.

6

Mendoza Drive, near Stanford University,
California.
The same day. 9.12 p.m.

'She didn't even seem excited when I told her the news,' Kathy Kerr complained, taking another sip of Earl Grey tea. 'It's been almost nine years of damn hard work and we've actually gained FDA approval to start Phase-Two efficacy trials. We've proved that Version Nine is safe on animals and now on healthy human volunteers. Finally we can go ahead and see if Project Conscience actually *works* on violent criminals. But is the great Alice Prince excited? Is she hell?

'And she was pretty quick to put those vials back in that precious safe of hers when I came in. She might be brilliant, but at times she can be bloody paranoid.'

Kathy looked at the face opposite hers and smiled. 'You don't know what I'm talking about, do you, Rocky?'

As if to prove her right, the large chimp cocked his head to one side and proceeded to scratch his chin. Then he turned back to the flickering portable TV on the step outside his pen, its extension cable trailing back across the yard to the house.

The night air was cool as she sat on the stoop by Rocky's pen in her backyard on Mendoza Drive. Mendoza Drive was a grand name for the rough track. Her house was at the end, surrounded by woods and fields. Her nearest neighbour was hundreds of yards away, which was just as well considering how noisy Rocky could get.

At well over four feet tall Rocky was a massive chimpanzee. If he put his mind to it he could easily tear a man apart. He had been one of the original primates on Project Conscience. In Kathy's laboratory at the Stanford Medical Research Center as many as eight apes used to be housed in the adjoining primate compound. But since the project had moved on to human volunteers three years ago the apes had been found homes in local zoos and wildlife sanctuaries.

However, Rocky was too old, and after his contribution to her work she felt obliged to care for him. So under the instructions of a keeper from the Charles Paddock Zoo down in Atascadero she had built this enclosed ape house in the garden of her home on Mendoza Drive. Rocky had been instrumental in testing her discovery of the seventeen genes that code for aggressive violent behaviour.

Rocky had been unusually violent when younger, almost killing one of the other apes. But ever since receiving one of the earliest somatic gene-therapy serums, taken from the genes of a smaller, gentler bonobo chimp, Rocky's behaviour had changed markedly, prompting many of the developments on Project Conscience. The reformed bruiser was now only ever violent when he thought Kathy was in danger; otherwise he was as mild as the proverbial lamb.

She put her half-empty mug of tea down on the ground next to her mobile phone and briefcase. After the Tice hearing this morning she'd returned to her laboratory on Pasteur Drive at Stanford University. Any thoughts of Luke Decker were quickly pushed from her mind when she received the fax from the Food and Drug Administration giving her approval to test her viral vector on criminal volunteers. Grinning from ear to ear she had broken the news to her two research assistants, Frank Whittaker and Karen Stein, and the lab technicians. An impromptu party in the lab had followed. So when she'd rushed off to ViroVector to share the good news with Alice Prince she'd felt deflated by her less-than-enthusiastic reaction. Still, tonight's farewell drinks for her assistants had doubled up as a celebration. Kathy had taken them and the lab technicians out for a meal before dropping Frank and Karen off at San Francisco airport.

She didn't begrudge them their six-week field trip to the Congo; after all she had helped arrange the sponsorship from ViroVector. And even though the timing wasn't ideal, Alice Prince had arranged for two fully qualified scientists from ViroVector to stand in while they were away. It was just that Frank and Karen had been with her from the beginning and had become more than colleagues; they were her closest friends in California. Staring up at the clear night sky Kathy saw an aeroplane pass overhead. In a few hours theirs would be doing the same.

Reaching into her briefcase she pulled out the folder she had prepared for tomorrow's meeting with Dr Prince and Director Naylor. Just reading the title, 'Project Conscience – Next Steps' gave her a thrill.

Would Project Conscience actually work? Alice Prince could be strange at times, but her work was brilliant, and Kathy had learnt a huge amount from her in the last nine years at the cutting edge of gene therapy and viral-vector technology. And although her other main sponsor, Madeline Naylor of the FBI, was paranoid about secrecy, at least she gave clear direction on the few occasions they met.

Kathy stood up and patted Rocky's arm through the wire of the pen. Picking up her briefcase she unlocked the door and walked to the back of the pen, bending down to an old school trunk screwed to the wooden floor. Taking a key from her pocket she unlocked the trunk and lifted the lid. She then reached into her briefcase, took out a computer disk and a copy of the folder she'd prepared for her meeting with Madeline Naylor tomorrow and placed them in the trunk. She put the disk into a plastic case, along with another thirty or so disks already there, and laid the folder on a pile of similar files.

Along with a few personal photos and artefacts of sentimental value the trunk contained copies of every major document, journal and experiment marking the development of Project Conscience. This was her personal record of her life's work.

Proof of what she had done, regardless of what anyone else might claim or say in the future. She regarded it as safe because no burglar would think to look here – and if they did, they would hesitate about disturbing Rocky.

In the trunk were recorded all the disappointments and triumphs that had led to this moment. And in the early days she and the team had experienced their fair share of scares. There had been a marginal risk of her original serum increasing the chance of testicular cancer in the test primates and their first-born males. Although the numbers had been small they had changed the calibration four times, fine-tuning them in iterative steps until any hint of the problem was removed. When other concerns, minor but possible, had come to light, they had done the same. Nothing was left to chance, and Kathy had been pleasantly surprised by how keen her FBI and ViroVector sponsors had been on finding her work so thorough. 'Don't cut any corners,' Alice Prince had said with that distant smile of hers. 'Spend all the time and money you need. Just make sure that when we go to the FDA we gain approval.' That patience was rare and made up for many of the other constraints.

Now, nine versions later, the team had developed a viral vector that the FDA had deemed safe to use on normal human volunteers. Kathy still had years of trials to go before she could *prove* it actually worked on violent offenders, but, given how few real changes she'd had to make from her original primate thesis to get to this point, she was confident. Plus all the data she'd used from the genomes of violent criminals on the FBI DNA database had allowed her to fine-tune the calibrations.

As Kathy left the pen and locked the door behind her she noticed a woman on the TV screen. She stood behind a lectern in a tailored navy-blue suit that set off her trim figure. Governor Pamela Weiss was over fifty, but the camera loved her. Her neat auburn bob was almost devoid of grey and her exquisite bone structure had fended off time better than any plastic surgeon's scalpel. And with her piercing blue eyes she seemed to look right out of the screen, directly at Kathy. The woman had true charisma, and Kathy found herself sitting down on the stoop, turning the screen towards her and increasing the volume.

She had no real interest in politics, but since gaining US citizenship she'd become more aware of the upcoming election, and she got a kick out of seeing a woman run as the Democratic candidate, with a chance of becoming the first-ever female president. Not only was Pamela Weiss media-friendly, but she seemed to possess real integrity.

By contrast, her opponent, the grey-haired, grey-suited Republican Senator George Tilson, had the bland good looks of a soap star. But he was a general who'd fought in Desert Storm eighteen years ago and, with the Iraq crisis looming, he was leading in the opinion polls by thirteen points. Despite Weiss's appeal the Republicans were on track to succeed the outgoing Democratic President Bob Burbank next Tuesday.

Kathy never watched live political debates because they were invariably boring set pieces of hollow rhetoric. But Weiss interested her. The candidates stood on a bare stage, facing each other from behind their lecterns. A moderator, the famous news anchorman Doug Strather, stood between them and a large studio audience. The TV debate had obviously been going for some time, but according to the commentator no particular points had been scored either way.

Doug Strather turned to the Republican candidate. 'Senator Tilson, do you think the gender of the President of the United States of America is relevant?'

Tilson smiled at Weiss and then at the camera, as if to apologize for what was clearly in his view a dumb question. 'Of course, in principle I have nothing against a woman becoming President of the United States. However, with the immediate threat of Iraq retaking Kuwait, China's expanding ambitions, and North Korea still far from settled, what the world needs now is strong, experienced leadership. I'm not saying that my experience in the Gulf War makes me more qualified than Governor Weiss to stand for the highest office in the land, but there is an argument for saying that now is not the time for experiments.'

Weiss shook her head. 'But surely, Senator Tilson,' she said, 'now is not the time to let history repeat itself. Particularly not with the weapons of nuclear and biological self-destruction that humanity now has at its disposal. Yes, women may historically have had little experience of waging war, but that's because we rarely start them.' She paused as the studio audience laughed. 'As a rule women are better known for promoting consensus than creating conflict. And frankly, I still think there's no such thing as a good war or a bad peace. However, when necessary, women can use force to end wars. Margaret Thatcher, Britain's first female prime minister, demonstrated that when she led the British to a successful victory in the Falkland Islands – thousands of miles from her country. She also stiffened our own President Bush's resolve when Iraq last invaded Kuwait before Desert Storm. And, if you remember, the initially nervous George Bush was both a man and a Republican.'

'So, Governor Weiss, as far as you're concerned gender is irrelevant?' asked Strather.

'Of course it is. As Senator Tilson said, what America needs now is strong leadership. Not male leadership or female leadership or black leadership or white leadership, just *good* leadership. And if you really want to look at gender, you could argue that when the world is poised on the brink of war the one person you *do* want in charge is a woman, particularly one who hates the very notion of armed conflict. The last candidate *I'd* vote for is an old warhorse with something to prove.

'And as for experience in running the country, eight years as Governor of California must count for something. Certainly more than Senator Tilson can lay claim to. Don't forget that I also have the full support of the current president as he nears the end of his second successful term. I intend to build on his administration's achievements by injecting new blood – both male and female.'

'But the current administration's record is appalling,' challenged Tilson. 'Vice-President Smith is a laughing stock; his comments on the UN and his involvement in recent sex scandals have destroyed his credibility and, by association, weakened that of the president. The issue of crime is of even more relevance. Violent crime is soaring at an unprecedented rate across the nation. Surely Governor Weiss doesn't think that record is good enough to simply carry on the good work?'

'No, of course not, there's always room for improvement. And, if you looked at the crime figures in more depth, you would know that my own state of California is already showing the way forward. Violent crime is down, particularly in the trouble spots like South Central LA.'

'That is true, Governor Weiss,' acknowledged Doug Strather. 'Can you explain why California has bucked the trend over the last five years?'

Tilson cut in quickly, 'It's clear to me that building more prisons and having a death penalty we are willing to enforce goes a long way towards cutting down crime. The sooner we as a nation get tough on crime, and *stay* tough on crime, then the sooner this country will be safe for normal citizens like you and me.'

Some of the audience clapped at this hollow rhetoric, but Weiss laughed and shook her head. 'But that simply isn't true. Texas, which has a Republican governor and a zero-tolerance programme in every major city, is the execution capital of the Western world. Outside of Islamic countries no other administration has more draconian laws, or carries them out with more vigour, than Texas. Ten people a month are currently being executed there, and many other states aren't far behind. But it's not working. Texas has the second-highest crime rate after Michigan.

'Time and time again an increase in the number of prisons and death penalties has failed. We need to reduce the incidents of crime by influencing the small minority that commits them, *before* they offend. The Philadelphia study and countless others have shown that over seventy per cent of the homicides, rapes and aggravated assaults attributed to any group of men are committed by a hard core of only six per cent. If we could target this six per cent, and stop them, we would significantly reduce crime. And apart from the obvious social benefits there are huge financial ones. If we reduce violent crime by just one per cent we save the country over $1.2 billion dollars. That must be worth doing.'

'But how do you do this? How do you reduce crime?'

The camera again focused on Weiss. 'First of all we must stop simply viewing crime as an external enemy to be fought and vanquished. Let's be clear on one thing: violent crime is almost the sole preserve of *male* criminals. In this country, a man is roughly nine times more likely to commit murder than a woman, seventy-eight times more likely to commit forcible rape, ten times more likely to commit armed robbery, and almost six times more likely to commit aggravated assault. Altogether, American men are almost ten times more likely to commit violent crime than women. They account for over ninety per cent of all these crimes. In addition to this, the majority of all penal reform is devised and implemented by men, therefore they are fighting against themselves – and that's a fight no-one can win.'

Kathy Kerr was mesmerized by the screen. Pamela Weiss was citing her own research, voicing her own arguments for tackling violent crime.

'Are you saying that being a woman makes you better equipped to fight crime?' asked Strather.

'Of course not. My gender makes no difference. Certainly not when it comes to *fighting* crime. What I *am* saying is that perhaps "fighting crime" is the wrong mindset. Perhaps it would be better to think of *treating* crime. Diagnosing its causes and, as with any health strategy, seeking prevention as well as a cure?'

'Again, how?'

'By looking not just at social factors but others as well. By looking beyond sociology and turning to the harder sciences, such as biology and genetics.'

Kathy Kerr couldn't believe it.

'But that's preposterous,' scoffed Tilson. 'Even the governor must have heard about the disastrous double-Y-chromosome study in the late 1960s. Back then scientists believed that men with an extra Y chromosome were more likely to be violent, but that was later entirely discredited. The only way to—'

'I know that particular study was discredited,' cut in Weiss, 'but we need proof rather than just theories. There have been no conclusive results proving that any of the conventional methods of preventing or punishing crime actually work. Indeed, all indications are that they fail – *miserably*. It's time for a change.'

Doug Strather adjusted his glasses. 'Governor Weiss, there's a lot of talk in the media about getting proof, *biological* proof of what causes violent crime, but are you saying that through your success in California—?'

'This is ridiculous,' interrupted Tilson. 'She's part of a defunct administration exhausted of ideas, trying any gimmick to retain power. First the Democrats play the feminist card, choosing a woman to run for president, despite the threat this may pose to national security, and now they're trying to claim responsibility for the *one* state in an otherwise crime-riddled nation that has a half-decent record. It's preposterous, not to say downright dishonest. Unless she knows something specific which the rest of us don't about curing crime, then she should keep her counsel.'

'Did you hear that, Governor Weiss?' said Strather smiling. 'I think you've been told to stop talking the talk and walk the walk. What do you say to that?'

At that moment the camera zoomed in on Pamela Weiss's face. Looking totally in control, she gave a wide, relaxed smile and said, 'What I say is this: the election is less than a week away. And don't worry, I'll walk the walk before then. I can assure you of that.'

Kathy turned from the TV and looked at Rocky. 'Did you hear that?'

Rocky gave a bored snort and scratched his chest.

She reached for her mobile phone, wanting to talk to someone. With Karen and Frank gone she considered calling Alice Prince, but then she remembered her lukewarm reaction to the FDA approval and thought it best to wait until their meeting tomorrow. There was no way she could get hold of Director Naylor. Then she thought of having a chat with her parents back in Scotland, but they were on holiday. Usually she would have gone with them, but because of the expected FDA approval she had postponed her trip this year. Anyway, the time difference ruled out a call to Britain, which also ruled out talking to her best friend in Edinburgh. Suddenly she had an overwhelming impulse to ring the one person who had always disagreed with her work, to see what he thought of the Weiss announcement.

Reaching into her bag she pulled out his card. But by the time she read it, she realized what a stupid idea it was to call him. Shaking her head, she replaced the card. It had been years, she reminded herself. Luke Decker and she lived separate lives now.

7

San Quentin State Penetentiary, California.
Thursday, 30 October 2008. 7.00 a.m.

The director of the FBI stood perfectly still in one of the two soundproof viewing rooms looking into San Quentin's renovated execution chamber. At five feet ten Madeline Naylor was two inches taller than the prison warden standing beside her. She wore a well-cut charcoal-grey trouser suit, which accentuated her sinewy frame, and had her white hair scraped back severely. Her face was pale, and the only colour in her otherwise monochrome appearance was the liverish red of her thin lips.

Director Naylor had come here personally to persuade herself that there would be no obstacles. She had personally arranged the execution papers with the governor. Ensuring that all appeals were quashed had been a formality for such a notorious criminal so close to an election. She only wished Alice Prince would hurry up and get here. She hated it when people were late.

To her sensitive nose this place reeked of sweat. Not the healthy physical perspiration from running in the sunshine or playing sport, but the acrid, emotional stench of adrenalin and fear. Even the warden, Neil Tarrant, standing beside her, gave off the tang of nervous sweat through his aftershave. She hated that smell; it signified man at his basest. And looking through the airtight porthole of re-inforced glass into the small execution chamber only confirmed her prejudice.

She looked down the corridor, past the second viewing room, where relatives of the victims sat waiting for justice, to the guards dragging the convict towards the airtight capsule. She had rarely seen a man look so pale before. He didn't struggle or betray any emotion. But then, how could he?

'What a farce! What a goddamn farce!' The words the warden muttered under his breath were almost inaudible, but she heard them. The irony that Tarrant, a man who had unflinchingly over-seen the deaths of tens, if not hundreds, of men in that airtight steel capsule, found this more shock-ing than the executions he usually sanctioned did not make her smile.

'It's necessary,' Naylor said as she watched the guards open the capsule and slump the man in the crude chair inside. 'You do understand that, don't you? We have to bring it forward to break the pattern, to avoid drawing attention to the other five men. That would look bad for all of us.' She paused. 'Not least you.'

Tarrant refused to look at her; he just rubbed the dark stubble on his chin and shook his head. 'This is a mistake. I hate it when someone else's mess becomes mine.'

'But that's the point; the mess is yours now. You

might not know everything, but after all these years you are involved. You understand that, surely?'

Tarrant gave a sullen shrug and Naylor's face hardened. She knew her strengths. Blessed with both a decisive mind and a will of adamantine rock, she had smashed through the glass ceiling in one of the most male-dominated arenas, shooting up the ranks of the FBI, finally becoming its first female director eight years ago, after a seven-year break as a federal prosecutor and district court judge. Madeline Francine Naylor was not about to let some sulky warden jeopardize everything. Her tone dropped in temperature when she spoke.

'Tarrant, you do of course realize that the presidential election is only a week away? And that we – and when I say *we*, I very much include *you* – have been involved in something that could have a direct effect on that result. Something that *all* of us have been working on successfully for years. Several extremely powerful people have far too much resting on this to see it fail. This mistake, as you call it, has happened and, regardless of whose fault it may or may not have been, it won't jeopardize our plans. No-one, least of all you, will be allowed to compromise what we're doing when we are so tantalizingly close. It just won't happen. Is that clear?'

The warden stared at her, nervously playing with his tie. He looked scared now and that pleased the director. Naylor liked men to be afraid of her; it made them easier to control. Tarrant nodded.

'Good,' said Naylor as Alice Prince arrived,

escorted by a guard. 'Could I have a moment alone with Dr Prince, please?' The dismissal was absolute; she didn't even wait for his agreement. Instead she turned to the door and watched Alice enter. As usual she was flustered and apologized to the departing warden for being late.

With her humble manner, shapeless navy skirt and jacket, greying hair and large glasses her friend looked more like a timid librarian or confused primary school teacher than one of the great minds of modern science. Only the doctor's cool grey eyes betrayed the fierce intelligence behind the bland façade, and the passion that fuelled it.

Madeline Naylor had known Alice Prince since they were children. They'd attended high school together and later Vassar college. She regarded Alice as a younger sister and the closest thing she had to a family. Madeline felt even closer to her than she did to Pamela Weiss – the friend they both met at Vassar, who was the current Governor of California and who, next week, was running for the highest office in the land.

'Sorry I'm late, Madeline.'

'It doesn't matter,' she said, embracing her friend. 'Come and stand next to me. We've got this room to ourselves so we can talk.' She smiled at Alice. 'Don't be so nervous. Everything's going to be OK. In all the years we've been together, have I ever let us down?'

Alice smiled back. 'No, I suppose not. It's just that as we come closer to Crime Zero I worry about all the things that can go wrong – and it's becoming so . . . so . . . *real*. It frightens me, Madeline, and makes me think that perhaps . . .'

Naylor smiled. She knew how Alice hated getting too close to the practicalities of what they were doing. She gestured to the man being strapped into the chair in the airtight capsule. 'Look, we're on schedule, aren't we?'

Alice nodded. 'Yes. TITANIA was out by a few hours, but no more than with the younger convicts. It was obviously an accelerated test, but it verifies the principles of the Phase-Three Crime-Zero vector. And I've just heard that the orphanage scare was nothing.'

'Excellent. Well then, once this unpleasantness is over, you can forget about Crime Zero and let TITANIA handle the phasing issues. Just concentrate on Project Conscience for now. I've blocked out most of today to deal with this. The immediate concern is to ensure Pamela is happy with everything. Her campaign manager has only given us an hour today to brief her for Friday's announcement. So after we leave here we'll go back to ViroVector and make sure everything's buttoned down before she arrives. How is Kathy Kerr? Will she keep quiet about the FDA compromise when she finds out about it?'

'Yes, I'm sure she won't be a problem.'

Madeline Naylor nodded but she felt less sure. 'Have you isolated her like we agreed?'

'Yes, yes. Her two closest colleagues are on a field trip to Africa and all the relevant files have been moved to a different directory in TITANIA.'

'How about hard copies?'

'I imagine she'll have those at Stanford.'

'OK, Jackson's people should already have removed those.' William Jackson was an associate director based at FBI headquarters who reported directly to her. A powerful African-American, with high cheekbones, fierce eyes and a distinctive nasal voice, Jackson ran a team of four special agents, who helped Madeline tie up loose ends and keep her abreast of any developments she should be aware of in the Bureau. She regarded them as her law within the law.

'But, Madeline, is this really necessary? Kathy'll be fine. It's in her interests to co-operate.'

'Perhaps.' Madeline understood Alice's loyalty. It had been Kathy Kerr's thesis that had inspired Alice's recovery from her breakdown nine years ago after her daughter Libby had been abducted and Alice's spineless husband had deserted her 'to rebuild my life' with his young secretary. 'Anyway, we're seeing Kathy before Pamela,' Naylor said. 'I can find out then how co-operative she's going to be. We can't afford any dissenting voices now.'

Saying nothing, Alice gave a small, acquiescent nod and nervously fingered the unusual pendant around her neck. It was a platinum-mounted glass teardrop the size of a thumbnail, which contained liquid that moved as she touched it. Naylor shifted her attention back to the prisoner. The guards remained expressionless as they went about their routine task. Alice Prince looked away, her face pained by the spectacle.

But Naylor didn't turn away. She knew all about Karl Axelman; she had studied his files, both criminal and medical. He had no family, which is why he and the other five death-row convicts had been selected for the Phase-One Crime-Zero trial. Most of Axelman's victims had been about sixteen –

little older than Alice's daughter, Libby, when she'd disappeared ten years ago. Naylor was Libby's god-mother and she had taken it personally when the FBI – *her* FBI – couldn't find her abductor. They still didn't know who he was, although for a time they'd thought it might be Axelman, but the absence of Libby's effects among his trophies made that unlikely.

Still, if a person deserved to die, then Karl Axelman did. Naylor was sure of it. But she wanted more than justice for men like him. She wanted punishment. Revenge. So she felt cheated when the door to the execution chamber was sealed and the warden in the other viewing room nodded twice, authorizing the release of the lethal gas pellet. Unlike his victims, the man being executed in front of her could feel no fear or pain.

Karl Axelman was already dead. He had died almost eleven hours ago.

Naylor gleaned some satisfaction from the way he'd killed himself. Last night he had stuffed a sheet into his mouth to stifle his cries and, despite terrible self-inflicted injuries, the prison doctor estimated that he had taken at least three hours to die from loss of blood. It was gratifying to know that, far from being the error Tarrant thought it was, the manner and timing of Axelman's death vindicated their plans.

Her only small concern was that a senior FBI agent had interviewed Axelman yesterday. She had asked Deputy Director McCloud to keep her informed of what Axelman might have revealed, but on past evidence she thought it was unlikely to be anything significant.

As Director Naylor watched the gas fill the chamber, she wished she could have witnessed Axelman's agony. Only what they had learned from his death, and what they still had planned, tempered her frustration. He was beyond their justice now. After all, only God could punish a dead man.

But there would be others, she consoled herself. There would be many others.

8

The Cold Room, ViroVector Solutions, California.
The same day. 9.11 a.m.

If TITANIA could have expressed an emotion it would undoubtedly have been satisfaction as it updated the status on both Project Conscience and Crime Zero.

TITANIA was housed in the Cold Room, a sterile room at the heart of the ViroVector dome. Embodied in a twelve-foot steel-and-glass cube, it was protected by an air-cooled white Kevlar jacket. Air ducts blowing sterilized eight-degree-centigrade air emitted a slow, rhythmic sound, as if TITANIA were breathing. Any service engineer entering this domain had to pass through an anti-static air-shower to remove dust, before donning white overalls, overshoes, hairnet and face mask.

TITANIA was born of the genetics age, when the need to sequence the three-thousand-million-letter sentence of the human genome had spurred computer programmers and hardware designers on to greater heights. The breakthrough came with the invention of the Genescope by the GENIUS Corporation of Cambridge, Massachusetts just months before the last millennium ended. That revolutionary gene-sequencer eschewed the use of electronic logic gates in its processor, using the primitive photo-responsive protein bacteriorhodopsin instead. This multiplied processing speeds a thousandfold within an industry that, until then, had prided itself on doubling speeds every year. Of the ensuing new generation of 'living' biosupercomputers TITANIA was one of the most powerful.

TITANIA controlled myriad projects within ViroVector. Its programs included payroll, inventory control, smart-building security and maintenance, the ordering of raw materials, production planning and distribution. It also controlled the data flow of the company's ten Genescope gene-sequencers. In its database were the DNA records of every ViroVector employee or associate, plus the gene sequences of every known virus in existence and every genetically engineered viral vector ever worked on or produced by the company.

Both Conscience and Crime Zero were controlled by a program located in its project management suite of applications. These applications controlled the schedules and status reports on every project managed by the company. They were updated automatically, with suggestions submitted to the human managers based on TITANIA's constant roaming of the information superhighway. Although physically based at ViroVector, TITANIA could be omnipresent in cyberspace. Driving a variety of search engines to probe and, if necessary, steal relevant data, its mission was to learn everything and convert what it learnt into usable information. It used this omniscience to maximize the success of each project's outcome, whether launching a new product, coping with imminent new legislation or choosing a new menu for the staff canteen.

Currently, a small section of its powerful neural net was focusing on the Crime Zero program, the most complex and secure system under its control.

First it noted the related Project Conscience inputs and data, although that project was almost complete. Conscience had always had two objectives as far as TITANIA was concerned. One was to act as a learning process to develop viral vectors for the infinitely more complex Crime Zero. The other was to help Pamela Weiss win the presidency – again vital for Crime Zero. Checking back over time, TITANIA noted the key dates for Project Conscience.

PROJECT CONSCIENCE MANAGEMENT SUMMARY: 0900hrs. 30/10/2008

V1 criminal-efficacy trial [non-FDA approved]	10/02/2001 to present
V9 Vector optimization complete	12/10/2004
V9 FDA human safety trials commence	06/01/2005
V9 FDA safety approval	29/10/2008

. . . .

| Democratic crime policy statement | 31/10/2008 |
| Pamela Weiss elected as Democratic president | 04/11/2008 |

There was nothing more TITANIA could do. The Version-Nine FDA-approval lag had been suboptimal, but with the forthcoming policy statement this Friday and next Tuesday's election Project Conscience had almost fulfilled its purpose. It could do no more to effect the outcome, merely record when it would happen. Next TITANIA checked Crime Zero.

PROJECT CRIME ZERO MANAGEMENT SUMMARY:
0900hrs 30/10/2008

Phase One: Telomeres Trials

San Quentin patient trial commenced	02/09/2008
Final patient #SQ6 terminated	29/10/2008
Cartamena patient trial commenced	11/02/2005
Patient #C78 confirmed as post-pubescent	30/10/2008

Phase Two: Controlled Trial

| Bioshield batch #VV233456H dispatched | 10/10/2008 |
| Microchip confirmation of batch activation | 23/10/2008 |

The Phase-One telomeres trials had been a complete success, with the suicide of the sixth and final

San Quentin patient less than twenty-four hours ago, and the Cartamena incident proving to be an isolated false alarm. But the escalating crisis in Iraq had necessitated pulling forward the Phase-Two controlled trial before Phase Three could confidently be launched. Interrogating its search engines, TITANIA scoured the Internet for feedback on what might be happening in Iraq. Knowing what it was looking for made its quest efficient.

One definition of intelligence is the ability to see patterns in apparently random data. If this were true then TITANIA was a genius. Logging into hospital databases in Baghdad and Iraqi military systems, while at the same time piecing together apparently unrelated snippets of information from Reuters, CNN, the BBC and the other syndicated news agencies on the World Wide Web, TITANIA continuously searched for the pattern. But it was still too early. The reports TITANIA was looking for would only surface in the next few days. Still, for the moment Phase Two appeared to be active and on schedule.

Only now did TITANIA look at Phase Three, the most complex stage of all. This was much harder to predict.

Given that Phase Three hadn't yet begun and Phase Two was on track the computer could only check the delivery and replacement schedules of the modified bacteriophage air-purifiers at Heathrow airport. Once it had confirmed these were in place it kept its original forecast unchanged, putting the final outcome of Crime Zero still some three years away – assuming nothing altered in the meantime.

As TITANIA compiled its Project-Conscience and Crime-Zero status reports for the two humans with gold level clearance, the biocomputer's air-cooling ducts seemed to exhale more loudly for an instant, as if breathing a sigh of satisfaction.

9

San Quentin State Penitentiary, California.
The same day. 9.25 a.m.

Life was looking less than satisfactory for Luke
Decker as he drove towards San Quentin for the
second time in two days, with Axelman's letter on
his mind.

That morning he had woken late in his old bed-
room at Matty's house. Cracking open his eyes as
he used to as a kid, he'd watched the morning light
reach its impossibly long fingers beneath the
curtains and stretch across the polished wooden
floor towards his bed. For a brief moment he had
felt like a child again. Only when he'd rolled over
did the dull throb in his head remind him that he
was a stupid adult who had drunk one too many
bottles of Budweiser with Hank Butcher last night.

Butcher wrote mainly for journals like *Vanity
Fair* and had a gift for tapping into the Zeitgeist. He
had made a name for himself with his witty pieces
commenting on the main issues and personalities
of the day. As always, he'd been excellent company, knowing all the trivial gossip that rarely

touched Decker's life. And he'd managed to push all thoughts of Axelman from Decker's mind.

But then, over breakfast, Matty had given Decker the sealed letter delivered by Axelman's lawyer and the doubts had come flooding back. Decker had read Axelman's handwritten confession with growing horror and Matty had sensed his shock. But when his grandfather had asked what was wrong, Decker refused to elaborate. What Axelman had written about Decker's mother and father was so preposterous, so poisonous, that he couldn't tell, or indeed *ask*, Matty about it. Not until he had to.

The letter had been clever because only half of it related to him, explaining why Axelman couldn't talk to Decker yesterday and detailing why he believed he was Decker's father. The other half contained the revelation Axelman wouldn't give yesterday, namely the general whereabouts of the twelve girls he'd abducted. To complicate matters Axelman had also confessed to murdering a thirteenth victim, indicating that this girl's parents unwittingly knew the exact location of all the bodies.

It was these final revelations which meant Decker couldn't just screw up the poisonous letter and throw it away. He was professionally obliged to acknowledge this information, check it out and then share it with the rest of the FBI. But Decker didn't want Axelman's sick little joke made public in the Bureau yet. Not until he'd made more sense of what currently seemed totally irrational.

His first thought had been to go to the San Francisco FBI field office and use a computer to check out the facts on the thirteenth victim. But then he'd remembered that, although Rosenblum had lodged yet another appeal, Axelman's execution date was scheduled for today. So he'd rushed to San Quentin penitentiary.

Squinting in the bright light Decker parked his hire car in the visitors' parking lot. As he killed the ignition his cellphone rang. He answered it and heard the deputy director on the line.

'Spook, it's Bill McCloud. I hear the Tice hearing went well yesterday.'

'He's not going to be able to kill anyone else, Bill, if that's what you mean.'

'That'll do for me.'

Decker liked Deputy Director Bill McCloud. The laid-back Texan was a healthy foil to the chilly absolutism of Director Naylor. McCloud had once worked in the behavioural sciences unit and had campaigned hard to maintain its budget and status within the Bureau, which is why he'd refused to accept Decker's resignation.

'How did your meeting with Axelman go? Her man Jackson told Director Naylor about it, and for some reason she's taken an interest in what you found out.' McCloud always called Associate Director William Jackson 'her man Jackson'. Jackson had no real role as far as Decker could make out, except spying for Naylor and carrying out her dirty work. He was universally hated and feared within the Bureau. 'Perhaps she values your famed psychological powers after all.'

Decker hesitated, feeling the letter in his jacket.

'I assume you struck out with him – nothing new, huh?' said McCloud before Decker could say anything. McCloud threw the words at him, a rhetorical question that required no response. So Decker didn't supply one. 'Don't feel bad about it, Spook. That guy was cold. One of the worst. Didn't even know the meaning of the word remorse.'

'You're using the past tense, Bill. I thought he had an appeal.'

'Cancelled by the governor. He was executed a few hours ago. So anyway, where are you now?'

Decker took a deep breath and sat back in his car seat. With Axelman dead there was only one way of proving what he'd claimed. Plus he had an over-whelming urge to see him again. 'Look, Bill, I need to check a couple of things out for a day or two.'

McCloud sighed, and when he spoke again he sounded suspicious. 'You're not still sniffing around Berkeley, are you, Spook? The Bureau needs you, boy. Don't you forget that.'

Decker wasn't going to be drawn on that issue now. 'Bill, I'll keep in touch via our field office here,' he said and hung up. Then he called Quantico to warn his team that he'd be away for a couple of days. Putting the phone away, he got out of the car and walked towards the prison gates, mentally ticking off the little he knew.

Axelman was a classic sociopath: controlled, self-centred and vain. He was incapable of showing any empathy for his victim's pain or remorse for his actions. He had killed twelve girls and delighted in keeping the whereabouts of their bodies a secret. Every psychological test showed that Axelman had no real fear of death or punishment.

And yet yesterday he had looked a physical wreck. He had acted completely out of character, hysterical with guilt and shame. And last night

Axelman had arranged, through his lawyer, to deliver a sealed letter to Decker. A letter containing personal details of why he had chosen to confess to Decker and a full confession indicating where the twelve bodies were buried – plus the existence of a thirteenth body.

Now the man was dead and the answers had died with him.

Decker felt torn as he approached the guards' window by the main door. The professional in him calmly tried to figure out how a man incapable of remorse could suddenly become so consumed by guilt that he confessed all. But on a personal level Decker ruminated on Axelman's outlandish paternity claim. It was no longer enough that Axelman was unable prove he was Decker's father. Decker now had to *disprove* it.

Clarence Pitt was one of the guards manning the gate. He looked bored and smiled when he saw Decker. 'Hey, Decker, what are you doing back here? This place is becoming like FBI central. Had the big boss herself in earlier.'

'Director Naylor was here? Do you know why?'

'Nope. But I guess it had something to do with watching that Axelman guy meet his maker.'

Decker frowned but said nothing. It was hardly usual for the FBI director to attend the execution of a killer.

'That's what I'm here for, Clarence, I need to see Axelman's body.'

Pitt checked a computer screen to his right and screwed up his face in a pained grimace. 'The Axelman stiff's been flagged. That means the warden wants it left alone. You got authorization?'

'Come on, Clarence, don't make me go through all the paperwork. I just want to look at the body. I saw him yesterday when he was alive. What harm can it do if I see him today when he's dead? Five minutes is all.'

Pitt scowled for a bit longer, then pulled out a form from his desk and handed it to Decker. 'Sign this, and then if anyone asks questions it's your butt that gets kicked.'

Pitt handed over his post to another guard and led Decker through the prison to the hospital building. The only sounds Decker heard as he followed Pitt down four flights of steps and along the corridor to the morgue were the occasional shouts of far-off human voices, the click clack of heels on the tiled floor and the whispered rustle of Pitt's starched uniform.

Turning through an arch, the guard pointed at a pair of swing doors. 'This is it,' he said, pushing them back. As he did so Decker was hit by a wave of cool air that reeked of chemicals. Inside was a large white room. The floor and the lower two-thirds of the wall were tiled. Two stainless-steel autopsy tables dominated the middle of the room and an unoccupied gurney stood on one side. Along the far wall were three basins. Part of the left wall was made up of stainless-steel drawers. A skinny guy in a soiled white coat stood by the drawers mopping the floor. Walking over to him, Pitt introduced Decker. 'Steve, this here is Special Agent Decker. He's from the FBI. He needs to see the Axelman stiff.' Pitt left him then, telling Decker he'd be back in exactly five minutes.

With the casualness of a clerk locating frozen

peas in a grocery store, Steve wandered over to the row of stainless-steel drawers and pulled out number seven. Extended to its full length the drawer acted as a table, displaying its contents. The body lay on its back, a sheet loosely draped over it.

Steve picked up a tag next to the corpse's head, then read in a bored voice, 'Executed on Thursday, thirtieth October 2008 at seven twenty-three a.m. Cause of death: asphyxiation from gas.' Steve checked his watch. 'I got to go clean up a few things. What else d'you need to know?'

Decker continued to stare at the contours of the shrouded corpse below him. 'Nothing.'

'OK, I'll leave you to it. But you'd better hurry. This one's on a fast track for cremation.'

As the sound of the man's footsteps receded, Decker tried to maintain some professional detachment. Taking a deep breath he pulled the sheet back off the head. Luke had seen many corpses in his life, but rarely one so white. The man's face had the pasty bluish pallor of soft cheese.

Luke examined Axelman's face more closely, trying to see a likeness in the features. The more he looked, the more he imagined his own features reflected there – the high cheekbones, the wide forehead. Reaching forward he opened one eyelid, revealing a cloudy iris as green as his own. Then he pulled the sheet back further and reached for one of the hands, comparing his with the cold digits curled on the slab. There was only one way to be certain.

With careful fingers he plucked three hairs from the dead man's head, checking each follicle was still intact. He stared at the bare patches of scalp,

115

amazed by how much hair the man had lost since his recent file photograph. Placing the hairs in a small plastic evidence bag Decker again studied Axelman's face, this time staring at the unusually pale acne-pitted skin. It was as white as the victims he had examined in the past who had bled to death.

Suddenly wishing his task over he pulled the sheet off the body. At first he couldn't see the wound, because it was only detectable by what had been removed. Grimacing, he moved down the body and examined the jagged, torn flesh beneath the grey penis lying inert on the man's left thigh.

The scrotum was missing, severed by what must have been a dull blade. By the look of the wound, Decker guessed it had been done before the execution. But it was still recent, and there were flakes of congealed blood on the hairs of Axelman's inner thigh. Peering more closely he studied the angle and nature of the purple cuts and the surrounding bruises.

Decker straightened and tried to mimic the cutting action required to make such a rough laceration. It wouldn't be the first time a convict had been castrated in gaol by vindictive or vengeful inmates. But Decker couldn't see how any other inmates could have reached him on the row. He didn't believe the guards would have done this. However Luke tried, he couldn't get the required angle to duplicate the wound. Then, with an insight that chilled his blood, he mimed one more series of movements, and the angle of the ripped cuts tallied perfectly.

Karl Axelman had inflicted this on himself.

It was incomprehensible and went way beyond mind games. Why had a serial killer, notorious for his lack of remorse, castrated himself? What could have motivated Karl Axelman to do this?

Hearing footsteps approaching, Decker quelled his feelings of disgust and reached out to pick two small flakes of blood from Axelman's inner thigh. The hair follicles would be enough for the paternity test, but blood could tell him much more. His fingers brushed the corpse's flesh and the cold waxy texture sent a shudder through him. Quickly he placed the flakes of blood in the evidence bag with the hair and put the bag in his pocket.

When Steve returned, Decker asked him about the wound. The morgue attendant gave a disinterested shrug and pulled the sheet back over Axelman's face. 'That's the way he was when he came down here. You'd be surprised what happens to folks before they go to the chamber. I just deal with 'em after they come out.'

'How often do they come down with their balls cut off?'

'Not often enough, in my opinion,' said Steve, looking at Decker suspiciously. It was a look Decker had seen on the faces of countless witnesses. It said, I'm not involved in any of this shit and don't want to be. So stop asking your fool questions. Then Steve smiled a thin fuck-you smile. 'The warden's coming down soon to authorize the body for cremation and possible autopsy. You can ask him about what happened to his balls if you like.'

Decker smiled. 'That's OK.' The last thing he

wanted was to have to explain to the warden what he was doing here. He had got what he came for. 'Thanks for your help. I've seen enough.'

After a nervous Pitt walked him back to the main entrance, Decker strolled over to his hire car and tried to collect his thoughts. Something very weird was going on, but he didn't know what it was. For the time being he would focus on the one thing that really mattered: checking the validity of Axelman's letter – particularly Axelman's claim to be his father, and the revelations about the whereabouts of the bodies, including the thirteenth victim.

Holding the transparent evidence bag up to the light, Decker studied the flakes of blood and the three hairs. Then he pulled another evidence bag out of his jacket pocket and plucked two hairs from his own head. Ensuring the roots were intact he placed them in the empty bag. Placing each bag in separate pockets he thought of what to do next.

He needed to ensure the test was done discreetly. And he couldn't involve anybody in the Bureau. He had only one option, someone who was trustworthy and near by. The thought of involving her made him squirm inside.

He reached for his wallet. After a brief search he found what he was looking for. Checking the address on the card, he climbed into his car. He had no choice. He had to ask for her help. But that didn't make him feel any better.

He knew that Kathy Kerr would regard his sudden dependence on her genetic wizardry as some kind of moral victory.

In the Baghdad barracks of the Northern Corps of
the elite Republican Guard, Dr Uday Aziz was
worried. The more he looked at the corpse
sprawled on the barrack-room bunk the more he
couldn't escape the conclusion that this wasn't
good. This wasn't good at all.

Aziz stroked his thick moustache and studied
Colonel Ali Saadi standing opposite him. The
colonel was a squat, powerful man, with a massive
stomach and thick eyebrows. He was glaring
angrily at the corpse. For a moment Aziz thought
he was going to kick the dead soldier.

'This is the fourth in two days,' Aziz said softly,
looking at Private Jaafar Hammadi's medical file,
trying to find some reason why a perfectly fit
twenty-four-year-old should have had a brain
haemorrhage. 'That's if you ignore the suicides and
the Khatib shooting.'

'I don't understand it,' the colonel said. 'He
hadn't complained of being ill to any of his immediate superiors.'

'Was he under any particular strain?'

'He'd been training hard for his transfer south,
but no harder than the other men.'

Aziz scratched his head and studied the corpse
again. Apart from the acne and the recent hair loss
there was hardly anything remarkable. After the
first unusual death two days ago, Dr Aziz had
ordered standard post-mortems on the corpses.
Most had died of either a brain haemorrhage or
were suicides. All had been in excellent physical

condition with no history of mental problems. However, their blood tests had all revealed similar abnormalities. These abnormalities all pointed to one possible explanation – particularly given the hair loss and acne – but he would need to make more tests. 'We need to find out what's happening,' he mused, as if talking to himself.

'You're damn right we do,' said the colonel. 'You need to make it top priority. We've managed to keep it quiet for now, but morale is suffering and people are talking. If this gets any worse and the Rais hears of it so close to a possible offensive, he will demand an explanation.'

'I understand.' Aziz returned to stroking his moustache. The suicides and the shooting couldn't be blamed on him, but the others could. Why did this have to happen now? In the past his job as senior military doctor had been comfortable. The army, particularly the Republican Guard, was well fed and resourced. And apart from the obvious risks of war, the health of the men wasn't an issue. But over the last few months Aziz had been working all hours in a bureaucratic role, preparing for the Rais's planned offensive on Kuwait, organizing field-hospital contingencies and the vaccination of hundreds of thousands of troops. And now, already with more problems than he could handle, he was being confronted by this . . . *annoyance*.

'Are you sure these men haven't been taking any unauthorized medication?'

'Well I haven't authorized any, if that's what you mean?' said the colonel with an angry frown. 'What sort of medication are you talking about anyway?'

Aziz studied him closely, trying to decide if he was telling the truth. It wouldn't be the first time officers had tested drugs on troops to improve their combat capabilities, especially so close to an offensive. Aziz shrugged, still looking at the colonel. 'I'm talking about anabolic steroids. You know? The drugs some athletes take to improve their performance.'

The colonel shook his head in disbelief. 'You think these men have been taking steroids? And that's why they're dead?'

'I don't know, yet,' Aziz said, closing the corpse's staring bloodshot eyes. 'But I'm going to find out.'

10

Stanford University, California.
The same day. 12.53 p.m.

Kathy Kerr checked and double-checked her proposal. She didn't want any last-minute obstacles.

All morning she'd been preparing for her meeting with Madeline Naylor and Alice Prince. Pacing round the small private office in her lab at Stanford University she re-read the recommendations she had made for taking Project Conscience forward. However she looked at them, she was sure each one stacked up. The funding budgets were realistic; the timings were ambitious but achievable. Then she turned to the 1,000 prison inmates she'd selected from the FBI DNA database of convicted violent criminals. As she registered each name she tried to memorize their files, double-guessing any objections Madeline Naylor might have for using them.

She also made a mental note to ask about Pamela Weiss's TV debate last night, and whether Alice Prince or Director Naylor knew anything about her apparent plans to use biology and genetics to treat crime.

Sitting at her desk Kathy watched the two lab technicians clearing the incubators and loading soiled Petri dishes and beakers into the autoclave. No-one else was present. Frank's and Karen's replacements would arrive next week, which was just as well, because until the forthcoming procedure had been agreed there wasn't that much to do.

A minute later the main doors to the lab suddenly swung open, startling Kathy. In that split second she thought Director Naylor and Dr Alice Prince had arrived early and she thanked God she was ready.

But she wasn't ready, because the visitor wasn't Madeline Naylor or Alice Prince.

When the tall, blond man tentatively walked into the main lab, she saw one of the lab technicians talk to him and point to her office. Kathy could only stand and stare through the blind as the man strode through the laboratory and knocked on her door.

'Come in,' she said, suddenly wishing she'd worn her contacts to work today rather than her old glasses.

The door opened and Luke Decker walked in. He seemed nervous, his eyes wary above a tight smile.

'Hi, Kathy. I hope you don't mind me popping in unannounced?'

She smiled. 'No, not at all.'

'Impressive set-up,' he said, indicating the laboratory.

123

'Thanks,' she said, putting her proposals for the forthcoming meeting down on the table. 'So what brings you to this neck of the woods?'

Luke's face became more serious as he turned and closed the door. 'Well, to be honest I need a favour – a discreet favour. Do you have a minute?'

Kathy's curiosity was piqued. 'Sure, I've got Director Naylor arriving in about half an hour, but I'm OK until then.'

At the mention of the FBI director Luke frowned. 'Sounds important.'

'It is. We've just got FDA approval for a big project we're working on, and she's coming round to discuss the next steps.'

'That's great,' he said. 'Congratulations.' But he was still frowning.

'What's the matter?' Kathy asked.

'Let's just say that I don't want this favour to become Bureau business just yet.'

Kathy nodded. She was studying Decker now, genuinely intrigued. 'Don't worry, my lips are sealed. So, what do you need?'

Decker paused. He seemed to be weighing up how much to tell her. Reaching into his jacket pocket he pulled out a small plastic bag. Then, from a side pocket he pulled out another. 'Well,' he said, lifting the first bag, 'I need to compare the DNA of the hair in this bag with what's in this one.'

'How do you mean, compare?'

He opened the first bag, revealing three grey hairs and two flakes of dried blood. 'I want to know if there's a relationship between the two people these came from?'

She narrowed her eyes. 'Relationship as in family

124

relationship? Brother-sister, father-daughter, that kind of thing?'

'Exactly.'

Kathy took the bag and peered at the hairs and flakes of blood, then placed it carefully on her desk. Then she took the other bag and looked at the two blond hairs there. 'You're not going to tell me what this is about, are you?'

'Not unless you make me. No.'

She could see from Decker's face that he disliked asking for her help, as if he were somehow endorsing her belief that understanding genes was at the root of understanding everything. And for a fleeting moment she felt an irresistible urge to draw attention to his sudden dependence on the very technology he had so openly derided in the past. She needed him to realize the significance of what he was requesting and recognize that the work she had dedicated her life to had meaning. 'OK, I'll give it a go.'

'How long will it take?' he asked, checking his watch. Now he'd told her, he seemed anxious to leave.

'How long? Well, in the old days we had to use the dot-blot technique, or RFLP analysis, to isolate the sections of DNA that highlight the genetic relationship between individuals. You'd be lucky to get the results in two weeks.'

His face fell.

She pointed at the black swan-like Genescope in the main laboratory and picked up the first bag. 'But with that thing out there we can read all ninety thousand or so of the genes in the samples here, and compare them with those in the other bag, in a fraction of that time. Leave it with me and give me a call in a couple of hours. I should have a definite result by then.'

Decker nodded, and in his face she could see both relief and dread. 'Thanks, Kathy. I appreciate it.'

'Are you sure, Luke? You don't look like you want to know the answer at all.'

He shrugged and flashed a deceptively casual smile. 'Let's just say I need to know.'

At one thirty precisely Director Naylor and Dr Prince arrived.

Moments earlier Kathy Kerr had given the lab technicians both batches of Decker's mystery samples to scan through the Genescope gene sequencer and analyse for any relationship. She couldn't help wondering why he had asked her to conduct the scans and why he was so keen to avoid the FBI. But for now she focused on her visitors.

Smart in a charcoal trouser suit, her white hair immaculate, the usually stern director was smiling. Alice Prince wore a shapeless navy jacket and skirt and seemed strangely nervous.

Within the opening minutes, in the privacy of Kathy's office, Alice told her that the FBI and ViroVector were increasing Kathy's funding by a further $5 million a year. This money would be deposited as a lump sum in a special project account to use at her sole discretion. 'Naturally,' Naylor said with a grin, 'you will be expected to fund your personal salary – as much as you deem appropriate – out of this additional grant.'

Kathy was dumbstruck. Her current grant was

126

already more than enough to continue her work within the tight budgets she'd set herself, especially as ViroVector subsidized much of her lab-equipment costs at Stanford anyway. But with additional funding she could recruit more people, speed up the whole programme.

'I don't know what to say. It's very generous. In fact, it's much more than I need.'

'Nonsense,' said Naylor. 'The first rule about seeking grants is that you can never have too much funding.' She smiled again, the skin creasing beneath her dark eyes, and her lips stretching over her teeth. Kathy had rarely seen her smile before and it seemed unnatural, more unnerving than her usual stern expression.

'Anyway,' said Naylor, rising from her seat at the small circular conference table. She moved closer to Kathy, bending over her, 'you deserve the additional funding and we want you to realize how much we appreciate all you've achieved.'

Flattered, but slightly embarrassed, Kathy reached for her notes in the middle of the table. 'Well, thank you, I'm very grateful. But what I most want to gain is your agreement on the next steps for the project.' She waited for Naylor to retake her seat and then handed her and Alice a folder each.

Kathy opened her proposal. 'As well as outlining the next steps, rationale, budget breakdowns, objectives and timings this proposal contains a list of all the subjects I'd like to test Conscience Version Nine on – subject to their approval. And yours, of course.'

Neither Prince nor Naylor said anything for a

127

moment; Naylor didn't even look at the papers Kathy had given her.

Then Alice Prince cocked her head to one side and appeared to study a spot just above Kathy's head. 'What would you say if I told you we could reduce the next eight to ten years of your research?'

Kathy didn't understand. She looked from Prince to Naylor. 'What do you mean? Accelerate the tests on criminals?'

Naylor nodded slowly, her smile gone. Unblinking, she stared at Kathy, a snake watching its prey.

Kathy shrugged. 'Well, that would be great if it didn't compromise the results. Accelerate it by how much?'

There was a pause as the dark eyes studied her even more closely. Kathy had the distinct impression she was being tested, judged on her reaction. 'Let's say we wouldn't so much accelerate the trials', said Naylor, 'as *bypass* them.'

'But we have to do tests. To make sure it works.'

'Not if they've already been conducted,' said Alice.

'But that's impossible; that would have taken years.'

The director nodded as her thin lips twitched into a small smile which failed to reach her eyes. 'Eight years in fact.'

Kathy stared at Naylor, searching for the teasing irony. 'Come on, Director, I don't understand. Tell me you're kidding.'

But the director of the FBI was no longer smiling.

Kathy put a hand over her mouth and looked at Alice, but she was looking down at the table. 'You've been conducting secret trials on our work . . . on *my* work?'

'It's not quite as simple as that,' said Naylor. 'Without our knowledge a group of over-zealous senior FBI officers and ViroVector scientists found out about Conscience and began a secret, unauthorized trial. Naturally, all the people involved will be severely disciplined, but the point is, their trials worked.'

For some seconds Kathy's disbelief numbed her to any other feelings. Then, realizing that this was serious, her anger surfaced. Standing, she pushed her chair away from the table and paced around the office. 'But who are these people? Why weren't they discovered earlier?'

Naylor sat cooly in her seat. Alice Prince squirmed in hers.

'It doesn't matter now,' said Naylor, 'but, Kathy, you must be aware of the improved crime figures in California.'

Kathy was so furious she could feel her nails digging into her palms. Of course she was aware of the state's improved crime figures. The news and current-affairs shows were full of theories to explain them, especially now that the governor credited with them was standing for president.

'Well,' continued Naylor, 'they are a direct result of tests conducted on violent criminals using your theories on gene manipulation.' Naylor held up Kathy's proposal. 'The people who did this test have done nothing different from what you planned. Indeed, some of the criminals on your list have already been given the treatment. In one way you could argue that it's good news: your theories have been proven to work. You've been saved ten years.'

Kathy reached across and snatched her proposal document from Naylor. 'Well, this was a bloody waste of time, wasn't it? My team and I worked our butts off for nothing. And how the hell could the tests have started eight years ago? The safe Version-Nine serum approved by the FDA was only developed four years ago.'

Naylor paused and gave a small sigh.

Kathy felt sick as understanding dawned. She could see her life's work, the hours of dedication and sacrifice, wasted. The whole of her research discredited and put back decades. 'Good God,' she shouted, 'they used the original serum, didn't they? Christ, I bet the subjects weren't even volunteers.'

'No, they weren't. But you could argue that after the crimes they committed they weren't given any choice about going to gaol or death row either. The criminal subjects might not have been aware of the tests, but almost all have benefited. Kathy, consider one thing. No-one has been harmed by the treatment. Some sixteen thousand convicts have been tested, and not only does it work, it's safe.'

'How the hell do you know? The effects could manifest themselves years into the future. God, our own research indicated that testicular and prostate cancers could be caused and accelerated by the early vectors. Not just in the subjects themselves, but in their children too. Male babies born with testicular cancer could be—'

130

Alice Prince shook her head. Her voice was almost pleading. 'Kathy, I saw your early reports. Causation was never proved. I've looked into it.'

'How can you say that, Alice? You know it was.'

'OK, OK. But the percentage risk was minute. Come on, Kathy, the difference between the early vectors and the final Version Nine is negligible.'

'Negligible? What gives you the right to say that?'

Alice looked flustered and looked towards Naylor. Alice Prince had always hated conflict.

'Why don't you wait outside, Alice,' said Director Naylor. 'Let me handle this.'

Alice paused and then, with a look of shame and relief on her face, she stood up and walked out.

Without missing a beat Naylor continued. 'Kathy, the negligible differences are vital for gaining official FDA approval, I grant you, but hardly necessary to be safe. Kathy, the money and lives that have already been saved by doing what these people did more than offsets any minute risk involved. And after Pamela's pre-election announcement all future treatments will use the FDA-approved Version Nine anyway.'

'What announcement?' said Kathy. She couldn't believe this.

'This Friday, Pamela Weiss—'

Kathy stopped her pacing. 'Is that what Weiss was talking about on yesterday's TV debate?'

Naylor nodded. 'Yes, and that's what we want to talk to you about. Once we learnt that the un-authorized tests worked and your Version Nine had received full FDA approval we decided to use the crisis to the project's advantage. A scandal could push Conscience back decades, but a brave visionary announcement that seizes the opportunity might not only save the project, but actually accelerate its acceptance.

'So, with the full support of President Burbank, Pamela Weiss will take responsibility for the successful results of the criminal tests, putting an end to all the speculation about the positive California crime figures. She will also announce a proposed policy to treat all convicted violent criminals across the nation with your FDA-approved version of Conscience. She will tell the American people that if they elect her she can guarantee to reduce crime across the country. What's more, Kathy, Alice – who is just as horrified about the unauthorized trials as you are – suggested you share full credit for the successful tests.

'Think about it, Kathy. You'll be famous. A Nobel Prize isn't out of the question. But more important, with the full political power of the presidency behind it, you'll see your life's dream of a cure for crime realized sooner than you could ever have imagined. Not just in this country, but worldwide. However, it's important that no-one is left in any doubt that the tests conducted over the last few years were done with the FDA-approved vector. Although we know the trials were safe, we have to be seen to have known all along. Pamela Weiss must appear as a bold visionary taking calculated risks, not as irresponsible or dangerous.'

This was unbelievable. Kathy walked back to her desk and leant against it. 'But she *is* being irresponsible and dangerous.'

For the first time Naylor looked angry. 'No she

132

isn't. The future president still isn't aware of the minor differences between Version One and Version Nine. As far as Pamela Weiss knows, the FDA approved what was tested in the unauthorized trials. And that's the way it has to stay.'

'You can't do this to me. It's completely un-ethical. You want me to lie about my life's work?'

'No, of course not. This whole project is based on your life's work. We just need you to see the bigger picture and make the most of the opportunity. This irresponsible test threatened to ruin the credibility of everything you worked for. But this way you can use it to your advantage to make the world a better place. How can that be a bad thing?'

Kathy sat on the desk and shook her head. Minutes ago her future had been bright and challenging but most important of all it had been her own. Now all her dreams were being ripped away. 'But it's a lie. I'm not sure I can go through with it.'

'Come on, Kathy, you have to be pragmatic to protect your ideals. The choice is simple: You can embrace what has happened and make the world a better place, or you can denounce it, merely because some petty rules were broken and a tiny percentage of convicted violent criminals were *possibly* exposed to a *negligible* risk of disease. If you do the first, you will achieve everything you've ever dreamed of, including the realization of your vision of a gentler world. If you do the second, then you will destroy any hope of your vision becoming reality.'

'But it's still wrong. Don't you see that?' Kathy said, her mouth dry with anger. 'You want me to break the law to promote something that's supposed to *stop* crime.'

Naylor stood slowly and spoke calmly and forcefully. 'What's done is done. The question now is, what do we do next? Do we build on your work or destroy it? Think about it. This is important. I need to know your decision by six o'clock tonight. Is that clear?'

Kathy said nothing for a moment. Her head ached with the unfairness of it all. If she kept her integrity she would compromise, perhaps even ruin, her life's work. But if she compromised her integrity she would see her dreams realized in a fantastically short space of time. It was a deal with the devil.

'Six o'clock. Is that clear?' Madeline said again, her face impassive as she opened the door to leave.

'No, it's bloody not,' said Kathy eventually. 'Nothing's clear any more.'

Alice Prince squirmed inside as she waited in her car in the parking lot. She felt a coward for walking out, but she was secretly glad to let Madeline deal with Kathy. Alice knew she owed Kathy a great deal, and it made it difficult to lie to her. But Madeline didn't care. She was fearless.

Alice could remember the first day she met Madeline as clearly as if it were yesterday. When Madeline arrived at St Joseph's school in Baddington, in upstate New York, she was the oddest-looking girl Alice had ever seen.

Madeline was only thirteen when the principal introduced her to Alice's class, halfway through the Fall semester. She had white hair, worn in an

134

aggressive, spiky cut and dark defiant eyes which stared out of her long face. All the other kids laughed at Madeline because she looked so odd, and because she lived with her grandmother, mad Mrs Preston, the stern old lady who lived in a rambling house on Oxford Street, not two houses from Alice's family.

No-one knew then that Madeline was living with her grandmother because her mother had abandoned her when she was small and that her policeman father had been shot dead in front of her two weeks earlier, the shock of which had turned her hair white. Instead they teased and bullied her. Alice was glad at first because it took the heat off her.

But when the two biggest boys in the class, the Tyndale twins, picked on Madeline in the yard Alice felt sorry for her. At least until Madeline turned on them like a wild cat, scratching and punching them, and not stopping until the boys limped off. Afterwards Alice picked up the bag and books the boys had knocked out of Madeline's hands and returned them to her. 'Hi, I'm Alice,' she said. 'So, what's it like living at mad Mrs Preston's? Is it true she's got dead bodies buried under the floorboards?'

Brushing herself off, Madeline shrugged. 'I don't know,' she said. 'Let's go take a look.'

Alice still loved Madeline's fearlessness and she was still frightened of her. She only hoped she wouldn't do anything to Kathy.

Striding into the sunlight of the Stanford University parking lot Director Naylor wasn't too disappointed with the meeting. In a perverse way the fact that Kathy Kerr had been so openly combative pleased her. It made her decision easier.

Naylor had lied about who was responsible for the criminal tests on Project Conscience in order to probe Kerr's true feelings. She had feigned innocence of the unauthorized tests to convince Kerr they were on the same side and were both forced to make the best of the situation. But Kathy hadn't bought the pragmatic approach. She was opposed on a matter of principle. Naylor had learnt that when it came to compromising, people with principles could never be trusted. Whatever she said at six o'clock tonight Kerr was too much of a risk. Not only would she jeopardize Conscience, but she could also raise doubts in Pamela Weiss's mind when Crime Zero was activated. Kerr had to be taken out of the mix. Fast.

Approaching her official car, she saw Alice sitting in her Mercedes. As soon as Alice saw her she got out of the car and walked over.

'How did it go?' Alice asked.

'You heard her. Kerr isn't listening.'

'Really?'

'Don't feel bad about it, Ali. I gave her every chance, but she's adamant.'

'Are you sure?'

'As sure as I can be.'

'So what do we do?'

'Don't worry, I'll handle it.'

A note of panic appeared in Alice's voice. 'You aren't going to hurt her, are you?'

'No, of course not,' soothed Naylor. 'I'll just make sure she's put somewhere safe until after the election. It's nothing for you to worry about.' She looked around the parking lot, searching for Jackson. He should have arrived by now. 'It'll look like she's gone away for a short vacation. It's all arranged.'

There was a pause. 'If it's the only way.' Alice looked unhappy but resigned.

'It is, Ali. Trust me, it is. Anyway, we'd better get ready for our meeting with Pamela. I'll see you there.'

As Naylor walked back to her official car, two agents stepped out; classic G-Men in their dark suits and short haircuts. The tallest agent opened the door for her, but before she stepped in she watched two other cars enter the lot and park next to each other a short distance away. The first was a grey Chrysler. A powerful black man with a hand-some face and fierce eyes sat in the passenger seat, with a weasel-faced agent beside him at the wheel. The second car was identical and contained three men.

That was one of the things she most liked about Associate Director William Jackson; he was always exactly where she wanted him to be. Jackson had been with her for years. His team were all highly motivated agents who had faced disciplinary charges in the past, which, if pursued, would have landed them in gaol for a long time. Naylor had used her influence to lose the charges and they were now unquestioningly loyal to her. Through Jackson, who acted as a buffer, they kept her informed of what was happening within the Bureau and sorted out any local difficulties without anything being traced back to her.

Jackson and his men didn't leave the cars.

'Banion, get me a phone,' she said to the agent holding the car door open for her.

As soon as Naylor was seated and the car door closed, a handset was passed to her. She dialled a number. Across the lot she saw William Jackson pick up his cellphone.

'Jackson,' he said in a deep, distinctive nasal voice.

'I want you to handle this personally,' she said. 'Don't forget, only Dr Peters is to know about it. Don't involve anyone else there.' She paused, levelling her gaze at his across the lot. 'And, Jackson, don't disappoint me.'

11

Sitting at one of the desks provided for visiting agents, Luke Decker tried to keep his mind off Kathy Kerr's test. Instead he placed his laptop computer on the docking station provided and proceeded to check out the thirteenth victim mentioned in Axelman's letter.

First of all he re-read part of the relevant section.

'. . . This last girl, the thirteenth, recognized the place I left all the girls. She told me her parents took her to play near there. The tree that covers the entrance to my tunnels was just one of many, but she called it a name. She told me she and her mom called it the Snake Tree. It's in a large forest near their home. Contact the girl's parents; they will know the place. That's where you will find the bodies – all thirteen. That's where I kept them safe.

I don't want you to go straight to the bodies. I want you to approach the parents of

139

this last victim. Please, make my peace with them. I will die soon, and only now do I realize what I have done. The knowledge is killing me, but the one thing I cling to is that my evil produced something good. I produced you. Perhaps, as my son, you can help me find peace, by helping me make amends for my crimes . . .'

Decker dropped the letter onto his desk, an unclean thing. He hated the very notion of somehow helping Axelman find redemption. Going back to his computer Decker used the mouse to run a search on the FBI-case-files database, entering the victim's name and the abduction date given in the letter, and as the files were retrieved he printed them out on the printer by his desk, favouring the lowest-tech option available.

He pulled the four-page document from the printer and scanned the text. It confirmed that a girl of the same name had been abducted at the time given in Axelman's letter and that her body had never been found. But her disappearance would almost certainly have been reported in the newspapers, so that proved nothing. Decker could go and visit the girl's family and ask about the tree, but if this was one of Axelman's hoaxes – a clever, cruel attempt to inflict more pain after his death – then Decker wanted no part of it. Instead he read all the available details about the victim and her family and studied the photographic images in the case file. One of the saddest consequences of Decker's work was that whenever he walked down a street and saw a young girl or woman he would

140

unconsciously grade her for risk, instinctively knowing signs of vulnerability – clothing, age, looks, make-up, bearing and personality all played their part. Knowing the victim was as important as knowing the killer. The girl in the file photographs was high-risk for a person like Axelman. She looked young, pretty and innocent. It was possible Axelman was telling the truth about his thirteenth victim. But why weren't her personal effects found in one of the boxes at his house?

Decker moved the cursor over the Internet icon and clicked twice. He keyed in his America online password and used a search engine to enter the area where the thirteenth victim's parents still lived. In seconds he was looking at a list of possible data sources. He clicked on one – the Los Altos Verdes Community web site. The welcome page was decorated with a stunning picture of soaring trees in a forest; a forest not unlike the one described in Axelman's letter.

Los Altos Verdes, San Bruno Mountains, California.
The same day. One hour later.

Eighteen miles from Palo Alto, Luke Decker stood by his rented Ford in a clearing overlooking one of several multi-million-dollar houses that studded the wooded estate of Los Altos Verdes.

From the web site he had learnt that some thirty years ago these luxury homes had been built on the site of a vast private zoo. Despite the beautiful natural setting, the zoo had fallen on hard times, and eventually the owners had sold out to a real-estate company, who had built ten prime properties on the existing terrain and planted new trees. It was a magical place, but the prospect of visiting the house below gave Decker no pleasure. It belonged to the family of the thirteenth victim.

Taking a deep breath, he looked up the hill to the towering trees that lined the denim-blue sky. The web site had made no mention of any Snake Tree, and if it did exist then it had to be a name known only to the victim's family. Scanning the oak, fir and bay trees, Decker knew he would never find it without their help – assuming Axelman had been telling the truth.

Telling the truth.

The notion that Axelman was telling the truth about anything in his letter was chilling.

Checking his watch, he wandered back to the car, picked up his cellphone and dialled Kathy's number. His heart was pumping so hard he was sure the whispering forest could hear it.

The phone rang five times before it was answered. With each ring he braced himself for the news.

'Kathy Kerr.' Her voice sounded strained.

'Kathy, hi. It's Luke. I was wondering if you had the results yet.' There was a pause. 'Kathy? Are you there?'

'Sorry, Luke. Yes, I'm here.' But she sounded distant, as if her mind was elsewhere. 'Yes, yes, the samples. I'll just get them. I'm sure they're ready by now.'

Her apparent diffidence only made him feel worse. She sounded more focused when she came

142

back on line. He could hear her fingers tapping on a keyboard. 'Luke, I'm in front of the Genescope. I'm scanning for the top-line results and . . .'

'Yes? What is it?'

'Hang on, let me just double-check something.'

He could hear surprise in her voice. If his heart had been beating fast before, it was racing now, a gallop of anticipation. 'Well?'

'Luke, is this official?' She sounded guarded.

'What do you mean?'

'The samples in the plastic bags you gave me have thrown up a virtual match with a subject on the FBI DNA database. A killer on death row. What's going on here, Luke?'

'Kathy, trust me. You don't want to know. Just tell me. Is there a relationship between the samples?'

'Luke, there's something very weird here—'

'I know that,' he almost shouted down the phone. 'Is there a goddamn relationship or not?'

There was a heavy sigh, followed by a long pause. For a heart-wrenching second he thought she was going to hang up. When she spoke again her voice was calm but strained. 'Yes.' She seemed unwilling to reveal the results. 'According to the Genescope the samples are both from the same family. Father and son.'

Decker's knees buckled and he leant against the car. On the phone he could still hear her fingers tapping on a keyboard. 'But, Luke,' she was saying, her voice insistent, 'there's something really strange here. We need to talk urgently.'

He was no longer listening. He had hung up, turned off the phone and thrown it in the car, as if

143

it were somehow unclean. But the phone wasn't contaminated; he was. His stomach contracted and he dry-retched. The words in the letter swam before his eyes, taunting him.

. . .I asked to see you because for some reason I suddenly feel real bad about all the things I've done. I thought by telling you – my son – you could help me put things right. But when I saw you today I couldn't tell you to your face. You look just like my father. He was a strict man, a religious man, and I felt kind of ashamed.

I've guessed you were my son for months. Ever since I saw your picture in the *Examiner* after you'd saved some girl in a graveyard. Your face in the picture looked exactly like one of my father when he was about your age. And I remembered the name. I've got a good memory – too good a memory. I wish I could forget all the things I've done. I raped a woman once near Union Square in San Francisco, at about the time that fits with your age. I know her name because her husband tried to help her. He was the only man I've ever killed. According to the papers he was a Captain Decker in the US Navy, but they never said anything about the woman being raped . . .

Decker sat on the ground, his back against the car, taking deep breaths. Looking up, the tall tree-tops seemed to dance around him, a giddying carousel in the clear sky. Not only was he

Axelman's son. But Axelman had killed the man Decker had worshipped as his father all his life. Decker felt his very being called into question. Every constant on which he'd based his assumptions of who he was, what he did, and his place in the wider world had been irrevocably destroyed. Even the validity of his work was suddenly doubtful. If Kathy Kerr and Director Naylor were right, and humans were little more than their genes, then what did that make him?

Standing up, he replaced the letter in his inside pocket and looked down at the house below. A chill formed in his gut and spread through his body. He got in the car and glanced at the brand-new spade and flashlight he'd bought on his way out here, sitting ominously on the rear seat.

Gunning the engine into life he turned the Ford around. Looking in the rear-view mirror he saw two green eyes staring back at him, judging him. And for a second those eyes weren't his at all, but Karl Axelman's.

12

Stanford University, California.
The same day. 3.12 p.m.

In her laboratory at Stanford University Kathy Kerr
sat staring at the Genescope monitor in a state of
shock. What the hell was Luke Decker up to?

After her meeting with Madeline Naylor, Kathy
had been so furious she'd been unable to concentrate on anything else. But when she'd calmed
down a little she'd tried to think through the consequences. What would she really achieve by
exposing the unauthorized criminal trials? Apart
from undermining the credibility of the Version-
Nine serum she had gained approval for. Not to
mention the personal damage she would cause herself. However hard she protested her innocence
she would undoubtedly be tarnished by her
involvement with Project Conscience. And she
could kiss goodbye to any dreams she might have
of fulfilling her ambition of treating violent crime.

But what she saw on the screen in front of her
eclipsed these concerns, making them seem
academic by comparison. Studying the DNA

profile from the blood-flake samples Luke had brought in, and comparing it to the matching profile on the FBI DNA database, her anger turned to ice.

The genome of the convicted killer Karl Axelman had subtly changed.

Switching to voice control she instructed the Genescope to search Axelman's DNA in chromosome one. As the lights blinked on the neck of the black swan there was a grumbling noise, and then its mellifluous male voice said, 'Subject's 5-HT1Da receptor gene is instructing boosted serotonin production − Three hundred per cent higher than normal levels.'

Kathy took a deep breath. 'Go to chromosome nine.'

The monitor shifted out of focus and then back, revealing a multicoloured double helix. Beside the coloured image was a table showing codons of triple letters. CGA AGT TGA. Each codon represented an amino acid, and the order of amino acids determined the genes, which in turn instructed the production of proteins. Part of the multicoloured double helix was highlighted, and a battery of codons showing the code at that particular part of the DNA strand scrolled down the screen.

'Genetic abnormality present,' said the honeyed voice. 'The dopamine b-hydroxylase gene instructing boosted production of dopamine. In excess of four hundred per cent typical levels. Effect exacerbated by similar boosting of dopamine receptor genes.'

When Kathy asked the Genescope to search out

all similarly boosted genes throughout Axelman's genome she discovered that the changes centred on the seventeen key genes her work had been focusing on. Karl Axelman had received gene therapy to modify his behaviour. But it wasn't Kathy's Conscience Version-Nine therapy. In fact, it didn't look like therapy at all.

Kathy's FDA-approved Version-Nine serum was a genetically engineered viral vector, which carried control-genes to reduce excessive aggression and increase appropriate emotional inhibitors to violence. It did this by reducing a patient's key drivers of aggression, including the dopamine receptor, nor-adrenalin receptor and testosterone genes, and boosting impulsive behaviour inhibitors, such as the 5-HT1Da serotonin gene.

But Axelman's modified profile indicated that *all* his hormones and neurotransmitters had been boosted to intolerable levels. Far from harmonizing and calming him, this gene therapy would have made Axelman implode. On the one hand it would have boosted his aggressive impulses to unprecedented levels, while simultaneously burdening him with huge emotional anxiety and guilt. She had never seen levels this high before, not even half as high. It was like pushing a foot down on a Ferrari's gas pedal and revving it to the limit, while at the same time pushing your other foot down hard on the brake pedal. Eventually something had to give.

She went into the Genescope's PACT menu, and chose T for threats. 'What are the implications of these genetic changes?' she asked.

'Subject's original genome shows no other major defects. Eighty-seven per cent probability of prostate cancer in his late eighties, but otherwise healthy. Realigned genome indicates intolerable levels of stress and anxiety. Subject's life expectancy reduced to days. Projected causes of death: brain haemorrhage, heart attack or positive choice.'

'What do you mean by positive choice?'

'Suicide,' the soft voice said.

Kathy's hands were shaking as the implications began to sink in. Had Axelman been treated in the unauthorized criminal tests? He was certainly a prime candidate. Suddenly this looked bigger than just being a cover-up over FDA approvals.

She reached for the phone and tried to call Luke, but his phone was still switched off. Shit, she really needed to talk to him about this. Perhaps he knew what was going on here? Was this why he was so paranoid about going through authorized channels and involving the FBI labs?

Inserting a hi-data-storage zip disk into the base of the Genescope, she made a copy of Karl Axelman's genome from the DNA database and another of his modified genome from the blood samples Decker had brought in. Given how sensitive this data was she wanted to keep it safe.

Taking the disk out of the Genescope she walked across the main lab, past her two lab assistants, busy emptying the autoclave, and retreated into the relative privacy of her office. Closing the door behind her she rushed to her desk, turned on the computer and moved the cursor to the folders holding all historical Conscience files. She wanted to check if she'd overlooked anything in the original viral vector that

149

might have caused Axelman's fatal genetic mutation. Moving the cursor she clicked on the directory folder marked: *FDA Approval: Clinical Trials History*.

A message appeared over the folder: 'This file has been moved to a different directory. Please seek authorization.'

Only hours ago she'd had open access to this data – *her* data. An irrational paranoid thought rose in her consciousness, but she quelled it. Nervously she looked out of her office at the technicians in the laboratory. She didn't know any of them well enough to trust. Christ, if only Karen and Frank were still here and not somewhere in the middle of Africa.

Still keeping calm, she rose and walked back into the lab, to the two large filing cabinets by her office. Although most of the data was stored electronically, a number of the text-based reports and completed approval applications were stored as hard copy too. Opening the middle drawer of the left-hand cabinet she immediately spied the blue folder marked *Project Conscience Trials*. It seemed significantly thinner than she remembered it. The paranoid thought nagged at her again. With trembling fingers she opened the folder. Seeing the batch of files on the FDA-approved Version-Nine vector she breathed a sigh of relief and admonished herself for being so foolish. But when she looked for documentation on the original serum – the one used in the unauthorized trials – there was no trace of it.

The paranoia returned with a rush. What the hell was going on? Someone was shutting her out, isolating her.

She turned to one of the laboratory technicians stacking up clean culture bottles by the autoclave. 'Warren, do you know what happened to these files?'

He put the bottles down and shook his head. 'Nope, I haven't touched any of them in days.'

She looked at him for a moment. Had he or one of the other technicians taken the files under orders from Director Naylor to ensure she didn't rock the boat? Or had men come in the night and removed them? A shiver ran through her. This was getting way out of hand. 'No problem,' she said, 'I must have left them at home.'

As casually as she could, she strolled back to her office and sat at her desk. Something was happening which she didn't understand. And after her less-than-constructive meeting with Director Naylor, she didn't know who to turn to – and that included Alice Prince. There was only one person who might be able to shine some light on this, someone who, despite what she felt about him, she still trusted.

Taking a pen, she quickly scribbled a note to Decker. When she was finished she pulled a small brown envelope from a pile by her desk and placed the note and the Axelman disk inside it. Then, using block capitals, she addressed the envelope to him at his grandfather's house, using the address Decker had written on the back of his card. Finally she stuck a stamp on the envelope, checked that she wasn't being watched through the window of her office and discreetly placed the envelope in the deep pocket of her lab coat.

She walked out of her office, through the lab to

the swing doors that led to the corridor outside and made her way to the toilets. When she reached them she doubled back and cut through the biology section to the reception area of the Medical Research Center. Here she smiled at the woman at the main desk, strolled as nonchalantly as possible towards the two large mailboxes attached to the wall and, as surreptitiously as she could, palmed the envelope out of her pocket and into one of the slots as she passed. Now, regardless of what was going on, at least this piece of evidence was safe, even if she and all her computer files were searched.

Back in her office she picked up her handbag and took out a well-thumbed road map of San Francisco. She decided that if she couldn't phone Luke she would go home to pick up a couple of things, drive to his grandfather's place and wait for him there. She quickly pinpointed Matty Rheiman's street and put the map back in her bag, then she took off her lab coat, picked up her laptop and handbag and left.

Out in the parking lot she climbed into her old Volkswagen, started the engine and turned out of the campus.

Kathy began to feel better as she left Palo Alto. Turning into Mendoza Drive she passed a grey Chrysler parked off the road near one of her neighbour's houses, and saw her house up ahead. Its cheerful white stucco façade made her reconsider whether she was over-reacting. Parking the car, Kathy picked up her cellphone and dialled Luke's number again, this time leaving a message on his voice mail. Explaining her fears, she told him she was going over to his grandfather's house now and that they needed to talk urgently. Just saying her concerns aloud helped put them into some kind of perspective. She jumped out of the car and ran across the lawn to her Mexican-style wooden front door. Even as she put her keys in the lock she felt calmer.

As Kathy opened the door to her house she would undoubtedly have felt less calm if she'd seen the three men step out of the grey Chrysler parked 200 yards back, or seen the second identical car pull up beside it. When she entered the house and confronted a dark face and fierce pair of eyes staring at her, she almost stopped breathing.

She froze on the spot as the man pointed his gun at her with one hand, while wielding a hypodermic in the other. Her own right hand was in her bag, replacing her house keys. Trying to keep her voice calm she asked, 'What do you want?' while her fingers reached for the top left-hand button on the cell phone and pressed it.

'Just to keep you safe and silent for a while,' the man said in a deep nasal voice.

She couldn't believe this. Despite her fear she felt angry. 'Why?' she shouted. 'This is something to do with Project Conscience, isn't it?'

The man smiled at that. 'All I've been told is that you're over-stressed and are likely to say things you may regret.' He moved closer. 'We're going to take you somewhere you can calm down. Somewhere you can have peace and quiet.'

'Keep that damn needle away from me, you bastard!' she shouted, backing out of the front door. But three men blocked her path. Two held her while the first man approached with the syringe. The fourth man covered her mouth with a cloth that smelled of sour water. Struggling as hard as she could, she felt a sharp prick as the needle entered her arm. All the time she kept her hand in the bag, her finger on the redial button of the cell phone, hoping it had called Decker's number. A silent cry for help to a man who wasn't there.

13

On her return from the meeting with Kathy Kerr,
Alice Prince felt calmer as she viewed the data with
Madeline Naylor on the presentation screens in
ViroVector's Smart Suite. The large interface room
was adjacent to TITANIA'S carefully controlled
chamber. It was populated with the usual equipment, such as monitors, printers, microphones,
speakers and keyboards, allowing TITANIA to communicate in every possible way with its human
colleagues.

There was also a long conference table and five
workstations. At the back of the room were four
small monitors, each showing quickly shifting
views of the ViroVector complex, as seen through
the series of sixty closed-circuit security cameras
which TITANIA controlled around the campus. But
these were peripheral to the two main display
media.

The first was the screen-wall dividing the Smart
Suite from TITANIA's Cold Room. The fifteen-by-

ten-foot liquid-crystal display was currently running through a series of projection charts on Project Conscience in anticipation of Governor Weiss's arrival.

The second was the hologram floor pad at the head of the conference table. Using leading edge laser-hologram-imaging technology from KREE8 Industries in San José, TITANIA could holo-project virtually anything over the pad, making the projected 3D 'object' appear at such high definition that to all intents and purposes it existed in the room. On display now was a rotating double helix of DNA, showing the 5-HT1Da receptor gene on chromosome one, which instructs for the production of serotonin in the human brain – the neurotransmitter that controls impulsive behaviour.

Two identical hard-copy briefing packs lay on the table for Pamela Weiss and her campaign adviser, Todd Sullivan. The black-bound document was labelled, *Project Conscience – Scientific Data and Crime Statistics.*

'Everything seems to be in order,' said Madeline Naylor, checking her watch. 'Pamela should be here any moment now.'

Alice thought she'd try it one last time. 'Perhaps we should tell Pamela about the FDA findings, explain why the differences don't really matter? She'll understand.'

Madeline raised an eyebrow and flashed that look of hers, both bullying and protective. It was the same look Madeline had used on an icy pond over forty years ago when, as children, they had witnessed an act which still bound them

156

together in an invisible web of guilt and dependency.

'Come on, Alice,' Madeline said patiently. 'We've agreed this already. That's why it was so important to get Kathy organized. Pamela can't be told anything that might compromise her. She must believe that the original Conscience vector used in the criminal trials was exactly the same as the FDA-approved version. And on no account must Pamela know anything about Crime Zero. She can't be told about the San Quentin deaths and suicides. As far as she's concerned they were normal executions to which she signed the papers. She wouldn't understand. Not like we do. Come on, Alice, we're doing this for Libby and for all the Libbys in the world.'

Alice Prince looked into Madeline's dark eyes, and despite her doubts she knew Madeline was right. She had always been the stronger one, able to make all the tough decisions.

Just then the phone beside her rang and Alice picked it up.

'Dr Prince,' said the voice on the line, 'Governor Weiss has arrived.'

Pamela Weiss had left most of her election entourage behind. This was a private meeting to discuss delicate matters. So her campaign manager and would-be chief of staff, Todd Sullivan, had adroitly slipped her away like a reclusive rock star from the huddled press battalions and shuttled her down to ViroVector by helicopter.

'We've got fifty-nine minutes before Governor Weiss has to leave for Los Angeles,' were Sullivan's first words as Alice Prince greeted them in the foyer and escorted them to the Smart Suite. Two Secret-Service men in dark suits and glasses followed behind and stationed themselves outside the closed door. They neither acknowledged nor spoke to the two FBI agents already standing there to escort Director Naylor.

'Relax, will you, Todd,' said Weiss, embracing Alice and Madeline with the affection of an old friend. Sullivan seemed vaguely discomfited by the obvious closeness of the three women and sat down. He was a lean man of forty-eight, with dark hair and a neat face, remarkable only for a small scar on his chin.

When everyone had been offered a drink Alice adjusted her glasses and began. 'The first thing to say is, we've got FDA approval. So Friday's announcement can go ahead as planned.'

'Excellent,' beamed Pamela.

Sullivan looked relieved. 'We really need this announcement. The national crime figures are scaring voters and we're seen as too soft. Iraq isn't doing us any favours, either.'

'And it looks as if it's going to get worse,' said Madeline. 'I was talking to Mike Clanton at Langley yesterday. His people believe the Iraqis have definitely got the bioweapon they've been bragging about. They probably paid some rogue scientist from Russia. The CIA reckon there's a real danger they'll use it if we stop them retaking Kuwait.'

Pamela Weiss nodded in agreement. 'And although the polls say the people want to vote for us,' Weiss said, 'it's the same old story: they don't believe a woman has the toughness and vision to handle either Iraq or the crime rate. So anything we can do to change their minds is vital.'

'Oh, I think this will help change their minds,' said Alice, pressing the console on the desk in front of her. Suddenly the lights dimmed and all the monitors on the screen-wall went dead except for the largest screen in the centre. *Project Conscience* appeared across the top in white letters and below it the line, *A Proven Treatment for Crime.*

'On the table you'll each find the bound briefing pack we'll be supplying to the press, complete with computer disks, slide-show presentations and summaries. At the front you'll find the crime statistics and results from the Project-Conscience field tests. At the back you'll find all the details of the formulations and scientific data, including all the pre-clinical and safety information. The first section should reassure you that Conscience works and the second that it's completely safe. At the beginning of each section you'll find the summary pages. I suggest you look at those now while Madeline and I go through the presentation.'

Alice sat down and gestured to Madeline. 'Madeline will take you through the statistics and then I'll take over for the scientific findings. If either of you are unclear about anything, just holler, OK?'

Sullivan and Weiss nodded as Naylor stood and walked to the screen.

'To recap,' Madeline Naylor said in her low, professional voice, 'every year for the past eight years, two thousand prisoners convicted of a cross-section of violent crime have been selected from

159

Folsom, San Quentin and the other major penal institutions in California. Under the pretence of a flu inoculation, this sample population was unwittingly injected with non-infectious stem-cell gene therapy – the Conscience viral vector. Over the last eight years we've amassed and tracked a total of sixteen thousand treated men. This tracking has been done with the assistance of four senior members of the Bureau, all of whom report directly to a person on my staff. None of them has any knowledge of the treatment or the project's overall objectives.' As Naylor spoke, the screen shifted, showing charts and slides that demonstrated her points.

'Since we started the trials two per cent of the treated subjects have been executed, one per cent have died of natural causes, and twenty-one per cent are still incarcerated. But even this twenty-four per cent performed well in aggression studies, showing significantly reduced testosterone levels and increased frontal-lobe activity. More importantly, of the remaining seventy-six per cent who were released, only a tiny percentage has re-offended. Recidivism is down to less than ten per cent, against a norm of over sixty. And their repeat crimes tend to be minor felonies.

'But the most interesting finding is that not only have the individuals benefited, but also the communities to which they returned. Genetic and environmental factors appear to become inextricably entwined – one influencing the other. Watts in South Central Los Angeles is the best example of this.' The screen shifted to show black-and-white TV coverage of the Watts riots in 1965;

160

Alice could clearly see the skeletal Watts Towers towering above the mayhem.

The screen shifted again, showing a colour view of the same scene five years ago. The place was relatively quiet, but it still looked run-down, with graffiti and boarded-up shops.

The last screen change revealed the same scene taken a week previously. It looked similar except that freshly painted thriving storefronts had replaced the boarded-up windows daubed in graffiti, and that people were walking down the street as if pursuing their normal business.

To Alice the differences were subtle, but the overall contrast was striking.

'You can't see much from this footage,' said Naylor, 'but when you go there on Friday to make your announcement you'll notice the difference. And, more importantly, so will the voters. The clincher, though, is that the overall crime rate in the test state of California has defied the national trend of escalating crime. Homicides are down fifteen per cent, assaults down five per cent, robberies down eighteen per cent, rapes down twenty-five per cent.

'Furthermore, from a financial point of view, the results are just as dramatic. If the positive trend in California is maintained the state will reap hundreds of millions of dollars from keeping crime off the streets. More people in work, plus fewer gaol, policing, hospital and urban-rebuilding costs, will all contribute. Each percentage-point drop in violent crime as a whole releases over thirty million dollars. On a national basis, a conservative estimate puts the savings at over two billion dollars *per year*.'

As Alice Prince listened to Madeline Naylor's steady, authoritative voice recite the facts she knew by heart, her mind drifted back in time to Vassar college, where she and Madeline first met the glamorous Pamela Weiss.

Vassar was a revelation. Madeline, with her tall powerful physique, excelled at sports and soon became a key player in the college track-and-field team. For the first time in her life she was not only accepted but admired. And Alice found she was similarly nurtured. Her teachers recognized her intellect and pushed her hard. Socially, Madeline and Alice still kept to themselves.

Alice didn't want to go to the party at West Point Military Acadamy, but everyone was going and some of the women from Madeline's team had space in their van. The party was in full swing when they arrived and both of them hated it. Packed with students drinking, dancing and making out, Alice couldn't see the point of it. The music was so loud she couldn't even talk to anyone.

Then she saw a woman standing in a quiet corner encircled by people hanging on her every word. Amidst the hellish chaos there was this radiant, poised creature holding court. She was laughing and drinking, but she was in control. Like some brilliant sun, everyone was drawn to her, rotating in her orbit like lesser planets needing her light and warmth. Seeing her made Alice yearn to be one of those planets – to belong. Turning to Madeline, she saw that she was equally enthralled.

An hour later, after drinking too much and

talking to Madeline's team-mates, Alice and Madeline went outside to walk in the grounds, waiting for the other girls to take them back to Vassar. It was a dark night, with the moon making only brief appearances from behind the clouds, so they stayed close to the main buildings and the well-lit paths.

They heard the commotion before they saw it. The sounds of a struggle came from the bushes at the dark end of the grounds. At first Alice thought it was an animal, then she heard the scream. Madeline immediately ran towards the noise and Alice followed. In the shadows she saw two men holding a woman down; one had his hand over her mouth and the other was pulling up her dress. An open bottle of Jack Daniels lay on its side, spilling its contents onto the ground, its smell heavy in the warm air. Bile rose in Alice's throat and her left leg began to tremble. The woman was struggling, but the men were too strong. Suddenly the moon broke through and Alice saw that it was the beautiful woman they had been watching only an hour ago. Her blue eyes were angry more than scared and her evident courage helped Alice find hers.

Alice shouted for help as she saw Madeline lunge at the man covering the woman's mouth. Madeline made no noise; she just steadied herself for a moment and kicked the man as hard as she could in the face. She was wearing spiked heels and Alice heard the man's nose break. Like a ballerina, Madeline turned and kneed the stunned second man in the temple, rolling him over. Alice reached for the woman and pulled her up, but

Madeline wasn't finished. Her face was white with rage, her eyes as dark and cold as midnight lakes. Methodically, she stood over the two dazed men and proceeded to kick them in the genitals until Alice and the woman pulled her back.

Both men were charged and one had to have a crushed testicle removed. That single act of saving Pamela Weiss from rape opened up a whole new world for Alice and Madeline. Pamela Weiss had connections and friendships that made Alice and Madeline popular simply for being her friend. Madeline in particular blossomed at that time. She idolized Pamela and learnt from her social ease, acquiring a public poise Alice could never emulate.

Alice never understood why the gilded Pamela became their friend just because they helped her once. It was almost as if Pamela felt guilty about all her privilege and found others like herself too shallow. She never tired of listening to Madeline's and Alice's accounts of their childhood. Pamela seemed to be ashamed of the fact that she came from a powerful banking family, that both her parents were alive, wealthy, happily married and loved her – as if it starved her of a perspective on the world and disqualified her from being taken seriously as someone who wanted to make a difference.

'Alice, do you agree it's empirically proven that the gene treatment calms violent men?' Pamela Weiss said, reading through the briefing-pack notes.

Alice sat forward in her chair, looking at Pamela, Madeline and Todd Sullivan, quickly regaining her bearings. 'Absolutely. The overall benefits will still take time to come through, but the proof that it works is irrefutable. This data is more than enough to make your announcement.'

'And we're sure safety isn't an issue?' asked Pamela, turning to the back of the briefing pack.

Alice smiled. 'Pam, we've been testing the treatment for the last eight years with no ill-effects at all. We've just undergone successful safety trials on human volunteers. The FDA have approved these and given us their blessing to go to the next step of efficacy trials. For good measure, we've also shown Conscience Version Nine to the National Institutes of Health and got their approval too. This means that, as far as the two most stringent bodies in the United States are concerned, the treatment won't harm anyone. And since our secret tests already prove its efficacy, we're in an unassailable position. Any concern over the timing of the premature criminal trials will be forgotten once everyone realizes this. I've spoken to Calvin Briggs at the FDA and asked a few hypothetical questions. Basically, for all their bureaucracy, the FDA are there to facilitate progress, not stop it. So long as the treatment is *safe* and it *works*, that's all they and anyone else cares about.'

'And don't forget,' added Madeline, 'with all the press interest in California's improved crime figures, you and Bob Burbank are going to be seen as heroes, visionaries. And let's face it, Pamela, our guinea pigs weren't children or defenceless old ladies. They were violent criminals, hated and feared by society.'

Pamela leant forward in her chair. 'So, Ali, the treatment you used is the same as the one approved by the FDA?'

Alice paused and caught Madeline's eye. Madeline just gave the smallest nod. She disliked lying to Pamela, but she had no choice. 'Yes,' she replied. Alice smiled then, allowing her genuine excitement to shine through. 'Trust me, Pamela,' she said, 'Project Conscience is both safe and effective. Politically, scientifically, socially and morally you have every reason to make your announcement.'

Pamela Weiss smiled but said nothing for a moment. She looked down at her notes, then up at Madeline and finally back at Alice. Her clear blue eyes rested on each of them for some seconds. Alice thought she was going to ask one of her difficult questions, and for a horrible moment she wondered if Pamela had somehow found out about Crime Zero or the San Quentin deaths. But she needn't have worried. A beaming smile suddenly lit up Pamela's face. 'Well done,' she said. 'We've all taken some risks, I know, but I promise that if I become president—'

'You mean *when* you become president,' corrected Todd Sullivan with a smile.

Pamela laughed. 'Then I will make sure we realize this vision of a gentler society – a society with a conscience.'

Todd Sulllivan stood up. 'Sorry about this, but we're going to have to run.'

'I'll see you both at the dinner tonight in LA with Bob Burbank,' said Pamela. 'It's a celebration of the Conscience announcement tomorrow and a chance for me to brief the president on the latest developments. It's going to be a good evening.'

14

Los Altos Verdes, San Bruno Mountains, California.
The same day. 5.25 p.m.

Alice Prince loved the way the afternoon sun filtered through the tall branches of the surrounding trees, dappling the grass and earth of the broad forest clearing. This was a private enchanted place, full of happy memories. Only a brisk fifteen-minute walk away from home, she often came here with her two golden Labradors. She liked to smell the sweet air, watch the sun move over the swaying treetops in the valley below and be alone with her thoughts.

After the meeting at ViroVector with Pamela Weiss she had been driven the eighteen miles home. She'd gone straight out into the garden and called the dogs, put on their leashes and taken them over here for a quick walk before taking the company Gulfstream to LAX and dinner with Pamela and the president.

Alice wished they could have persuaded Kathy to see their point of view. In many ways their objectives were the same. Alice admired the fact that she had stood up to Madeline. But she was frightened that Madeline would do more than just keep Kathy quiet until the election. She knew how far Madeline could go. Alice loved her friend, but Madeline was never happy with doing only what was necessary. She always had to go further.

Alice sat on a tree stump in the middle of the thirty-yard clearing and tilted her face to the sun, enjoying the warmth on her skin. Around her she could hear the trees whispering in the breeze and the dogs barking as they played together. If she closed her eyes she could even hear Libby's voice.

Alice used to come here often with Libby. Her husband, John, and Madeline would sometimes come too. Even Pamela Weiss had come once or twice, with her husband, Alan, and the three boys.

After Vassar Pamela became a successful lawyer in the Los Angeles District Attorney's office; then she married one of the partners of the law firm she most often opposed in court. Her marriage had remained strong and she now had three sons; the youngest, thirteen-year-old Sam, was Alice's godson. Pamela's husband was one of the few men Alice was genuinely fond of.

Madeline, who had also gone on to study law before joining the FBI, married next, despite her increasingly obvious ambivalence towards men. She'd said at the time that it would be good for her career and that she wanted children. Unsurprisingly it failed and there were no kids. Still, divorce aided her real marriage, the one to the FBI, which blossomed spectacularly.

Alice's own marriage had been a disaster. After a

Ph.D. at Stanford and a spell with GeneCell Industries, where she met her husband, John Prince, she started up ViroVector. At first Prince had seemed to live up to his name, especially compared to her father, but she soon learnt that John was far from being a prince. However he did contribute to the single most wonderful thing in her life: Libby.

Even now, if Alice squeezed her eyes shut and listened hard to the wind, she could hear Libby's laughter in the clearing.

But of course she was no longer there. Plucked away, as if she'd never even been here.

As Alice sat, she allowed her mind to fold in on itself. The present no longer existed, only the past and the future. An acid pain burned in her chest, the anger and grief as intense as when Libby was first taken. What had the monster done with her? How had she died? If only Alice knew these answers she could bury her daughter and grieve for her properly.

But her anger and grief were no longer impotent. Madeline had seen to that. Soon no other Libby would ever again fall prey to the evil that stalked every street in the land.

Suddenly the warmth left Alice's face, and through her closed eyelids she could tell the sun had disappeared behind a cloud. The dogs barked. She shivered involuntarily and opened her eyes.

Then she saw the tall man standing at the edge of the clearing, his car parked on the dirt track. He was looking directly at her.

She looked so peaceful sitting in the sun that he

was loath to disturb her. But Luke Decker's course was set. He had no choice but to carry this through to its conclusion. Dr Alice Prince was the mother of Axelman's thirteenth victim, and to find where the bodies were buried he had to ask her the location of the Snake Tree.

He had driven to Dr Prince's house only to find she was out. After some persuasion her maid had said she was walking the dogs and given him directions. He had come straight here.

Prince looked like she did in the case-file photographs, older but otherwise unchanged. She wore flat shoes, a pleated skirt and a navy cardigan over her cream blouse. She didn't look like the founder of a major multi-national corporation.

Walking towards her he introduced himself and showed his badge. 'Dr Prince, my name is Special Agent Luke Decker. I run the FBI's behavioural sciences unit, which specializes in serial crimes. I want to talk to you about your daughter, Libby.'

Her shoulders slumped momentarily and the pain in her eyes told Decker more about her damaged psyche than any record of her divorce or breakdown in the FBI case file. Time didn't always heal. Alice Prince was still a devastated woman. She stood up and folded her arms in a defensive gesture, barely looking at Decker's badge; instead she kept her eyes locked on his face. For a moment they both stood in silence, listening to the wind blowing in the trees.

'If you prefer we can talk back at your house,' he said.

She didn't appear to have heard him. 'Have you found Libby?' she asked.

'Not yet, but I believe I know who was responsible for her murder. And with your help I might be able to locate her body.'

'Who killed her?'

'A man named Karl Axelman.'

'Karl Axelman?' she repeated, her face frowning in disbelief. She said his name as if she was familiar with it. Her right hand moved to the unusual teardrop amulet around her neck, stroking it like a worry bead. She suddenly seemed miles away, her eyes peering off into space at some scene Decker would never see. 'How can I help you find where Libby was buried?' she asked him, her voice barely above a whisper.

'As you might be aware, Axelman also committed a number of other similar crimes. And something we believe your daughter said to him could identify the resting place of all his victims.'

'What? What did Libby say to him?'

'Apparently Axelman gained access to his victims' resting place through an entrance near a tree your daughter called the Snake Tree. Does that mean anything to you?'

Prince's eyes suddenly misted over and she smiled, the saddest smile Luke had ever seen. 'Yes. Yes, I know the Snake Tree.'

Decker's mouth felt dry. 'If you can tell me the location I'll get it checked out.'

Alice Prince gazed at him silently for some seconds, before suddenly turning away. At first he thought she might be collecting herself, stopping herself from crying. But then she pointed to the other end of the clearing, towards the setting sun. 'See the big oak. That's the Snake Tree.

That's the tree Libby always used to climb.'

Squinting into the dying light he looked at a silhouetted clump of trees. Slightly by itself was a vast, gnarled oak that looked much older than the younger trees around it. It had low branches and a thick trunk. Around the base some of the roots were exposed and seemed to coil round the tree like slumbering serpents.

'Thank you,' he said. 'I'll get the place checked over. If we find anything we'll inform you immediately.'

She opened her mouth as if to protest. But then said nothing.

'Can I give you a lift home?' he asked. 'Can I call anyone for you?'

'No,' she said, leashing her dogs. 'I prefer to walk. I want to be alone.'

Alice Prince was numb as she walked her dogs out of the clearing to the path that led back home. It seemed wrong somehow. She was sure she ought to feel hysterical relief or grief or something, but she could feel nothing. There was a cold void in her soul that robbed her of all sensation, as though she'd just put her hand under a tap of scalding water and was awaiting the pain.

When Agent Decker had told her about Libby she'd been less shocked than she expected. Over the last ten years she had been subconsciously preparing for this day. But the news about Karl Axelman had been a blow. She had thought it could be him, as indeed had the FBI. But since none of Libby's effects were among the killer's trophies it was deemed unlikely. It seemed ironic now that she had unwittingly used Axelman as one of the guinea pigs to verify TITANIA's projections on Crime Zero.

Axelman's abduction of Libby had been the catalyst for both Conscience and Crime Zero. When Libby was taken Alice's husband deserted her for a woman he had been secretly seeing for years. After this betrayal Alice collapsed and was admitted to an upstate sanatorium. Madeline and Pamela visited often, vowing to do everything in their power to help. Alice took great comfort from them, but it had been science that had saved her sanity.

Making them bring the papers and books she required to the sanatorium, she devoured everything she could find on the topic, believing that if she could discover the answer then she could repair her fractured mind. Just as she was about to give up she read an article in *Nature*, published by a Ph.D. student from Harvard called Kathryn Kerr. It was an ingenious theoretical model based on primates and, like an epiphany, it made sense of everything. It was to be her salvation.

Within weeks she was back at ViroVector Solutions. Taking Kerr's detailed theories, Alice used her expertise with viral vectors to put them into practice; not only to diagnose violent behaviour but to modify it. Most science is built on failure and disappointment, but Kathy's theories on gene calibration were rigorously thought through and extremely well documented. Within months of leaving the sanatorium Alice lured Kathy Kerr to Stanford University and, using her expertise on gene calibration, developed a genetically engineered retrovirus which successfully modified chimpanzee genes. Within another three months, without Kerr's knowledge, Alice perfected a viral vector which she was convinced could deliver Kathy's control genes into man.

She laid out her plan to Madeline and Pamela when they next met. If they really wanted to help, as they had vowed to do, then she had found a way to stop crimes like Libby's abduction happening again. But she would need to conduct tests on criminals; and to do this without FDA approval she would need the backing of her now-powerful friends.

Dr Kerr wasn't told about the criminal trials, instead she was given the brief of following the usual painstaking stages of pre-clinical screenings, primate studies and human-volunteer trials to gain FDA approval. Once she had done this and won their consent, and assuming their secret efficacy criminal trials had worked, they could go public. The FDA approval would vindicate conducting human experiments years before they should have done.

Pamela, who by then was being groomed as the new governor of California, had been difficult to convince. But in time she came aboard, especially when she realized how political correctness and the notoriously conservative FDA were stifling research in this area. Some black-rights groups even protested against conducting research on black males because they claimed the findings would be used to reinforce white prejudices. Even though these fears were completely unfounded, the National Institutes of Health avoided using black subjects, making any broad-based research meaningless. Pamela eventually realized that secret trials would not only speed things up but also get them started. She even approached the new US president, Bob Burbank, and, using her formidable powers of persuasion, she gained his broad agreement that curing crime was a good idea. Making no commitments, Bob Burbank made it easier for them to cut through red tape and keep the project secret, whilst always maintaining a distance in case anything should go wrong.

But it was Madeline who had taken the project to the next level. She had been even more excited about it than Alice. In fact, her initial reaction was that Conscience didn't go far enough. And over the following months she convinced Alice of the controversial but shockingly logical next step: Crime Zero.

Turning back to the clearing Alice saw Decker standing motionless in the slanting sunlight, staring at the Snake Tree. No doubt he would call his colleagues soon and then they would conduct the search. She felt compelled to stay, even though she knew he wouldn't allow her to. She was desperate to find the body. The nightmare of not knowing had poisoned the past ten years.

Walking farther on, she paused behind a bank of bushes and watched Decker walk back to his car. To her surprise he didn't get in and drive off or reach for a phone. Instead he opened the back door and pulled out a spade and a flashlight.

She watched Decker carry the spade on his broad shoulders and switch on the flashlight. Wielding the torch like a sword he cut through the encroaching shadows and moved towards the Snake Tree, its massive trunk silhouetted against the sun.

15

The Snake Tree, Los Altos Verdes, California. The same day. 5.47 p.m.

Luke Decker had embarked on a course of action from which he could not deviate. Yet as he approached the looming tree with its serpentine roots he couldn't remember such fear. A band of steel tightened around his chest and a film of sweat covered his skin. In his time he had faced all manner of killers, but physical danger had never affected him – not in the way psychological danger could. Not like now, when he couldn't escape the bizarre notion that somehow he was returning to the scene of his own crimes.

After Decker's breakdown, Sarah Quirke, the FBI shrink at the Sanctuary, had warned him not to inhabit the minds of the killers he hunted so completely, particularly when working simultaneously on a number of traumatic cases. 'If you play with too many fires, one of them's bound to burn you,' she'd said. He'd always believed he could handle it. Entering a killer's mind didn't mean he had to bring something of them back with him.

Now, as he sat down on the roots of the large tree and tried to think the way the killer might have done, he wasn't so convinced. This time the killer had been his own flesh and blood. He was walking in his father's shoes and he shuddered at the thought of how snug the fit might be.

He began to compile a mental profile from what he remembered of Karl Axelman's files. The teenage girls had been abducted over a twenty-year period, with at least eighteen months between each one. This told Luke that Axelman had some-how preserved the bodies, allowing him to revisit them again and again and staving off his need to kill for long periods. Since Axelman was a hoarder he would have wanted to keep all the bodies intact, not just the most recent kills. That required space. A lot of space.

Decker looked around him and then studied the huge Snake Tree. He stood up and moved round the trunk, tapping the bark for clues, testing for any hollow sounds. Nothing.

It was unlikely that Axelman would have squirrelled the bodies in the trunk of the tree; they would have rotted too fast. But in his time Decker had seen stranger hoarding sites.

It was far more likely that Axelman had buried the bodies, perhaps in protective wrapping, to pre-vent the ingress of worms and other predators. But he needed access to them. This place was remote but not unfrequented. Axelman would have had to have some means of viewing the corpses without fear of being disturbed. Just the thought of dis-covery would have seriously inhibited his fantasies and curtailed his enjoyment.

But Axelman had been a builder; he would have known how to construct some kind of concealed storage facility, which he could easily enter and exit without being detected. Decker could only guess at why Axelman had chosen this particular site.

Stepping over the gnarled roots, Decker moved closer into the base of the tree and studied the trunk. It was at least eight feet in diameter. From one angle the base of the tree resembled an upside-down Y, as if the tree stood on two squat legs. Walking further round the trunk, to the side that still caught the last rays of sun, he noticed an area of earth, three feet square, partially sheltered under the low crotch of the two legs. He jabbed the earth with his spade and the impact jarred his shoulder.

Moving in closer, he scraped away the scrubby grass, leaf litter and topsoil, revealing dark wood. More roots, he thought, before scraping away a wider area. Gradually he uncovered more wood, until there was a flat platform a yard square. His heart beat faster; the wood was too regular to be natural. Then his spade hit something metallic, and in the dying sunlight he saw a glint of dulled brass. Throwing the spade to the ground he dropped to his knees and began to brush away the damp dirt from the centre of the panel, revealing a brass hand-ring. Gripping the ring, he pulled it upright so that it formed a handle. Then he stood and tugged it as hard as he could. There was a groan and a creak from the damp wood, and then the panel hinged upwards – a trapdoor opening to the underworld.

Grimacing at the stale air emanating from the hole, Decker reached for the flashlight and shone it down into the dank darkness. To his surprise there was a timber-lined hole that went down about ten feet, with an iron ladder attached to one side. The timber was green with damp, but there was no sign of rot and the workmanship was impressive.

Finding a stick, he wedged the trapdoor open, took the flashlight in one hand and eased himself into the hole. He tested the ladder with his right foot and, when he was convinced it was firm, made his way down into the darkness. At the bottom of the ladder a tunnel sloped gently away from him and the tree. The ceiling and walls were made of interlocking beams and the floor had a matted non-slip surface. Every ten yards or so there were perforated panels in the ceiling, which looked like ventilation ducts. And all around was the smell of damp earth and decay.

Tentatively he walked forwards into the blackness, his feet testing each step before trusting his full weight to it. All the time he sought out tell-tale cracks in the ceiling with his flashlight, but aside from the occasional creak and groan the tunnel appeared robust. Then, after some twenty yards, he turned a bend and came to an abrupt dead end. Using the flashlight he saw that there were broad concrete steps to his right, leading deeper down. To his left the wall was a square plug of cement, as if the passage to an earlier entrance had been filled in. The wall on each side of the concrete steps was no longer timber but brown tiles caked in mould.

Decker suddenly understood why Axelman had chosen this place. It was part of the old zoo, which had been bulldozed over thirty years ago to build the exclusive estate where Alice Prince lived. Evidently not all of the zoo had been destroyed. The underground sections that didn't interfere with the foundations of the new houses were simply sealed and returned to nature, and new trees were planted on top. Axelman had built the wooden tunnel to gain unauthorized access to the sealed area.

The smell coming from the base of the concrete steps was different; it was no longer earth but something else – a chemical smell Decker recognized but couldn't place. He had encountered it only recently, but he couldn't remember exactly where. The flashlight shook in his hand as he gradually walked down the steps. He tried to tell himself it was the damp and the cold, but it wasn't.

The flashlight beam reflected off a rusting steel sign screwed onto the tiles: *Reptile House and Aquarium*. At the base of stairs, discarded on the floor, was another sign. Dented and buckled it was barely legible. *Carolan Construction* was painted on it in black letters. Axelman must have worked on this area thirty years ago and earmarked it for his own private use. It wouldn't have been that difficult to seal the area, as he was contracted to do by his employers, while at the same time making plans for his secret tunnel.

Decker came to a junction in the brown-tiled maze. A faded arrow marked *Aquarium* pointed right and a virtually invisible arrow with illegible markings pointed left. The chemical smell was now so strong it made his eyes water and stung the back of his throat; it was coming from the aquarium. Taking a handkerchief from his pocket he tied it over his nose and mouth. Suddenly he remembered where he'd last encountered that smell: the morgue at San Quentin. With leaden legs he walked towards its source.

A few yards into the aquarium he realized that the torch beam had narrowed – he must have twisted the end of the Maglite when tying the handkerchief round his face. He quickly adjusted the flashlight, and as the beam broadened he realized that the corridor had narrowed dramatically; each wall was now less than an arm's length away. He also realized that the claustrophobic walls were no longer tiled but smooth.

As smooth as glass.

A chill ran down his spine and the skin prickled on the back of his neck.

As if chancing upon some slumbering beast, he slowly lowered the beam to the floor in front of his feet, highlighting the mould-stained tiles. Then, gripping the Maglite white-knuckle tight, he inched the flashlight to his right. Where the floor met the wall there was a strip of chrome, and above that a thick black band of rubber. The rubber was a seal and the smooth reflective material making up the rest of the wall was a thick plate of glass. Moving along the base of the glass he saw a typed label. The label didn't identify the species of some rare fish or carry notes on its preferred diet and geographical origin; there was simply a name, date and location.

Mandy James. 7 April 1979. Sausalito.

His chest was so tight and the smell so noxious that Decker could hardly breathe. He remembered the girl's name from the Axelman case files. One of his earliest victims, her belongings had been found in a box in his house in San José. On auto-pilot, Decker moved the torch upwards so that its beam shone through the glass into the greenish, clear liquid beyond.

The first thing he saw in the ghostly green light was Mandy James's foot, attached by a rope around her right ankle to a heavy rock on the base of the tank. Moving the torch upwards he saw the rest of her naked body, floating perfectly preserved in formaldehyde.

Pressing a hand to his mouth he switched off the torch; he couldn't bear to see the girl's face. Turning away, he stood in the dark, pressing his forehead against the opposite wall, forcing down the bile rising in his throat. Gradually he regained control and straightened up. Not daring to turn around he switched the torch back on.

In that instant his blood ran cold. Staring out at him was a face so heartbreakingly beautiful and so wide-eyed with terror that he could only scream and run. Disoriented in his panic, he ran as fast as he could down the dark corridor. And as he ran, the beam of his flashlight flailed wildly, cutting through the darkness to reveal the horrific tableaux on both sides of him. An avenue of glass tanks, each containing the perfectly preserved body of a young woman. Typed names and con-torted faces were intermittently thrown up in the beam of light, names and faces he remembered from the files.

Only when he reached a tiled wall on his left did he realize he had run the wrong way. Standing panting in the dark, focusing on the tiles, he clapped a hand over his mouth and took deep breaths of his own exhaled carbon dioxide. Gradually his heart slowed. To find the exit he would once again have to run the grisly gauntlet of bodies in the dark. He looked around for an alternative.

Turning slowly to the opposite wall of the corridor he saw that it was also tiled. A red kerosene can sat on the floor, and halfway up the wall he noticed a box with a red button and a lever protruding from the front. Calming himself, he steadied the flashlight and read the bold red letters on the box. *Fuel Powered Generator. To Start: Push Button and Hold for Ten Seconds Before Pulling Lever.* Taking a deep breath he followed the instructions, and after two attempts he heard a motor start up. Suddenly the protective darkness was gone and the full horror of his surroundings was illuminated by a row of lamps along the ceiling and a light shining out from each tank. But at least in the light he could prepare himself for the sights around him.

He was in the middle of Axelman's horrific collection. To his right, towards the exit, there were ten tanks, five on each side. Each contained one of the murdered girls, in chronological order of abduction. To his left there were a further ten tanks, but only three were full. The other seven were no doubt reserved for subsequent ac-quisitions. Keeping his eyes straight ahead, he walked past the last pair of victims to the final occupied tank. On the tiled floor in front of it was a cardboard box, similar to those found in

183

Axelman's house, and in it were a set of mouldy clothes, some trainers and a pair of glasses. There was also an audiotape with a name scribbled on it. He now knew why Karl Axelman had never been a suspect for Libby Prince's abduction: all her personal effects were here.

With terrifying clarity Decker could see what had happened.

Unlike the others in this macabre gallery, Libby Prince's murder had not been planned. Visiting his trophies one fateful day, Karl Axelman had probably seen her wandering in one of the nearby lanes and had abducted her on impulse. Eventually he must have planned to take her effects to his house in San José, but he'd been caught before he was able to do so.

Bending to his knees, Decker studied the pitiful personal effects laid out neatly in the box, finding them as hard to look at as the body suspended in liquid to his left. Ever since he could remember, Decker had believed that each man made his own choices. That a man's life should be judged at its end by what he had done. Not at its beginning by what he had been born with. To Decker, free will was everything, without it there was no point in living.

But now, as he willed himself to look at Libby Prince, he felt less sure. He had steeled himself against seeing the remains of his father's victims, preparing to view them as bones or body parts, not the humans they once were. But seeing this perfectly preserved innocent girl floating in the tank made that impossible. Seeing her beautiful face frozen in a silent scream, for ever young and for ever in pain, he couldn't help but feel the sins of his father crushing down on him. Whatever he did he would be tainted. Nothing he could do would ever remove that stain from his soul. His career had been based on the premise that a man's capacity for good or evil was shaped by a host of influences throughout his life. But now he wasn't so sure.

Perhaps his knack for tracking down evil in others stemmed from some genetic 'gift' he had received from his biological father? Perhaps it did take a thief to catch a thief?

Lost in his thoughts, the sound of echoing footsteps made him suddenly turn his head. Then he heard the scream.

16

When Kathy Kerr woke, any sense of time and place had been taken from her. Her mind kept somersaulting, playing tricks on itself, as if all sanity had fled. She could see a man's dark face coming towards her with a gun and a needle, yet she knew her eyes were still closed. There was a pumping in her ears, which she slowly recognized as the sound of her own racing heart. Her mouth was tinder dry.

What had happened to her? What *was happening* to her? Why couldn't she think straight or remember anything?

And why couldn't she move her arms?

She opened her eyes and stared up at a bare bulb of head-splitting brightness. Groaning, she closed her eyelids again, desperately trying to orient herself. She recognized a smell from her past, an underlying tang of human sweat, masked by disinfectant and fresh paint – the smell of hospitals or prisons.

Trying to move her hands again, she realized her arms were strapped to her body, as if she were hugging herself. But when she peered down and saw the straitjacket she drew no comfort from its embrace.

Kathy was breathing more quickly, close to panic. She had no idea where she was, or how long she'd been there. She had never felt more alone or abandoned in her entire life.

Rolling away from the bright light above her, she gradually forced her eyelids open and waited for her blurred vision to focus on the surroundings. She was lying in a featureless cube, every surface – wall, ceiling and floor – an identical off-white. Pushing her head against the floor, she felt it give beneath her. This was a nightmare. She was in a padded cell.

Inhaling deeply she tried to order her fractured thoughts. She remembered her angry conversation with Madeline Naylor about the unauthorized criminal trials, the terrifying revelation of Karl Axelman's lethal gene therapy, the missing files and the shock of opening her front door to be confronted by the man with the gun and syringe.

Calming down, she told herself she must have been drugged and brought here to keep her out of the way and discredit her. No doubt Madeline Naylor and Alice Prince, and whoever else was involved, had already prepared a credible story to explain that their brilliant young scientist had been taken into hospital for the sake of her mental health.

She tried to remember what her kidnapper had said before injecting her – something about taking her somewhere quiet to recover for a few days. Did that mean until the election, so she couldn't jeopardize Pamela Weiss's precious announcement? Kathy took momentary solace from regaining her memory, but as her awareness increased, so did the realization that her predicament was hopeless.

She thought of shouting for help, but her mouth was dry and the cell would undoubtedly be sound-proofed. Lying stranded on the soft floor, a suffocating helplessness descended on her.

As she lay there, her mind questioned why she had started working on curing violent crime in the first place.

It was during her early teens at school in England that Cesare Lombroso, a nineteenth-century Italian physician, had first put the idea into her head that a person's violent nature could be explained scientifically. From his research on criminals Lombroso believed that certain primitive instincts resurfaced from time to time in 'modern' humans and could be identified in the structure of their facial features. For example, sexual offenders could be identified by their full lips, and murderers by their sloping foreheads.

Even then Kathy had known Lombroso's theory of phrenology was nonsense. But as simplistic as Lombroso's ideas were, they opened her mind to the possibility that violent crime was *caused* and that guilt was in our natural make-up. To her way of thinking, there had to be a reason for everything.

It was when her younger brother Mark suddenly committed suicide in her last year at school that her curiosity became a crusade. Unbeknown to anyone, he had been suffering since childhood from a mental illness called obsessive-compulsive disorder. In his mind he was convinced that he had murdered people, even though he'd done nothing of the kind. He would secretly wander the streets at night in search of his mutilated victims, convinced he would find them if only he looked hard enough, even though he knew at a rational level that his anxiety and guilt were ridiculous.

If she'd known she could have helped him. Drugs existed to moderate the serotonin in his brain and treat his symptoms. After his death, the whole concept of guilt obsessed her. Why did some people have too much and others have none? She was convinced it was genetic. And if these genes could be identified and modified then senseless violence and guilt could become a thing of the past.

But now her dream had become a nightmare.

Suddenly she heard the lock turn, and as the door opened she saw a pair of black shoes enter and walk towards her. Looking up, squinting against the bright light, she saw a tall man in a white coat.

'How are we feeling?' he asked, not unkindly.

'Who are you? Where am I?'

He stooped down towards her and she could see he had grey curly hair and round glasses. 'Come, come. So many questions.'

'I shouldn't be here. You must let me out.'

'On the contrary, we can't possibly let you out. You must have done something very wrong for me to have to give you this.'

She looked up and saw that he was holding a syringe and she tried to roll away. 'No, no more drugs. Just let me talk to someone.'

But the man was smiling now, humouring her. 'Oh, we can't allow that. That's why you're here. Let me give you this and it'll help take away all your

189

unpleasant memories.' He held the stainless-steel syringe up to the light and tapped it twice. She could see a bead of liquid form at the tip of the hypodermic needle and dribble down the side. 'Don't worry, the first few injections don't do any lasting damage.' He spoke in a calm, helpful voice, as if informing her of the weather forecast. 'They merely prepare you for the fourth one, which I'm afraid does have more long-term effects. I understand you have a history of mental illness in your family. Your brother, I believe?'

'But why?' she screamed. 'Why?'

'I'm afraid I don't know that. But whatever you did or saw, I'm afraid that the time for regrets is over. I think you should sleep now. Everything always seems less confusing after a little sleep.'

She panicked now, screaming for help as loud as she could. When he knelt down beside her she tried to struggle, but the straitjacket was too tight.

'Relax, there's nothing you can do about it. So try not to worry yourself,' he said soothingly, easily holding her still and injecting her arm.

But she refused to stop struggling. Awake, she could at least think, but as she felt the drug work she knew that even this freedom was being denied her.

In her despair, fighting to maintain consciousness, one fragile thought, like the flicker of a distant flame in the darkness, gave her hope: that Luke Decker had somehow heard her improvised phone message and would know how to do something about it.

The Snake Tree, Los Altos Verdes, California.
The same day. 6.15 p.m.

Alice Prince only screamed when she saw the other girls. As soon as she saw Libby she stopped.

She had waited as long as she could before following Decker down here. She had always thought that nothing could be worse than the nightmares in which she'd witnessed Libby endure every conceivable horror. But now, as Alice stared at the glass tank two feet ahead of her, she realized she'd been wrong. No nightmare could be as bad as this. Raising her hand, she placed it against her daughter's palm, pressed flat against the cold glass.

Decker's voice was gentle when he spoke. 'Dr Prince, you shouldn't be here. Come, let me take you out.'

Pushing him away, she approached the glass, placing both hands flat against the glazed wall of Libby's grave. 'Of course I should be here. I should have been here years ago. I should have been here to save my daughter from a monster.'

'Come,' he said softly, directing her away from the tank and carefully guiding her down the avenue of grisly exhibits to the exit.

'But why?' she demanded, her voice brittle. 'Just tell me that.'

'I can't. I don't know.'

But she wasn't asking about what happened to Libby. 'Tell me, Special Agent Decker, why did Karl Axelman tell you about this? Why did the killer tell *you*?'

His green eyes were pained when he turned and met her gaze. Pale and tired, he looked a broken man.

'Because he was my father,' he said.

17

FBI field office, San Francisco, California. The same day. 8.12 p.m.

Director Naylor didn't know what enraged her more: the fact that she hadn't been informed about Axelman's revelations to Decker, or that Decker had let Alice Prince into the chamber of horrors.

Naylor was supposed to have been in Los Angeles with Alice, attending the campaign dinner for President Bob Burbank and candidate Pamela Weiss on the eve of the Project-Conscience announcement tomorrow. But just as the Bureau jet was about to take off for LAX the call had come through from George Raoul, the special agent in charge of the San Francisco office, telling her that Decker had found Axelman's stash of bodies. Raoul had told her because Dr Prince was involved and had asked for her.

After rushing back to see Alice, who was now sedated at home, she had viewed the chilling exhibits and then commandeered the SAC's office in San Francisco.

She sat at Raoul's desk, facing Special Agent

Decker. To her left, on the video-conferencing screen, Deputy Director Bill McCloud looked on tiredly. His craggy face frowned as he scratched his head. It was midnight in Washington.

'Why the hell didn't you pass on what Axelman told you?' she asked Decker. 'On my instructions, Deputy Director McCloud expressly asked if you'd received any new information before Axelman's execution, and yet you said nothing. Axelman may have claimed to be your father, but that's no excuse. You're the head of a major unit and you should know better. That's why we have procedures, dammit: to avoid the complications of personal involvement. Did Axelman tell you anything else?'

She waited, but Decker said nothing. He looked beat; he had dark rings under his eyes, his hair was spattered with mud and his face was pale. She pressed on. 'Decker, are you going to talk to me, or am I just going to have to suspend you on the spot? Alice Prince, a very good friend of mine, is now sedated, having seen her daughter's corpse. And for that alone I would happily kick you out of the Bureau. But for some reason McCloud here's been begging me to save your sorry soul. He says that we need you, but frankly I don't believe him. Your record's good, but if you can't fit in with my Bureau, then you're out of here. Do you understand that?'

Again she waited, and again Decker remained silent. She was as surprised as she was annoyed. On the occasions in the past when they'd met they had always sparred. She didn't like him, and thought the psychological mumbo jumbo he practised in the behavioural sciences unit was obsolete. But she had always grudgingly admired Decker's independent spirit and the fact that he got results. Now he looked drained of all passion or care. She wanted to know what else Axelman might have told him, or whether Decker's famed powers of observation might have gleaned something suspicious about Axelman's behaviour before he died. But any concerns that Decker might expose Crime Zero seemed groundless.

As if to prove her right, Decker slowly reached inside his mud-encrusted jacket and pulled out his badge. 'You don't need to suspend me. I resign.' He said it with no anger or emotion, as if he were reading lines.

McCloud spoke then. He shook his head on the video screen. 'Hey, Spook, don't be so hasty. Just go home, get some rest and think it over. OK?'

McCloud turned to Naylor. 'Director, surely it would be better to discuss this later, when everything's calmed down? We can get everything into perspective then. Decide things away from the heat of the moment.' McCloud looked at her, pleading. Decker didn't seem to care either way.

Naylor stared at Decker. He stared back. 'You're fired,' she said. 'Now get out.'

As soon as Decker and McCloud had gone the phone rang. 'I have Governor Weiss for you,' said a voice.

'How's Ali?' was the first question Pamela asked.

'She's back home now, sedated, but she's bearing up better than might be expected. In a perverse way she says it's helped. At least she can now bury Libby and grieve for her, knowing she's

195

finally at peace. And you know, Ali, she's stronger than she looks. She even made me tell you to use this as added ammunition in your announcement. I doubt she'll make it tomorrow, but I'll still be there.'

'Can I speak to her?'

'Pam, I'd leave her to sleep for now. I'm staying over at her place tonight. I'll tell her you called. She'll appreciate it, I know.'

'So what happened exactly?'

Naylor told her the bare bones, including what she herself had seen in Axelman's gruesome exhibition chamber. 'It's sick, Pam, but don't worry about it. Focus on the announcement tomorrow. It's exactly this kind of crime that Project Conscience is designed to end.'

'OK, but give my love to Ali.'

'Of course I will. Good luck tomorrow. I'll see you there.'

Feeling tired, Naylor checked her watch. It was gone nine and today had been a full day. Tomorrow was important, too. She looked forward to a glass of Jack Daniels and a bath before hitting the sack. But first she had one more call to make. Putting the desk phone to her ear she punched in the numbers.

'Jackson,' said a deep nasal voice. She could hear from the background noise that he was in a bar. Involuntarily she licked her lips.

'How is everything?'

'Fine, Director Naylor.'

'Did you give her the injection?'

'Yes, and everything's been arranged. We delivered her a few hours ago. Dr Peters handled it.

196

No-one else was involved. And the doc confirmed that he knows exactly what to do.'

Madeline nodded into the phone. Dr Peters had too much at stake to be unreliable. If she revealed just a portion of the abuse Peters had been involved in he would spend the next decade or so in gaol, and when he got out the only medicine he'd be allowed to practice would be opening a pack of Tylenol.

'Anything else?' asked Jackson.

'No, that's fine, for now. Goodnight.' With that, Naylor replaced the phone and stood up from the desk. As she left the office and made her way out of the building, she thought again of the horrors she'd seen that afternoon.

The timing was advantageous, though. Crime Zero was approaching the critical stage, and seeing Libby and the other dead girls would have hardened Alice's resolve to see it through to the end. After all, Axelman might be gone, but there were countless others like him still walking the earth.

18

Marina District, San Francisco, California.
Later that night.

Pulling up outside his grandfather's house, Decker
was grateful that neither Barzini nor any of Matty
Rheiman's other friends appeared to be visiting.
Emotionally drained, Decker was desperate to talk
to his grandfather alone.

Inside the house, Matty gave him a delighted
hug. 'Luke, what a surprise. I didn't know you were
still in town.'

'It's been quite a day, Gramps. And there are a
couple of things I need to talk to you about.'

Within seconds of hearing his voice Matty sat
him down in the lounge. 'Luke, what's up?'

Feeling like a child, Decker let everything spill
out. He unburdened himself of all the fears and
doubts he'd felt over the last few days: Axelman's
letter claiming he had raped Decker's mother and
murdered his father; the results of the paternity
test; his discovery of Axelman's grisly collection of
preserved corpses.

When he'd finished, Decker took a deep breath

and asked his grandfather to tell him everything he knew. The old man sat silently for a while, gently patting Decker's arm, before speaking of his daughter's ordeal.

'It was an awful night. Your mother was having a drink with friends downtown. Richard was away on Navy business, but he'd agreed to meet up with her for a meal in town on his return. The police say her assailant must have been watching her all night, because her friends had only just left her where Rachel and Richard had agreed to meet when she was attacked.'

Decker's stomach churned. His mother had been a pretty, petite woman. She must have looked vulnerable and childlike to Axelman.

'According to the police she was attacked from behind and knocked unconscious. Then her attacker dragged her into an alley. When Richard arrived and couldn't find your mother, he must have started calling her name. The police think the killer ran out of the alleyway and called your father over, saying a woman had been attacked and needed help. Richard probably ran to your mother then. And, while he bent over and tried to revive her, the killer stabbed him five times in the back. Then he ran off.'

'Did he rape my mother before my father . . . before her husband . . . began calling her?' Correcting himself brought bile rushing to his throat.

'Yes,' said Matty in a soft voice. 'And the man was never found.'

Decker groaned and shook his head. If the crime had happened a decade later the police could have

199

used DNA fingerprinting to help catch Axelman. 'What happened then?'

'Your mother was beside herself with grief. They'd been married for less than a year and Rachel had even converted to the Catholic faith for him. He was her world. When she discovered she was pregnant she wouldn't have an abortion; not only was it against her faith, but she felt sure the child would be Richard's. She was convinced that something good would come out of something bad.'

'And she never suspected I might have been the rapist's child?' Decker asked.

Matty shrugged and his ancient face, which itself had experienced so much suffering, creased in compassion. 'She may have done, but she never talked about it to me. And anyway, what difference would it have made? You were her child, and no parent could have loved a son more.' Matty placed his right hand on Luke's face, and with feather-light fingers he described the contours of Luke's features. 'I don't know what this Axelman looked like, but I can tell you that you resemble Richard so closely I can feel his face in front of me now. He was a good man, and although you never met him, his memory and your mother taught you who you are. Whatever science says, he was your real father as far as all that's important is concerned. And don't forget you've got your mother's genes, too. They were good people, Luke, and you're a good man.'

Decker held his head in his hands, his temples throbbing with exhaustion, desperately wanting to believe Matty's words of reassurance.

'Anyway,' said his grandfather, patting him on the shoulder, 'I regard you as my son, as much as my grandson. I helped bring you up. And I couldn't be more proud of you.'

Friday, 31 October 2008. 1.51 p.m.

It wasn't until the next day that Decker's mind began to focus on other anomalies relating to the Axelman case. He had been so obsessed with the paternity claim that he'd pushed everything else to the back of his mind. But now the questions came forward, demanding attention, and Decker encouraged the distraction they offered.

Why had the cold remorseless Axelman not only revealed where his victims' bodies were buried, but also castrated himself? And why had his physical appearance changed so radically and so quickly?

Something must have happened to him. He wouldn't have done those things naturally; they were totally against his personality. And why was Director Naylor so interested – over and above her friendship with Dr Alice Prince?

Decker mulled over these questions as he sat in front of the TV with a bottle of Michelob. Rhoda was pottering about the house and Matty sat quietly with Decker in the corner of the lounge, reading a Braille book.

Clicking the remote to escape the blanket coverage of Karl Axelman and his victims, Luke felt almost grateful to see the faces of Governor Pamela Weiss and President Bob Burbank smiling out from the screen. They stood behind a lectern bearing the presidential crest at the foot of the Watts Towers in South Central Los Angeles, the crime capital of the West Coast. A crowd gathered around them, along with a battery of media. Decker even recognized the rake-thin, curly-haired Hank Butcher in the press pack. The TV commentator promised a 'ground-breaking announcement in the war against crime'.

Bob Burbank introduced Pamela Weiss, without hesitation, as the next President of the United States. He praised Weiss's record as governor of California, particularly when it came to cracking crime.

Decker took a sip of cold beer and listened numbly to the rhetoric as Weiss began her announcement.

'Last night we all learnt of the true horror of the notorious Karl Axelman's crimes. What you might not know is that the recently executed killer's last victim was the daughter of Dr Alice Prince, a close personal friend of mine.' Decker groaned and almost switched channels immediately, but he was curious. At the same time Matty looked up, his fingers pausing on the page he was scanning.

'Sadly, Karl Axelman is hardly unique. Although he has been executed, there are many other Axelmans at large. Violent crime in this country is an epidemic. Murders are up over ten per cent nationally, rape by even more. Armed robberies and assaults are increasing so rapidly our over-stretched police forces have to prioritize which crimes they deal with first − if at all.

'Aside from the incalculable human costs of

violent crime, the financial cost runs into billions. A drop of just one percentage point in violent crime would free up almost one and a quarter billion dollars a year to invest in health care and other more necessary areas.

'But this isn't a political point. Crime is a social cancer which has riddled society throughout history. For all the rhetoric and well-meaning schemes that have been attempted, no society has yet found a way to stop the few malignant individuals who corrupt the rest of the social body. And, unfortunately for Dr Prince and the other victims of Axelman's crimes, we can't undo what he did. Or indeed help the victims of the countless other crimes. But I believe we can – we *must* – ensure that these crimes don't happen again. And that is what we have been trying to do here in California.'

Decker stared at the TV, open-mouthed. Pamela Weiss was going to claim credit for the California crime figures. To do that she'd have to explain something that had baffled police chiefs, sociologists and media pundits for the last three years.

'Eight years ago, with the backing of a visionary president, senior-level support from the FBI and the involvement of Dr Alice Prince, we embarked on a bold project.'

The camera panned from Weiss and President Burbank to the right of the small podium, where Luke could see Director Naylor standing motionless and unsmiling.

'A project designed not to fight crime but to treat it – to reawaken the good in all of us. We called this initiative Project Conscience. And it is

Project Conscience which is behind California's improved crime figures.'

As she said this Pamela Weiss's confident face filled the screen. Luke was sitting forward in his seat now, his full attention on the TV. In the corner Matty was listening no less intently, his book forgotten.

'All men possess genes that make them less or more predisposed to commit violent crime. And over the last eight years we have proved that fact beyond any doubt. Through modifying the genes of some sixteen thousand convicted violent male offenders in California we have been able to improve their behaviour, achieving the reduced crime figures that have dominated the domestic headlines over the last few years.'

Pamela Weiss stopped and gestured with her hand, taking in the surrounding area. 'Just look at this regenerated area around Watts Towers, where the president and I are now standing. This was once a symbol of all that was bad about our inner cities, but now, through Project Conscience, it represents a soaring example of improvement and hope. And let me reassure you that the gene therapy which yielded these results has been rigorously checked and approved by the FDA as completely safe.'

Decker sat on the couch stunned, as the camera panned round the regenerated shop fronts and houses of Watts. This had to be the project Kathy was working on; the one based on her original thesis back at Harvard and the one she had the meeting about with Naylor yesterday.

'I understand that many of you will have

204

concerns about this bold decision to test a radical therapy outside normal channels, but hard crime requires hard choices. Of course there were risks, but the risks of doing nothing were far greater. Crime has become so entrenched that we believe drastic action was required; not political rhetoric or posturing, but hard, decisive deeds.

'This project wasn't undertaken lightly. Rigorous research involving the best-available minds was conducted over a period spanning almost a decade. This research was conducted on the most intractable violent criminals – people who had already forfeited their right to live in normal society. And the results show that, far from being inhumane and punishing them for their old life, we have given them a new one.

'I believe in free will. It is my firm conviction that genes only predispose us to behave in a certain way by virtue of our hormones and the chemicals in our brains; ultimately we *consciously decide* what we do. We must still all take full responsibility for our actions. But this therapy stacks the odds in favour of a subject being better able to cope with inappropriate aggressive responses. It reawakens his conscience, allowing him to decide to walk away from a senseless fight, avoid initiating a brutal attack, or curb his base urge to rape a defenceless woman.

'Let me share a vision with you. A vision for America. With this therapy, violent men will be freed to channel their energies into more productive areas, which benefit society rather than undermine it. Imagine a society where all convicted criminals are given this treatment – where the majority of offenders are enabled to rediscover their better selves, creating a more productive, tolerant, kinder world. Imagine it. A kinder, stronger America. Your America.'

Weiss raised her right hand and pointed directly at the camera.

'And I tell you now, if I am elected president on Tuesday, I will turn this dream into a reality.'

Decker watched as Pamela Weiss paused for a moment, staring at the camera with just the right amount of concern and warmth. She was making this all sound plausible – even commendable. The beer suddenly tasted sour in his mouth.

'Don't they ever learn?' Matty shouted suddenly.

Luke whipped round at the sound of his angry voice. He had never seen his mild grandfather so enraged before. His face was red and the veins stood out on his temple. 'What's wrong, Gramps?'

'What's wrong? You've just heard what that woman's been saying and you ask me what's wrong? They are judging people by their genes and trying to change them. '

Decker found it hard to match his anger. 'They're only going to give the drug to convicted criminals.'

'But that's just the start. First they use this drug to change the genes of criminals, and then they decide to give it to those young people who perhaps have genes they don't like, *before* they have done anything wrong, because they *might* do something wrong. Soon they will separate those with good genes from those with bad, ignoring the fact that people *choose* to do evil. I remember

206

when the Nazis first began to separate *us*. They made us wear the Star of David on our jackets so they could tell who we were. Not humans. Not people like them. But Jews. Luke, we are more than our genes. You are more than your genes. Hasn't anybody learnt anything?'

'But this is different, Gramps.'

'Is it? What if they decide that you have Karl Axelman's genes and are therefore a potential criminal who should be "treated"?'

Decker couldn't answer that. He put the beer down on the table beside him.

'Yes, my fellow Americans, with the support of President Burbank I have taken risks and challenged conventional procedures. But I firmly believe that what America needs now more than ever is a leader. Someone who will serve the people, not by slavishly *following* changing opinions, but by taking tough decisions and *leading* them to a better, more peaceful tomorrow. If you share this vision then vote for me on Tuesday, so that together we can reawaken the conscience of America.'

Even before Weiss finished uttering the last syllable of her speech the crowd on TV erupted in applause. Decker turned to watch his grandfather shaking his head in disbelief. At that moment the door opened and Rhoda walked into the room. 'Luke,' she said, handing him a brown envelope. 'This came for you in the mail.'

'Thanks.'

Tearing open the buff envelope he found a computer disk and a scribbled note inside. To his surprise it was from Kathy Kerr:

Luke, we've got to talk.

The samples in one of the bags you gave me match the DNA profile of a killer on the FBI database – Karl Axelman. Except there are some subtle, lethal differences, which might be connected to my work on a project called Conscience.

What's going on, Luke? You must suspect something, otherwise you wouldn't have asked me to analyse the samples instead of using the FBI labs. I've enclosed a computer disk for safekeeping. It includes a copy of Karl Axelman's original genome and the modified one taken from the samples you gave me. But don't worry, I should see you before you receive this. I guess this is just a precaution.

We really need to talk. This is scary.

Kathy.

Decker frowned as he read the note, unsure what to make of it. He picked up the disk and placed it on the coffee table. She'd said she should be here before the disk, but she wasn't. She'd also said that Axelman's genes had been changed. Could that explain his physical appearance, the hair loss and acne? And could it explain his sudden remorse and radically changed personality? Did it also explain why Director Naylor had been so interested in what Decker may or may not have found out from Axelman?

He looked up at the TV again and the closing shots of the Watts rally. Pamela Weiss stood triumphant, arms raised. FBI Director Naylor stood close by, staring out across the crowds, a look of cool satisfaction on her face. Had Axelman been one of the criminals tested in the unauthorized Conscience trials, and had something gone wrong? Something that had been covered up?

'What is it, Luke?' Matty asked.

'I'm not sure yet,' he said. Rising from the couch he fetched his jacket and retrieved his wallet. He pulled out Kathy's card, picked up the phone and dialled her number at Stanford. But there was no answer. Then he reached into his jacket pocket and pulled out his cell phone. It had been switched off since their last conversation. Perhaps she'd left him a message?

Sitting forward on the couch he replayed the messages. Matty rose from his chair and came to sit next to him. Kathy had left a message, but it sounded much the same as her scribbled note. There were also a couple of old messages from the Bureau, and one other, but it was such poor quality that Luke almost dismissed it.

'Play that again,' said Matty suddenly, his head cocked to one side, as if listening to a musical instrument. 'Can you turn it up? I heard voices. One sounded frightened.'

Luke turned up the volume and held his ear closer to the phone. Matty was right. A woman's voice was audible now. It was muffled, but Luke knew it was Kathy's. 'What do you want?' she said, her soft Scottish lilt brittle with shock.

'Just to keep you safe and silent for a while,' said a distinctive nasal male voice which Decker recognized but couldn't place.

'Why?' Kathy shouted. 'This is something to do with Project Conscience, isn't it?'

Decker heard the man again. 'All I've been told is that you're over-stressed and are likely to say things you may regret. We're going to take you somewhere you can calm down. Somewhere you can have peace and quiet.' He was sure he'd heard that voice before.

Then there were sounds of interference, or a scuffle.

'Keep that damn needle away from me, you bastard!'

The message stopped then as it reached the end of recording time, but Decker had heard enough.

'Is she a friend of yours?' asked Matty.

'Not exactly,' Decker replied, still trying to place the voice. Then he thought of Director Naylor and he knew who the nasal voice belonged to. It was someone who kept his nose stuck up the FBI director's ass: Associate Director William Jackson, Naylor's senior Rottweiler in the Bureau. Madeline Naylor had to be behind Kathy's abduction; Jackson wouldn't scratch his own balls without clearance from her. But why did Naylor want Kathy Kerr out of the way? It must be serious for Jackson to get personally involved and not just leave it to his goons.

Kathy was right; they did need to talk. Holding the phone to his ear Decker played the message back again, this time listening to exactly what Jackson said.

'. . . take you somewhere you can calm down. Somewhere you can have peace and quiet.'

Decker's first thought was a Bureau safe house.

210

He scanned his memory, remembering all the ones he knew near San Francisco. They were definitely options, but even safe houses were manned and maintained. Naylor would want as few people as possible to know about Kathy's abduction. But it had to be near San Francisco; a long journey would risk discovery. Where was there a discreet institution, controlled by the Bureau, which could accommodate an individual in secrecy? Somewhere that guaranteed peace and quiet?

Suddenly it came to him – the perfect place. Filled with dark memories, Decker pressed a pre-set number on the phone and waited for the dialling tone.

The phone line clicked in his ear and he heard a polite, professional voice greet him.

'Hello,' he replied, 'my name is Special Agent Luke Decker. You should have me on your books. I need an urgent appointment.'

'What are you going to do?' asked Matty.

Decker shrugged with a casualness he didn't feel. 'Find her and get her out, of course.'

19

'As far as I'm aware, no-one's been admitted in the last three days. Certainly not to the secure wing, Luke.'

Dr Sarah Quirke spoke softly, with the trace of a Welsh accent, as she sat at her desk in the main building of the Sanctuary. A petite woman in her late forties, with auburn hair and a round face, her kind eyes frowned with concern behind elegant spectacles. Behind her, half the wall of the office was a vast picture window, through which Decker could see the distant purple haze of the High Sierras etched against a faultless blue sky. Sunlight flooded through the glass, highlighting the copper in Dr Quirke's hair and bathing the wooden desk and chairs in a warm, honeyed light. His sessions with Dr Quirke were the only positive memories Decker had of his four-week stay here after his mother died.

'Luke, what's this all about? I only came in on a Saturday because you said you needed an urgent

212

check-up – although in my opinion you're saner than most of the doctors here. But all you seem interested in are patient admissions to the secure rooms. You know full well that this is an FBI-funded retreat for agents with stress-related difficulties. We deal in counselling and therapy for temporary mental disturbances and dependencies, *not* insanity. We have only two secure rooms and those are for short-term emergencies. It's rare for them to be used at all. So tell me, Luke, what exactly are you after?'

Decker sat back in his chair and rubbed his temples. He didn't like coming back here, and it wasn't just because of the memories. If, as he suspected, Kathy had been abducted and was being held in the Sanctuary, then somebody very senior had to be involved, and that meant Decker was exposing himself just by being here. He'd only approached Dr Quirke because he trusted her absolutely. 'Sarah, you probably know me as well as anyone, so please don't be alarmed. Something very strange is going on that I need to investigate. But the last thing I want to do is involve you. Trust me, it's safer this way. All I want to know is, have you a record of all the inmates and their rooms?'

Quirke frowned. It was clear that although he trusted her it wasn't entirely reciprocated.

'I don't want to know any names,' he reassured her. 'I just want to know if there's *anybody* in the secure wing.'

She paused for a while longer and then gave a small nod. 'All right,' she said, looking at the computer screen on her desk as she tapped on the keyboard. 'I've got all the patients on my computer

213

and, like I said, no-one new has come in over the last three days. As for the secure rooms in the garden wing, they haven't been used for three and a half months. The last time was when a patient became violent and had to be restrained overnight in room A.'

'So as far as you're concerned, there's nobody in any of the secure rooms now?'

'Correct.'

'Does anyone physically check them?'

'No, because they're usually empty. Dr Peters does occasionally.'

Duke nodded, remembering the grey-haired doctor. They'd never met, but Decker had often seen him around the place when he was staying here, and he knew the doctor's reputation. Peters was more of an administrator than a medic. He was a drab career man, who worked for the FBI first and the patients second. 'Does he still manage the place, making sure it escapes the Bureau budget cuts?'

She gave a small smile. 'Yes.'

'But you have access to the secure wing as well, don't you?'

'Well, like most of the senior doctors here, I have keys. I can easily check the rooms. Or I can call Dr Peters. Like I said, he's probably seen them most recently.'

Decker raised a hand. 'No, don't do that. If I'm right, I don't want to involve you or Dr Peters in this. Just let me see inside the rooms by myself. No-one need know I've even been here, and if the rooms are empty then no harm's been done. Please, Sarah, help me. If I'm being paranoid, I promise I really will book myself in for a check-up.' He smiled at her, but he could see she was taking him seriously.

After a brief pause, she opened a drawer in her desk and reached for a bunch of keys. 'Perhaps I should come with you,' she offered.

Luke was tempted for a moment, but then he thought of Jackson and Naylor. He couldn't endanger one of the few people who had genuinely helped him in his life. 'Trust me, just give me the keys to the rooms, tell me when the secure wing will be quietest and tell no-one of my visit here. No-one at all, even if they ask you directly.'

Dr Quirke frowned again and then handed over three keys. 'The large key gets you into the wing, the two smaller ones open each of the two rooms. Go now.'

Decker took the keys and thanked her.

'I don't know what this is all about,' she said as he left her office, 'but I hope to God you don't find anyone there.'

He jangled the keys in his hand and smiled back at her. 'I hope to God I do.'

Madeline Naylor and Alice Prince's terrible objective came to Kathy Kerr in her drugged sleep. It made no sense, but that hardly mattered. What mattered was that it flouted every reason she'd embarked on Project Conscience, and this made her cry aloud in her sleep – so loud that she woke herself up.

As she came to full consciousness she became aware of a raging thirst; her tongue was so swollen she could hardly swallow. Her arms ached from being strapped in the jacket and she needed to urinate. So she felt relief as much as fear when she heard the key turn in the lock. Rolling over, she opened her eyes and saw the pair of black shoes enter the cell.

'Water,' she croaked. 'I need water.' Still groggy with drugs she closed her eyes and waited, too exhausted to struggle, hoping she wasn't going to be injected again. 'I need to pee as well.'

Bending to her level, the man with curly grey hair adjusted his round glasses and smiled his kindly smile. In his right hand he held a bottle of liquid. It had a teat like a baby's milk bottle. 'Drink this. It'll quench your thirst and it's rich in vitamins and minerals. I'll feed you some solids later. As for peeing, you're wearing diapers, so please go ahead. You'll be changed when you're next sedated.'

'I'm not a bloody baby,' she croaked, sounding angry in spite of her exhaustion. 'I demand to speak to someone. You can't keep me here.'

'Come, come,' he said in his condescending voice. 'Don't over-excite yourself. Just drink.' Kneeling down, he raised her head and laid it on his lap. Then he placed the drinking bottle in her mouth. The liquid was cool and smelt of orange Gatorade. Briefly she tried not to drink, to exercise the only control she had, but she was so dehydrated she couldn't stop herself sucking on the teat, gulping down as much as she could.

As she drank she felt him bend over her, so near his coat brushed her face. To control her claustrophobia she closed her eyes and tried to ignore his suffocating closeness. Then she felt his hand move

216

to her left breast and start to probe its contours through the fabric of the jacket.

The narrow tiled corridor leading to the secure wing was enough to bring back the memories. And a glimpse of the small confined rooms on either side of him made Decker quicken his step. Just being in a place like this and contemplating the possibility of losing control of his mind made his pulse beat faster.

When he'd been a patient here he had been terrified of his obsession with hunting down the evil in others, scared it was an addiction that somehow indicated he was evil himself. He hadn't even seen his own mother in the nine months before she died because he had been so busy tracking down criminals.

Now the fears came flooding back, and this time there was a firmer basis for them. He *knew* he possessed the seed of evil in him.

Banishing these thoughts to the back of his mind, Decker pushed through a set of fire doors to the secure wing. He tried to focus all his thoughts on one aim: finding Kathy Kerr and getting her out.

At first she couldn't believe he was touching her breast with any sexual intent, but when Kathy heard the catch in the man's breathing and felt him push his crotch against her cheek she spat out the bottle teat. 'What the hell are you doing?'

'Relax,' he soothed, smiling down at her, as if humouring a troublesome patient. Beads of sweat had formed on his forehead below his fringe. His eyes, magnified behind the glasses, had a glazed look that sent a cold rush of fear through her abdomen. Putting down the bottle he began to stroke her face, rubbing his fingers around her mouth, tracing the line of her lips. She could taste salt on his skin as he moved his fingers over her slick lower lip. She tried to bite him, but his fingers stayed just out of reach, slowly tracing the moistness of her lips. Totally helpless, she could feel her chest tighten in panic, especially when his hand moved to his crotch and began to unzip his pants. This can't be happening, she thought. Only a few hours ago she'd been on the verge of embarking on the final stage of her life's work, and now she was here in this hell. She struggled as the man began manoeuvring her head. Out of the corner of her eye she could see him pull his penis out and begin to rub it.

'I'm warning you, I'll bite anything that comes near me,' she shouted.

This seemed to excite him more as he tried to manoeuvre himself over her face. And as his breathing increased so did her panic and desperation. 'Relax,' he said. 'In a few days you won't remember any of this. You won't remember anything at all.'

She closed her eyes and gritted her teeth. Then suddenly his heavy breathing stopped, and from the door behind her she heard a sound that made her gasp with relief.

'Dr Peters? What the fuck are you doing?' Crisply controlled, Decker's words were thick with anger. She tried to twist round to see him, but he was already moving into the room, pulling her tormentor to his feet. Looking up, she saw Decker hold the man with his left hand and punch him hard in the face with his right. It was an easy, powerful movement, like a golf swing. The blow was followed by the satisfying sound of the doctor's glasses breaking and a hoarse groan. As the doctor crumpled, Decker pumped his knee up into the man's groin. Peters bent double, holding both hands over his open zipper, his face white. Kathy felt such rage she wanted Decker to hit him again and again, but he didn't, he just let Peters collapse squirming on the floor. As he lay there, Decker gestured to Kathy and barked, 'I've been sent by Associate Director Jackson, on the orders of Director Naylor, to take her to a new location.' Luke's face was expressionless, but his green eyes burned with rage. 'I'm supposed to deliver her unharmed. So I hope you haven't hurt her. Because if you have I'll be coming back.'

'No, I've done nothing,' the man whimpered, moving his hands from his groin to his broken nose.

'Then get out of here and leave me to my job.'

'But I haven't given her all the injections yet. Director Naylor told me I was to hold her here for at least four more days.'

'Well, the plans have changed. If you want to check you can call Jackson or the director. But Jesus Christ you'll piss me off if you do, and I'll tell them what you've been doing. Now get the hell out of my sight, you sick fuck. I don't want to see you again before I leave this shithole.' With that, Decker hauled the man to his feet and threw him out of the cell. Decker waited for a moment, listening to Peters scurry off, before bending down and silently unbuckling Kathy's jacket.

The hands that had just demolished her tormentor were now gentle as they rolled her body and began untying her arms from around her body. He focused on the straps and knots, careful not to hurt her as he undid them. All the time she stared at him, terrified he might not be real. As soon as the jacket felt loose, his strong fingers massaged her arms, pulling her up. 'You came,' she said, still not believing it. 'You found me.'

'Of course I came,' he said, his face breaking into a grin. 'I want to – I *need* to know what the hell's going on.'

'We've got to stop them, Luke,' she said. 'Something terrible is happening.'

'I kinda gathered that,' he said, supporting her as her legs gave way. 'I know about Project Conscience and them trying to cover up the mistake over Axelman.'

'It's worse than that,' she said, trying to think straight, realizing what little sense her revelation made. 'Axelman's death might have been more than a mistake. I think it was a test for something else. Something far worse than Conscience.'

'What do you mean?'

Before she answered him, Kathy again questioned the insight that had come to her in her drugged sleep. Surely they weren't prepared to go that far, she thought.

'Luke, I don't think they want to treat violent criminals at all,' she said. 'I think they want to kill them.'

PART 2

THE PEACE PLAGUE

20

The New Military Hospital, Baghdad, Iraq.
Monday, 3 November 2008. 1.07 a.m.

Dr Uday Aziz knew time was running out. Over the last week the elite Republican Guard had suffered eighteen cases of suicide and sixteen lethal brain haemorrhages. And there was every indication that this was only the beginning. All the deceased had been supremely fit, mentally stable soldiers under the age of twenty-five.

Three days ago the furious Iraqi president had demanded, via his generals, that Aziz and his team uncover what lay behind the problem. The Rais would not countenance delaying the planned offensive on Kuwait to reclaim their rich oil reserves. The loss of face was unthinkable. And after tomorrow's US elections there would be a lame-duck government in power, making it an ideal time to invade. Aziz knew he had to find the source of the problem and identify the solution as soon as possible or risk joining the ever-growing list of dead.

But it wasn't the Rais's threats that drove Aziz as

he sat in his office on the top floor of the drab brownstone building that made up the main wing of The New Military Hospital. Tapping away at his laptop, trying to complete his report for presentation to the generals tomorrow afternoon, Aziz was desperate to solve the riddle for more personal reasons. He had never been emotionally involved in his work as a doctor, seeing it more as a comfortable, lucrative job than a vocation. But now, for reasons he didn't understand, Aziz felt an almost intolerable responsibility for the deaths, as if he were in some way responsible for them. And as each new case was recorded Aziz knew the only way he could ease this crushing burden was to find a cure.

A desk lamp was the single light in his otherwise dark office. It was after one in the morning, and for the last four days he hadn't returned home to his wife and two children or slept for more than a couple of hours at a time. Over that period he had returned to the first recorded incident – a twenty-one-year-old called Salah Khatib, who had been shot for refusing to shoot four deserters – and had studied the autopsies and relevant test. Aziz had then charted each subsequent suicide or brain haemorrhage, recording every link between Khatib and the others.

Khatib's urine had yielded the first clue. That and the other victims' samples had contained an exceptionally high level of androgens, hence his initial belief that they were suffering from steroid abuse. The hair loss and acne, plus pronounced testicular atrophy in many of the men, had seemed to confirm this. Suicide was also a known side effect of steroid abuse.

But the blood told another story. It confirmed the androgen levels, but it also contained massive amounts of the enzyme monoanime oxidase. MAO is a marker for the level of neurotransmitters in the brain, particularly the inhibiting transmitter serotonin.

Aziz conducted a full DNA scan on Khatib's blood, using one of the two Genescopes in the military hospital. These expensive gene sequencers were two of only three in Iraq. The third was in a private medical bunker below the main presidential palace two miles north of Baghdad.

Comparing the DNA profile in Khatib's military records with the DNA profile in the blood taken from his corpse, Aziz found a subtle but significant difference. Seventeen of Khatib's genes had been modified by the addition of a series of control sequences; sequences that weren't present in his original genome and which certainly weren't present in the standard human genome. At first Aziz had been at a loss to understand why this should be the case. Then he checked whether Khatib had received any gene-modifying drugs in the last few weeks. In the man's records, among the battery of jabs and inoculations every soldier receives, Aziz noted one DNA vaccine: the standard Bioshield injection given to any soldier about to go into combat to immunize him against biological weapons, particularly those used by Iraq. This allowed them to use these weapons in battle without harming their own troops. Despite the numerous wrangles with the UNSCOM inspection teams, it was common knowledge that the Rais had secretly developed a powerful

225

biowarfare capability. It was this that allowed the Iraqi president to consider defying the US-led UN Security Council and invade Kuwait again.

But the Bioshield viral vector wouldn't change the particular genes that had been modified in Khatib's genome. The Bioshield vaccine merely modified stem-cell DNA, immunizing the body to most of the standard threats while making the cells receptive to more specialized booster vaccines, designed to counter the ingress of newer bioweapons. But Khatib had only received the standard Bioshield vaccine and no boosters. And even if he had they wouldn't have had this effect on his genome. Something had subverted Khatib's genes in a way that had killed him.

Looking at the other suicide and brain-haemorrhage victims, Aziz's team discovered that they shared the same anomalies in the key seventeen genes. Studying these genes and understanding how they boosted aggression hormones, fuel neurotransmitters and inhibition neurotransmitters had convinced Aziz they were the cause of the problem. But how and why had they been changed?

He had also checked with Yevgenia Krotova, the Russian scientist heading up Iraq's biological-warfare programme. According to her team not all of the deceased had received the Bioshield DNA vaccine, and many of those who had were given it years ago. So how could it be the source? Especially as all the batches of vaccine his team and hers had subsequently checked revealed nothing unusual. What was the link? If only he had been a more committed doctor he might now be able to explain this. He might be able to prevent more men from dying.

Pausing from writing his report, he rubbed the painful spots on his chin and picked up a small blue cardboard carton from beside the laptop. He had studied medicine at University College London two decades ago and could easily read the Western lettering on the pen-sized carton. The text told him nothing he didn't already know, but as he stared at the carton four dark hairs fell onto the keyboard of his laptop computer. Instinctively he scratched his scalp. A cold tremor ran through him as he watched the dark strands fall like fur from a moulting dog.

Suddenly everything was as clear as ice.

The source of the epidemic wasn't in *all* the Bioshield serums at all, only a few, perhaps just *one* random corrupted sample. That was why his team hadn't found anything in their batch checks. It would only take one person infected by a rogue viral vector, providing the vector hadn't been attenuated and rendered non-infectious. That person would then spread it to all the people he came into direct contact with, starting a chain of infection.

Which included himself.

With a trembling hand Aziz began to type on the laptop, rewriting parts of the report. He had to record what he'd discovered and alert his team and Yevgenia Krotova. Khatib was probably the index patient and had infected others before he died. The army lived in such close quarters that the troops could be decimated within weeks if not days. His team had to search their stocks for any other corrupted samples of vaccine and analyse them to find a cure. And he must tell the generals about what had happened; tell them to call off the advance. Yes, he thought, as he typed feverishly, suddenly painfully aware of all those soldiers going to war, perhaps he could avert the conflict and save all those lives, too.

Sweat streamed down his forehead and he felt so tired he wanted to sleep. But he couldn't rest; he had too much to do.

When he stopped typing fifty-eight minutes later he wept with frustration. His left hand lay limp on the keyboard, refusing to obey his instructions. Then the whole left side of his body went numb, and his forehead felt as though a band of steel had tightened around it. He could only gasp as he tried to focus on the screen in front of him.

'Oh no,' he groaned. 'No.' But the brain haemorrhage wouldn't abate and, when it struck, the seizure was so massive that Aziz only felt pain for fractions of a second. Disturbing half the contents of his desk as he fell, he pulled the laptop with him, closing it down. His body was lifeless by the time his head and the laptop struck the hard, cold floor, deleting the report he died writing.

Next to the doctor's face, inches from his open, unseeing eyes, lay the blue carton of Bioshield vaccine. Under the Bioshield brand name was the manufacturer's logo: a target made up of rings of chromosomes, with an arrow shaped like a double helix striking the nucleus. *Targetting a better future* was the tag line next to the company name and address: *ViroVector Solutions Incorporated, Palo Alto, California, USA.*

'I feel like I'm going mad. all the signs point to a bigger picture than Conscience, but I can't believe it. Whatever's going on, we can't just let them get away with it,' Kathy Kerr said, sipping her tea in Matty Rheiman's lounge.

Matty Rheiman sat listening quietly in the corner while Decker paced around the room. 'Do we have a choice?' Decker said, bending to the coffee table and pushing the pile of photographs towards her. He took a picture from the top and handed it to her. 'Look, I've been to your house on Mendoza Drive twice now. And Jackson's people are crawling all over it. They're probably waiting until after the election, just to make sure that anyone who comes looking for you doesn't cause a fuss. They don't give a damn who sees them, either. Which means they don't know you've escaped yet. But it also means they think they're above the law. And they're probably right.'

Kathy Kerr looked at one of the photographs of her house that Decker had taken. It showed three men, looking relaxed, leaning against a grey Chrysler parked outside her front door. She recognized all of them. They had been with Associate Director Jackson when she'd been abducted. Another photograph showed them going into her house. Going inside *her* home, as if it belonged to them.

'Jackson hasn't been around,' said Decker. 'He's doubtless trying to distance himself now. He's pretty senior within the Bureau and he's

229

probably back in Washington. I bet his rogue agents don't even know Director Naylor's involved – not directly anyway.'

'But we've got to do something, Luke.'

'What?' Decker's voice rose in exasperation. 'Kathy, it's your word and mine against the director of the FBI, the head of a major biotech company and the future President of the United States. I've just been fired from the Bureau. Shit, after Weiss's "Conscience against Crime" announcement, the polls are putting her in the lead – a long, long way in the lead. The press and the police love her. *Everyone* loves Pamela Weiss and her miracle cure for crime. And sooner or later Naylor and her cronies are going to find out that you've escaped from the Sanctuary and they'll come looking for you. They don't know I'm linked to you yet, but you should get away.'

Kathy clenched her jaw but said nothing.

Almost two days had elapsed since Decker had rescued her from the Sanctuary and taken her back to his grandfather's house in the Marina District. All of Saturday night and most of Sunday she'd slept fitfully through drug-induced nightmares while Decker watched over her. By Sunday afternoon she'd felt strong enough to talk, and that evening they had shared their discoveries.

Using Decker's over-specified but under-used laptop, she had re-examined the changes in Karl Axelman's genome from the disk she'd posted to Decker, and she used his FBI access codes to probe other suspicious deaths at San Quentin.

She probably owed Decker her life, but if she

expected him to share her outrage and be totally sympathetic to her plight she was disappointed. After they'd pieced together all they knew, Decker shook his head and gave her a weary look, as if to say, What did you expect? Project Conscience had been her dream since their arguments at Harvard, so why was she complaining now, just because the methods weren't entirely ethical?

'Luke, if nothing else we've got to find out what they're really up to.'

'Isn't it obvious what they're up to? Face it, Naylor and Prince took your idea and used you to dupe the FDA. They screwed up with Axelman and the others at San Quentin, or maybe they didn't. And because they don't want Conscience to be compromised they've covered everything up and put you away. It's as simple as that. I want to see them pay and I'm pissed at what they did to you, but you're out now and perhaps you should just walk away.'

Kathy looked at Decker long and hard. 'Shit, there was a time when you'd have turned over every stone if you felt a crime had been committed. Don't you care any more?'

'Of course I care. I'm just being realistic. Let's say we did get into your house and got to your trunk in Rambo's pen—'

She frowned. '*Rocky*'s pen. The chimp's name is Rocky.'

'OK, Rocky's pen. Let's say we did get out all your disks and files, what would that prove?'

She sighed. God, she'd been through all this already. 'It would prove that Conscience was based on false data; that the original vector used on

231

unsuspecting convicts wasn't the Version-Nine vector approved by the FDA.'

Decker shook his head. She could see the muscles working on his jaw. 'OK, but who's going to *care*? Look, everyone *wants* this miracle cure for crime *you* helped create. And since all future treatments will be done using your safe Version-Nine vector, who gives a shit that violent cons were given potentially unsafe stuff?'

His voice rose in volume. 'Christ, Kathy, apart from the fact that you were kidnapped, why do *you* care? This is your dream. I've got reason to be pissed off. I've never believed in all this "genes means everything" shit. I've spent my whole working life hunting down killers and rapists based on the notion that the way they think and behave is dictated by their pasts. I've done a pretty good job of it, too. But now I discover that my own father was a particularly unpleasant serial rapist and murderer. And, according to this brave new GENES "R" US world of yours, I'm suddenly no better than the scum I've been hunting down.'

He lowered his voice and turned away from her. 'Kathy, I've always hated the whole Fascist notion of genetic predetermination, but this is what you wanted. An ordered society where unpleasant variables are cancelled out. So don't accuse me of not caring.'

Kathy bit her lip. Matty was still sitting quietly in the corner of the room, his dead eyes levelled at her. She had the unsettling feeling that not only could he see her, but that he could also read her thoughts.

'Luke, that's not fair,' said Matty quietly. 'Hear her out. I don't agree with Kathy's ideas, either,

232

but I'm sure her motives are good. Kathy didn't want this, did you?'

'No, of course not. Certainly not like this. Luke, I can understand why you're angry, but I'm angry too. And I want to try and stop them. Look at Axelman's death: the disk I sent you shows that his genome was altered, and any scientist with half a brain cell can plug the disk into a Genescope and tell how lethal the alterations are. Axelman wasn't corrected to make him behave better. The corrections killed him.'

'But he would have died anyway. He was on death row. And if it was just an accident, who really cares?'

'But that's the whole point. I don't think it was an accident. Trust me, I know a bit about viral vectors; I had a good teacher. What killed Axelman and the others at Sàn Quentin was too well designed to be an accidental mutation. Something very strange is going on. I don't know what, but it's more than Conscience. I'm sure of it.'

Decker sighed and turned towards her. His eyes searched hers, as if seeing her for the first time. She could see his analytical mind working, weighing up the implications of what she was saying.

'You can't do nothing, Luke,' said Matty simply.

'Gramps, I'm sorry, but would you please stay out of this.' He turned back to Kathy. 'You're really sure this was no accident?'

She paused. 'Pretty damn sure. Yes.'

'Sure enough to risk your life trying to prove it?'

She swallowed hard and took a deep breath. 'This was my life, so I guess so, yes.'

* * *

233

Decker kept staring at her for a moment and then gave a small nod. She looked vulnerable wearing his baggy jumper and rolled-up jeans, especially with her ruffled dark hair and pale skin. But there was steel in her eyes.

During the last few days he had watched her sleeping form toss and turn, jettisoning the drugs that had been injected into her system. And he'd been consumed by anger that the director of the FBI could have justified this, and whatever else she'd sanctioned, in the name of fighting crime.

He was also incensed with Kathy for being so naïve. She seemed to think that everything in the big bad world could be smoothed away as neatly as variables in one of her experiments. That people – especially senior people - obeyed set rules and laws. But his anger was outweighed by a real fear for her; he knew that if Naylor's people got hold of her again they'd have no choice: they would kill her.

He didn't believe in her conspiracy theory, but the cover-up was real enough. And he did want to get to the bottom of it. He hated the whole idea of Conscience, and his continually churning mind couldn't help throwing up anomalies. Kathy wouldn't have blown the whistle on the FDA scam; she would have been pissed off initially, but after calming down she wouldn't have risked her life's work. Naylor and Prince must have known that, so kidnapping and murdering Kathy seemed excessive. Alice Prince didn't seem a person who would willingly allow Kathy, someone she knew and trusted, to be hurt – not of her own volition anyway. The San

Quentin deaths weren't a factor, either. As far as Naylor was concerned no-one knew about those – least of all Kathy. The bodies had been officially executed and cremated.

Still, Decker couldn't see how Kathy's life was worth the futile goal of thwarting a project she herself had initiated. However, he realized that if he refused to help her, she would go it alone and she probably wouldn't last five minutes. Plus Matty had been fussing over her for the last two days, telling him something had to be done to stop this.

'Let's say you could prove all this – and that's a big assumption, because I bet Naylor and Prince have already got plans to discredit you – then who would you tell?'

'Pamela Weiss.'

'What makes you think she isn't involved?' he asked. It didn't fit with his impression of her, but he wouldn't bet on Weiss not being involved.

'Because when Naylor and I argued about this, she insisted that Weiss knew nothing. She seemed furious even at the idea of her finding out. I'm telling you, we've got to get to Weiss.' Kathy stabbed her finger towards one of the photographs. It showed her house viewed from the rear. The top of Rocky's pen was just visible over the backyard fence. 'And to make her believe us we have to get the evidence that proves her friends are deceiving her.'

'I assume Rambo' – Decker corrected himself again – 'I mean *Rocky* can be noisy. And he'll get pretty excited when he sees you?'

'Yes,' said Kathy, 'he'll make some noise.' Her face fell. 'Are you saying we can't get to

235

the trunk until the men have gone?'

'Not if we don't want to be found out.'

'Shit.'

Then Decker smiled as an idea came to him. 'But that doesn't mean we can't start stirring things up before we get all the evidence. We've got the Axelman disk and you know what's in the trunk, yes?'

'Yes.'

'And you reckon Pamela Weiss should be informed of what we know as soon as possible?'

'Of course, but how? There's no way I can get to her and, even if I could, Naylor would get to me first.'

'You're right,' said Decker, reaching for the phone, switching it on to speaker. He dialled a number he knew by heart. 'So we need a go-between. Someone with access to the great and the good.'

Kathy gave him a quizzical look, but he didn't say anything. Matty smiled as if he'd already guessed what Luke was going to do. The phone rang five times before the familiar voice answered. 'Hank Butcher,' the journalist said, his voice filling the room. He sounded harried.

'Hank, hi, it's Luke. Do you remember the other night, when you said you were tiring of just doing profiles and witty stories and that you wanted to get your teeth into something big? What did you call it? A real Pulitzer prize-winner?'

Butcher laughed. 'Yeah, buddy, isn't beer great? Hey, Luke, now isn't a great time, OK. You might not realize it, but one of the most historic elections in American history is taking place tomorrow. This

Project Conscience announcement has changed everything. I've even got myself invited to a celebration party on Thursday, assuming Weiss wins and becomes our first female president. Frankly, I don't think any story of yours is going to cut it right now.'

'What if I said my story involves the star of that historic celebration bash you're going to on Thursday.'

'Oh, yeah?'

Decker looked over at Kathy, who was nodding her head in understanding. 'How about an exclusive on Weiss's Project-Conscience announcement from the scientist behind the original idea?'

Hank gave a dismissive snort. 'You mean Alice Prince?'

'No, the person she got the idea from.'

'Go on.'

'And what if I told you that Project Conscience isn't all it seems?'

'Meaning?'

'There's a huge cover-up underway, including the abduction of the scientist behind the project, the deception of the FDA and covering up deaths related to the Conscience treatment?'

'Luke, this is on the level, right?'

'Yup.'

'I assume you've got evidence?'

'Let's just say I've got enough for you to ask our future president some pretty searching questions. And there's more evidence coming.' Decker could almost hear Hank's mind working, preparing his Pulitzer-prize acceptance speech. 'So, Hank, do you want an exclusive or not? Of course, if you're not interested I can call someone—'

'Cut the crap, Luke,' Hank interrupted with a short laugh. 'You have my undivided attention. Tell me more.'

21

ViroVector Solutions, California.
Wednesday, 5 November 2008. 6.00 a.m.

As the United States of America awoke to the news that they had elected their first female president TITANIA was not surprised. It had planned for Pamela Weiss's victory and based many of its far-reaching projections on it coming to pass.

TITANIA had no vote to cast in yesterday's election, but since it never slept it had been busy all night raiding the computer-controlled electronic ballot boxes, counting up the results. TITANIA knew within a matter of hours that Pamela Weiss had won with the biggest landslide victory since Reagan in 1984. And the reason for TITANIA's lack of surprise was that this victory represented yet another domino falling in a sequence it had long predicted.

As always, a small proportion of TITANIA'S vast neural net was focusing on Crime Zero, continually updating progress on the differing phases and fine-tuning its predictive sequences.

Phase One was now complete, as was the

239

related Project Conscience. TITANIA needed to check how Phase Two was developing. Its progress against predicted action standards was vital to the launch of Phase Three. Interrogating its search engines TITANIA scoured the Internet for feedback on Iraq.

Logging on to hospital databases and military systems in Baghdad, while at the same time piecing together apparently unrelated snippets of information from Reuters, CNN, the BBC and the other syndicated news agencies on the World Wide Web, TITANIA soon found the pattern it was looking for.

The above-average number of deaths listed on the computers at the military hospital in Baghdad – all under-twenty-five males with suspected brain haemorrhages, and isolated reports of an unexplained rash of suicides within the Iraqi armed forces – told TITANIA all it needed to know. The Iraqi military was fast becoming an amplification zone, and the reports were increasing in number. TITANIA would continue to monitor these reports, feeding the findings into the predictive model. But for the moment Phase Two appeared to be on schedule.

Only now did TITANIA look at Phase Three, the most complex stage of all. First of all it interrogated the control computers at the target airports, ensuring that the radio-activated bacteriophage filters were in stock, awaiting its command. Only then did TITANIA rerun its predictive sequences.

Phase Two employed an infectious vector, which was transmitted by touch. But Phase Three was transmitted via the respiratory system. It was airborne and, once launched, the spread would be much faster and harder to predict.

Using earlier test data, TITANIA knew how fast the Crime-Zero-Phase-Three viral vector incubated within the human body. It could also predict the spread through a population by extrapolating the diffusion characteristics of past airborne pandemic plagues, particularly the Spanish Flu epidemic of 1918–19, which killed almost 50 million, and the more recent Chinese Flu outbreaks of 1957 and 1961. Using this base model, and continually checking empirical data on the World Wide Web, TITANIA was able to give a real-time prediction for when Crime Zero would meet its final objective.

The original forecast was more or less unchanged, putting the end still some three years away. Assuming nothing changed and the human entity Madeline Naylor carried out her next task, then TITANIA only had to launch Phase Three at the designated time and wait for the final dominoes to fall.

As TITANIA e-mailed its Crime-Zero status report to Prince and Naylor it had no conception of the morality of what it was doing, only that it was technically possible and increasingly inevitable.

The White House, Washington DC.
Thursday, 6 November 2008. Noon.

Director Naylor hated being kissed. At social functions she always tried to avoid the European affectation of greeting people with a kiss on each cheek – air or otherwise. A handshake sufficed. But at the White House champagne reception Bob Burbank held in the magnificent East Room Madeline allowed herself to be kissed. She even manoeuvred her face so the president's lips momentarily brushed against hers. And as she did so, Alice Prince looked on, a nervous frown of fascinated horror on her face.

The grand room, with its Bohemian crystal chandeliers and Fontainebleau parquet floor, was filled with the party faithful who had helped Pamela Weiss win. Campaign advisors, secretaries, canvassers and a few journalists mingled and congratulated each other as liveried waiters ferried around endless trays of canapés and champagne.

Naylor stood with Alice Prince and Pamela Weiss, talking to Bob Burbank, as his wife, Nora, chatted with Pamela Weiss's husband, Alan, and Todd Sullivan, Weiss's campaign organizer.

The president was all charm and bonhomie, beaming his Gregory Peck smile at Prince and Naylor. 'So, since you guys are the real heroes in winning this election, can you tell a simple country boy like me *how* Conscience actually works?'

'Don't ask me,' said Naylor with a smile, resisting the urge to wipe her lips. The president was no country boy and he was only laying on this charm offensive because Project Conscience had made him look good – a visionary president, assured of his place in the history books. But that was OK. Bob Burbank's charm offensive had already allowed her to achieve what she had come here for.

She turned to Alice, who now appeared to be coming to terms with the shock of seeing Libby. The funeral had been two days ago and she already seemed calmer. She had been typically reluctant about today, though, forcing Naylor to remind her of their plans. 'It's the science that makes Conscience work,' she said, smiling at Alice.

'Well?' Burbank said turning to Alice. 'Can you explain it to me?'

Alice looked at Madeline and then back at the president. 'Vectors, Mr President.'

'Vectors?'

'Yes, viral vectors,' said Alice, nervously, clearly annoyed that Naylor had focused the spotlight on her. 'You see, Mr President, Project Conscience is all about getting the right control sequence into the right cells, and to do that I must create the right virus. Like a cross between a parcel and a cruise missile, a viral vector can target and deliver any DNA I insert into it. Viral vectors are gene changers. With them I can alter the very essence of a person.'

Burbank took a sip of his champagne. 'How targetted can they be?'

'Well, with the right engineering, I can create a virus that will target a particular cross-section of humanity, or a particular person, or even a particular type of cell.'

'You mean it will ignore any other target and only hit what it's supposed to? Like a smart bomb?'

'That's the idea.'

'I wish we could be as precise in solving the Iraq crisis.'

At that moment the tone changed. The escalating problem with Iraq was casting a shadow over the celebrations.

'Yes, what's the latest?' asked Alice Prince.

Burbank shrugged and Naylor fancied she saw relief in his eyes, as if he was glad to pass on this particular baton to his successor in the new year. 'Well, we're doing everything we can. I only hope the Rais will see reason. But as you know Iraqi troops are still gathering north of the thirty-second parallel.'

'Surely he realizes that if his troops cross that line, for whatever reason, then the coalition allies will stop them?' asked Alice.

Burbank nodded. 'Oh yes. French and British carriers, as well as our own, are already on standby in the Gulf. Troops and fighter planes are on alert in Saudi, Kuwait and Turkey. We're ready for him, but he doesn't appear to care.'

'Why?' asked Alice.

'He has warned that he'll view any attempts to thwart his repossession of what he calls "the Iraqi province of Kuwait" as extreme provocation and will unleash an "appropriate response".'

'But he hasn't got nuclear weapons, has he?'

'No, not yet. Not nuclear. But we believe his biological capability is pretty awesome. Despite all our inspections, our intel suggests he's got something special up his sleeve.'

'And if the Iraqi president does launch something?' Alice asked.

Burbank frowned. 'Then the allies will have little choice but to escalate to nuclear weapons, razing Baghdad to the ground.'

Naylor turned to Pamela Weiss and she could see that this very real scenario filled her with dread. Becoming the first-ever woman president was fine, but becoming the first to launch a nuclear warhead in anger was not.

As if to reinforce the urgency of the situation a tall, African-American in dress uniform appeared beside Burbank. General Linus Cleaver was the chairman of the Joint Chiefs of Staff. 'Mr President, can I have a word, please?'

No sooner had Burbank turned away than he turned back again, leaning towards Weiss. Speaking to his successor he kept his smile fixed and his voice low, but Naylor heard him. 'I'm sorry to break up the party, but something's just come up involving Iraq. I've arranged a briefing in the conference room. I think you should be there. We need to keep a united front during the handover. I suggest we meet in the Oval Office in ten minutes.'

Naylor watched Weiss clench her jaw. 'Thanks, Bob, I'll be there.' Burbank smiled once more before walking back towards the chairman of the Joint Chiefs of Staff. With him was the secretary of state, Jack Manon, and the defence secretary, Dick Foley.

'You OK, Pamela?' asked Alice.

'Yup. But it looks like I'm not going to get much of a honeymoon period. I'll see you guys later.'

'Good luck,' said Naylor, watching her say good-bye to her family, then walk towards the door in the direction of the Oval Office. As Weiss neared the door Naylor saw a compact, sandy-haired man in a dark suit appear from the throng and shadow her. Naylor knew it was Toshack, the Secret-Service agent assigned to organize her protection. She didn't like him. He never showed her fear, only politeness. And, being Secret Service, she had no jurisdiction over him.

Then, just as Weiss reached the door, a rake-thin

man with curly hair suddenly stepped out in front of her and extended his hand. Toshack tensed but held back. Everyone here had been vetted and searched. Weiss shook the man's hand, although she carried on walking, clearly not intending to stop. He smiled at her and appeared to be congratulating her.

'Who is that?' Alice Prince asked Naylor.

Squinting her eyes, Naylor stared for a while then gave a small nod. 'I think it's a journalist. You know. He does all those pieces for *Vanity Fair*. He interviewed Pamela about three years ago, when she was being launched as a major contender for the White House. It was a big piece in all the magazines at the time. Did her a lot of good. Hank . . . er, Butcher, I think.'

Suddenly Weiss stopped in her tracks, her face no longer smiling. Butcher was saying something and Weiss was listening intently. Then Weiss darted a quick look in Naylor's direction before shaking her head at the journalist and pointing to her watch. After exchanging a few more words the journalist pulled an envelope out of his jacket and handed it to her. Then they shook hands and Butcher left. Weiss quickly looked in the envelope and then called Toshack over. She said something to him before turning to leave the room.

'I wonder what's going on?' Alice asked Naylor. 'She doesn't look too pleased.'

To Naylor's surprise, Toshack turned and approached them. The agent was courteous but unsmiling as he addressed then. 'Excuse me, Dr Prince, Director Naylor, but Governor Weiss would like you to meet her tonight to discuss an urgent matter relating to Project Conscience. Eight o'clock at your offices, Director Naylor?'

'Fine,' said Naylor with a tight smile. Next to her Alice fingered her pendant nervously.

'She also has a question for you,' said the agent, his face impassive.

'Oh yes?' said Naylor again. 'And what's that?'

'Who is Dr Kathy Kerr?'

22

The Mandrake Hotel, Washington DC.
The same day. 1.17 p.m.

Hank Butcher felt pretty pleased with himself as he walked to his rental-car in the underground lot beneath the new Mandrake Hotel, where he'd stayed last night. The evidence Decker had given him about irregularities on Project Conscience had been enough to challenge the president-elect, and she'd appeared suitably shocked. And with more evidence to come, he was sure there was a huge story here.

His story.

This could dwarf the Watergate and Lewinsky affairs of the last century. And if he handled it well he could be credited with blowing the first-ever female presidency wide open – *before* she was even inaugurated.

He blew onto his hands. The temperature had dropped dramatically since election day. Washington was in the grip of a cold snap and snow was forecast. After getting into his car, Butcher opened his briefcase and checked his airline ticket. His American Airlines flight from National to San Francisco left in an hour and a half.

Pulling out his cellphone he pressed a pre-set button. Decker's phone was turned off so he left a voice mail.

'Luke, hi; it's Hank. I've spoken to Weiss. She put on a pretty good show of looking shocked. I'd even go so far as to say she knows nothing about this. Let me know when you've got the rest of the stuff. I should be back home tonight.'

Just then a figure entered the deserted underground lot. A tall woman in a thick winter coat. Although he recognized her face he couldn't believe it was her: she was so rarely alone; her entourage usually accompanied her. She stopped and checked her watch, as if annoyed that whoever was supposed to be picking her up hadn't arrived. She must have had a clandestine meeting at the Mandrake. It wouldn't be the first time deals were struck in the discreet hotel. She had probably arranged to be picked up down here so as to avoid prying eyes.

Butcher had thought of approaching her at the White House reception earlier, but had wanted to get a response from the president-elect first. And Decker had warned him to leave her alone until they knew more. But this was a heaven-sent opportunity. He opened his door.

'Director Naylor?'

Turning to face him she looked startled and wary. 'Yes?'

'The name's Hank Butcher. I saw you at the White House reception. Can I ask you a few questions?'

249

She gave him a withering glare. 'You can do what you like, but I doubt I shall answer them. I'm in a hurry.' She checked her watch again and turned away from him towards the exit sign.

He left his car. 'C'mon, Director. It'll only take a few moments. I need to ask you about Project Conscience. I was going to ask you at the White House, but I wanted to get a comment from Pamela Weiss first.'

'I'm sorry, but like I said, I'm in a hurry. I have to get to National.' She pulled a cellphone out of her pocket with her gloved hand.

'No, don't call for your car. I'm going to the airport, too. Let me give you a lift there. We can talk on the way, OK?'

'I don't think so.'

Butcher gave her a sly smile. 'What if I told you I know all about the cover-ups on Project Conscience? And that I'm going to get all the evidence I need to blow it right open. Would you still refuse to talk to me?'

Naylor's eyes narrowed and he saw shock on her face. 'What if I told you that you've been misinformed by people who wish to sabotage the most significant initiative against crime since DNA fingerprinting?'

Butcher opened the passenger door of his car. 'I'd say you might be right. But I'd need to hear your side of the story. The president-elect was too busy to give me an immediate response, perhaps you might like to instead.'

Naylor hesitated for a moment and then let out a defeated sigh. 'OK,' she said eventually. 'Let me tell my agents where I'll be. She put the cellphone to her thin lips and left a curt message. 'But, Mr Butcher,' she said after she hung up, 'what I'm going to tell you is off the record. And I'm only telling you so that you understand this initiative mustn't be sabotaged.'

'Fine, whatever you say,' he said as she got into the car.

By the time they reached the Potomac it had begun to snow. But as Butcher asked his questions he ignored the large flakes falling from the sky.

'So, tell me about Dr Kerr. She's made some serious allegations.'

'Look, Dr Kerr is brilliant, and the origin of Conscience undeniably comes from her work, but over the last six or so years she's been acting more and more unstable. Her work hasn't been a success and most of the recent step changes on the project have come from Dr Alice Prince, not her. Kathy's been feeling very insecure about her role in a project she still regards as hers.

'Alice offered to share the credit, but Kathy wanted a ridiculous financial reward and full credit or she threatened to trash it. Naturally, we can't allow a project as important as this to be held to ransom by one person – however much they've contributed. So we accepted her resignation, and now it appears she's trying to discredit the whole project.'

Ahead, the sprawl of the airport rose through the thickening blizzard. Butcher peered through the windshield. 'She claims you had her put away in some mental asylum.'

Naylor laughed at that. 'What proof do you have of all this nonsense? I thought you were supposed to be a responsible journalist.'

251

'It isn't just Kathy Kerr who claims you put her in an asylum. I've got another witness.'

'Oh yes? Who?'

'I'm not telling you that,' he said. 'Not yet, anyway.'

'Look, Mr Butcher, there's no way anyone can corroborate a story that didn't happen, unless they're lying. I asked for proof not hearsay.'

'I'm expecting more proof any time now,' he said. 'Dr Kerr says she's got records going back ten years or so.'

They were heading for the main terminal building and the rental-car drop-off points. As he turned to ask her where she wanted to be dropped off, Director Naylor calmly reached into her jacket and, in one fluid motion, pulled out a gun and pressed it into his crotch. 'Mr Butcher, please take the turning for the long-term car lot. If you do not do exactly as I say I *will* pull the trigger.' The pistol was pushed hard into his balls, but for a good second or two he didn't react. His brain simply couldn't believe what was happening.

Butcher exhaled suddenly, and Director Naylor watched in satisfaction as his grin faded and his face paled.

It hadn't been easy to make her prey think he was the predator. But she'd no choice. She couldn't get one of her minions to handle Butcher because she needed to know what he knew. And she needed to do it quickly and discreetly.

Immediately after Toshack had asked about Kathy Kerr, Naylor got on the phone to Jackson. Kerr had been delivered to Dr Peters as agreed.

252

Naylor hadn't been able to contact Dr Peters, but he wouldn't have released Kathy; he had too much at stake. She had to find out who'd got her out and why. Just the thought of Kerr shooting off her self-righteous mouth to Weiss made Madeline squirm. This had to be stamped out fast.

It had taken Director Naylor just two phone calls to discover where Hank Butcher was staying in Washington. She'd learned that he had checked out of the recently opened Mandrake Hotel this morning and had a reserved American Airlines seat to San Francisco from National airport at four forty-six in the afternoon. But his rental-car was still parked under the hotel.

After a brief talk with Alice to sort out what they were going to tell Weiss that night, she'd taken a taxi to the Mandrake, then waited. Once Butcher spotted her the rest had been easy.

Now *she* could interview *him*.

'What are you doing?' he demanded, his voice at least an octave higher than before. 'You can't possibly hope to get away with this. I'm a journalist, for Christ's sake.'

'Be quiet and drive to the long-term parking lot.'

It was now so white outside she couldn't see more than a few yards ahead. Butcher kept pleading with her as he drove through the automatic barriers and followed her instructions to the middle of the vast lot, eventually parking in a space surrounded by hundreds of increasingly snow-blanketed cars. His face had a greenish cast and was covered in a film of sweat by the time he switched off the ignition and turned to her. She could tell from his eyes that he was close to panic. Good.

'Hand me the keys.'

He took the keys from the ignition and gave them to her. 'What do you want?' he asked.

'Who got Kerr out of the Sanctuary?'

'I can't tell you that. I promised him I wouldn't. I've got to protect my sources.'

She pushed her gun further into his groin until he grimaced in pain. 'I'd think about protecting more than your sources right now, if I were you. Trust me, Mr Butcher, unless you tell me what I need to know, I will shoot you and feel justified in doing so. We are embarked upon something that is vital to the future success of our species. Something far too important to allow a couple of individuals to hijack it.'

Butcher looked really scared now. 'But if I tell you, how do I know you won't kill me anyway?'

'God, you journalists always ask questions. You don't know. But I assure you that if you don't tell me you'll beg me to kill you.'

She stared into his eyes and cocked the gun.

'OK, OK, I'll tell you. His name's Luke Decker; he contacted me by phone.'

'Decker? As in Special Agent Luke Decker? Jesus.'

'Yeah. He told me about getting Kathy Kerr out of the Sanctuary and how you'd deceived the FDA. And also how Axelman was possibly a mistake you wanted to cover up – or something else.'

'Did he tell you what this something else might be?'

'No, he said Kathy Kerr had some suspicions,

254

but nothing concrete. That's what I was asking Pamela Weiss about at the reception, but she seemed completely in the dark.'

Naylor smiled at that. 'Oh she is, Mr Butcher, she is. And that's exactly how it's going to stay. Would you please get out of the car now?'

A look of relief and then renewed fear crossed his face. 'Why? What are you going to do with me?'

'Mr Butcher, get out of the car or I will shoot you where you sit. If you run or shout for help I will shoot you dead. In this blizzard, no-one will see or hear you anyway.'

Once out the car she steered him to the back. 'Open the trunk.'

Shivering with terror and the sub-zero temperature he did as she asked. There was a small case and a laptop inside. Otherwise it was empty.

'Get in the trunk.'

'But it's freezing.'

'Now! Or I will shoot you.'

For a moment she thought he was going to struggle, but then he sat on the bumper, allowing her to push him into the trunk. Butcher lay there trembling, his eyes staring up at her through his glasses, pleading with her.

'Let me leave you with two points of consolation,' she said to him. 'One, you aren't dying much sooner than you would have done anyway. Two, you got off lightly compared to what I'm going to do to Dr Kerr and Special Agent Decker.' With that she fired one perfectly placed bullet into Butcher's forehead and closed the trunk.

Checking she hadn't been seen in the vast snow-swept lot, she retrieved a Swiss Army knife from her inside pocket and unscrewed the rear and front plates from the rental-car. She swapped the rear one with a Saab's plate ten cars down and the front plate with a similar one on a Chevy two rows back. The whole process took her twelve minutes, but it would ensure that Hank Butcher's rental car, and therefore his body, wouldn't be found for weeks, especially if the weather stayed cold. And by then it wouldn't matter.

Walking toward the courtesy bus shelter she turned to watch her footsteps disappear in the falling snow. Despite her reservations about exposing herself, there was something satisfying about doing a job personally and doing it well. It took her back to her early days as an agent, when she'd finished in the top percentile in her class at the Quantico FBI academy and helped bust two murder cases in her first six months, receiving a bullet in her left leg and right shoulder for her troubles. She certainly felt no remorse for what she'd done. It was necessary, and in the long run the morality of the deed would cease to be relevant. In the bus shelter she reached for her cellphone and dialled Associate Director Jackson's number.

'Jackson,' she ordered when he picked up, 'find Dr Peters and get rid of him. He allowed our guest to escape. Then find Luke Decker; Dr Kerr will be with him.'

'Decker?'

'Yes, the same Decker who beats you every year at the Quantico shooting meet. Find them both and bring them to me. Naturally, no-one else in the Bureau must know about this, except your people. Understand?'

'Yes, but what if I can't bring them to you alive?'

Naylor looked up as the courtesy bus approached through the snow. She checked her watch, calculating that she could get a cab from the terminal building in plenty of time to rendez-vous with Alice before their meeting with Pamela Weiss.

'Director,' pressed the voice on the phone, 'if I have to, can I kill them?'

Madeline Naylor looked back across the rows of cars, already unable to identify which contained the rapidly cooling corpse of Hank Butcher. 'Of course you can, Jackson. You can do whatever you like. Just make damn sure you get them.'

257

23

Iraq. The same day. 10.07 p.m.

The presidential palace in Babylon, 100 kilometres south of Baghdad, was one of over fifty built since the 1990 war. Its unrestrained opulence seemed obscene in a land where continuing international sanctions meant many people lived in poverty. Including the older palaces, the Rais and his family now owned over eighty such residences around the country.

Standing in one of the military planning rooms, Dr Yevgenia Krotova shifted the weight of her heavy frame from one foot to the other and stared at the six silent television screens on the far wall; each showed a different cable channel. These flickering images of the modern world contrasted sharply with the palace's old-world splendour – the marble pillars, the thick rugs, the gilt high-backed chairs and the alabaster water fountains visible in the floodlit courtyard beyond the arched windows.

The ostentatious show of wealth didn't shock Yevgenia Krotova. After selling her soul to the devil nothing shocked her any more. Ten years ago she had been deputy director of Russia's State Research Centre of Virology and Biotechnology in Koltsovo, helping to run their illegal germ-warfare programme. But Russia was poor and unable to maintain even the meagre salary she was paid. Iraq had outbid both Iran and North Korea to purchase her expertise, and whatever secrets she could bring with her.

One freezing night in January 1998 Yevgenia had decamped with her husband and three daughters and for the last decade she had headed up Iraq's formidable biological-warfare programme. She was paid more money than she could ever use and had a good life, but she was a guarded prisoner, a bought possession of the Rais. She was forbidden to leave the country and her family were continuously watched. Dr Yevgenia Krotova didn't allow herself to question her decision, though. Regret served no purpose.

But now she was in trouble. Aziz had died before he could explain the escalating deaths in the Republican Guard, and because he'd involved her in his investigations she had been summoned to the palace to supply answers. Any sadness she may have felt for Aziz's death was more than countered by frustration. She'd been left to explain the unexplainable to the three generals. Why couldn't Aziz at least have left a few clues before he'd died? The only consolation was that the generals were here and not the Rais himself.

After greeting the generals she stood in the middle of the room. It was late and she felt tired. She wanted to sit down, but they didn't invite her to join them on one of the comfortable-looking high-backed chairs surrounding the long table. Instead they left her standing and proceeded to interrogate her. Frowning, she tried to ignore the flickering screens over the generals' shoulders and concentrate on their questions.

'Dr Krotova, do you, or do you not, know what the cause is?' General Akram was the tallest of the three men. His eyes searched her face as he spoke and his voice was brusque. Ostensibly, Akram had overall responsibility for medical matters in the army, although the man was an idiot who was only given the role because of his distant blood relationship to the Rais.

'Not exactly, but I'm convinced Dr Aziz was close. He thought it was steroid abuse at first, but now he has died showing the same symptoms, which implies that whatever killed the men is infectious.'

'Infectious?' asked General Rashani, a short bald man with glasses. He sounded incredulous. 'But these men have been dying of brain haemorrhages and committing suicide. How could that be infectious?'

'That's what Aziz was trying to confirm. It might be a complex virus or a prion, or else something entirely new, which changed the men's DNA and brain chemistry. Aziz was writing up his work on the night he died and I tried to recover his report, but his computer was damaged and most of it had been deleted. However, from the fragments we salvaged from his hard drive I think he may have found something.'

'But you don't know the cause, or how to cure it?'

'Not yet. My people are reviewing all the tests Aziz's team conducted on the patients, and we are currently conducting detailed autopsies on the men's brains to shed more light on the pathology. But we need more time.'

'You haven't got more time. We haven't got more time. We await the Rais's order to march on Kuwait at any moment.'

'But you can't wage a military campaign until we know more. This phenomenon is no longer confined to the Al Taji Camp. At least a hundred men are now dead, and the rate is increasing. We need to check how widespread this epidemic has become in order to contain it. If you don't you will lose even more men.'

'Men always die in war,' said General Akram. 'Unless you can explain what's wrong we shall proceed as planned. If it's non-infectious, then there's no problem. And if it is, then at least they can serve a purpose before they die.'

'But that's—' she started to say before the third general gave her a dark look.

'This is not open to debate,' he said.

Yevgenia bit her lip, framing a more positive response. It was dangerous to anger them any more than she had done already. But before she could say anything else she heard a loud voice speaking in English. The three generals swivelled round to face the wall of televisions, and Yevgenia realized the volume had been increased on the top right-hand screen. The channel was CNN and the voice she could hear was that of the US president. He was standing in front of a podium, and at the bottom of the screen was a subtitle, which read,

Bob Burbank, Live from the White House. Behind him were four men and a woman. One of the men was in uniform. The president had been speaking for some minutes when Yevgenia, who spoke English well, picked up what he was saying.

'I hope and pray that the president of Iraq sees reason and doesn't cross the thirty-second parallel. But if he does, then the coalition allies are committed to crush his offensive. He must understand that we will execute this ruthlessly and decisively, because we firmly believe that to delay would only encourage him further. We have the conventional force in place to destroy his army and we will employ that force *immediately* one Iraqi boot, tank or plane crosses that line in the sand.'

As the US president spoke his face was pale and his eyes tired. His face worried Yevgenia; he had the look of a man telling an awful truth.

'We are aware that the Iraqi president has promised to retaliate with unconventional weapons, but we will not appease him. We *cannot* appease him. The very last thing we want to do is start a conflict, let alone escalate one. But he must be in no doubt that if he raises the stakes one notch we will have no choice but to end this decisively. The game of bluff and counter-bluff he has been playing with the UN for the last eighteen years has come to an end. There is no more patience.'

President Burbank seemed to sway on his feet and as he did so he wiped beads of sweat from his brow. At first Yevgenia thought the president was affected by the import of his speech, but then she realized it was more than that. He looked ill. 'As I speak, the president of Iraq controls the greatest destructive force we have ever seen. His actions will determine whether our nuclear response remains unused or whether it is unleashed on him and his country.' Burbank paused and looked into the camera, his face haggard. 'I hope he chooses his actions wisely.'

When he finished there was a hush, not only in the palace but also in the White House briefing room on the screen. Yevgenia could see the generals craning over the backs of their chairs, staring at the screen. Then, just as the journalists began asking their questions, the most unimaginable scene unfolded before her eyes: Bob Burbank clutched his chest, reached for the podium as his knees buckled and collapsed to the floor. There was a second of shocked silence, then the screen went mad. Secret-Service men in black glasses formed a circle around him. Journalists left their seats to rush forward and the president's aides panicked.

The camera suddenly focused on one of the men who had been standing behind the president. A tall thin man, identified by an excited commentator as Vice-President Smith, he looked shell-shocked, paralysed by terror. 'I'm sure somebody will take control of this awful situation soon,' said the CNN commentator, more out of hope than knowledge. But Yevgenia could see from his stricken face that the vice-president wasn't going to be that some-one.

At that moment there was a thumping noise and the camera shifted back to the podium. The woman who'd been standing behind the president was now tapping her hand on the microphone, her eyes looking straight at the camera, her gaze unflinching. She was a striking-looking woman with a thick bob of auburn hair. Her face was open and strong, and although she was clearly in as much shock as everybody else was she was not debilitated by it.

'Please resume your seats; this briefing isn't yet over,' she said. Her voice wasn't loud, but the tone was so calm and clear it cut through the collective panic, stopping everyone and making them turn towards her. Gradually the journalists returned to their seats and a semblance of order was restored as the Secret-Service men and two paramedics lifted the president and removed him from the room. One man, who looked like a doctor, came over and whispered something in the woman's ear, and her chest heaved as she took in this new information.

'My name is Pamela Weiss. I am the President-elect of the United States of America. I have just been informed that what you have witnessed was a heart attack. President Burbank is now being rushed to hospital, where he will receive the very best medical care. A full bulletin will be issued as soon as his condition is known.'

For the briefest of moments she paused and glanced behind her at the vice-president, who still stood frozen to the spot, his eyes dead with shock. Pamela Weiss cleared her throat and Yevgenia could see her steeling herself. She couldn't help but admire the woman as she continued: 'I'm sure that the country's thoughts and prayers are with the president and his family at this moment.

But let no-one be unclear – friend or foe – this changes nothing. The US and UN position on Iraq is unambiguous. The president's words stand.'

The volume faded then, leaving just the silent screen. Turning, Yevgenia wondered who had the controls. But all the generals stood silently, taking in what they'd just witnessed, their hands loose by their sides.

Suddenly one of the high-backed chairs at the large table in front of her swivelled round, revealing the Rais in full military uniform. In his right hand he held the TV remote control. His thick black hair and moustache were still unnaturally devoid of grey and his jowls heavy. As was his wont he had been listening in on her meeting, trying to hear what she really thought.

'We definitely can't delay now, Dr Krotova,' he said in a delighted voice. 'We have the wonderful weapon you made me, and we have this opportunity.' His face was smiling as he stared at her, though she knew that his smile stemmed from what he had seen on TV, not from what he'd heard her say to the generals.

'General Akram,' he said, not taking his eyes off her, 'you and the others will organize for the invasion to begin as discussed. The timing is perfect. Whatever the Weiss woman says, the Americans will be distracted.'

'Come,' he said, beckoning to Yevgenia with the remote, as if controlling her.

Nervously, she walked past the generals and stood in front of him. Smiling, he beckoned her to come closer, until she was bending down, his thick moustache almost scratching her cheek. His breath smelt of stale cigars. 'Find out what is killing these soldiers,' he whispered, 'or I will kill you and all your family.' The smile didn't leave his face as he spoke, but she believed every word he said.

24

Waiting outside Kathy Kerr's isolated house on Mendoza Drive neither Kathy nor Luke were aware of the events on Capitol Hill. Their only concern was to steal into her house unnoticed.

'They've gone,' said Decker, getting back into the car after checking out Kathy's house for the third time in the last hour. 'But we still shouldn't stick around when we go in. They're gonna find out you've escaped soon. Five minutes, like we agreed. No more.'

Kathy nodded her agreement as she sat silently in the passenger seat of the rented Ford Taurus.

He turned to her. 'You sure you want to go through with this?'

'Yes,' she said, staring at her house. It looked the same as before, but now the white façade, which she'd always viewed with such affection, seemed sinister, as if concealing some threat behind its darkened windows. In her mind's eye she could see Jackson waiting behind the front door, armed with a gun and a syringe, like the last time. 'You sure no-one's waiting inside?'

'As I can be,' said Decker. 'I've checked the whole place. There's no-one there. You've got no security alarms or lights I should be aware of, have you?'

She shook her head. 'Nope. Before we go in, should we call your journalist friend again to see if he's heard anything more from Pamela Weiss yet?'

Decker shrugged and dialled the cellphone resting on the dash. The phone rang in the cabin of the car and then Hank Butcher's voice mail kicked in. Decker hung up. There was no point in leaving another message.

'Shit,' she said, 'why doesn't he turn his phone back on?'

'Don't worry, we know from his message that Pamela Weiss probably isn't involved. And she's not likely to get back to him until she's checked things out herself. Hank isn't shy. He'll call back if he gets any response. And when he does he'll want the rest of your precious evidence.' Decker smiled at her, his eyes glinting in the half-light. 'Ready?'

She took a deep breath, picked up the empty canvas bag she'd brought with her and got out of the car. 'Let's go.'

Taking the spare key from under the right plant pot she opened the front door. The house was silent and apart from a vague mustiness in the air there was nothing different about the place. It was as if the last few days had been nothing more than a bad dream. Feeling her way through the darkened rooms she led Decker to the back of the house and the yard beyond.

As soon as she stepped into the yard Rocky began to screech with excitement. In the moonlight she could see him standing by the wire mesh of the large wooden pen. His teeth shone white as he grinned madly at her, delighted to see her. Running to the door she released the bar and latch and walked in. He jumped on her, chattering and screeching, almost knocking her over as he hugged her. Decker moved to support her and Rocky suddenly turned on him, baring his fangs.

'No, Rocky,' she said quickly, stroking Decker's face. 'He's not hurting me. He's a friend.' Decker froze and didn't move while Rocky sniffed him suspiciously. Then Rocky reached out a long hand and roughly prodded his shoulder. It was a grudging gesture, done more for her benefit than Decker's, but it signalled that the ape accepted him.

Kathy checked Rocky's store of food in the automatic dispenser at the far end of the pen and could see it was almost exhausted, as was the tank of drinking water beside it. The pen was in need of a clean, but otherwise he seemed unaffected by his recent neglect. Once she was reassured on this point Kathy went to a tyre hanging from a tree in the middle of the pen. Reaching into the bottom of the tyre she felt for a ridge of duct tape and pulled it off. Attached to the tape was a key.

Then she walked over to the trunk, unlocked the padlock and raised the lid. She felt a rush of relief when she saw her files and personal memorabilia inside – all untouched, all safe. She reached for her canvas bag. 'It's all here,' she said.

Decker checked his watch as he stood guard. 'Great, now hurry up.'

'Don't worry, it'll only take a moment. Then I'll just get a few of Rocky's things and we can go.'

'Rocky's things? Why?'

She busied herself sifting through her journals, taking all the important ones and putting them in the bag. Then she picked up the computer disks and stacked them in, too. 'Well, we can't leave him here.'

Decker shook his head in exasperation. 'Why the hell not?' he demanded. 'He's big and ugly enough to look after himself. For Christ's sake, Kathy, he's not the one in trouble, you are. Where the hell are you going to keep him?'

'I know somebody in a zoo down at Atascadero who'll take care of him until all this blows over. Come on,' Kathy said casually, picking up the bag, 'let's go.'

Decker frowned but said nothing as he led her out of Rocky's pen, past the tall Douglas fir to the house. She smiled up at the dark sky, bejewelled with stars, as Rocky walked beside her, his hand in hers. She began to feel hopeful for the first time in days when suddenly Rocky let go of her hand and disappeared into the dark. Turning in surprise she saw Decker drop the bag of disks and files and launch himself at her, pushing her to ground and rolling her behind the fir tree.

Then she heard them – two men came out of the house, whispering to each other. Then one of them raised something in his hand and the whole yard was bathed in light so bright she could only look down at the ground. Three yards beyond the shelter of the tree trunk the bag of files was illuminated in the blinding light, its contents spilling onto the grass.

'Shit,' said Decker beside her, pushing her tight against the trunk. 'What the hell are they doing back here?'

'I don't know,' she said in shock, as if he actually expected her to know the answer.

'Rambo was a great help, wasn't he?' spat Decker.

'*Rocky*,' she corrected automatically. The light was now shining directly on the tree they were hiding behind.

Decker scowled and retrieved a gun from his shoulder holster. 'More like Bambi, if you ask me.'

'I told you, he's no longer violent.'

'I wouldn't sound so goddamned proud if I were you. Right now we could do with some good old-fashioned aggression.'

She heard the men walk towards the upset bag of evidence and pick it up. It was frustrating, but there was nothing they could do about it. The light was so brilliant that if she or Decker moved a fraction beyond the protection of the tree they would not only be blinded but starkly visible, too. 'I told you,' she hissed, 'Rocky only gets aggressive when I'm threatened.'

Decker turned and gave her a wry grin which, despite the circumstances, made her smile. 'Kathy, I don't know about you and Bambi, but I've been under threat before, and trust me, this qualifies.'

Suddenly the spit of a silenced gun cut through the night and she felt the thudding impact of a bullet hit the tree. Then a man's voice said, 'Come out, or we'll come and get you.'

271

25

The Hoover Building, FBI headquarters, Washington DC. The same evening.

'Madeline, this is getting out of hand. Perhaps we should slow down and look at what we're doing.' Alice Prince adjusted her glasses and toyed with her pendant.

The FBI director sat back in her chair and drummed her fingers on the desk. They were alone in Naylor's office on the fifth floor of the Hoover Building in Pennsylvania Avenue. It was an oppressive masculine room, designed to thwart electronic surveillance devices, with dark wood panelling covering the lead-lined walls along with photographs of Naylor's famous predecessors. But the most striking feature was the obsessive neatness of the office. The piles of reading were stacked so perfectly that not one book or leaf of paper protruded. Even the pads and pencils on Naylor's desk were in regimented lines. But then, even as a child she had exerted extreme control over her environment. Even more than Alice had. 'Relax, will you, Alice. Everything is under control.'

Alice Prince rose from the small conference table and paced around the room. Everything was not under control. Most importantly, she wasn't under control. She was used to planning projects like Conscience and Crime Zero at an academic level, but generally she left the operational aspects to others. Madeline Naylor had murdered two men today and she had participated.

Even though Madeline had administered the kiss of death to Burbank, Alice felt a direct responsibility for killing the president. After all, she had genetically engineered the viral vector Madeline had smeared on her lips; she had created it to target the heart cells of a particular individual – the president – matching his unique DNA sequence, seeking out any fatal flaw it found there and bringing it forward in time. Harmless to any other human, Madeline's kiss had been fatal to Bob Burbank.

It had served its purpose. Citing the constitutional amendment of 2002, both the Senate and Congress had sworn in Pamela as president two hours ago, effectively bringing forward her inauguration. The vice-president had expressed no objection.

But Madeline had killed the journalist, too – just for asking the wrong questions. Kathy Kerr was now on the loose, and she was probably the only person on earth with comparable knowledge of viral vectors. If anyone had the technical talent and experience to stop Crime Zero it was Kathy Kerr.

As far as Alice was concerned, things were far from under control.

'Perhaps we should cancel Crime Zero and

just stick with Conscience. There's still time.'

Madeline Naylor sat forward and shook her head. 'Stop worrying. You know that Crime Zero is the only long-term option. We've discussed this already and you know the arguments better than I do. Everything is going to be OK. Kathy Kerr isn't going to be a problem. Look, Pamela's going to be arriving any moment now. I'll explain everything after she's gone. Just stick with what we agreed to say. No more. No less. OK?'

Alice sat down and released a huge sigh.

'C'mon, Ali, you know I'm right. Haven't I always been right in the past? Think of Libby. Think of the future. Think of our vision. Just focus on the benefits – for everyone. OK?'

The phone rang and Madeline answered it. She listened for a second then looked up, her dark eyes willing Alice's collusion. 'She's here.'

The recently sworn-in President threw two sheets of paper on the table. 'I've got ten minutes. Tell me what the hell's going on. I've got enough on my plate without worrying about Conscience. The last thing I need now is some journalist raising questions about the very project that got me elected.'

Pamela Weiss was dressed in black and her face was pale.

'Pamela, we can explain any concerns you have,' said Madeline coolly. She sipped a glass of mineral water and looked completely unfazed by Pamela's anger.

'OK, this journalist Hank Butcher has given me a list of issues and questions to respond to before he goes public with new evidence.' Pamela slapped her hand on the papers she had just flung on the table. 'I'll go through them for you. First of all, who the hell's Dr Kathy Kerr? She claims that Project Conscience is little more than a test before moving on to something more drastic, which apparently involves *killing* criminals with dangerous genes rather than curing them? This of, course, would be preposterous, except that apparently there have been some deaths at San Quentin caused by a mutation of your vector.'

Pamela straightened and walked round the table with her arms crossed, the fingers of her right hand drumming on her left arm. She wasn't just angry, Alice realized now, she was hurt.

'And that's not all,' said Pamela through gritted teeth. 'She also claims that the serum we secretly tested on criminals is different from the one that gained FDA approval. And that you had her committed to a mental asylum so she couldn't expose this "conspiracy".'

Alice fingered the teardrop amulet round her neck and breathed deeply. Madeline was staring right at her. 'Well, let's start with Dr Kathy Kerr,' Alice said. 'I may have mentioned her before. She's a British-born scientist, and it was her initial project on curbing aggression in male primates that gave me the idea for Conscience. I recruited her nine years ago to head up one of the research teams and she has been working for me ever since. She's brilliant but unbalanced. Apart from her original work she has contributed little over the last few years and she's bitter. When we gained FDA approval for a serum she played no part in

275

developing she became defensive and angry. I promised her shared credit, but she refused.'

Alice felt uncomfortable with the lies, but it was necessary. Madeline said so.

Pamela frowned. 'So what are you saying? That she invented these claims out of spite?'

'Mainly, yes.'

Pamela's frown deepened. 'Mainly? You mean some of them are true? What about the San Quentin deaths? A whole list of symptoms have been listed on this sheet of paper; symptoms which result either in suicide or a brain haemorrhage.'

'That did happen, yes.'

'What!'

'But it was a mistake.'

'A mistake? That's not what Kerr told Hank Butcher. It's no goddamn wonder he thinks our endgame is killing violent criminals. How did it happen?'

Alice adjusted her glasses. 'Those men received corrupted samples. It was a one-off. A routine check highlighted the bad batch and we managed to stop it before it was sent out to any more test subjects. The fatal samples had nothing to do with the proper serum we tested on the others. Somehow the batch was tampered with.'

'Tampered with?'

'We can't prove anything. But in checking all our procedures, the only weak link was Kathy Kerr. She has access to most of the ViroVector facilities and she has the knowledge. It would appear that she has been disaffected for some time, and perhaps she sabotaged the batch to hijack the project.

Luckily we discovered it before the problem became more widespread.'

'But what about Axelman, Alice? It could look like you tried to kill him in revenge for Libby.'

Madeline stepped in before Alice could reply. 'Alice didn't know Axelman was responsible for Libby's death until after he'd been executed. That was entirely coincidental. And before you ask, Pamela,' she added, 'yes, we did cover up their deaths. There was nothing we could do about them. They were on death row anyway, and any scandal would only have jeopardized the success of Conscience and your election. Right or wrong, whatever we did we did for you because we wanted to protect you. The country needs you as president and it needs Project Conscience. Nothing we did was intended to betray you. We are your most loyal friends. We would never intentionally hurt you. You have to believe that.'

Pamela stared at them, thinking through what they were saying. She looked so tired and beleaguered that Alice could tell she wanted to believe them in order to focus on other, more important issues. 'What if the journalist can prove Axelman's DNA was changed?'

'It doesn't matter,' said Madeline emphatically. 'His scare story about intentionally killing criminals doesn't add up. Sixteen thousand men have been treated over the last eight years or so and they are all fine. And Axelman's body has been cremated, along with the other five dead inmates in San Quentin, so no further proof can be found as to *why* their DNA changed. But, more to the point, Axelman was a killer. He had no family and nor did

277

the others. Even if the journalist could get all the proof in the world no-one would care. Kathy Kerr has obviously done some digging and is using whatever she's found to cause trouble. But she has no real proof of anything.'

Pamela rubbed her temples. 'But what about the FDA-approved serum? Kerr claims it was only developed four years ago – long after you started unauthorized trials on criminals. Are the serums different?'

Alice shrugged. 'Again, strictly speaking, yes. There are minute differences, but nothing important. Certainly nothing to trouble the FDA.'

Pamela sat down and held her head in her hands. 'Then why the hell didn't you gain FDA approval for the one we did test?'

'Because we improved it. There were some minor concerns with the original serum, involving possible side effects.'

'Such as?'

Alice paused and Pamela leaned forward, waiting.

'There was a low-level risk of causing testicular and prostate cancer,' said Alice.

'Cancer?' Pamela almost shouted the word. 'The treatment we tested? The treatment that won me the election gives men cancer?'

'No, it doesn't. There is a very slight risk that it might. So low it's hardly statistically significant. But we thought it best to iron it out, so we developed an improved serum, which we tested on healthy human volunteers to gain FDA approval. That vector is Version Nine. Naturally all subsequent treatments will use this new vector.'

Pamela struggled to remain calm. 'So you lied to the FDA? And you lied to me?'

Madeline Naylor shook her head. 'Pamela, you're missing the point. We've tested over sixteen thousand men and all have benefited. Some risks needed to be taken, otherwise the whole project would have collapsed. Perhaps we should have been more open with you, but I decided against it, because if we told you it would compromise your position.'

'Well, I'm compromised now.'

'No you're not. If the journalist had anything concrete he would have used it. Dr Kerr is simply stirring things up for reasons of her own. She's a bitter woman with a family history of mental instability. She has no real proof and frankly, even if she did, it wouldn't matter now. The public and the media have bought into your vision of a crime-free future. They want it to work. Pedantic quibbling about the finer points of how one genetic vaccine differs from another won't change anything. The fact is that in the future all criminals will be treated by an FDA-approved vaccine that works. That's all anyone cares about. The journalist doesn't have a story. Trust me on this.'

Pamela looked down at the sheet of paper, clearly wrestling with the issues. But Alice could see she was weakening. 'Still, what we did was wrong.'

Madeline set her jaw. '*You* did nothing wrong. We did. But if you want to come clean and resign, go ahead. Throw away the chance of the millennium to cure one of the main scourges of society. I'll resign too, if you like, but it would be pointless. Yes, we did a few small wrongs, but we achieved a far greater good.'

'What about Dr Kerr's claim that you authorized her abduction and held her in an FBI mental facility to keep her quiet?'

Madeline snorted and clapped her hands together. 'Well, that just proves she's making trouble. A mental asylum sounds the perfect place for her, but I didn't put her in one. Pamela, frankly you have more important things to worry about than some deranged scientist with a grudge and a journalist trying to win a Pulitzer prize. Ignore them. I'm sorry if we hurt you by not telling you everything, but this is exactly why we didn't. Let us handle these minor annoyances, while you prevent Iraq starting the Third World War.'

Before Pamela had time to answer, a cellphone rang on the table. Alice picked it up and listened. 'Yes, Special Agent Toshack, the president is here. Yes, she will be with you in five minutes. Thank you.' She smiled and put the phone down. 'Well, Madam President, your Secret-Service detail is waiting to escort you to the Pentagon.'

Pamela stood and Alice rose from her seat to embrace her. 'Please, Pam,' said Alice, 'always remember that we are your friends. If you can rely on anyone, you can rely on us.'

'The way I see it, Pam,' said Madeline, moving to hug Pamela in her sinewy arms, 'you have embarked on a great journey and it's our job to keep you from falling. I for one will do anything to stop that happening. Anything.'

Pamela studied them both for a moment then gave a small nod and a smile. She seemed satisfied, even touched. 'Just tell me one thing before I go. What are you going to do about Kathy Kerr? She sounds a real loose cannon.'

Madeline laughed at that. 'Don't worry about it, Pamela. She isn't your problem. She's ours. We'll talk to her.'

Alice watched Pamela leave, escorted by two Secret-Service agents. It appeared that their performance had allayed Pamela's fears, but Kathy Kerr was still most definitely a problem.

After the president had left, Alice silently reviewed the meeting, and Madeline seemed to be doing the same. Alice checked her watch; she had arranged for the company jet to fly her back to San Francisco in an hour's time.

'Do you think she believes us?' Alice asked, preparing to leave.

Madeline nodded. 'Yes, because she has no proof. And because she wants to.'

'But what do we do about Kathy?'

Madeline smiled and lay back in her chair, putting her hands behind her head like a man. Her dark eyes glowed and she looked surprisingly confident. 'Well, Hank Butcher told me that Dr Peters let her escape. And Jackson called me just before Pamela arrived to say that Dr Peters has now been punished – permanently. Jackson's hot on Kathy's trail. He's pretty sure he knows where to find her. He knows who helped her get out.'

'Who?'

Madeline paused and raised her left eyebrow. 'Luke Decker.'

Alice felt something hard and cold contract in her stomach. The last time Alice had seen Decker was when he'd led her out of that macabre gallery of death which his father had consigned Libby to. 'So that's how Kathy found out about Axelman?'

'Yes, it seems they know each other from way back. Anyway, it doesn't matter now. Jackson's people are specialists in this area.'

Leading her out of the office, Madeline said, 'By the way, did you read TITANIA's latest e-mail? Everything's in place. Now we've got rid of Burbank we just have to sit and wait. As for Kathy Kerr and Luke Decker, they won't be standing much longer. Much bigger dominoes than them have fallen already.'

In the black limousine driving her to the Pentagon, President Weiss reached into her coat and retrieved Hank Butcher's list of questions and the computer disk he had given her. She handed the disk to Toshack, the head of her Secret-Service detail. He was a broad-shouldered man of medium height. He had sandy hair and a dimple in his chin, which made him look like he was just about to smile. But he rarely did.

'I need you to get this disk to Major General Allardyce at USAMRIID. Tell him I want a full analysis done. I also need you to check out someone called Dr Kathy Kerr. Don't involve any other agencies. How soon can you get me some answers?'

'How soon do you want them?'

'Yesterday.'

'That shouldn't be a problem, Madam President.'

26

Pushing Kathy Kerr closer against the tree trunk, Luke Decker's guts churned with frustration. He was trapped. Checking the magazine of his Sig pistol he wondered if he could reach around the tree and shoot out the light. He doubted it.

Judging from the intensity of the dazzle, it was an FBI-issue handheld max light. Fitted with a 2000-watt bulb and a two-inch-diameter reflector, it could send out an adjustable beam so searing it bleached night, blinding the naked eye to anything, including the source. It was the flashlight equivalent of a power water hose.

'I suggest you come out from behind that tree,' said the voice with the light. 'If we have to come and get you we can't guarantee your safety.'

'Yeah right,' grunted Decker. 'Like our safety is their big concern.' He looked to his left and, shielding his eyes, could just make out Rocky's pen but little else. All he knew with absolute certainty was that the voice wasn't Jackson's. And as Jackson would almost certainly have done all the talking he probably wasn't here. But there would still be at least two of his cronies here. And that was enough. One could hold the light while the other circled round.

'Kathy,' he said as calmly as he could, 'keep your eyes peeled behind us for anyone coming round to cut us off. Use the beam's light to see any shadow or movement.'

To her credit, although Kathy's eyes were wide with fear, she was calm. 'What are you going to do?' she asked.

'No fucking idea, but whatever it is, I'd better do it quick.' Taking a deep breath he considered his options. But there was only one: to roll round the right of the tree and fire at the voice. He probably wouldn't hit anything, but at least it would make the man move the damn flashlight and then Kathy could make a run for it. He guessed they would hesitate before shooting Kathy here: even the director of the FBI would find it difficult to explain shooting her in her own house without a good reason. He, on the other hand, was going to shoot at whoever he damn well could. 'Kathy,' he said, not looking at her. 'When I start firing, run to the left and get the hell out of here.'

'But what about you?'

'For Christ's sakes. Just this once, don't argue with me.'

He heard her start to protest, then sigh. 'OK.'

Tensing his muscles he gripped the gun in both hands, and was just about to roll around the tree and let off as many of the Sig's seventeen slugs as possible when he heard a fierce roar and a blood-curdling scream.

The intense light suddenly faltered and Luke heard the spitting thud of a silenced gun being fired. The torch beam began to flail about madly, describing arcs of light in the night sky like some frenetic laser show. In the stroboscopic chaos Decker could just make out a man wrestling with a ferocious beast. A second man was sprinting towards them, training his gun on the two figures dancing their frenzied jig. The man with the gun was obviously scared of hitting his screaming partner. Without waiting another second Decker grabbed Kathy by the arm and dragged her to her feet.

'Come on,' he shouted, 'let's go.'

'What about the evidence?'

Decker yanked her arm, pulling her behind him. 'Forget it. Run.'

'But we can't leave Rocky!'

Just then the screaming stopped and the torch flew through the air, landing on the ground in front of them. Its beam pointed away from them, and in his rush Decker almost missed the fact that the flashlight was still held by a severed human limb. He jumped over it and grimaced. 'I wouldn't worry about Rocky,' he said, pulling Kathy past the debris, hoping she hadn't seen it. 'I think he can look after himself.'

But Decker knew he was mistaken when he heard the hiss of two more shots. Rocky groaned once and then fell silent. The sound of his body falling to the ground was unmistakable. 'Come on,' he shouted, dragging Kathy through the French windows into the house.

Outside the front of the house they passed their pursuer's grey Chrysler. Firing four silenced bullets into the two front tyres Decker ran to his rental-car and clambered in, waiting for Kathy to climb into the passenger seat. Calmly he placed the key in the ignition and gunned the motor. As Decker turned his car round and accelerated down Mendoza Drive, he glanced in the rear-view mirror and saw a figure emerge from the house and raise his arms into the firing position. Suddenly Luke felt a cold feeling in the pit of his stomach. But it wasn't the shots that worried him, it was the fact that they would have seen his car and could now easily trace it to him.

What if they had already discovered his involvement? The fact that he could be in danger didn't bother him – the novelty of that had long worn off. He wasn't worried about himself.

This was getting out of hand. Way out of hand.

He turned to Kathy beside him. She looked pale. 'We've got to hurry,' he said and put his foot down.

Kathy Kerr swallowed the bile in her mouth as they sped along Route 101 towards the lights of downtown San Francisco. The evidence they needed, their only hope of proving the allegations, was back at her house.

She didn't notice another grey Chrysler speeding past in the opposite direction. Every car she saw seemed to contain smiling people, living normal unworried lives, oblivious to how hers had changed.

Passing the sign to the airport she turned to Decker, but he kept his face staring straight ahead.

He drove as fast as he could, but it seemed he wasn't fleeing *from* their pursuers so much as rushing *to* somewhere. Decker slapped his hand on the steering wheel. 'Shit, shit, shit. How could I be so goddamned stupid?'

'What?'

'If they find out about me, they'll use Matty to get to us. We've got to get him somewhere safe as fast as possible.'

Realizing what he was saying put their situation into perspective for Kathy. This wasn't only about stopping Madeline Naylor and Alice Prince any more. Perhaps Luke had been right when he'd said she should just walk away. What had she achieved by staying? Except putting those who'd helped her in danger.

Entering San Francisco, Decker took South Van Ness Avenue toward the Marina District. They passed Pacific Heights and then turned into Broadway. Driving in silence, Kathy saw Decker's frown deepen and his eyes narrow as they pulled up outside Matty's home. The front door was wide open and the windows were dark.

Pulling the car into the kerb and killing the engine, Decker's voice was hushed when he spoke. 'Gramps always leaves at least one light on,' he said. 'And even he doesn't leave the front door wide open. Kathy, wait here while I check inside.' He jumped out, ran up the steps and disappeared into the house.

Ignoring his request, Kathy opened her door and cautiously followed Decker inside. She clicked on the hall light switch, but nothing happened. It was as if all the lights had been fused. Gradually her eyes adjusted to the gloom, using the moon-light and illumination from the street lamps filtering through the windows to make out her surroundings. To her left the dining room was a wreck. Drawers had been pulled out, their contents strewn over the table and floor. Chairs had been upended and the upholstery ripped out. To her right, through the open double doors of the TV lounge, she could make out similar carnage. This was either a burglary or it was meant to look like one. But if this was the work of Jackson and his men, how could they have found out about Decker and Matty so quickly?

'Gramps? Where are you?' Decker's voice came from the landing on the next floor. Kathy went up the stairs after him. Before she got to the top she heard Decker call his grandfather again, but this time it was less a question than a cry of disbelief.

At the top of the stairs Kathy ran to her left, into the music room that overlooked the bay. There was something on the landing ahead of her. Looking down she saw Matty's golden Labrador, Brutus; his tongue hung out of his mouth and his eyes were wide open and glassy. Two red holes punctured the glossy fur of his neck. A shiver ran through her. The bastards had shot a goddamn guide dog. Stepping round Brutus she saw that the door to the music room was open, as were the large French windows looking out on to the balcony and the bay beyond. A brisk breeze was blowing into the room, seeming to carry the moonlight in with it. Light streamed through the open windows forming a ghostly trapezium on the rug. The rest of the room was in shadow, but she could see the debris:

photographs knocked off the piano; a violin thrown to the floor, the metronome shattered beside it.

In the moonlight, in the centre of the rug, she saw Decker crouching down, silver tears on his cheeks. He cradled his grandfather in his arms, studying the man's hands. When Decker spoke, his words were so choked that she had to put her hands to her mouth to stop herself from crying out. With her horror came fresh guilt. They had done this to find her.

'They broke his fucking fingers,' Decker said, turning to her, his eyes almost luminous in the light. 'Even the goddamned Nazis didn't do that to him.'

Luke Decker gripped his grandfather tighter, trying to contain the grief and fury welling up inside him.

Acid guilt seared through him when he thought how this brave old man had suffered and died alone trying to protect him; this man who had already endured and given so much. Jackson must have uncovered his involvement with Kathy's escape and then sent one car to check on her house while he had come here. But how had Jackson found out about him? Dr Peters couldn't have told him, Peters didn't know who he was. And they couldn't have traced his car this quickly. The only answer that made sense was that Hank Butcher had talked.

Decker's rage and guilt were nothing compared to his feeling of loss. He wanted to scream aloud. Without Matty he felt cast adrift, anchorless in a fickle sea, his compass gone, and with it a lifeline

289

to his own decency. Matty was the antidote to the knowledge that Axelman's blood ran in his veins; just knowing he was descended from Matty gave Decker hope.

But now his grandfather was dead.

Looking down on Matty's lined face Decker closed the staring blue eyes. He stroked Matty's head and vowed that he would avenge him and make some sense of his death.

He heard Kathy kneel close beside him and felt her arms move around his shoulders. 'I'm so sorry, Luke,' she whispered in a small voice. Her soft hands moved to his neck, caressing him gently just as he had stroked his grandfather. 'If you hadn't helped me, perhaps this would never have happened.'

'But it has happened,' he said. He turned to look at her, seeing the hurt in her eyes. 'Kathy, you were right. This has to be about more than just Conscience. We've got to find out what they're really doing and we've got to stop them. I couldn't stand it if Matty had died for nothing—'

Then he heard the sound.

Decker froze, and he could tell from Kathy's sharp intake of breath that she'd heard it too.

A footstep – no more than a yard or two behind them.

Then a man's voice, deep and smooth. 'You'll need help,' was all it said.

Swivelling round Decker saw an enormous figure step out of the shadows and tower over him. Two other men stood behind him. It took Decker a moment to recognize the blue-black hair and strong patrician nose of Joey Barzini. The man knelt, but he was so tall he still appeared to be standing. In the moonlight his clear blue eyes were moist, and his chin was set in a determined cast as he looked at Matty's crumpled body. Like a father tentatively touching his first-born he reached across and gently inspected Matty's broken fingers. Decker watched the big man wince and shake his head.

'My friend, my friend. What have they done to you?' he whispered. Then he turned to Decker, his voice suddenly harsh. 'Your grandfather called earlier and told me you were in some kind of serious trouble. He explained the problem and I said I'd come round tonight to see if I could help.' He paused. 'I wish I'd come earlier.'

Barzini looked at Kathy and then back to Luke. 'The only way I can help Matty now is by helping you two. Come with me. I need to know more about what's going on.' He paused for a moment and Decker considered what he really knew about him. Although Joey Barzini was supposed to be legitimate, his list of friends and family read like a *Who's Who* of organized crime. But his grandfather liked and rated him as highly as anybody – highly enough to call Barzini for help when he and Kathy were in trouble. If Barzini was good enough for Matty then he was certainly good enough for him.

'Luke,' Barzini said, as if reading distrust in his look. 'I know from Matty how you feel about my family connections. Often I'm not too proud of them myself.' Suddenly his noble face creased into a smile, a momentary flash of gleaming white teeth.

'But trust me, at times they have their uses.'

291

27

Alexandria, Washington DC.
Friday, 7 November 2008. 2.30 a.m.

FBI Director Naylor was annoyed that a group of them had somehow escaped detection. She pulled the trigger and then moved on. It infuriated her that however fast she killed them they always came back. She could never totally eradicate them.

Brandishing her insecticide spray like a pistol she patrolled the neat rows of yucca plants, African violets and rare orchids in the conservatory of her house in Washington's exclusive suburb, Alexandria. Above the glass roof of the climatically controlled room a frigid moon looked down from a cloud-riddled sky. The interior garden adjoined the spacious lounge and was effectively another room in her house. Entirely made of glass, it allowed her almost total control over everything that grew there.

When she was satisfied that everything was as it should be she opened the inner door to the lounge, poured herself a glass of Jack Daniels and lay back on her recliner by the large TV in the corner. There were few paintings in the lounge.

292

Two walls were taken up with a large stone fireplace and the entrance to the conservatory, a third was covered from floor to ceiling with books covering every theme, particularly history and gardening, and the fourth was similarly bedecked with tapes and compact discs.

Naylor had showered and wore a blue robe, her long white hair flowing loose to her shoulders. Her pale face, now devoid of make-up, looked almost translucent, like paper-thin mother-of-pearl. She pointed the remote at the multimedia system, and as Wagner filled the room her mind travelled with it, away from the responsibilities of the office, away from Crime Zero, Kathy Kerr and Luke Decker to a kinder, more peaceful place.

According to TITANIA everything was in order, so Naylor convinced herself that, for now, she could do no more. She would retire soon and set the alarm for six o'clock; she only needed a few hours' sleep.

As always when she wanted to relax, Naylor thought of the garden and protecting her beloved plants. And as she allowed her mind to wander she went back to her fourteenth birthday and Alice's gift.

Apart from Alice, Madeline has no friends at school. Most of the other kids regard her aggressive manner and white spiky hair as too weird or too frightening. So it's not surprising that on her fourteenth birthday she receives no presents and cards, especially as it falls on a Saturday.

But she's not unhappy. Her grandmother, Mrs Preston, is pretty cool really. The old woman forbids her to invite any boys round and won't allow men in the house, saying they're 'different' and can't be trusted. But Madeline doesn't mind that at all, and her grandmother lets Alice come round. On her birthday the old woman makes Madeline a special breakfast of strawberries and cream with a glass of chocolate milk.

It's June and the sun's shining. After breakfast Madeline goes out into the garden. Her grandmother's house is a rambling mansion and Madeline loves exploring all the old rooms, but the best part is the garden. It's so big that Madeline is allowed to have a small walled section of her own. Here she can plant and do what she likes. She's put up a sign on the rickety gate forbidding entry. Even her grandmother knocks before entering with Madeline's cold lemonade and stale Oreos.

On her birthday Madeline tends her flowers and pulls out the weeds as usual. She has created a strictly ordered world, with regimented beds and weed-free paths. Rows of sunflowers stand to attention next to manicured marigolds. But today, as with most days, much of her time is spent killing the ants infesting the pathways and beds. This is the one place where she can banish everything she hates in the world outside. Here she can pretend that the bad men who killed her father will be punished; and that her mother, who left her, will return. Here she can control everything.

But the invading ants keep wrecking the fantasy. And whatever she does, whatever she tries, she can't get rid of them. The beds are pockmarked with holes she's dug trying to find their nest. And in each corner of the square walled garden there's an empty mayonnaise jar full of dead ants. The jars are intended to act as a deterrent to the others, but they seem only to intensify the problem. However fast she kills them, they return.

'Madeline, Madeline,' calls a small, excited voice from over the wall. 'Are you there?'

'Yeah, come over.'

Alice's backyard is on the other side of the far wall. And she often climbs over to play in Madeline's secret garden. Watching her friend scrabble awkwardly over the wall makes Madeline laugh.

'Don't laugh or I won't give you your present,' warns Alice as she falls to the earth by the sun-flowers. Her glasses are crooked, and despite the warm weather she wears a long-sleeved dress.

'Present?' Madeline couldn't help feeling excited. 'You got me a present?'

'Only a little one.' Alice looks at the holes in the ground. 'But it's a good one.' She reaches into her bag, and as she does so one of her long sleeves rides up and Madeline sees a purple-and-yellow bruise on her forearm. It's so livid Madeline can see the finger marks, where a large hand has squeezed her arm.

'Who did that to you?' she asks. She doesn't need to ask what it is. Madeline's own father hit her enough times to teach her about bruises.

Alice gives a flustered shake of her head and quickly pulls down the sleeve. 'It's nothing.'

'Was it your dad?' probes Madeline. Alice's father is a respected doctor, but this doesn't sur-prise Madeline. Her dad was a respected cop and he still beat her. She feels angry for her friend, but she also feels a small stab of satisfaction. She's always envied Alice having a perfect mum and a dad, so it makes her feel closer to her knowing that her dad's bad too. 'Does he hit you a lot?'

But Alice won't be drawn. 'Do you want your present or not?'

Madeline drops the matter, but stores it away. 'Yeah, sure.'

When Alice pulls the tiny parcel out of the bag and puts it in her hand, Madeline's initial reaction is disappointment. The tube wrapped in blue paper is smaller than one of her fingers. 'Open it,' says Alice nervously, straightening her glasses. 'I hope you like it.'

Madeline peels off the blue paper to reveal a tiny bottle. It looks like one she's seen her grandmother use for her eye drops.

Madeline opens and smells it. 'Maple syrup?' She starts to squeeze a drop on her finger so she can taste it, but Alice screams at her.

'Don't eat it! You mustn't eat it!'

'Why not? What is it?'

Alice takes it from her and bends down near a line of ants at the bottom of the wall. Taking a leaf from one of the sunflower stalks she places it on the floor in the path of the ants, then she takes the small bottle and drops one bead of syrup on the leaf. 'Watch,' she says.

Madeline sees how at first the ants walk round the drop, and then some start to circle the syrup and feed off it. 'Is it poison?' she asks, delighted.

'It's better than just poison.'

The feeding ants move on after a moment and continue in line, making way for other ants to feed on the droplet. 'So what does it do?'

'Well,' says Alice with a frown, 'according to the stuff I've read, the maple syrup and chemicals I mixed together should attract the ants to make them eat it. Then, when they go back to their nest, they'll puke up what they've eaten for the queen ants to feed on. The chemicals should kill the queens before they lay any eggs. The base poison is trichlophon, but I've added some refinements. It's slow acting, so it doesn't just kill the ants that eat it, but the whole nest as well. And you haven't got to dig up anything; the ants do the work for you.'

Madeline is so impressed and delighted that she laughs for joy. 'Awesome. You made it yourself?'

'Oh yes. It wasn't very difficult. Dad had some stuff in his shed and the school labs had everything else. It should get rid of your ant problem though – completely.'

Beep beep beep.

The insistent tone of the speakerphone by the TV interrupted Naylor's reverie. The volume automatically lowered on the laser disc and a soft, feminine voice issued from the speakers: 'You have an override phone message on the multimedia system. Please pick up.'

Naylor thought for a moment, regaining her bearings, resenting the intrusion into the dome of self-reflection she had built for herself. Reaching for the phone she was still thinking back to how, in a matter of weeks, Alice's magic potion had eradicated virtually every single ant from her garden.

'Madeline, it's Bill McCloud. I'm in the incident

room at headquarters looking at the satellite screen. You might want to come in and see this. I think Iraq is about to invade Kuwait.'

The Hoover Building, Washington DC.
The same day. 3.07 a.m.

Half an hour later Director Naylor was in the FBI incident room on the ground floor of the FBI's headquarters on Pennsylvania Avenue, looking at an eight-foot-by-five-foot screen. To her right was Deputy Director Bill McCloud. He looked even more grizzled than usual. Three other senior Bureau officials sat around the table in the dimly lit room. A flask of strong coffee was on a hotplate by the door and its aroma filled the air.

'They're going to goddamn do it,' McCloud said, rubbing his steel-grey eyes. His normally laid-back Texan drawl was tense.

'Looks like it,' Naylor said, staring at the screen. She tried to sound calm, but it was difficult. According to TITANIA this shouldn't be happening. 'Are all national contingencies in place?'

'Absolutely,' said Associate Deputy Director Ray Tate, a short barrel-chested man who ran the investigations section of the Bureau. 'We've updated our list of Iraqi sympathizers. The key threats are under surveillance and can be pulled in at a moment's notice. All major terrorist targets across the country are on full alert.'

Naylor nodded silently and kept her eyes on the screen. The picture she was seeing was a feed from CNN, which was as good as any government

298

satellite surveillance. In the top right-hand corner the gold CNN logo looked faint against the pale background. At first the overall image meant nothing to her, thousands of dark shapes moving over a light-yellow backdrop. It looked like a microscope picture of diseased cells spreading across an organism.

'Do you want to hear the CNN commentary?' one of the agents behind her asked.

'Yes,' she said, not wanting to engage in conversation, her eyes riveted to the screen.

'This is incredible,' said a male commentator with a British accent. 'Using our access to the Kamagachi high-resolution satellite we are able to bring you what might prove to be the first-ever live pictures of a war starting. You are watching history in the making. As I speak, our engineers are trying to increase the magnification still further. It's a clear day in Iraq and soon we should be able to make out each individual tank. They are now less than twelve miles from the thirty-second parallel – and I don't need to remind anyone watching how, eight years ago, that line in the sand moved from being simply a no-fly area to a no-go area for any Iraqi military personnel. If the Republican Guard cross that line into southern Iraq they will be declaring their intent to invade Kuwait. Once that happens, and it looks like it will, then the United Nations coalition forces, led by the United States, will be forced to act.'

Naylor sat forward in her chair. At least this vindicated the decision to target the Iraqi Army as the amplification zone for the Phase-Two launch of Crime Zero. Not only had that nation shown itself to be the most belligerent, but it was also an excellent 'real world' test before giving final sanction to the Phase-Three roll-out. They had even pulled Phase Two forward because of the Iraq crisis. However, now it looked as though they hadn't pulled it forward far enough. This shouldn't be happening. Not a war. Not after this much time had elapsed.

Taking a deep drink of black coffee she watched as the screen faded and then returned at a higher magnification. She could now clearly discern the contours of the sand and the markings on individual tanks; thousands of them were moving across the arid plain in ordered rows. She could even make out the helmets of the commanders protruding from the gun turrets. She wondered if Alice was watching this. Pamela certainly would be, probably in the War Room deep below the Pentagon.

'President Weiss and other world leaders have confirmed that the UN forces will attack Iraq's tanks and destroy them if they cross the line,' continued the reporter. 'The question on everyone's lips is, what will the Iraqi president do next? Reports suggest he has at least ten warheads loaded with a new doomsday virus aimed at selected sites around the world. Each one is ready to be launched if his troops are stopped from reclaiming what he regards as the Iraqi province of Kuwait, together with all its oil.

'But if Iraq unleashes biological weapons then the coalition allies have pledged to mount a nuclear strike on Baghdad. This is surely a baptism of fire for Pamela Weiss, the new American president. If there are any who still question whether a woman has the necessary resolve to fight a war, then their questions may soon be answered.'

As the satellite camera panned across the expanse of desert the screen mottled with the dark shapes of the machines of war. Perhaps TITANIA was wrong, Naylor thought. Perhaps the computer's projections were out by a day or two and she was watching the last war unfold before her.

Staring at all those troops she was reminded of the ancient historian Herodotus's account of the Persian emperor Xerxes watching his vast army march across the Hellespont to Greece. As he watched them the emperor had wept. When asked why, Xerxes had replied that he was weeping for all the thousands of men he could see before him, because in one hundred years not one would be alive.

Dry-eyed, Naylor sipped her coffee. Only a man could feel such sentiment watching other men about to engage in barbaric war. She knew that all those on the screen in front of her would be dead in a fraction of that time – and many more besides. But she felt no sadness, no remorse.

On the screen some of the tanks appeared to be breaking ranks, then the camera angle widened and the picture shifted back to lower magnification. A red superimposed line suddenly appeared on the screen and it seemed impossibly close to the approaching swarm of ordered black dots. Naylor could imagine Weiss in the War Room, along with her advisers, making decisions, thinking that *she* held the future in her hands.

Squinting at the screen she noticed the ordered phalanx of dots now appeared to be breaking up. Some even seemed to be stopping. But because she was willing them to stop she couldn't be sure she wasn't just imagining it.

'They are less than ten miles from the thirty-second parallel,' continued the commentator, his voice increasing in pitch. 'The red line indicates the barrier they must not cross. Wait! Something's happening . . .'

And it was, although for a time Naylor couldn't determine what. Sitting forward, clenching her coffee cup, she watched the tanks slow and then stop.

'Increase the damn magnification,' said McCloud beside her.

As if in answer to his command the screen shifted again to such a high level of resolution that Naylor could almost see individual faces. But still nothing seemed to be happening.

'The world is on tenterhooks,' announced the commentator. 'What are they going to do? Are they waiting for the final command to advance?'

Then gradually the ordered pattern began to dissolve into apparent chaos. Some of the tanks were turning round. And so were many of the troop carriers. Soldiers in the stationary trucks were jumping out, throwing down their guns and walking away.

'Jeez,' said McCloud softly. 'What the fuck's happening here?'

Naylor just stared, willing it to carry on.

'If I wasn't seeing this with my own eyes I wouldn't believe it,' said the commentator. 'Scores of tanks and troops are turning round. Many are throwing their weapons down and just walking back into the desert. It appears that fellow officers and soldiers are forcibly trying to obstruct them. But short of shooting them, which many are now doing, they are helpless to stop them. And what is incomprehensible is that the apparent deserters – and there are thousands – are not retaliating. They're simply turning their backs and walking away.

'In over twenty years of reporting on conflicts from around the world I have never seen anything like this. And as the deserters' numbers continue to swell, the rest of the tanks are now turning back too. It appears that at the eleventh hour, on the very brink of war, Armageddon has been averted.'

The men in the room with Naylor burst into spontaneous applause.

A surge of euphoric vindication swelled her chest. TITANIA had been right, its projections were perfect. A potential nuclear war had been averted. Mankind had been saved from the mindless aggression of men.

She could imagine the rest of the world, including Weiss, breathing a huge sigh of relief. Surely after seeing that display, even she might begin to understand the merits of what they were trying to do. Crime Zero was finally happening and the future was beginning to look brighter.

28

Tiburon, California.
The same day. 12.11 a.m.

Sipping her red wine and picking at a plate of steaming tagliatelle Kerr couldn't relax. The guilt she felt corroded her stomach, but she forced herself to eat because she needed the focus and strength. She couldn't escape the conclusion that this was somehow all her fault.

She sat with Luke Decker and Joey Barzini around a plain stripped-wood kitchen table. Despite Barzini's obvious wealth his large, beautiful house in Tiburon was first and foremost a family home. Pictures showing their five, now adult, children at various stages of development were dotted around the large kitchen. But despite the warmth of the place she still felt on edge, and she could tell Decker did too. There were obviously servants here, but Kathy hadn't seen any yet. Carmela, Barzini's wife, had made the pasta and was now checking on their rooms.

Decker quietly sipped his wine and left his food untouched. He still appeared to be in shock after leaving Barzini's men to handle the police and ensure his grandfather's body was properly taken care of. Barzini had concocted a story of how he'd been visiting his friend Matty when he'd found the body, keeping Luke and Kathy out of it. A limousine had swept the three of them across the Golden Gate Bridge to Tiburon.

On arriving at his house Barzini told them that the president had died and Pamela Weiss had been sworn in. Neither of them had really been able to digest the information in the aftershock of the evening's events. Now, just after midnight, Decker looked as exhausted as she felt. But despite Barzini's pleas for them to rest, she and Decker insisted they resolve what was to be done before retiring.

'Start from the beginning and tell me everything,' said Barzini, nursing an oversized espresso.

Kathy looked at Decker, still unsure whether to trust Joey. Decker returned her look and shrugged, as if in concession.

So for the next fifteen minutes she outlined Project Conscience and the subsequent events. She told Barzini about Decker's paternity test and how this had alerted her to Axelman and the other death-row prisoners in San Quentin who had received lethal gene therapy similar to Conscience. She recounted her abduction by Madeline Naylor's people and her rescue from the Sanctuary by Decker.

She then explained how Decker had contacted the journalist Hank Butcher, using him to pass the evidence to Pamela Weiss, and how their evening had unravelled.

305

'And that's where you were tonight, getting the evidence?' Barzini asked.

'Yes,' said Decker quietly. 'While Matty was being killed. And we didn't even get it.'

'How important is this evidence?' asked Barzini. 'What does it really prove?'

'That the unauthorized Conscience criminal trials used a potentially unsafe vector,' said Kathy.

Barzini frowned. 'Even though the final vector they were proposing to use in future was FDA approved?'

'Yes.'

Barzini looked puzzled. 'Let me get this straight. These people's unauthorized tests had risked the health of a few hardened criminals in order to develop a refined FDA-approved cure, which would help radically reduce violent crime. If this had got out before the election I could understand it being embarrassing, but now that Conscience is accepted and Weiss is in power, why should they care who knows? They could easily rationalize it. They certainly don't need to kill people to keep it quiet. Not any more.'

'But the Axelman disks prove their tests have killed at least one person,' said Kathy.

Barzini shook his head. 'Surely they could say it was an accident, a mistake. And again the unfortunate casualty was death-row scum. The benefits of their work far outweigh any harm. Why kill Matty to get to you? Why kill anyone now? There must be another reason.'

Kathy sighed then. 'But that's the point. I can *prove* that they intended to kill Axelman. I understand how complex it is to create the viral vector

306

that did this, and how close it is to the more benign Conscience vector. That's why they can't let me alone. They're planning something and they're worried I might jeopardize their plans.'

Decker leaned forward. 'The question is what are those plans? Once we know that, and can prove it, then we can stop them.'

Barzini slowly sipped his espresso. 'What do you *think* they're planning.'

Kathy shrugged. 'Well, I thought they were trying to kill criminals, but Luke doesn't believe that's politically feasible. But I can't think of a better hypothesis. Perhaps it's just category-A prisoners they're targeting? It would save money if the worst criminals in prison quietly fell ill and died, and thinning the prison population would be much easier to keep quiet. As far as the voting public is concerned, they don't give a damn about what goes on in a high-security prison. What's out of sight is out of mind. And if taxes fall, who's going to complain?'

Decker frowned. 'It doesn't sound right to me but I can't think of a better theory. All I know is that they killed Matty because of it and I want to find out what it is and stop it. Come on, Kathy, you've worked with these people. Where would they keep proof of a secret project?'

Kathy Kerr thought for a moment. 'I don't know. I've got pretty good access to ViroVector, but I haven't come across anything. Christ, I didn't even know about their secret trials on Conscience.'

'Can't you think of anything suspicious?' asked Decker. 'I don't know – documents, that kind of thing.'

307

'The information must be kept somewhere,' said Barzini, warming to the theme. 'Could Dr Prince have it locked away in her office? Perhaps in a safe?'

It was the word 'safe' that did it. Kathy suddenly remembered the last time she'd seen Alice Prince at ViroVector. It had been in the Womb, just after she'd been told about the FDA approval. When Alice had tried to shield a tray of vials before hurriedly placing them back in her safe, Kathy had assumed it was her usual paranoia. Alice Prince's refrigerated strongbox had always been a standard feature in the Womb – somewhere for her pet projects – and no-one, least of all Kathy, had ever paid it much heed.

She rose from the table and went to the small pile of belongings they'd taken from Matty's home. She picked up the laptop and cellphone and brought them back to the table. Plugging the laptop modem into the cellphone she logged on to the main menu of ViroVector's network manager and clicked on to the access authorization schedule. She let out a small 'yes' of satisfaction. Her hunch had been correct: her name was still there with a silver key beside it. Alice and Madeline had been so confident she was going to be out of the way that they hadn't bothered to tell TITANIA to deny her physical access to the buildings.

'Have you found something?' asked Luke.

'Well, I know one place we can look.'

'Yes?' said Barzini.

'In the storage fridges at ViroVector all samples are tagged with an electronic barcode. And when a laser wand is waved over this code it automatically opens a file in the main computer, regardless of who's waving the wand. That file contains all the technical data on the sample and a summary of the project's objectives and background. It makes it easy for scientists working in difficult conditions to get quick access.'

Decker nodded, renewed fire in his eyes. 'The barcode gives you the project background and the formula specs for each sample? And there's no other code you need to access this?'

'No, but you do have to get hold of the sample and run TITANIA's computer wand over it. You see, the vials I'm thinking about are already in a very secure place.'

Barzini smiled. 'No place is completely secure.'

'This comes pretty close. It's in a safe in a biosafety-level-five lab called the Womb. And, believe me, it's not as comfortable as it sounds.'

Briefly, she told them about the Womb – its security measures, the protective-clothing procedure, the contamination risks and the vials in the locked steel safe she had seen Alice Prince closing when she was last there. 'I reckon I can still get in because they haven't wiped me off the security register. TITANIA controls all security with cameras, alarms and steel barriers. The locks are DNA-coded, but my profile appears to still be active. Once inside, though, I'll need help breaking into the safe. And help getting stuff out.'

'Don't worry about the safe,' said Barzini. 'If you describe it or give me a model name I can probably find someone who'll rig up something to help you.'

Kathy thought for a moment. 'It's black, about

309

waist-high, with a large silver dial on the front. And it's refrigerated. There's a brand name in big red letters across the top of the door. Something like Lemka, with a number after it. One hundred and one, I think.'

Barzini nodded his head. 'Big red letters? Refrigerated? Sounds like a Lenica One Zero One. Swiss. Very good, but not impregnable with a correctly set-up quantum pulse box.'

'What?' asked Kathy.

'Don't worry, it's an electronic code-breaker,' explained Decker. 'We'll go into that later. But if we find anything, what do we take out as evidence? Surely everything will be contaminated?'

Kathy had thought of this already. 'We only take out information; nothing else.' She turned to Barzini. 'Have you got a pencil and paper?'

He passed her a biro. 'Use your napkin.'

Quickly she sketched an elevation view of the main dome showing the concentric circles of the underground biosafety laboratory complex and the hospital and morgue beneath it. 'Much of the action at ViroVector happens underground. Apparently there are safety tunnels leading to and from the lab complex, but only gold-clearance employees know the codes to the airtight doors. We'll have to use the ground-floor entrance of the main dome to enter the lab complex.'

She pointed to the centre of the underground lab complex. 'I'll go down to the Womb here. Assuming Joey can tell me how to get into the safe, and that I find something, then I'll be able to scan it.' She pointed to the ground-floor level of the dome. 'But, Luke, I'll need you to wait up in the anteroom above the complex. There's a terminal and a printer there. The terminal can be used to transfer data onto a hi-data digital disk and the printer will generate hard copy. You turn on the printer and insert a blank disk into the terminal. I then send topline data from the Womb terminal to the printer and copy the detailed stuff to the blank disk. It's standard practice in order to get info out of the Womb whilst avoiding contamination.'

Decker nodded. 'OK, but how do we get in and out without being spotted or challenged?'

'Well, with silver clearance I can sign in one other person, so long as they submit to a DNA scan. But we've still got to—'

'Hey, hey, hey. That's enough for tonight,' said Barzini, standing up and raising his two huge hands. 'You know what you're after and where you think it is. That's great. Now it's time for you both to get some sleep. Let me make a few phone calls, and by tomorrow morning I should have some people to help you with surveillance, transport and equipment. They'll know the best way to get in and out of the campus, and they'll supply you with a pulse box and a safe to practice on.' Barzini smiled. 'These people are very good at what they do, but I must stress they're nothing to do with me.' His smile broadened. 'Sadly, not all of my family are as law-abiding as I am.'

29

The White House, Washington DC.
The same day. 9.30 a.m.

First came relief and euphoria, then concern, and
finally fear. The United States administration ran
through the extremes of emotions on the morning
after the dramatic Iraqi retreat. The concern and
fear came later, though, when Pamela Weiss
received more information.

The secretary of defence and the secretary of
state were tired but smiling when they accompanied the uniformed chairman of the Joint Chiefs
of Staff into the Oval Office at nine thirty that
morning. The usually sober trio had an almost dis-
cernible spring in their gait; they were men who
had received a stay of execution.

At first the Iraqi volte-face had seemed inexplic-
able. The first reports of a mystery epidemic
ravaging the Iraqi Army arrived via the CIA and
Britain's MI5 at eleven that morning. Again, the
initial reaction was positive. The nation was a
known belligerent and therefore anything that
affected its military capabilities was regarded as

beneficial. Such infections were common on military bases where troops lived in close proximity to each other.

At one forty in the afternoon sketchy intelligence reported that the mystery illness was more serious than the usual epidemics, that it led to either suicide or brain haemorrhage, and that it appeared to be already spreading to the civilian population. Another report claimed that all the sufferers were male.

The fact that the epidemic – if that's what it was – wasn't understood and was spreading caused the president and her advisors grave concern for the wider implications. It was immediately agreed by the UN and the World Health Organization that all Iraq's borders, which were already strictly patrolled, should be sealed, allowing no-one in or out. The country was effectively put in quarantine.

But it was the symptoms the more detailed reports were outlining that gave cause for greater worry. Reaching into a drawer in the impressive desk that dominated the Oval Office, President Weiss pulled out two sheets of typed paper, frowning when she read the second page. Asking her advisers to leave the office for a moment she reached for her secure phone and began dialling a number she knew by heart. Then she stopped, pausing for a second before deciding against it.

It was a minute past 2 p.m. in Washington, therefore just gone 11 a.m. in San Francisco. She dialled one of the two numbers given at the bottom of the sheet of paper. When she received no reply she tried the second number, hoping it might be his office. A woman answered.

'I'm sorry,' the woman said, not even asking who was calling, 'I'm Mr Butcher's personal assistant and I was expecting him to return from Washington last night, but for some reason he missed his flight. I'm expecting him to turn up or call in at any moment. I apologize, but it's very unusual for him not to tell me his whereabouts. Can I take a message? I'm sure he'll get back to you as soon as he can.'

'No, that's fine,' said the president, her face pale. 'I'll call later.' Taking a deep breath she asked the White House operator to put her through to Fort Detrick in Maryland. 'This is the president. I need to speak to the commander immediately.'

Within seconds Major General Thomas Allardyce MD of the United States Army Research Institute of Infectious Diseases was on the line. 'Hello, Madam President, I assume you're calling about the computer disk Special Agent Toshack brought me.'

'Yes, I hope you've told no-one else about it. Not even within USAMRIID.' She drawled the acronym phonetically – 'you sam rid'.

'Of course not.'

'What can you tell me?'

'Well, it contains two copies of an individual's genome. Except they're not exact copies. The second contains subtle changes in seventeen of the genes.'

'What would those subtle changes do?'

'Well, quite a lot.'

'Such as?'

Listening to his answer Weiss stared down at her desk, comparing the intelligence reports with the

314

two sheets of typed paper that Hank Butcher had given her with the disk. When the doctor had finished she asked him one more question, then thanked him and hung up.

For a long while she sat in silence, trying to marshal both her thoughts and feelings. Finally she came to a decision and pressed a button on her desk, summoning the head of her security detail.

Special Agent Mark Toshack entered the room. He held a file in his hand. Without saying anything he passed it to her. Opening it, she scanned the photograph and notes. It only confirmed her thoughts. 'Thank you, Mark,' she said. 'Now I would like you to do something else for me. Again I want you to use only Secret-Service personnel, and I need you to do it fast.'

Overlooking ViroVector Solutions, California. The same day. Noon.

'Well, if you want my advice, I wouldn't do it. the first rule of this business is you don't go into a rat hole. You always make sure you've got a way out. And this Womb sounds like the mother of all rat holes.'

Decker groaned and took the binoculars off Barzini's cousin, Frankie Danza, training them on the main dome of ViroVector. 'Thanks, but that's not really the kind of advice we're after.'

Luke Decker and Kathy Kerr sat inside Frankie's Mercedes van on a raised part of the main road overlooking the ViroVector campus. The other two men with Frankie hadn't volunteered their

315

names and their faces didn't invite further questions.

The irony of his current situation didn't really register. It was probably one of the less-weird things that had occurred to Decker over the last few days. Working with the opposition was only part of it. Earlier that morning, after Joey Barzini had made a few vague introductions, Frankie and his men had taken him and Kathy to a warehouse near Fisherman's Wharf. There the two nameless men had given Kathy a pulse box and taught her how to use it on a safe similar to the one in the Womb. Throughout the three-hour session their conversation never once strayed outside the narrow confines of the task in hand.

And now Frankie Danza, a whip-thin guy with nervous hands, no hair and a Camel cigarette surgically attached to his lower lip, was trying to explain the problems involved in getting into and out of smart buildings.

Frankie's van was parked next to an imposing blue sign with *White Heat Science Park* written on it in three-foot-high letters. The park of the same name – a cluster of small high-tech start-up companies – comprised the only buildings adjoining the relatively isolated ViroVector site. A large man-made lake and the eleventh hole of the Bellevue Golf and Country Club bordered its other perimeters.

The ViroVector campus itself was an emerald blanket of manicured lawns and perfectly proportioned trees, only interrupted by a few tennis courts, a helicopter pad, parking lots and large production warehouses. But the most striking feature was the crystal dome sitting like a vast alien moon in the centre of the site.

A lightweight steel fence encircled the campus and on the road there was a gateway. All around the perimeter and at key locations on the campus, on twenty-foot-high poles, Decker could see what looked like sensors and closed-circuit TV cameras.

'Getting in ain't the problem,' said Frankie, 'especially if Kathy's got clearance. The guardian computer don't question you or give you no trouble if your clearance is OK. But it'll watch you and sometimes it'll splash your face up on the monitors inside the dome. And if this Dr Prince is inside and sees you, then you're in deep shit. But you can wear headgear to disguise yourself. The other risk is being eyeballed in the flesh. But again, if you go late in the day you can minimize that.

'Your big problem is that there's only one way out. And if you don't leave in time that computer mother's gonna close you down. And if Dr Prince catches you on one of the monitors while you're in the Womb and sets off the alarms. Kaboom! You're history.

'A guy I knew did a bank job in Hong Kong. A brand-new grade-A smart building overlooking Kowloon Harbour. He got in easy, outmanoeuvred the computer, fooled all the sensors. Got right into the vault. Even tripped the time-lock codes with a quantum code-breaker. Then, when the team was in the heart of the vault, the computer closed 'em down. Two-foot thick steel doors shut 'em in, then sucked all the air out. Game over. They were found the next day – a pile of stiffs. That's what smart buildings do. They let you check in, but they don't never let you check out.'

'Thanks for the encouragement,' said Kathy. 'Any ideas?'

'Well, if you gotta go in, the only real advice is timing. From what you've told me the whole place closes down to all personnel except those with gold clearance at ten. That means you must be out by ten. If you're inside the dome the computer will seal you in. Even if you're outside it'll get you. Those flimsy fences around the campus are like the computer's skin. If you try and break through it, it'll feel you and send a few thousand volts your way. So, rule number one: you *gotta* be off campus by ten.

'Rule number two: go in as late as you can to avoid most of the working suits. When do most people leave the site?'

Kathy shrugged. 'Most are out by seven. Few if any people work after that. It's virtually unheard of to go into the Womb after six. It's not the place to be when you're tired and prone to making mistakes.'

Frankie nodded. 'Rule number three: give yourself enough time. This is the hardest rule to stick to because no-one knows what enough means. How long d'you need to get your stuff? Give yourself at least half an hour to get into the safe.'

Kathy thought for a moment. 'I've got to get into a biohazard suit beforehand and then go through the decon showers when I come out. Assuming we find a sample of something it shouldn't take more than ten minutes to scan the file and for Luke to copy it onto disk in the anteroom above. I'd say we need an hour, tops.'

318

Frankie nodded. 'Give yourself two. That means we drop you off outside the main gates at eight, and we pick you up before ten. In the meantime you betta get some more practice with the pulse box. And then you betta start praying no-one catches you in the Womb. It sounds an awful easy place to die.'

ViroVector Solutions, California.
The same day. 7.59 pm.

By eight most of the ViroVector offices were empty, but the tireless TITANIA was still at work. The bio-computer's electronic receptors scoured the World Wide Web, monitoring any data even remotely related to Crime Zero, continually informing its neural net of any relevant information. Its air ducts breathed with precise regularity as it absorbed much of the same information President Weiss had received from her intelligence sources.

TITANIA had no moral compass against which to evaluate the escalating deaths it was recording. The supercomputer could only objectively compare the deaths and their causes against its predictions. The death of Bob Burbank and the swearing-in of President Weiss were logged, as were the Iraqi retreat and the spreading epidemic. TITANIA calculated that over 9,000 humans had died as a consequence of Crime Zero within Iraq and that the rate was increasing, all in the expected demographic groups. Unlike the President of the United States, these figures elicited no concern from TITANIA.

319

Similarly, TITANIA neither felt anxiety nor raised the alarm when, at a more basic level of artificial cognition, it registered the activation of one of the DNA scanners allowing entrance to the campus. Like a human's subconscious, TITANIA's base operating system controlling ViroVector's security noted that the genome taken from the palm of the human hand pressed against the sensor matched one on file. And since that genome possessed silver clearance and the second unauthorized person acceded to a DNA scan TITANIA simply allowed the two entrants access without troubling its higher-level consciousness, in the same way that a human's subconscious automatically regulates breathing, only alerting the conscious mind when it perceives a problem.

TITANIA'S eyes, however, followed the two entrants, watching their every move.

30

ViroVector Solutions, California.
The same day. 8.00 p.m.

'Please place your palm against the sensor,' said the voice at the main gate of ViroVector. Decker did what he was told, but he was disconcerted by the fact that the gate wasn't manned. Not by a human anyway.

The tall guard in the gatehouse was a life-like hologram; his face a composite of leading male film stars. It was standing above a KREE8 version-six holo-pad, according to the sticker on the window. 'Is he meant to scare off people or welcome them?' Decker whispered to Kathy.

Kathy shrugged and removed her palm from the sensor, where his was now being read. She looked nervous and he didn't blame her. 'Don't worry about it. He's just there to impress you with how technologically advanced ViroVector is.'

'It's working,' he said, feeling a slight heat under his palm as the sensor peeled a microscopic layer off his skin, scanning his DNA. Suddenly a rush of irrational panic hit him as he wondered whether

321

the scanner would somehow be able to identify Axelman's genes in his DNA and bar him access.

'Welcome, Dr Kerr,' said the hologram after Decker's palm had been read. 'Please state your guest's full name.'

'Luke Decker.' She spoke into a small microphone on the guardhouse wall.

'Thank you, Dr Kerr.'

Suddenly the large gates slid silently open and they were in.

He turned round briefly and saw the lights of Frankie Danza's van a 100 yards further up the road. They had brought Decker and Kathy here an hour ago. In that time they had sat in the van watching the last stragglers leave work and had waited a further half an hour after the last ViroVector employee had left. The parking lot was empty and the whole place appeared to be deserted. At eight o'clock precisely they'd approached the gates, trusting Kathy's clearance was still live. It was a gamble, but now they were inside. But as Frankie had said, that was the easy part.

As Decker followed Kathy towards the large dome, which glowed in the evening gloom like some implacable spaceship, he felt the sting of hundreds of invisible eyes watching him.

'There shouldn't be anyone here,' said Kathy, as they neared the steps that led up to the entrance. 'But, if there is, just smile.' Ahead he could see a pair of thick glass double doors, with *ViroVector* etched into them. Looking in, Decker was relieved to see that, apart from two people talking intensely by the restrooms, the reception was empty.

'To open the door put your hands on the sensor again,' said Kathy.

'Does every door have these damn sensors?'

'Yup. TITANIA likes to know where everyone is.'

'Great,' said Decker as he placed his hand on the steel pad.

As they walked into the foyer he turned to see a set of car headlights pierce the darkness of the parking lot. A limousine drove past the dome. It could have been his nervousness, but he was sure he glimpsed Director Naylor's white hair in the passenger seat.

'Shit,' he said.

Kathy had seen her, too. 'Don't think about it. Let's go,' she said, clutching her bag. She led him through a door at the end of the foyer, which opened out on to a long corridor. At the end was a yellow door with a black biohazard symbol on it. 'Be quiet,' she hissed as they walked past a steel door with *TITANIA Smart Suite* written on it in black. A dull hum could be heard from within.

When they reached the yellow doors their palms were read once more. As the door opened Decker could see a white sterile environment, totally devoid of warmth or colour. And just as the door closed behind him, sealing in the air, he was sure he heard the door to the Smart Suite opening.

But it wasn't the door to the smart suite Decker had heard, it was the sound of TITANIA thinking.

The Smart Suite was humming with activity. The main display media – the fifteen-by-ten-foot screen-wall and the KREE8 hologram floor pad at the head

323

of the conference table – were both in use. And at the rear of the room, four small monitors showed quickly shifting views of the ViroVector complex as seen through TITANIA's sixty closed-circuit security cameras.

The hologram being displayed on the pad was a five-foot-diameter, three-dimensional globe, rotating slowly a yard off the ground. The definition of the hologram was so precise that the silver globe looked solid, as though it were made of real metal. Each country's border was demarcated by thin black tracing and was layered with three coloured strata forming population mountains, like a topographical three-dimensional map – red, green and blue – graphically demonstrating the demographic breakdown of each country. Unlike the static colours in the rest of the world the red in Iraq pulsed with light, as if alive.

Simply by touching a country with a fingertip the layers of colour would separate to display a percentage figure and an absolute number, showing the importance and size of that demographic group within a particular country. The absolute numbers were constantly changing, reflecting new births and deaths collated from the numerous data sources on the World Wide Web. The rising Total World Population number shown on the screen-wall also fluctuated. The last number stood at 6,567,987,601.

Beneath the population counter was a cryptic legend, indicating what each colour represented. Red was labelled, *target*; green, *carrier*; and blue, *corrected*. Beside each colour was a number counter, giving a total for that segment.

324

Standing alone in the room Alice Prince's eyes were sparkling with excitement as she watched the globe, its iridescent colours reflected in the thick glass of her spectacles. After witnessing the Iraqi turnabout last night Alice Prince felt born again. The Third World War had been averted and any doubts she may have had ceased to trouble her. Crime Zero was a just project and it was going to work. Phase Two was performing so well it looked certain that they would be able to launch Phase Three within days. And the vision was so much cleaner and clearer when seen in its clinical entirety, far from the confusion of face-to-face human realities.

TITANIA began to run its global predictive sequence for Phase Three.

At the top of the screen-wall a time line appeared, showing today as time zero and then counting off the months and years as they elapsed in the simulated sequence.

The coloured layers started pulsing in each chosen index country for Phase Three. But no sooner had the epicentres been illuminated than black parabolic arcs, simulating air, sea and land travel, spread across the globe like the legs of a malevolent spider. Within days all the colour segments on the time line in most of the so-called First World were pulsing. Only the remoter regions of South America, such as the Amazon and Patagonia, Antarctica and central Africa, as well as the more remote islands north of New Zealand, remained unaffected.

Within ten days, in the major countries, the red band of colour representing the *target* stopped pulsing and began to glow. The other countries soon followed, and within weeks 90 per cent of the red sections on the globe were aglow and therefore in decline. In one month every single country had been touched in one way or another. On the main screen-wall the rising number on the counter slowed to 2,408,876,654 and then began to fall. Within two and a half months the figure had dropped by almost 300 million; within six months the decline had doubled and within a year the figure had dropped by more than one and a quarter billion. After thirty-six months and three days all traces of red in the world had disappeared.

There were only two colour strata left on the depleted population mountains: green and blue; *carrier* and *corrected*.

The total number on the population counter had reduced by almost two and a half billion humans in three years, a drop fifty times greater than that caused by the great influenza pandemic of 1918.

Rolling the time line forward another twenty years the counter gradually began to climb once more, with a new strata of differing shades of blue adding to the rising population mountains in each country.

The silver globe was now dominated by calming blues and greens. The angry rash of red was effectively extinct.

As TITANIA laid out their vision like the onslaught of the inevitable, Alice felt she was seeing something sacred: a purging flood she had played her part in unleashing. So transfixed was she by the globe that she hadn't even registered Madeline Naylor enter the room.

'It's beautiful isn't it, Ali?' said Madeline.

'Unstoppable,' said Alice with a sigh.

'There's just one small thing we need to make this perfect,' said Madeline.

'What now?'

'Decker and Kerr still aren't out of the way. Jackson's working on it but . . .'

'It doesn't matter now, does it?' said Alice, staring at the shimmering globe and the New Eden it represented.

'I suppose not,' said Madeline. 'I just wish I knew where they were.'

Ironically she had only to ask TITANIA and the biocomputer would have told her Luke Decker and Kathy Kerr's exact location. Or, had she looked behind her at the four screens continually monitoring the entire campus, she might even have snatched a hurried glimpse of a figure in a blue Chemturion biohazard suit entering the Womb.

31

The Womb, ViroVector Solutions, California.
The same day. 8.32 p.m.

As the glass doors of the womb hissed closed behind her, the first beads of sweat prickled on Kathy Kerr's skin inside the rubberized suit. Entering the campus she had felt nervous but in control, and even seeing Director Naylor had spurred her on rather than paralysed her. But now, here in the Womb, she could feel herself tensing, with only the sound of her breathing for company. This time was different to all her previous visits.

The clock above the door indicated 20:32. TITANIA would close down the Womb at 21:30. Including the essential half-hour to undergo the decontamination procedures, Kathy had to make her exit before TITANIA closed down the whole compound at 22:00 hours. That gave her fifty-eight minutes to use the pulse box, open the safe, find what she was looking for and capture the data on the computer and printer upstairs, where Decker should be waiting. It didn't seem enough. The prospect of another scientist entering the biolab complex in the meantime was beyond contemplation. If they did, she would be helpless.

Taking a deep breath she walked past the first bank of refrigerators to the corner, where the waist-high safe sat. On the front, covering the electronic keypad, was a flap about the size of a paperback book. It was as she remembered it and looked reassuringly like the Lenica 101 she'd practised on, but she couldn't be sure.

On the workstation beside Alice Prince's safe was a VDU. Kathy switched it on and opened up the link with the terminal on the floor above, where Decker waited with a new box of blank disks, ready to copy whatever data she found.

The keyboard was twice the normal size, with large flat keys covered in a sterile plastic sleeve. With her unwieldy gloved fingers she jabbed out a message.

'I'm in and have found the safe. Are you set up with disks and the printer?'

There was a heart-stopping pause.

'Everything looking good up here. Good luck.'

She looked down at the slim, chrome, cheque-book-sized slab resting in her left palm: the pulse box, and the key to the whole operation. Exploiting nuclear magnetic resonance and liquid molecules, the quantum code-breaker used qubits which, unlike classical binary bits, can exist simultaneously in multiple states, allowing it to decipher each element of a code in parallel time rather than sequentially. It was fast and efficient, but was it enough? Studying its liquid-crystal display and the two silk-thin wires trailing from one end like wispy antennae, she recalled the procedure. Using the magnetic pad on the back of the quantum pulse box she anchored it above the safe's electronic keyboard. Once she was satisfied it was secure, and with Frankie's words in mind – 'If you drop this thing it's history'– she carefully taped the spring-hinged plastic keypad cover back on itself, revealing the keys. Then she took the trailing wires in her fingers and searched for the two tiny holes in the top edge of the keypad. 'After a bit of practice it should be easy,' she'd been told.

But it hadn't been easy in practice and it wasn't easy now. At first she couldn't even find the holes and when she did she almost gave up with frustration. The protective gloves she wore were even thicker than the ones she'd used when practising. They'd been designed to give as much movement as possible, but inserting two silk-thin wires into the minute holes obviously hadn't been in the usage spec.

'Relax and take your time,' she told herself. But time was the one thing she couldn't afford. Maintaining composure, she straightened out the inch-long wires with one hand, aligning them with the two holes. If they met any resistance at all they began to bend, and she had to ease them in at a painstaking pace. It was vital that they connected with the inner electronics. Frankie's guys had taught her how to 'jiggle' them, as they put it, gently vibrating the wires until they found a way into the opening. But jiggling required sensitive fingers and her gloves didn't allow her that luxury.

She could feel perspiration on her brow as she concentrated on her task. She wanted to rip off her helmet and wipe the sweat away, but had to blink through the droplets instead. She lost count of the number of times both wires were in the holes when one became snagged and she had to start all over again. Finally, twenty-six minutes later, her arms aching with the effort, she heard a beep and the pulse box burst into life. The liquid-crystal display began racing through numbers as it simultaneously searched for every character comprising the code.

Kathy immediately turned to the computer terminal and plucked the wand from its bracket. She ran it over a barcode on one of the vials in the main refrigerator to check it was functioning. Instantly the screen displayed a contents menu, offering the genetic composition of the vial's contents, its history of clinical trials and topline rationale and objectives. Satisfied, she replaced it and waited for the pulse box to do its work.

It only took five and a half minutes for the chrome code-breaker to work its magic and show six characters illuminated on the LCD: 666%£5. Carefully she extended a gloved finger and punched in the code on the safe's electronic keypad. Silently the door opened.

'I'm in,' she typed on the computer, checking the time. She had a little over half an hour to copy what she needed. It should be enough. Removing a tray of cigar-sized coloured vials, she rested them on the work surface by the terminal and read their labels. The two red vials were marked *Conscience*, so she ignored those, but two words on the three green vials made the hairs on the back of her neck stand up.

Crime Zero.

In what way was each of the three vials different? To extract all the evidence she would have to capture the data on each one. Suddenly the remaining twenty-seven minutes didn't seem long at all.

She typed, 'Think project is called Crime Zero. You need to stand by with two more disks. At least three vials. All might be vital.'

'Do we have enough time for three?' Decker responded immediately.

'Hope so.'

Kathy picked up the vial marked, *Crime Zero (Phase One – telomeres test)* and ran the wand over the barcode.

Not bothering to scan what was on the screen she immediately clicked on the copy icon, selecting the disk drive on the computer upstairs.

The file was large. The clock symbol at the bottom of the screen moved painfully slowly, indicating it would take seven minutes to download. Assuming the other two were as big she'd be lucky to get them all out before TITANIA closed down the Womb. She looked at the two other terminals in the Womb but there was only one computer next to Decker, and she could only copy each disk sequentially.

While she waited she removed the quantum pulse box, extracted the wires from the safe, and searched for a place to conceal it. She couldn't take it out of the Womb now it had become contaminated, but its presence would alert someone, particularly Alice Prince, that she'd been in here. Eventually she dropped it in a sample tray, closed the lid and then placed the tray at the back of the lowest shelf in the largest refrigerator.

By the time she'd finished and returned to the computer screen the Crime-Zero Phase-One vector file had been copied. Eighteen minutes remained.

'Ready for disk two?' she typed to Luke.

'Ready.'

Barely pausing, she picked up the vial labelled, *Crime Zero (Phase Two – controlled trial)* and waved the wand over it. As soon as the screen registered the file had been opened she copied it upstairs to Luke. Again she checked the clock at the bottom of the screen. This file transfer would take eight minutes. There would be virtually no time for the third phase.

Fearing that time was slipping away she decided to scan the last Crime-Zero vial on a second terminal to check its contents. Switching on the terminal by the Genescope she did so.

At that moment a soft feminine voice interrupted her. 'The time is now twenty-one fifteen. The biosafety-level-five and level-four facilities will be closing in exactly fifteen minutes. If you have not yet done so you should clear the workstations and prepare to leave. The ViroVector campus will be sealed at exactly twenty-two hundred hours.'

Kathy glanced at the screen where Crime Zero Phase Two was being copied. Over three minutes to go. With one eye on the digital clock above the door of the Womb she turned to the data on the second terminal.

Scrolling to Crime Zero Phase Three's technical specifications she speed-read the summary. Words and phrases jumped out at her: 'engineered influenza vector – chimera – respiratory transmission – Y chromosome trigger – Project

333

Conscience control genes – hormonal imbalance – telomeres-determined time release.' Each word and phrase was innocuous on its own, but the cumulative implications were terrifying.

Her heart beating like the wings of a trapped bird, Kathy quickly scrolled to the summary objectives. What she read there was so outlandish it made her gasp. And yet what shocked her most was that at an entirely amoral, scientific level it made perverse sense. With horrible clarity Kathy realized that Crime Zero represented her life's work taken to its ultimate extreme. In part she had to take some perverse responsibilty for what Alice Prince and Madeline Naylor were doing.

A deeper chill clutched at her heart.

Or for what they may have *already* done.

'You now have ten minutes exactly before the level-five and level-four facilities will be closed down,' informed the soft feminine voice.

Kathy took a deep breath and rushed over to the first monitor.

'Ready for third disk?' she typed.

'No time,' Decker replied. 'Get out of there.'

'Make time. Explain later.'

'It's your call,' Decker's response was instantaneous. 'Third disk ready. Hurry!!!!!!'

Rushing back to the second terminal she selected Decker's disk drive and then pressed 'copy'. She wouldn't have more than a few seconds after the copying was complete, if she wanted to switch off the terminals before leaving. No-one must know that she'd been there.

Keeping her eye on the main clock Kathy quickly returned the vials to their tray, careful to

334

replace them as they were, before returning them to the safe.

'The biohazard level-four and level-five laboratories will be closing in exactly five minutes.'

'GET OUT!' she read on the screen from Luke.

But she still had to hide any trace of her intrusion.

'Four minutes.'

If Naylor or Prince knew, they might activate Phase Three prematurely. Assuming they hadn't done so already. She slammed the safe shut.

'Three minutes.'

Racing back to the large refrigerator she checked that the pulse box was concealed as discreetly as possible.

Two minutes.

She closed down the first terminal and checked everything was as she'd found it.

'One minute.'

Come on, she shouted at the second terminal, willing it to finish.

Then suddenly it was done. She switched it off and walked as fast as her suit would allow her to the door, pressed the open button and exited the Womb.

The airtight doors hissed shut behind her with forty-three seconds to spare.

'The womb is now closed,' said the disembodied feminine voice. 'The ViroVector main gates will be sealed in half an hour. This site will close at twenty-two hundred hours. If you have not yet done so, please prepare to leave.'

'OK. OK. I heard you,' Decker said aloud,

assuming Kathy had got out of the Womb in time. No alarm had sounded. Yet.

He stood in the sterile white vestibule next to the single computer and printer. To his left was the door leading to the transit station, through which Kathy had disappeared to descend to the biohazard labs and the Womb. To his right was the main exit, leading to the corridor and the foyer beyond.

Extracting the third disk from the computer, Decker labelled it and placed it with the others in his tote bag. He then switched off the terminal and sat on the desk. He could do nothing but wait. Every few seconds he would look at the main exit, expecting someone to walk in.

He checked his watch. Kathy still had to pass through the decontamination showers and change out of her suit before they could leave this technological nightmare. And they had to leave soon.

As he waited he wondered why Kathy had insisted on risking getting locked into the Womb in order to copy the third vial of Crime Zero. Surely two were enough.

'Let's go,' said Kathy, suddenly bursting through the doors of the transit room.

Picking up the tote bag, Decker rose from his chair and made for the door. 'We've got about twelve minutes. Let's get the hell out of here.'

In the corridor they ran past the Smart Suite and the Cold Room to the foyer. Outside the dome, the campus was as quiet as before.

At the main gates Decker put his hands on the scanner and only began to feel better when the gates opened for them. Seconds later Frankie Danza's van appeared and pulled up at the gates, its broad tyres screeching on the tarmac.

Breathing a sigh of relief, he walked up to the driver's tinted window with Kathy in step beside him. He opened the door and froze.

It wasn't Frankie Danza in the seat. Not that Decker really noticed, because the gun barrel staring him in the face held his attention.

'Drop the bag! Now!' said the man in the driver's seat, pressing the barrel against Decker's forehead.

32

The peace plague was how the media dubbed the epidemic raging through the ranks of the Iraqi Army. Some US and British tabloids even claimed it was a good thing; a divine curse sent to blight the warmongers.

After Friday's Iraqi retreat, the World Health Organization, with the full backing of the UN Security Council, had endorsed and enforced the quarantine of Iraq. Every country bordering that nation applied the quarantine rigidly, terrified the mystery plague might spread to them. Already deaths were being put at over 30,000, with more Iraqis – military and civilian alike – being stricken by the hour. So far, few if any women or children had been affected.

The World Health Organization, Médecins sans Frontières and the Red Cross immediately dispatched specially equipped teams to try to understand the nature of the mystery epidemic and offer advice on containment strategies. Even the US Army had released a team from the Epidemic Intelligence Service, based at the Center for Disease Control in Atlanta. Within a matter of hours, Iraq had been transformed in the eyes of the world from a dangerous bully to a needy cripple.

By Saturday, early findings suggested that the disease affected the patient's hormone levels and brain chemistry. It was speculatively hoped that the plague wasn't airborne, that it could at least be contained if ruthless measures were applied and adhered to.

Isolated reports began to surface that even the hitherto ruthless Iraqi president had expressed remorse to the Kurdish leaders for past atrocities, and had sent apologies to Kuwait for his aggressive stance. At first these acts – if they were indeed true – were seen as a cynical means to ingratiate himself with his enemies at a time when Iraq was collapsing. But increasingly they were seen as proof that he had also succumbed to the peace plague.

Against a backdrop of rising hysteria the press besieged the White House, demanding a statement from the new president. Some reporters from the more sensationalist newspapers asked if the plague had been intentional – a brilliant pre-emptive strike by the new administration. Inspired by the success of Project Conscience – a biological solution to crime – was the peace plague the next step – a biological solution to war?

These claims were strenuously denied by President Weiss, who stressed that she took the Iraq plague very seriously and that Baghdad was being offered America's full support. She claimed that, whatever their differences, humanity must always unite against its common enemy: disease.

Surprisingly few national journalists asked if the

peace plague could spread to North America. And, if so, how soon it would get there.

That was one question Pamela Weiss was unable to answer.

Saturday, 8 November 2008. Morning.

Kathy Kerr was made to wear the blindfold for a long time. The plane had been flying for at least four hours, perhaps more. The dull roar of the engines and the nylon wrist-binders increased her sense of isolation. The cabin smelled of cheap cologne and commercial airliner restrooms. But this wasn't a commercial airliner; that much she knew.

There were at least two other men in the cabin with them, but she didn't know where they were sitting. She took some comfort from the knowledge that Decker sat three seats to her left. They had hardly talked since they'd been bundled into the van and onto the plane. She'd only just had enough time to whisper the basics of Crime Zero – what she knew about Phase Three, anyway. They hadn't talked since. There was nothing to say.

A wave of hopelessness washed over her. The project was so huge, so outlandish, that alerting the authorities suddenly seemed irrelevant. Decker had been right: she should have gone home when she'd had the chance. Just because she'd helped start this nightmare didn't mean she could ever stop it. This was global, inevitable and final.

As Luke Decker tried to make himself comfortable in his seat he failed to understand why they were still alive. If what Kathy had told him about Crime Zero was true then they should already be dead. Naylor would have to assume that they knew about the project and would have made the necessary arrangements to kill them.

Decker shook his head; it didn't make sense. Alice Prince was damaged, and therefore probably not naturally vindictive. Her involvement in Crime Zero was almost certainly fuelled by idealistic fantasies, which denied the realities of the human costs. The dominant partner in this was Naylor. Instinctively he knew she always had been.

So why were they still alive?

When he heard the undercarriage drop and felt the plane coming in to land he guessed he would soon find out.

As the plane eased to a stop Decker was bundled outside into the cold and transferred with Kathy to another van. As it sped off, their blindfolds were removed, and Decker studied the two men sitting with them in the windowless rear cabin. His tote bag containing the disks was at the feet of the shorter, sandy-haired one. They were typical agents, with dark suits and impenetrable manners, but he didn't recognize either of them.

Decker assembled the facts. The plane had been government or military owned, and the ease with which the van had met it on the airport tarmac confirmed they hadn't landed at an ordinary commercial airport.

At least on the ground there was a chance of escape.

Decker smiled wearily at Kathy. She looked pale and tired, but she smiled back.

341

Decker turned to the shorter agent. From his relaxed body language he looked like the leader. 'Do you know what's on those disks you took from us?'

The man's face remained impassive, as if he hadn't heard the question. Decker spoke again, calmly, as if to an ally. 'Don't you even *want* to know what's on the disks?' he said, feeling the anger build inside him. 'You should, because it'll involve you too, sooner than you think. Doesn't that bother you just a little?'

Still the man said nothing.

Decker prided himself on his control, on using reason to solve most things, but now he allowed the hurt and anger of the last few days to build up. As his rage and frustration peaked, the van came to a sudden stop; then he made his move.

There was no plan, no coolly timed stratagem, only an opportunist explosion of vented energy. As the engine died, both of his captors visibly relaxed and looked towards the driver's cabin. At that moment Decker leapt forward and, using his bound hands as a club, brought them down on the side of the larger man's head, felling him to the floor. Extending the same fluid movement, he swung his clasped hand to the right in a double-handed tennis backhand, smashing against the smaller man's jaw and catapulting his head against the side of the van. His knuckles burned with pain as he felt one pop with the impact. 'Grab his gun,' Decker shouted, feeding off the adrenalin surging through him.

Kathy bent down and scrabbled through the felled man's clothes, producing a black revolver.

Decker did the same with the other man who, still conscious, lay sprawled against the side of the van, clutching his head. He also picked up the tote bag lying at his feet and kicked it towards the van doors. He paused for a moment, considering how to unlock them, when suddenly they opened.

Raising his gun he levelled it at a small group of outlines silhouetted against the night sky. An imposing female figure stepped forward, flanked by four men, their guns drawn and pointing directly at him.

'Oh my God,' said Kathy behind him.

Decker's jaw dropped. What was she doing here?

'What the hell is going on here?' the woman's voice was firm and commanding. Looking first at Kathy and then at Decker she peered beyond him at the sandy-haired man groggily rising to his feet. 'Special Agent Toshack, what happened?' the woman demanded. She looked tired and pale, but her manner indicated total control. 'I told you to bring them to me, not fight with them.'

Stunned, Decker turned and watched the man stumble to his fallen colleague, who was also beginning to stir. Toshack rubbed his chin and gave Decker a rueful grin. 'I think Special Agent Decker here had his own ideas about that. And he's got a pretty good way of expressing them.'

'How's Brown?' she demanded.

The man checked his groaning partner. 'He'll live.'

The woman shook her head in disgust and then, ignoring Decker's gun, extended an open hand towards Kathy. 'Welcome to Fort Detrick, Dr Kerr.

343

Now that I've ascertained we're both on the same side I'm very pleased to meet you. I'm Pamela Weiss.'

Kathy shook her hand in dumb silence.

Then Weiss turned to Decker and gestured to the tote bag at his feet. 'Special Agent Decker, are you going to shoot me? Because if you're not, can I have whatever it is you took from ViroVector?'

Decker didn't move for a second, still trying to work out whose side she was on. Finally he lowered his gun and picked up the bag, holding it close to him. 'I think we all want to see what's on these disks, Madam President.'

33

ViroVector Solutions, California.
The same day. 10.09 a.m.

Two senior ViroVector scientists discovered the chrome electronic gadget in the Womb on Saturday morning. Working to a deadline developing a viral vector for Alzheimer's disease, they'd been incensed to find that part of their allocated refrigerator space had been annexed.

When they complained to Alice Prince her initial reaction had been annoyance. The last thing she needed was a petty dispute about lab resources. But when no-one could identify the chrome box, or knew how it had got there, her irritation changed to concern.

Donning her biohazard suit, she entered the Womb to examine the box, which had apparently been concealed in a tray at the base of one of the refrigerators. She interrogated TITANIA, who informed her that only authorized personnel had entered the Womb in the last few days. As a matter of course TITANIA listed all the entrants to the biolab suite and the Womb. Scanning the list on the monitor Alice gasped when she saw Kathy Kerr's name, and was shocked to learn that she and Luke Decker had entered last night. It was impossible. Both Alice and Madeline had actually been on site. But then she remembered that she hadn't cancelled Kathy's silver clearance – Madeline had said it wasn't necessary. As far as TITANIA was concerned Kathy Kerr was still authorized to come and go as she pleased.

Alice quickly moved to the safe and punched in the code on the electronic keypad. Opening the door she peered in and pulled out the tray, checking the tamper-sealed caps on the vials. Everything appeared as it had been. Then she picked up one of the Crime-Zero vials and ran a computer wand over it. Looking at the nearest monitor she saw the project menu appear. In the bottom right-hand corner was the time and date of the last scan: 21:22 on 7 November. Yesterday.

Alice moved back to the speakerphone and with a heavy heart prepared to tell Madeline Naylor.

Heathrow Airport, London.
The same day. 2.12 p.m.

Heathrow has always been amongst the world's busiest airports. In 2005, when the first phase of Terminal 5 opened, it became the undisputed number one. The complex was a town in its own right, employing over 100,000 people and processing almost 80 million passengers a year.

Amidst the Saturday-afternoon throng of people, no-one was even aware that three of the

346

embarkation and disembarkation tunnels had been closed for two hours. Passengers were diverted to other departure gates and the disruption was minimal. Few paid any heed to the two men in blue overalls entering the closed departure gates with a trolley of white cardboard boxes, each bearing the same brand name as the one stamped on the back of their overalls: *AirShield Industries*. At the base of the carton was a small line of blue type to denote that AirShield Industries was a subsidiary of ViroVector Solutions Incorporated, Palo Alto, California.

It was a routine task. The computer had informed the operatives that certain cartridges were exhausted and had itemized the exact serial number of the replacement from the inventory. They were doing what they were told. Neither of them considered questioning the task. They had no way of knowing the consequences of their actions.

The departure gate ahead was deserted and the display that usually showed the flight number and destination now flashed, *Closed for Maintenance*. Like most major airports Heathrow used bacteriophage air purifiers in their embarkation and disembarkation tunnels. Passengers were largely unaware of being sterilized by the bacteria-destroying phage as they left or boarded the plane. Only a slight breeze, perfumed with a fresh, soapy fragrance, made them notice the phage-rich air. The process was simply accepted as a sensible precaution.

Stepping through the deserted passport and ticket control, past the empty rows of seats for

347

waiting passengers, the maintenance men entered a service hatch marked, *Authorized Staff Only*, which lead down to a series of interconnecting walkways beneath each tunnel and accessed the individual phage-purifier cartridges. Once inside, both men left their trolley at the top of the steps and walked down to a lower level, each with a carton. Ahead there was a long chrome corridor with rows of airtight doors to their left. Each door was numbered, corresponding with the individual departure gates above.

Using a key the first man watched door number twenty-eight slide open, revealing a crawl space beneath the bacteriophage air tunnel. The second man walked on to the adjacent gate. Crouching down, the first man made his way into the small inspection chamber and quickly located the two-foot-square flue of the air-purification system protruding from the ceiling. He removed the grill from the flue to reveal a red button marked *Seal* and a green light. Beside the button was a lever, which released the cylindrical magazine of six vials – each containing a distinct bacterium-specific bacteriophage – from its bracket.

Pressing the button he watched the airtight door slide shut behind him. When the green light changed to red, indicating that no new air was entering or leaving the tunnel, the man checked the number on the carton, opened it and removed the replacement cartridge, placing it on the floor.

He then reached up and pulled the lever, freeing the magazine already in place. Carefully checking there was no breakage, he removed the magazine and placed it in the empty carton. As always he briefly examined the cylindrical cluster of six glass vials, and was surprised that most of them seemed at least half full. He didn't question it; he only operated on the computer's instructions.

Without a second thought he quickly inserted the replacement cartridge into the purifier. There was no difference between the two canisters. Any slight change in colour in one of the vials didn't interest him. It wasn't his job. And he ignored the fact that there was a minute powerful radio antenna in one corner of the casing. Replacing the grille on the flue, he picked up his carton and left the crawl space. Another task completed.

Once he used to tell himself his job was important because he helped protect people's health, but now he didn't care about what he did. It paid the mortgage.

He might have cared today, if he'd known that ten maintenance men just like him and his partner, in five other airports across the globe, had unwittingly helped change the world for ever.

34

USAMRIID, Fort Detrick, Maryland.
The same day. 12.23 p.m.

'You've all seen the topline data from the disks Dr
Kerr and Special Agent Decker took from
ViroVector. We know from the Phase Three disk
that remote-control activation is planned for the
very near future. So we have to assume and plan for
the worst.

'We also need a full strategy for attacking the
Iraq Phase-Two epidemic, with contingencies
should it leak. No-one here should stand on
ceremony or rank. Say what you think. And if we
need anybody else on the team, for God's sake get
them on board now. This is a National Security
Directive Seven. It doesn't get more serious than
this.'

President Weiss looked drawn as she addressed
the task force gathered around the table in the
main conference room. Kathy understood why
the president was taking such a personal interest in
this. If *she* felt bad about Alice Prince and Madeline
Naylor using her work on Project Conscience to

350

develop and test their abomination, then Weiss must be devastated. They were her trusted friends. Project Conscience had helped elect her. And now Prince and Naylor had turned what she thought was their shared dream into a nightmare.

Kathy had since learnt that the alarming similarity between Axelman's symptoms and those of the peace plague in Iraq had galvanized Weiss into sending Toshack in search of her. Armed with a faculty photograph from Stanford, Toshack and his men had tailed the FBI director, believing she would lead them to her. And last night, after following Naylor to the ViroVector campus, they had challenged and neutralized the men in Frankie Danza's van, parked a short distance up the road from them and waited for Kathy and Decker to emerge.

Since arriving three hours ago they'd had time only for a meal, a scan of the disks and some hasty introductions. Now Kathy sat back and looked around the table: next to Decker sat the President of the United States of America, along with six other people trying to make sense of the madness.

The large, uniformed coloured man on Weiss's right was General Linus Cleaver, the chairman of the Joint Chiefs of Staff. To his right was a square-jawed man also in uniform. Major General Tom Allardyce MD was the commander of USAMRIID, although he asked everyone to call him Tom. Next to him was a thin-faced woman with long dark hair and quick, intelligent eyes. Dr Sharon Bibb ran the Epidemic Investigation Service at the CDC in Atlanta. Beside her was Deputy Director Bill McCloud of the FBI. A tall lean man with a buzz cut and a Southern drawl, he had experience with the Bureau's Hazardous Materials Response Unit. He and Luke knew each other already. The other two men were Todd Sullivan, Pamela Weiss's new chief of staff, and Jack Bloom, who headed up the Doomsday Committee. The Doomsday Committee was part of the National Security Agency and existed solely to brainstorm the bleakest of disaster scenarios and lay down plans should they arise. The very fact that he was there was implicitly terrifying.

Major General Tom Allardyce spoke first, indicating the deck of charts in front of them, which summarized the disks' contents. 'I suggest we make sure we all understand the full implications of Crime Zero and agree next steps before we assign responsibilities. Kathy, since you're the closest to this, would you summarize the three phases as you see them?'

Glancing at the charts, Kathy briefly outlined the background of Project Conscience. She could see Pamela Weiss grimace as she explained how Dr Prince and Director Naylor had used Kathy's research on Conscience to develop a gender-specific vector.

Kathy sipped at her glass of water. 'Phase One was a test on six prisoners at San Quentin, including Karl Axelman. They inserted the modified genes into an attenuated viral vector, which inserted itself into the stem cells of the patient. This meant that the treatment – if I can call it that – only affected the person it was injected into. The vector targeted the cells in the hypothalamus in the brain and the testes. The new genetic instructions

352

boosted the patients' hormone and neuro-transmitter levels to literally mind-blowing proportions; on the one hand it stimulated their aggression, while at the same time racking them with suicidal guilt. The main aim of that phase was to check whether the treatment would first render the patient incapable of violent deeds and then kill him within a given time frame.'

'Given time frame?' asked Todd Sullivan.

'If the vector and the modified genes within it were engineered correctly the patient's age at death could be genetically predetermined.'

'How?' asked Dr Bibb as she checked her charts. 'By using the length of the telomeres?'

'Exactly.'

'What are telomeres?' asked General Linus Cleaver.

Kathy looked at Sharon Bibb to see if she wanted to answer, but she smiled, as if to give her the floor. 'They are the protective tips on the ends of chromosomes, like those on the ends of shoelaces. As we get older our cells divide and the telomeres erode. If the virus is so engineered it can recognize a host's age by their length. You must understand that Alice Prince has an incredible array of vectors. She can do almost whatever she wants.

'Phase Two was intended to move from an iso-lated test to a real-life situation. They chose a belligerent nation because they wanted to show the power of their vision, I guess to impress people that they could stop war. After all, there is no greater violent crime.'

'I think they particularly wanted to impress you, Madam President,' said Decker quietly.

353

Pamela Weiss frowned but said nothing.

Kathy continued. 'The disk clearly shows that they used a single corrupted sample of Bioshield vaccine to start the infection. Iraq, like most military powers, is a client of ViroVector. They would have ordered a supply of DNA vaccines to protect their troops and it wouldn't have been hard for Dr Prince to instruct TITANIA, the computer that runs ViroVector, to insert one corrupted sample into the Iraqi batch. Unlike Phase One this vector is infectious. It's a hand-to-mouth agent, passed on by contact.'

'But why didn't they use a more infectious vector right off?' asked Jack Bloom.

'I think they needed to ensure it could be contained if it misbehaved,' Kathy replied. 'Iraq is effectively a trial of the treatment on a larger scale, both in terms of who it affects and, as importantly, who it *doesn't*. This vector is designed to *infect* everyone, whereas the DNA modifier within the vector is designed to *affect* only men. Alice Prince and Madeline Naylor wanted to make sure their smart assassin only killed what it was aimed at.'

'According to our intelligence, that's happening,' said General Cleaver. 'It appears that no women or children in Iraq have caught the disease yet.'

Kathy nodded and chewed her lip. 'They've probably caught it, they're just carrying it without any symptoms. The brilliance of the Crime-Zero vector is that it targets only what it's meant to, but it uses everyone as a carrier. Ebola and marburg burn out because usually their victims die before they can pass it on. Crime Zero isn't like that. Phase Two lives on; there's no end zone.'

'But how the hell are they co-ordinating all this?' asked McCloud. 'Pandemic plagues are a nightmare to contain. How do they expect to get one to do their bidding?'

'Through TITANIA, ViroVector's supercomputer,' said Kathy. 'Alice Prince and Madeline Naylor are the composers, but TITANIA is almost certainly the conductor, orchestrating everything and monitoring each phase before moving on to the next one. And the last phase is the really clever one. Phase Three is the killer.'

Kathy flicked through the deck of charts in front of her, her hands trembling as she came to the final ones. 'The Phase Three vector overrules everything that went before. If a person has been exposed to Phase Two, Phase Three will overwrite any genetic changes with its own. This vector is a piece of genius. Like Phase Two it infects everyone, but it only affects some of the population. And even those effects differ according to the age of the victim. This combines the best of Conscience and the worst of Crime Zero. It's frighteningly clever.'

'Explain,' said Weiss.

'OK, first of all this vector is designed to infect females of all ages, but not give them any symptoms. They carry the viral vector in the cells lining their respiratory tract and can pass the virus on, but they remain healthy, save for a mild cough. This means the virus won't burn itself out. With pre-pubescent male children their genome actually changes, but only in the way the Conscience vector modifies genes. It won't kill them. Infected pre-pubescent boys have their genes recalibrated

355

to make them less prone to violence, regardless of their natural predisposition. It will also affect their germ cells. This means that they will pass on these modifications to any children they sire. But they're lucky compared to any male past puberty who becomes infected.'

She paused for breath.

'As with the Phase-Two vector, every post-pubescent male who catches the Phase-Three virus will first be rendered emotionally incapable of committing violent acts and then die. But with this virus, guided by the telomeres on a target's chromosomes, the timing of death will be determined by the victim's age. Essentially the young will die first. Post-pubescent men under about twenty-five will die in a few months. The last to go will be the older men, those who are the least violent and have the most knowledge to pass on. They will die in about three years. The other key thing about this vector is that it's based on the influenza virus, which means it's spread through respiratory aerosol. It's airborne. Just breathing in the vector can infect a person. With modern air travel it will spread around the globe in twenty-four hours.'

There was a moment's silence, then Sharon Bibb spoke. Her voice had the monotone of someone in shock. 'Can I just put this into context. The greatest pandemic to date occurred in 1918 after the First World War. Influenza spread like wildfire through Asia, America and an already-exhausted Europe. We all know that millions of men died in the First World War, but that number was dwarfed by the fifty million who died of Spanish Flu.

Twenty million died in India alone. But this would make even those figures seem small. If Phase Three got out, almost two and a half billion people would die over three years.'

'All men,' added Decker. 'You can't fault the logic. Violent criminals cause violent crimes. Violent criminals are men. So no more men equals no more violent crime. Only females and boys with modified genes would remain on the planet. Violent crime, wars and all acts of senseless violence would be wiped out at a stroke by one enormous act of violence. Within a few decades a new stock of peaceful males would grow up and violent men would just be a memory.' He let out a deep sigh. 'You can't say it lacks vision. And, President Weiss, I think they've chosen you as part of that vision.'

Pamela Weiss turned to Luke, a look of horror on her face. 'In that case, can I make them see sense?'

After listening to the others discuss the three phases of Crime Zero it became increasingly obvious to Luke Decker what role the president was meant to play in Madeline Naylor and Alice Prince's brave new world.

Project Conscience wasn't just a precursor to Crime Zero, it had also been a means to get her elected. Although Prince and Naylor planned to stagger the deaths over three years, the logistical implications alone would still be enormous. They needed someone strong and female in charge to provide continuity and prevent the world, particularly the US, from sliding into chaos when the mass deaths began.

'Why haven't Prince and Naylor been arrested yet?' asked Jack Bloom of the Doomsday Committee.

'Because the third disk doesn't say how or where the airborne virus is going to be set off,' said Deputy Director McCloud. 'For all we know they could have numerous devices geared up to go. All we know is that, according to the strict timing plans on the disk, Phase Three isn't due to be released for at least a few more days. Director Naylor is one smart woman. We've got her and Alice Prince under surveillance, but I don't want to jump them until we're sure how to handle them.'

Bloom frowned. 'But they could be releasing it now. Surely the risks of taking them in and neutralizing them are less than letting them run free?'

Decker shook his head. 'I think Bill's right. The only thing in our favour at the moment is that Naylor and Prince don't know that we know. They aren't in any hurry and that's to our advantage. They don't see themselves as terrorists or psychopaths, more as physicians curing a great disease. They've planned this meticulously and won't make any knee-jerk reactions unless we force them to. They don't want to destroy the world; they want to save it. They think they're the good guys.'

'So what do you suggest we do?' asked Weiss. 'Just wait until they save the world?'

Decker smiled. 'No, Madam President, I think *you* should talk with them face to face. They're doing this partly for you, and they want you to help them. Don't alert them that you know anything before the meeting. Use the pretext of the peace plague to call a meeting. Appeal to them as friends. Focus on Alice Prince, and make her realize the human cost of what she's doing. She's the weak link. My guess is that Naylor is committed to this and you won't move her. From what I know Prince likes the concept of Crime Zero, but shies away from the real implications. Is she particularly fond of any of your family?'

Weiss blanched. 'My third son, Sam, is her godson.'

Decker nodded. 'How old is he?'

'He's past puberty, if that's what you mean. Thirteen.' Weiss took a deep breath. 'He would be one of the first to go.'

Decker nodded again. 'Use that. Show her your pain. Make Alice relate your potential loss to the loss of her daughter, Libby. Make her realize, in no uncertain terms, that she would be murdering your child as brutally as Axelman murdered hers. If Alice connects she might help us control Naylor and stop the genie before it gets out of the bottle. She might even help with the peace plague.'

Weiss's face was expressionless, as if frozen.

'I'll meet them both at ViroVector,' she said.

'Good idea,' agreed Allardyce. 'We could cordon off the campus, containing them and any hot agents they might have on site. Then, regardless of how your meeting goes, we'll have them in custody.'

Sharon Bibb tapped her fingers on the table. 'That's all fine and dandy. But surely we've got to assume the worst. We've got to work on a vaccine for the peace plague and Phase Three in case it gets out.'

359

Allardyce nodded. 'The problem is that these are extremely complex recombinant viral vectors. Most of my people don't have that kind of specific experience. Not to find a solution quickly, anyway. This has taken Prince years to develop; we have, what, a few months?'

Bibb sighed in agreement. 'The same at Atlanta. We tend to specialize in combating naturally occurring emerging viruses.'

There was a pause as all eyes looked to Kathy.

'Kathy, how long have *you* worked in this particular area?' asked the president.

Kathy nervously ruffled her hair and Luke could see her shoulders sag, as if suddenly laden down with a heavy burden. 'Almost ten years.'

'With Alice Prince?' asked Sharon Bibb.

Kathy nodded.

'And Crime Zero is based on your work,' said Allardyce, nodding slowly.

'Yes, I'm afraid it is,' Kathy whispered.

Pamela Weiss leaned forward then and looked straight at Kathy. 'I want you to lead the task force looking for a vaccine. Would you do that? *Can* you do that?'

Luke watched as Kathy hesitated and then gave a small nod.

The president then turned to Sharon Bibb and Allardyce. 'You will supply Dr Kerr with all the personnel and resources she needs.'

Both nodded.

'Where shall we base the main biosafety lab?' asked Bibb. 'Atlanta or here at USAMRIID?'

'I'd personally prefer to work somewhere I know,' said Kathy. 'And somewhere there's a large library of relevant samples to hand. How about ViroVector? The Womb there is the most advanced virology lab I've ever used.'

Allardyce gave a resigned shrug. 'Well, we would effectively be commandeering the site after the president's meeting with Alice and Naylor, so taking control isn't an issue. And it's got a slammer, hasn't it?'

'Yes, and a submarine,' said Kathy.

'What the hell's a slammer?' asked Todd Sullivan.

'A biosafety-level-four hospital,' said Allardyce.

'And a submarine?'

'A biosafety-level-four morgue,' said Kathy.

There was a short silence.

'OK,' said Weiss, 'that's agreed. Let's move on.' She turned to Jack Bloom. 'What contingencies are in place if it all goes down the pan?'

Bloom pushed a strand of black hair off his forehead and pulled a sheet of paper from an attaché case beside him. Decker could see the sheet was made of flash paper: one whisper of flame and it would disappear in a puff of smoke. 'Naturally this information doesn't go outside this room. We must plan for the worst-case scenario but present the best case to the media and the public. Panic must be avoided at all costs. Every exercise conducted by any agency in this or any other country involving the spread of an airborne pathogen has shown that once the population panics the shit hits the fan.

'This applies internationally as well. We tell no other world leader the full story about Phase Three until we're sure it has been released. The golden rule is we only give people information if they can do something positive with it.

361

'So the cover story is the peace plague in Iraq. We're helping to find a vaccine, while at the same time taking precautions in the extremely unlikely event that it spreads beyond those borders. These precautions will not be specified, but if they are discovered we'll just put them down to extreme caution.

'Let's start with the bleakest scenario. Fifty-five mass graves have been prepared across the nation, at least one in every state. These have been around for decades and the largest can hold up to fifty thousand people. Most of these are disused mine shafts, quarries and natural caves, but the current capacity won't cover our little problem. So we're already seeking more sites.' He looked up and gave a humourless grin. 'At least Director Naylor and Dr Prince, our two angels of death, allowed time for the dying to bury the dead.

'The key personnel list, including everyone vital to maintaining the nation's basic infrastructure, has been updated. And all those on it have been allocated space in quarantined accommodation. Again our angels of death have thought this through. By ensuring that women are trained to undertake all vital tasks disruption could be kept to a minimum, even if the worst happens.'

Bloom paused and looked around the table at their pale faces. 'Oh, it's not all bad. Not yet, at any rate,' he said drily, giving a sardonic smile. 'On a more positive note, there are numerous contingencies in place to contain this thing and stop it causing any damage.' He turned to McCloud. 'Bill, do you want to run us through what the Bureau's got?'

McCloud leaned forward, his hands clasped on the table. 'Basically it's all the standard stuff, but there's lots of it. On the operation side we've got a squad of hostage-rescue-team trained ninjas on standby in every major city, equipped with full body armour, Racal biohazard suits and enviro-chem sprays. Similar squads will be deployed to secure ViroVector when the president meets with Madeline and Alice. I'm also going to get a team of IT specialist agents to work on taking control of TITANIA.'

The hostage-rescue-team ninjas had impressed Decker when he'd seen them training at Quantico. He hoped they and their armour wouldn't be needed.

As the meeting drew to a close and Weiss confirmed what everyone had to do, Decker allowed himself to think about tomorrow. On arriving here three hours ago he'd called Barzini. Although forbidden to talk of Crime Zero he had been able to tell Joey that he and Kathy were OK. Barzini had told him that Matty's funeral had been arranged for the next day and Decker had said he'd make it.

He turned to McCloud as he rose from the table. 'Bill, keep me in the loop, won't you? I need to go to a funeral tomorrow for a few hours, but I want to be involved in this.'

McCloud patted him on the shoulder and gave a dry laugh. 'Involved? Shit, Spook, you're stuck right in the middle of this thing.'

35

Alice Prince tried to quell the worry gnawing at her stomach. She didn't think it particularly odd that Pamela had asked for their advice on the Iraq epidemic. They were her oldest friends and ViroVector could offer real practical help. She was only surprised that her advice hadn't been sought before. Finding the pulse box in the Womb was worrying. But just because Kathy Kerr now knew about Crime Zero didn't mean that Pamela Weiss did.

Alice sat on Madeline's right at the head of the conference table, and from their vantage point they could see the main door of the Smart Suite. Behind them was the screen-wall, its array of screens and cameras perusing the room.

Whatever Alice felt, Madeline had become so paranoid and had taken such extreme precautions that it made her think the unthinkable. What if the president really did know about their involvement in Crime Zero? The idea filled her with dread.

But if Weiss genuinely wanted help with the Iraq epidemic, then the meeting offered a great opportunity to plant the possibility of what *could* happen in her mind. To ready her for the reality of Crime Zero.

Coiling the pendant chain around her little finger Alice hoped that Madeline's man, Associate Director Jackson was correct in his hunch about where Luke Decker and Kathy Kerr might be today. They had to be taken out of the equation.

A voice on the intercom told them that the president had arrived and would be shown into the room within a matter of moments. Standing, but not moving away from the table, Alice watched two members of staff open the door and show the president to a seat before leaving again. To Alice's relief Pamela made no move to embrace them both, content with a cool verbal greeting. She looked strained, drawn.

To her surprise Pamela had come alone. No advisers. No back-up.

Alice's heart began to beat a little faster.

'How long have we known each other?' asked Pamela with a sad smile. 'It must be thirty years.'

Alice flashed a nervous glance at Madeline, but the FBI director kept her face expressionless.

'Yes, about that,' said Alice.

Pamela nodded. 'And we're friends, aren't we?'

'The best of friends,' said Madeline.

'And I've never lied to you, you know. I have never purposefully deceived you.'

Alice's heart was beating so fast now she was sure that Madeline, or even Pamela at the other end of the table, might hear it.

'And I've never lied to you,' replied Madeline.

'What about all the lies regarding Conscience?'

'They weren't harmful. They were to protect you,' said Madeline. Alice couldn't believe Madeline's calm.

Pamela paused and looked at Alice, those wonderful blue eyes staring right into her soul. 'Did you know that the symptoms of the epidemic in Iraq exactly match those exhibited by Axelman and the other death-row prisoners at San Quentin?'

Alice didn't know what to say.

'I need your help to solve a problem. I'm going to ask you one question, and if our relationship means anything I need you to tell me the truth – both as your friend and your president.' Pamela turned back to Madeline. 'Do you know what is behind the Iraq epidemic?'

Alice felt hot-and-cold rushes down the back of her neck. It was their chance to confess all, to tell Pamela everything and involve her in their plans.

'No,' said Madeline with a frown, as if the idea were preposterous. 'No, of course not. No.'

Pamela turned back to her and Alice thought she saw the glint of tears in her eyes. 'What does my other oldest friend say?'

Alice desperately wanted to say 'yes', but Madeline caught her eye and gave her an icy look.

'No,' said Alice, realizing the consequences of her denial even as the syllable left her lips.

Slowly Pamela nodded, still keeping her eyes fixed on Alice. 'And would either of you do anything to hurt me?'

'Of course not,' said Madeline quickly.

'Or my family?'

'No,' said Madeline.

But Alice found it harder to lie so quickly. 'No,' she whispered eventually.

'So, Alice, help me understand something,' said Pamela. Her eyes were definitely moist now. Alice hated confrontation, especially with her friend, and she was rigid with tension. 'Tell me then, why do you want to murder my husband and sons? Why do you want to kill your own godson?'

Alice gasped, her throat suddenly so tight she could barely breathe.

'Pamela, what are you talking about?' asked Madeline, still calm.

But Alice was far from calm. She began shaking her head. 'But I don't want to murder your family.'

'Well then, Alice, for the sake of my children, and for Libby, help me stop Crime Zero.'

The silence seemed to last for hours. Alice turned pleadingly to Madeline, but she looked just as shocked.

'You must understand, Pamela,' Madeline said, rising to her feet. 'We did this for you.' She sounded angry rather than concerned. 'We can explain everything.'

At that moment the president rose, walked to the door and opened it. 'I want someone else to hear this. Another old friend of yours, who'll understand the science a lot better than me.'

Alice watched as Kathy Kerr walked into the room. The second woman she'd betrayed.

'Tell us everything,' said the president, beckoning for Kathy to stand beside her. 'We're listening.'

36

Hills of Eternity cemetery, Colma, California. The same day. 11.00 a.m

Colma was the world's only incorporated city where the dead outnumbered the living. Just west of San Francisco airport, this necropolis had been home to most of the bay area's cemeteries since 1902, when the city and county board of supervisors had outlawed all burials in the city of San Francisco.

Contemplating this, Luke Decker felt a small shiver as he helped carry Matty's coffin over the rolling lawns of the Hills of Eternity cemetery – one of three specifically Jewish plots in Colma. As a child, a ghoulish teacher had once told him that if all the human dead from the beginning of time were added together the total would still fall short of the billions alive today. He wondered, if the third phase of Crime Zero were allowed to run its deadly course, whether that statistic would still be true.

As they neared the grave Decker and the other pallbearers lowered the coffin. Decker couldn't believe how heavy it was when Matty had been so

368

small. 'You OK?' whispered Joey Barzini as they laid the coffin on the straps to lower it into the earth.

Decker nodded and smiled at the big man. He was touched that in his absence Joey, who was Catholic, had taken it upon himself to contact all of Matty's friends and help to arrange the funeral in keeping with Jewish tradition. Decker had never been a religious man, although his mother had brought him up to follow her husband's Catholic faith. But he took comfort from the fact that Matty was being buried according to his most cherished values.

As is customary, the funeral had been arranged as soon as possible – to allow the healing process to begin. Then, following Kavod Hamet, the Chevra Kaddisha had carefully prepared his body, washing him and dressing him in the special hand-sewn soft linen clothes of Tachrichim before placing him in the Oron, the wooden casket.

Despite his sadness and anger at the circumstances Decker found the funeral and the service that preceded it an oddly joyous occasion. It was a glorious blue-sky day and over 200 people had gathered on the emerald lawns of the Hills of Eternity, including the two FBI agents McCloud had assigned to watch over Decker. At the service a selection of Matty's friends from the San Francisco Symphony Orchestra had played his favourite passages from Paganini and Debussy. At least Matty's funeral celebrated his zest for life as much as marking his death.

As he listened to the Kaddish, Decker felt suddenly alone. And, to his surprise, he thought how much he would have liked to have Kathy standing beside him. It seemed strange that after all they'd been through recently she wasn't there now.

He thought of what his grandfather had always believed in, Matty's conviction that we were far more than the sum of our genes. He recalled the night Matty had comforted him after he'd found out Axelman was his natural father: touching his face, telling him he was a good man; that he was more Matty's grandson and his mother's son than Karl Axelman's – regardless of blood.

In the madness of Crime Zero Decker realized the wisdom of his grandfather's words. A man could be judged only by his deeds. Nothing else mattered. There were influences brought to bear, from the past and the present, but those deeds were ultimately his choice, his responsibility. And for the first time in a long while Decker felt a kind of peace within his soul.

But as the grave filled with earth, hot tears stung his eyes. Decker was not a vengeful man – he'd seen too much and learnt too much to think that revenge brought anything more than fleeting satisfaction and then greater pain. But if he ever met Associate Director William Jackson or his cohorts again he might settle for that.

Blinking back tears of loss Decker didn't see the Chrysler pull up behind the copse of trees fifty yards from the edge of the mourners. Three men were in the car. The face of the powerful man in the front passenger seat was partially obscured as he held a pair of binoculars to his eyes, studying the crowd. Scanning the heads he smiled when he alighted upon Decker's flash of blond hair next to a huge man at the front.

If Luke Decker had turned at that moment he might have recognized the car and realized that meeting Jackson again wasn't going to be a problem.

Associate Director William Jackson had already found him.

Smart suite, ViroVector Solutions, California. The same day. 11.12 a.m.

Standing beside President Weiss in the ViroVector smart suite, Kathy Kerr was shocked by how passionately both women believed in what they were doing. And how desperate Alice Prince was for the president to understand her reasoning.

Madeline Naylor and Alice Prince had known Kathy for almost ten years, and just over a week ago they had tried to kill her. Yet there was no shame in Naylor's eyes, only hatred. Alice Prince wouldn't even look at her. Behind them, on the screen-wall, Kathy noticed the tiny cameras tracking her and the president, as if TITANIA was studying them.

'You must understand, Pamela,' said Alice Prince, standing and leaning forward, as if giving a sermon. Kathy had never seen her so animated. Behind her lenses her eyes shone with frightened zeal. 'Crime Zero is the cure for all the world's violence. Within three years we'll virtually eradicate all violent crime, including war. Surely, Pam, you of all people must realize that, with its weapons of mass destruction, *Homo sapiens* is the

371

one species on earth with the ability for self-annihilation. The Iraq crisis, which almost brought you to the brink of nuclear war, proves that humanity has only one mortal enemy left to fear: itself.

'Years ago we needed men. Apart from reproduction they protected us from predators and supplied us with food and nourishment. Their aggression and drive helped us to develop and eventually rule the planet. But as a species we have become too successful too fast. Evolution has lagged behind. Now that we dominate the earth, men's roles have changed – but men haven't. Technological advances in a host of areas mean that we no longer need their protection, or even their hunter-gatherer role. Physical strength – their key asset – is now redundant. We don't even need them for procreation.'

Alice spoke quickly and fluidly, her words bursting forth in a torrent. Her face glowed, as if she had a fever, and she seemed desperate for Weiss to not only understand her motives but approve of them. Even if the president wanted to interrupt her, Kathy knew it would be in vain. Alice Prince barely seemed to pause for breath. All the time Pamela Weiss stood stock-still, her weight seemingly on her toes, as if standing in a rushing stream, braced against a relentless current.

'Even men's drive, which years ago was such a positive asset,' continued Alice, 'means they aren't content to nurture our position as the lead species and husband the resources of the planet. Now they turn their predatory and protective impulses on each other. Pamela, they are no longer an asset to the species, they're a liability. Over ninety per cent of all violent crimes are committed by men. The rest usually involve them. Virtually every war has been waged and fought by men for no purpose that benefits us. We are a species imploding on itself because men haven't evolved.

'Evolution needs help, and with Crime Zero we can give it. Don't you see? In three years only women and children need exist. All the corrected boys will grow into and sire a new breed of men more genetically relevant to today's needs. Within a single generation the world will be born anew, its future assured. No more violent crime, no more wars, no more mass destruction. Don't you see?'

Before the president or Kathy could reply, Madeline spoke. Her voice was calmer and more pragmatic than Alice's, but still weighty with a searing conviction. Madeine's dark eyes shone like polished jet and her usually pale face was flushed. 'Think about it, Pamela: one purge, one cull and the world will be changed for the better. And it'll happen; we've tested it. After Iraq we know that men will be rendered incapable of violence. Crime Zero Phase Two stopped what could have become the Third World War. We also know that no children below puberty will be harmed. Boys will be allowed to grow into men – but better men. There need be no more rapes, no more senseless murders.'

'No more Libbys,' interrupted Alice.

'We won't need the FBI,' continued Madeline, 'or armies, or weapons. Christ, you wouldn't believe the things I've seen in the Bureau and in the law courts: the abominations men perform for no real motive. Their violence doesn't even bring

373

them any significant benefit. Pamela, Crime Zero is the only way to stop this. We are protecting man from destroying himself. If ever there was a necessary evil, this is it. Can't you see? This isn't about killing people, it's about *saving* them. It's about saving us all.'

'But why didn't you just go with Project Conscience?' asked Kathy, trying to make sense of their insane logic. 'I could almost understand you deciding to unilaterally infect everyone with the Conscience vector. But killing almost two and a half billion people in order to eradicate violence—'

'You're missing the point,' said Alice desperately, as if Kathy *must* understand her. 'Project Conscience was always going to be too little too late. All men alive today are genetically *and* environmentally tainted. Men have become a cancer. They were once healthy cells in the "body human", but now they are threatening the very existence of the species. To cure cancer you must *remove* the malignant cells – and you must remove them *all*, because any remaining cells will spread the disease. We must start afresh with a new wave that will benefit the "body human", not undermine it. We must do this precisely because we don't want to eradicate men. In order to protect them we must help them evolve.'

'Put it into context,' urged Naylor. 'What's a few lost decades and deaths in the grand scheme of things? We've been evolving for thousands of years, and if we act now we'll survive to evolve for thousands more. In thirty or forty years men will see the wisdom of what we've done. They'll live in

374

a more equal, matriarchal society and their aggressive, destructive past will be a bad memory.'

Naylor gripped her hands together. 'Pamela, you can, you *will*, lead the transition. You are currently the only female leader of a major power. You are perfectly placed to lead this country and the world through the transition.'

Weiss's face was grey with shock, as if her old friends were strangers she was seeing for the first time. 'But what about the good men? Not *all* men are bad. What about my husband? What about my sons, Alice? Sam is your godson, for Christ's sake, and he's just reached puberty. How can you justify killing *all* of them? Killing my children won't bring your child back.

Kathy saw Alice falter and look down, sadness creasing her face.

'Everything has a cost,' said Naylor. 'Surely you understand that? Nothing comes for free.'

'Alice, there must be vaccine for Phase Two and Phase Three,' demanded Kathy. 'You create a vaccine for every vector you develop. You've always told me it was good practice in case they mutated and needed to be neutralized.'

'Alice,' the president was almost pleading, 'it's not too late. We can still stop the deaths in Iraq. You can still help end this madness.'

Alice Prince glanced uncertainly at Naylor. Kathy tried to read her look but couldn't.

'There's no cure for Crime Zero,' stated Madeline firmly. 'Crime Zero *is* the cure. And, Pamela, you have to accept that.'

It was too much for Kathy. Instinctively she moved down the table towards the two women. As she walked towards them Weiss turned to the door and opened it. Bill McCloud and four armed men in black body armour entered the room. 'I can't believe I got you both so wrong,' she said to Madeline and Alice. 'How could you ever have thought I would want any part of this abomination?' She turned to Bill. 'Arrest them and keep them under armed guard.'

'You won't stop Crime Zero, Pamela,' said Madeline. 'You can't escape your destiny.'

Alice looked down at her feet. A study of discomfort.

'Oh yes she bloody well can,' said Kathy, standing two feet from Naylor.

Then Naylor opened her right hand and revealed a small black tablet which resembled a TV remote. 'I think Phase Three should start now,' she said.

At that point Kathy lunged for Naylor and the remote.

Or tried to.

Her hand missed and she almost lost her balance. Steadying herself, she took one step forward, knocking into Naylor. Except that Kathy didn't knock into her; she didn't make any contact at all.

In a split second of confusion Kathy looked down and saw the black pad on the floor beneath her and registered that the green light was on.

Suddenly everything was clear. She had used the KREE8 technology herself to present and examine enlarged three-dimensional images of viral-vector DNA molecules. She thought of the guard at the gate and the camera lenses watching from the screen-wall, which allowed Prince and Naylor to see them via TITANIA.

She turned to the stunned McCloud and an uncomprehending President Weiss. 'They're not here,' she said slowly, not wanting to believe what had happened. 'Neither Madeline Naylor nor Alice Prince are physcially here.'

'What do you mean?' demanded McCloud, the blood draining from his face. His men had seen Alice and Madeline enter the campus and were now in charge of the whole site. 'They have to be here.'

'This is a holo-pad area. TITANIA has projected their three-dimensional image from another source.'

'So where are they?' Weiss stared at the hologram, at the smiling faces of her old friends. 'Ali, Madeline, stop this madness. Where in God's name are you?'

'Finishing what we started,' said Naylor, looking at the remote. 'As I speak at least six airports world-wide are equipped to release Crime Zero Phase Three into certain bacteriophage air-purifier tunnels. And I can activate each of them from here.' Then, with a wintry smile, she and Alice vanished.

Kathy put her head in her hands. 'Christ, we've got to find them,' she said. 'They could . . .' She tailed off, not knowing what to say.

But from the look of horror on Weiss and McCloud's faces there was no need to say anything.

Private executive suite, San Francisco Airport,
California.
The same day. 11.47 a.m.

Anger and relief flooded through Madeline Naylor
in equal measure. Anger that Pamela Weiss had
found out about Crime Zero before they could
silence Kerr and Decker, but relief that she'd made
contingency plans. Perhaps Jackson would finish
Decker. That would be a bonus. As she packed up
the three KREE8 3D image-catchers she looked out
of the window at the main concourse below.

'Cheer up, Ali, it's not the end of the world.' She
smiled, fingering the remote, which had activated
the phage air-purifiers. 'It's the beginning.'

But Alice didn't smile back. 'I just wish we
hadn't lied. Perhaps we could have convinced
Pamela if she still trusted us; if she understood
what we were trying to do.'

Naylor shook her head. 'No way. Pamela was
always going to have to be protected from the
truth. She's a democrat, for Christ's sake, a liberal.
She'd never have gone along with this willingly.
But, whether she's willing or not, she has no
choice now. At least we didn't let her stop us.'

It had been Naylor's idea to go into ViroVector
before 6.30 a.m. with Alice to set up the Smart
Suite, and then use their gold-clearance code to
exit via one of the two main inspection tunnels
beneath the campus to their waiting rental-car.
They had immediately driven to the airport and
taken a private executive suite on the mezzanine
level above the main concourse, using one of six
valid credit cards Naylor held in different names.

With a conference room and adjoining bathroom the suite afforded them total privacy.

Then, using the suite's digital phone socket, Alice computer-linked their laptop and the three KREE8 3D image-catchers to TITANIA so that they could appear to sit in the Smart Suite for their pre-arranged conference with Pamela.

'Come on, Alice, we've got to get ready. There's no time to worry any more.' Naylor reached into one of her olive-green shoulder bags, which contained everything she would need as a fugitive, and pulled out the sachets of black and auburn hair dye and some contact lenses. Perhaps in a few years, when the dust had settled, the world would realize the wisdom of what they'd done and they would be heroes. But for now they had to disappear.

Naylor walked to the adjoining bathroom and turned to Alice, who still sat at the conference table looking off into space. 'We've things to do, and we need to catch that plane.'

'Have we done the right thing?' Alice said suddenly.

Naylor walked over to the laptop and clicked on to the departures programme. She checked Heathrow first. The British Airways flight BA344 from Gate 28 was already boarding. It was the same with Sydney, Rio, Singapore, Nairobi and Los Angeles. She smiled a smile of satisfaction. 'Of course we have. Anyway, it's too late to start worrying now. It's out of our control. Evolution has begun.'

37

Hills of Eternity cemetery, California.
The same day. 12.01 p.m.

A prickling awareness of being watched made Luke Decker turn his head. Otherwise he wouldn't have seen the car as he walked back across the lawns to the black Mercedes Joey Barzini had lent him.

The funeral was over. Most of the mourners had left for the wake at Barzini's house, but Decker had wanted some time alone to say goodbye to Matty before he joined them. He'd sent his two FBI minders on ahead, promising to join them in twenty minutes.

Climbing into the Mercedes he adjusted his rearview mirror and studied the grey Chrysler parked fifty yards away behind a copse. There were three men. A dark man sat in the front passenger seat: Associate Director William Jackson.

Gunning the engine into life Decker slowly pulled away, all the time keeping his eyes on the Chrysler. He felt no fear, only a cold sense of purpose. The car behind him wasn't a threat. It was an opportunity.

In his mind he recalled the winding lanes that led out of the vast complex of cemeteries and tried to pick the spot where Jackson would make his move. Then he selected the place he would make his.

He checked the gun in his jacket and clicked his seat belt into place. Behind him he could see the Chrysler pulling closer, but he made no move to increase his speed, keeping to a sedate twenty miles an hour. The road ahead was deserted, and beyond the cemetery gates the main road looked equally abandoned. He and the three men behind seemed to be the only living souls in this city of the dead.

The Chrysler was only a few yards behind. He could see Jackson's face clearly now. He was smiling.

Pulling out of the gates Decker turned right down the main tree-lined artery that cut through the patchwork of cemeteries. Still keeping his speed down to twenty miles an hour, Decker waited for the Chrysler to come closer. He could see indecision on the driver's weaselly face. Did the man speed up and overtake him, or did he pull up alongside, or wait? Jackson didn't seem to be giving him any guidance.

So Decker made up his mind for him. He suddenly braked to a standstill, put the Mercedes into reverse and slammed his foot on the gas.

The impact was bone crunching, but Decker was prepared for it. As the Chrysler stalled and Jackson pulled the driver's head off the dashboard Decker pushed the Mercedes's automatic gear shift into drive and again slammed his foot on the gas.

He'd gone 300 yards down the straight deserted road before the Chrysler started to pursue him. But instead of trying to make good his getaway, Decker again slammed on the brakes, jumped out of the car and walked into the middle of the road. Retrieving his gun, he held it in both hands and locked the barrel on the approaching Chrysler. The car accelerated. He wouldn't miss. He had hit far more difficult targets in practice.

The first bullet took out the front left tyre, pulling the car to the left. He didn't need a second. The Chrysler almost turned on its side as it spun round and hit a large gnarled oak. Decker ran to the wreckage and barely noticed the unconscious driver or the third man slumped in the rear seat. Jackson was fumbling with the door, trying to get out. He had a large gash on his forehead and his left arm appeared to be broken.

Decker opened the door and pulled him out of the car, depositing him on the bruised grass verge. He pushed the barrel of the Sig into the back of Jackson's neck and leaned towards him.

'Why the hell did you have to break his fucking fingers?'

'It wasn't my fault,' Jackson whimpered, his nasal whine incensing Decker. 'Director Naylor made me do it. I had to find you. If he'd told us where you were he'd have been OK.'

Decker tightened his finger on the trigger. 'Well, you've found me.'

'But I wasn't going to kill you. They wanted me to take you to the airport if I found you and Kathy. They called me to—'

A question suddenly cut through the heat of

Decker's rage. 'When did they call you?'

'I don't know. A few hours ago.'

'And you were supposed to take me to the airport?'

'Yeah, to meet them.'

Decker suddenly felt calm, numbingly calm.

Reaching into his left pocket he pulled out his cellphone and called Bill McCloud's number. Before he could say anything, McCloud told him about Naylor and Prince's disappearing act.

'They could be anywhere,' said McCloud, his drawl uncharacteristically strained. 'According to our IT guys they could have pulled off their hologram stunt from anywhere with a digital phone socket. The IT guys have taken control of most of TITANIA, but apparently a whole lot of its higher functions require some other kind of clearance. They're working on it, but until then we don't know where the hell they are.'

'I think I do,' said Decker abruptly.

'Yeah?' McCloud sounded stunned.

'I've got William Jackson here, and he says they're at the airport.'

'Shit. We'll get it closed down and cordoned off immediately. We'll do it from the outside in so we don't alert anyone inside.' Decker heard McCloud turn from the phone and bark an order.

He came back on line. 'We can have the whole airport sealed within minutes. But we've got to get close to Naylor and Prince before they set anything off, assuming they haven't done so already.'

'I've got an idea,' said Decker, 'but I'll need some help.'

'Whatever you need. What do you want to do?'

'The only thing I can: use myself as bait. Prince and Naylor have told Jackson to take me to them.' Decker pushed his gun into Jackson's neck. 'And I'm going to make sure my friend here does exactly what he's told.'

Private Executive Suite, San Francisco airport, California.
The same day. 12.37 p.m.

It took Madeline Naylor completely by surprise. Not one of her contingency plans could have covered it.

She stood in the private bathroom admiring her short, copper-flecked hair with black roots in the mirror above the basin. Her immaculate shoulder-length white hair had gone. Naylor had dyed her hair twice to look like a natural brunette who had coloured her hair. She was pleased with how different it made her look. Blue contact lenses helped the transformation, as did the long floral dress. She rarely wore dresses and never floral prints.

'Your turn, Alice,' she said, entering the conference room.

But Alice hadn't changed. She hadn't even moved.

'Come on, you've done nothing.'

'I know.'

'Well, hurry up! We need to get going.'

Alice frowned and fiddled with the pendant round her neck. She seemed distracted.

'Alice?'

The ringing interrupted her. Naylor went over to the green bags and fished out her cellphone.

'Yes.' She exhaled the word into the handset.

'I've got Decker,' said Jackson. The reception was poor, but despite the static she could still make out his nasal voice. 'You said you wanted him. I've got him at the airport. The new mall construction site on the east mezzanine by the Calvin Klein billboard. It's quiet.'

Naylor frowned. She didn't need this now.

'Who is it?' asked Alice.

'Jackson; he's got Decker.' Naylor spoke back into the phone. 'Kill him.'

'Wait!' shouted Alice suddenly, snatching the phone from her. 'No, leave him. I want to speak to him. Where is he?'

Naylor laughed in disbelief. 'You can't speak to him. Are you out of your mind? There's no time.' She tried to grab the phone back, but Alice wouldn't release it until she'd made her arrangement with Jackson and hung up. Then Alice turned her back on Naylor and rested on the bags.

Naylor was really angry now. She had never seen Alice so defiant before. 'Alice, you aren't seeing Decker. You're getting changed and leaving NOW!'

'No, I'm not,' said Alice quietly, with her hand in her bag.

Naylor moved towards her then, but before she could reach her Alice turned round, a small pistol in her shaking hands. 'Madeline, I don't want to shoot you, but I promise you I will. Just let me go.'

Naylor didn't know what to say; she could only stare at her friend. Alice's round face was red and her eyes were moist with tears. And Naylor had no doubt at all that, if she rushed her, her shy, gentle friend would shoot her. 'I don't understand. What are you trying to do?'

'Step back into the bathroom.'

Naylor did as she was told. 'We've done everything we planned to do. What the hell's wrong?'

Alice closed the bathroom door and locked it from the outside. Naylor heard her take the key out and put it in her pocket. 'I'll come back for you afterwards,' Naylor heard her say through the door.

Naylor couldn't believe this was happening. 'Just tell me what the hell you're going to do, for Christ's sake!

There was a pause and the faint echo of a sob. Then, slowly, in a faltering voice, Alice explained.

And as soon as she did, Naylor lunged at the bathroom door with all her force, trying to break it down.

38

San Francisco Airport, California.
The same day. 12.56 p.m.

Alice Prince could think of no other way but this.
Madeline would understand when she calmed
down. She had to.

Alice walked across the concourse, which
teemed with busy travellers. She looked up at the
Calvin Klein billboard and the unpainted concrete
pillars of the new, unfinished shopping mall.

Stepping over a strip of blue tape and a sign saying, *Construction Work. Please Keep Out*, Alice
opened a door and walked up a flight of service
stairs, negotiating an obstacle course of paint tins
and abandoned ladders.

Alice Prince regretted using the gun to threaten
Madeline. But she'd had no choice. Madeline was
just too dominant. She'd always had a hold over
her, twisting everything around. Ever since they
were children. Ever since Madeline had explained
why it was right to punish Alice's father. Just
remembering that day on the ice made Alice's
chest tighten. It also convinced her that she

was right to do what she was doing now.

The frozen lake close to her house in Baddington is beautiful and Alice loves skating there – except when her father joins her. Alice doesn't know if she loves her father, because when he gets drunk he hits her and her mother. But she's used to it now, so she's embarrassed that her friend Madeline knows.

In January, a week before her fifteenth birthday, Alice goes skating on the lake with Madeline. It's late on a Saturday afternoon and it's so cold her breath almost freezes. The sky is pale blue, and the small lake, lined with neat fir trees, dazzles in the late-afternoon sun. The far end is roped off with a sign saying, *Keep Off. Thin Ice.*

Because of the cold only a few other skaters are on the ice, so they have most of the lake to themselves.

Until her father comes out to join them. She can tell at once that he's drunk because he orders her to skate with him. She tries to leave, but Madeline holds her back. Madeline wears a bright-red jacket with a hood, and her white hair sticks out like icicles. Her dark eyes stare at Alice's father and confidently she skates over to him with Alice in tow. And like two ducklings they follow him round on the ice.

Alice's father is a large man with a red nose and face. His rheumy eyes stare out from under a furry Russian hat that makes him look like an angry grizzly bear. 'Follow me,' he shouts, 'both of you!'

Then he proceeds to describe joyless circles in the ice. Her father is a good skater, and as he goes round he increases his speed. It's a game Alice knows well. Eventually her father will gain such a lead that he will lap her, and when he passes he will push her over, laughing as he exhorts her to go faster.

But today it's different, because Madeline is with her. And, unlike Alice, Madeline is an athlete. She skates like the wind, and as she glides on the ice she tucks Alice into her slipstream and carries her along with her.

The faster her father skates, the faster Madeline goes; and Alice is sure Madeline isn't even trying. She just matches his pace – no quicker, no slower, keeping their distance on the ice. But her father is stubborn. He skates without respite for an hour, trying to close the gap.

As it gets late the lake is deserted by the few remaining skaters. But behind Madeline Alice feels exhilarated and safe. It is like she has wings on her feet, which can take her away from harm.

It takes another ten minutes before he tires of the game, realizing he can't win. The last stragglers have gone and suddenly he stops and points to the unsafe end of the lake.

'Skate by the rope,' he orders. His eyes have that cruel, bullying look she hates. 'Or are you too scared?'

But she's not frightened with Madeline by her side. Then Madeline pushes the game further.

'I'll skate to the *other* side of the rope if you follow me,' she says to Alice's father. 'Or are *you* too scared?'

His expression changes then and he frowns. He approaches them and Alice is scared. Then

389

Madeline turns and, taking Alice's hand, she leads her towards the rope.

'Come back here,' he shouts.

But Madeline just pulls her forward, their skates hissing on the ice. For the first time in her life Alice feels a surge of power. It doesn't matter what he does to her when she gets home, at this moment the fire of defiance runs through her veins.

'No,' Alice yells back. 'Come and get me.'

Then, ignoring the sign, Madeline crouches and skates under the waist-high rope, pulling Alice behind her. Cutting her skates into the ice Alice stops and turns back to her father.

He glowers at her from the other side of the rope. 'Alice, come back here. Do what I say. Now!'

'Don't move,' whispers Madeline beside her. 'You're safe here.' Madeline's eyes are bright and she has an excited smile on her frozen face. Alice looks down and the ice is so thin here she can see the dark water beneath her skates.

Madeline suddenly shouts at Alice's father. 'If you want to hit Alice, you'll have to come here to do it.'

His face reddens with rage.

'Be careful, Madeline,' she says. She knows how vicious her father can be. 'He might hurt you too.'

Madeline shakes her head. 'He won't hurt me. Watch.'

Alice admires her courage, but doesn't like the look on her face.

'We're waiting,' Madeline taunts. 'Or are you too scared?'

He waits for a moment, not believing they can be so defiant. Then he snarls like an animal and steps over the rope. Carefully he rests his first skate on the thin ice and then his second. And when he realizes the ice is taking his weight he gives them a horrible smile. 'Who's scared now?' he says, lunging for Alice.

For a second she's frightened, but then she hears a crack and Madeline pulls her further along the rope, stepping over to the safe side.

It happens in seconds.

One moment he is standing there scowling at her, the next he's falling through the ice, clawing at the side of the hole, trying to pull himself back onto the slippery surface of the lake. She waits for his splashing to stop before skating closer to the breach.

'Pass me the rope,' he orders her. His face is furious, but for the first time ever she can also see fear in his eyes.

She stands and looks down at him, but before she can move towards him, Madeline holds her back. 'Just watch!' she whispers.

'Hurry,' her father cries. 'I can't hold on much longer!' His voice becomes pleading as he realizes she isn't rushing to his assistance. He looks up at her, his hands trying to keep their purchase on the treacherous ice. His eyes now show naked terror. 'Please, Alice, help your papa,' he pleads. 'Help me. Throw me the rope.'

But she can't move. Madeline isn't exactly holding her back, but she legitimizes her inaction. Because looking down at her father and seeing him beg makes Alice feel good. She can't remember how many times he has towered over her, ignoring her pleas.

Still, as she watches his fingers slip on the ice and sees him slide deeper and deeper into the freezing water, she wants to go to him – to help him.

But Madeline is saying in her ear. 'Let him go. Let him slide out of your life. You don't need him. You don't love him. He only brings you pain.' As he sinks he starts to cry, but she can't move. Madeline isn't even touching her, but Alice feels as if she's pulling her back.

'Help me,' he screams in panic.

But Alice is too paralysed to help.

He struggles and tries to scream once more, but he slips further and the water drowns his cries. Alice stands there, watching as her father's flailing body floats under the ice beneath her feet. And as she stares in horror, Madeline takes her hand and leads her from the lake. 'You don't need a father,' Madeline reassures her. 'I haven't got a father. We just need each other. Your secret's safe with me. You've done nothing wrong.'

But that wasn't true. Deep down Alice had always known that she'd done something wrong. Something so evil that ten years ago her daughter had been taken from her as punishment. And all her life she'd been in Madeline's thrall, bound to her by guilt. She had always believed that Madeline must be right about everything; to believe otherwise was to face the truth that allowing her father to die had been wrong. But now she accepted it *was* wrong – like so much else.

When she reached the service door on the mezzanine level Alice paused. Jackson had said he would leave Decker by the Calvin Klein poster. Slowly opening the door she stepped out, ignoring a large sign, '*Please Keep Out. Work In Progress.*'

Turning to her left Alice looked through a break in the advertising boards, over the balcony to the teeming concourse below. At that moment a group of businessmen in dark suits entered through the main doors. They were obviously from some kind of convention and were late for their flights because they stormed impatiently through the crowd, cutting a dark swath through women and children, almost knocking over a baby in a pram.

As her eyes blurred, the milling throng no longer resembled humans at all, but cells in a Petri dish. Some of those cells were good and healthy but others were malignant – male. She imagined the dark, invasive male cells being eradicated and the remaining cells having more space to move. Then she imagined them all moving at a kinder, more peaceful pace, working together rather than struggling against each other. The vision briefly pleased and reassured Alice, but then she looked again and the reassuring warmth left her.

Turning, she saw Decker sitting against a pillar next to the Calvin Klein billboard, just as Jackson had promised. Dressed in a black suit, he was gagged and his hands were tied behind his back. When she looked into his green eyes he seemed more surprised than scared. He kept glancing beyond her, as if expecting there to be someone else.

Bending down to his level she reached forward to pull off the tape that covered his mouth. It wasn't strong tape and it came away easily. His lips were dry beneath it.

'Where's Naylor?' Decker asked. There was no time for subtlety. The whole plan was to have her here, too. If they took Prince, but Naylor was free and she had Phase Three . . .

Alice smiled. 'She's not important. She's safe.'

Decker tried to remain calm. After forcing Jackson to call Naylor, Decker had left him to McCloud's men and rushed here. McCloud had already sealed the airport, and although Decker couldn't see any of the ninjas he knew they were close by, waiting to pounce.

'What have you done with Phase Three?' he asked.

When Alice told him his heart sank.

Then she put her face close to his and explained everything else. As he listened he leaned forward, unsure he was hearing correctly. Then Alice reached for the teardrop amulet around her neck and made as if to bite it.

At that moment Decker saw two FBI ninjas appear over Alice's shoulder, their guns trained on her, anti-virus bleach sprays at the ready.

Suddenly everything slowed down.

Alice followed his eye and snapped a look over her shoulder. She stood up, pulled the amulet from its chain and broke it into two parts with her teeth. One part bore a tiny needle.

The ninjas ran at her.

'No,' he screamed at them. He could see panic in Alice's eyes.

She moved back against the waist-high parapet and slipped backwards. She made no attempt to steady herself, keeping both hands locked on the amulet. Suddenly she was falling over the parapet.

Decker reached for her, clutching at the ruptured amulet, its contents dripping onto the crowd below. His senses heightened, he imagined seeing fine droplets float through the air, beautiful in the refracted light, falling towards people on the concourse below.

'No,' he shouted again, throwing himself at Alice Prince. She spread her arms wide and received him in her embrace as she fell backwards over the balcony.

'Spook,' McCloud shouted behind him, but Decker was falling too. Beneath him, Alice jabbed the ampoule needle into his arm. Below him everyone was screaming.

Alice smiled. Clasping his face to hers, wrapping her body around his. 'For Libby,' she whispered.

Then there was nothing.

Alice Prince's body had jumped with shock when she saw the men in biosuits and with guns. But as soon as she realized it was a trap with no way out her terror left her.

She felt no fear of death. She would soon be reunited with Libby. And she'd done all she could It only seemed right that Decker, the son of her daughter's killer, should be the one.

Even as she positioned herself beneath Decker's body and crashed into the trolley of luggage beneath her, snapping her neck, dying instantly, Alice was smiling.

Madeline Naylor was too late. She couldn't believe it. She stood, stunned, in the teeming crowd, watching the two bodies fall through the air towards her. The sound of the impact was like two heavy mattresses falling onto dry kindling wood: a sickening, cracking thud.

After breaking her way through the flimsy bathroom door she had rushed here, trying to stop Alice and save her from herself. But she'd failed. Her friend was dead. Alice had gone.

Dazed, she pushed through the babbling crowd to see the two bodies lying on a pile of broken luggage. Decker was sprawled over Alice in a parody of two spent lovers. Squinting, she stared at Alice's neck and then turned away.

On autopilot, she registered the ninjas in Racal suits swarming around the bodies with bleach sprays and covering the main exits. Their unworldly appearance added to her sense of unreality. But even now she sensed the danger. Her disguise wasn't foolproof, and they would be looking for her. She had to get out fast. Her mind automatically clicked through all the processes required to close down an airport. She remembered the exercise she'd handled at JFK.

Pulling the green tote bag over her shoulder she pushed her hand inside and reached for the Glock. Then, keeping her hand on its grip, she walked slowly through the large, milling crowds on the main concourse, heading for the service door by the Barnes and Noble bookstore. Most of the ninjas were preoccupied with keeping the crowds from leaving the main exits. No-one seemed to be watching as she stole away into the labyrinth of service tunnels below.

Alice had mentioned once how the AirShield

maintenance men who serviced the bacteriophage air-purifier cartridges had a locker and shower room below the concourse. At the bottom of the stairs she found herself in a large corridor with pipes running along the walls and strip lights on the ceiling. Just as she was about to turn right she saw a sign pointing left towards the service lockers. Six company logos were on the sign; the top one was AirShield.

The door was locked, but it was flimsy and she easily kicked her way in. In the small, dark room she put on an AirShield overall and baseball cap and consulted an airport plan stuck on the wall behind a grimy perspex shield. Bending back the shield she pulled out the map. There was one passageway, which would take her past the baggage-handling area and out under the runways to the perimeter fence at maintenance exit 3C. From there she stood the best chance of escape.

Striding down long corridors beneath flickering spines of fluorescent strip lights, she ignored the few people she passed and calculated how much time she had before the FBI managed to seal the whole airport. Since Jackson's phone call, which was probably part of the trap, McCloud had had ample time to cover most of the main entrances and exits. Exercises she'd run to close down large airports in the past had always taken no more than fifteen minutes. Containing suspected airborne pathogens was more difficult, though. Every man in the front line of containment had to wear full biohazard protection. And men had to be concentrated where the biggest population of passengers was. The outer perimeters were left thin. At least for the first hour or so.

Following the map she saw a large junction ahead, from which all the main passageways under the runway branched out. If she were organizing the containment she would have placed a man there to cut off those routes. Knowing McCloud and the standard procedures, that was precisely what he and his agents had done. Naylor could try to go around or she could use the junction to her advantage.

Slowing to a walk she wiped the sweat from her brow. The large exposed pipes that ran down the right of the corridor were hot, and McCloud would have closed down the air-conditioning to prevent the distribution of contaminated air. Naylor stopped ten yards from the underground junction and rested her green tote bag on the floor. She stood listening for a moment before she heard the two voices. A man and woman. She listened for another minute to make sure they were alone, then she began walking towards the junction. She made no attempt to be particularly quiet. She just walked slowly and calmly: a maintenance employee in overalls going about her daily work.

She saw the eerie figure in the black biosuit before he saw her, but she made no attempt to avoid him.

'Halt, FBI,' said the man when he spotted her. His voice sounded strange through the suit's speaker, like he was on a long-distance phone line. 'Sorry, ma'am, but you can't come this way. You've got to go back to the main building.'

'What's going on?' she asked, roughening her voice, hoping the man wouldn't recognize her. 'I got to go check a thousand things.' She reached into her tote. 'Look, I got a pass and everything.'

The man levelled his gun at her and the female agent came and stood beside him.

'This isn't about passes,' she said. 'You can't go any further. Just go back now. We don't want any trouble.'

'What's wrong?' Naylor asked, feigning fear. 'Why you dressed like that?'

The man lowered his gun and smiled at her through his glass visor. It was a kind, reassuring smile. 'Don't worry. Go back to the main building and everything will be explained to you.'

She shrugged then. 'OK.'

'Take care, now,' said the man, already turning away with his partner.

Naylor's gun was out of her bag in less than a second and both FBI agents – *her* agents – were dead in under four.

Within two minutes she was wearing the female agent's black biohazard suit and using her headset to track the other agents' movements. In just over sixteen minutes she was outside the cordon sanitaire and in a stolen car making her way to the city.

Crime Zero Phase Three was out. But she'd heard something on the headset, something about Alice Prince and Luke Decker, which meant she couldn't rest yet. As she drove she tried not to think about Alice. There would be time enough to mourn her. But first she had to protect her legacy.

PART 3

CRIME ZERO

39

Flight BA186 to Calcutta, India.
Monday, 10 November 2008. 8.00 a.m.

Flight BA186 from London to Calcutta was the first flight carrying passengers infected by a bacteriophage air-purifier contaminated with Crime Zero Phase Three. For everyone on board the infection would begin unobtrusively enough with a slight cough and a cold.

Every virus has a chosen host cell, whether it's the leaf of a tobacco plant in Mosaic disease or the CD4 subset of T-lymphocytes in a human sufferer from AIDS. The genetically engineered Crime-Zero-Phase-Three virus was no different. An airborne virus, transmitted by respiratory infection, the first cells it targets are the lungs. Once it has been ingested it seeks out the relevant target cells in the brain's hypothalamus, the respiratory tracts and, in the case of males, the testes. It then begins to subvert those cells' DNA with its own. Using the genetic clues it finds there, the virus unbundles its own genetic contents for replication within the human host in three different ways.

In the 118 female passengers on board BA186 the virus would generate no symptoms, except the mild cough that would last for a few days and help transmit the infection.

In the thirty-six pre-pubescent boy passengers the cough would be the only uncomfortable symptom. Within days the viral vector would unload a battery of control sequences into target cells in the brain's hypothalamus. These control sequences would fine-tune the seventeen inter-dependent genes responsible for aggression and inhibition in the boys. Their genomes would alter, levels of the inhibiting neuro-transmitter serotonin would increase if deficient or be maintained if naturally adequate. The level of the more stimulating transmitters, such as dopamine and nor-adrenalin, would be modified if too high. Potential testosterone levels would also be managed to within predetermined tolerances. Unknowingly, the boys would be subtly changed. The default of violent aggression would be shifted to pacific co-operation and each would find it easier to 'behave well'. They would exhibit no other symptoms.

In the 210 post-pubescent males the cough would mutate into other symptoms, the onset of which would depend on age. The initial genetic programming would be the same as the boys', and each male would stabilize in this less-aggressive state, in the same way as a person with HIV may stabilize before contracting full-blown AIDS.

Melt-down would be determined by the age-indicative telomeres on the tips of their chromosomes. The youngest would enter melt-down and die within seven or eight days, the oldest in three years.

At the onset of melt-down the virus's dominant genetic code would boost the inhibiting levels of serotonin higher, while instructing full expression of the fuel neurotransmitters and stimulating androgens to kick in, flooding the men's systems.

Immediate physical symptoms of melt-down would include those associated with extreme clinical anxiety, in addition to hair loss, acne and shrinking of the testes. Psychological symptoms would include chronic anxiety, hallucinations, paranoid delusions and obsessive ruminations. Death by brain haemorrhage would arrive mercifully within a matter of days. A proportion would take their own lives.

All of the men on flight BA186 would die in the next three years. But not before each husband, father, brother, son, lover and grandfather had passed Crime Zero to whoever came within breathing distance of them.

Within a matter of days the flight from London to Calcutta would carry Crime Zero to every continent in the world. The number of humans infected would already be in the hundreds of millions. Within a week only the most remote areas of the globe would be uninfected. And then the youngest of the men on the flight would start to die.

ViroVector Solutions, California.
The same day. 3 a.m.

The other scientists were already calling it a loop virus. But to Kathy Kerr it looked more like a

405

hangman's noose, an indiscriminate viral executioner that would lynch all men unless it was stopped. The blown-up photograph from an electron microscope was pinned to the door of the level-one-laboratory conference room in the outer ring of the ViroVector biolab complex. It featured Luke Decker's blood at a magnification of 100,000. The picture was dominated by what looked like a loop with a curled devil's tail. It was the Crime Zero virus, and Luke Decker's blood was teeming with it.

Kathy was still troubled by the clear genetic differences between the virus Alice had infected Luke with and Crime-Zero-Phase-Three virus. But when she'd suggested studying them more closely Bibb and the others had argued that, although Luke remained in a coma, there were more pressing matters to contend with. Prince had probably developed various versions of Crime Zero, and the one she carried in her pendant was simply an earlier version, sharing greater similarities to the Phase-One vector than Phase Three. Despite her nagging doubts Kathy knew she needed to focus on Phase Three.

'A week's impossible. No way!' said Jim Balke, ViroVector's short, scruffy operations director, who ran the large-scale production plant on site. He nervously rubbed his red eyes and took another shot of coffee. 'We're going to have to aim at a more realistic target. We have to accept that people are going to die. Lots of them. We can't do anything about that.'

'But that's the whole reason we're here,' groaned Sharon Bibb. 'To see how we can limit the numbers.' Her dark hair was scraped off her narrow face and the stress showed in her eyes. In front of her an open laptop and piles of paper were evidence of the last few hours' work. On her left the brilliant Schlossberg twins, Mel and Al, brought in from her team at the CDC in Atlanta, scribbled away on charts, showing each other what they were working on but saying nothing as they communicated. It was past three in the morning and all around the room the walls were plastered with sheets of flip-chart paper. Every sheet was covered in brainstormed ideas scrawled by the team.

'But a week's just not long enough,' Jim Balke said again. 'You'd be lucky to do it in a year. Even if we had the vaccine now it would take the pharmaceutical industry six months to produce and distribute enough to treat the US alone. We're not going to have time to test it.'

'For God's sake, Jim,' growled Major General Tom Allardyce, squaring his jaw and rising from his seat to pace round the room. Two other USAMRIID scientists sat at the far end of the table, peering at a laptop, frantically checking oligonucleotide sequences against Crime Zero's genome, searching for clues that would lead to a vaccine.

'Of course a week's too damn short. But we've got no choice. If you want to start accepting death now, fine. But quit moaning. When we come up with a cure other countries will help produce it. Ever since Crime Zero's gone live, the president's informed all heads of state. Each has agreed with the US not to say anything to their people yet, but they're starting to make contingency plans. The Russians have already offered their production facilities and weaponization expertise. Jim, your role is crucial in determining *how* we can scale up production from shake flasks.'

Kathy Kerr rubbed her temples and looked at the flip chart by the door. Two axes were scribbled on it in blue marker pen. A steep exponential curve in red ink ran from the origin of the graph. The horizontal axis represented time – yesterday's date, 9 November, was written in as time zero – and the vertical axis represented the population of men, banded by age. Three black lines connected the red line with the horizontal time line: the first at seven days, the second at one year and the third at three years. By the first line was the scribbled legend, 'Men start dying – 30 million per week.' By the second, '1.2 billion plus men dead.' There were only three words by the third line, 'All men gone.'

She took a deep breath and tried to take some comfort from the calibre of the team assembled around her. Both Sharon Bibb and Allardyce had brought two of their brightest and best with them. As for the pessimistic Jim Balke, who as operations director at ViroVector was responsible for mass-producing serums and viral vectors, in a perverse way Kathy was glad he was being so downbeat: it seemed to fire up the others.

All the team were dressed in surgical greens and not one of them had slept since McCloud's agents had confirmed that an air-purifier tunnel at Los Angeles's LAX airport had been contaminated with Crime Zero, and at least two planeloads of infected passengers had spread the virus. Other major international airports were being checked and Crime Zero had been detected at London's Heathrow, but that was academic. One contamination was enough. Crime Zero was out. The world was hot.

'Let's focus on the main things we've got to do,' said Kathy. She turned to the two USAMRIID scientists working on the laptop. One was a large quiet man with a thick ginger beard called Floyd Harte. The other, Rose Patterson, was a slim coloured woman with huge eyes and an intellect to match. 'For the base vaccine we've got to concentrate on developing antisense oligonucleotides to block Crime Zero's genetic instructions. And yes, that's going to take time. But I still say Alice may have developed one already. She usually did. Once the IT boys have got gold clearance for TITANIA we can look for the code there. We might find a short-cut.'

Kathy looked at Jim Balke. 'And when thinking of how to distribute this vaccine to the world we shouldn't assume it has to be via a syringe, injected individually into every person. What we need to do is fight fire with fire. We need to develop a viral vector that spreads the vaccine for us.'

'Yes, that might work,' said Al Schlossberg suddenly, turning to his twin, Mel. Both virologists were educated at Johns Hopkins; they were both six feet four tall with dark curly hair, round steel-rimmed glasses and prominent Adam's apples. Out of their greens they wore matching bow ties. They were rarely seen apart and were brilliant enough to prove the maxim that two heads are better than one.

Mel seemed to muse on what Al was saying. 'Yes, it could, but we'd need to—'

Al nodded. 'Of course, but if we—'

'Yes, that might do it,' agreed Mel. Both spoke in a deadpan voice and assumed that everyone else was privy to their seemingly telepathic mutterings.

'What might work?' Bibb muttered in frustration.

'Well,' said Al, as if talking about the weather, 'we know that Crime Zero Phase Three uses a toughened influenza orthomyxoviridae virus, genera A, sub-type H2N28, carrying the H2 and N28 antigens on its spikes.'

'It's a good choice for a vector,' continued his twin seamlessly, 'because this genus is most often associated with serious epidemics and killer pandemics. Its drop nuclei are less than four microns in diameter and will remain suspended in the air for hours after being expelled.'

Al resumed, 'Its viral resistance to drying has been improved, so it will keep moist in an aerosolized droplet for longer even than the robust measles virus.' He paused. 'So what we need to do is find, or develop, a vector with even better infectious properties, in order to spread our vaccine through the population as fast as possible. Then, in the same way as Crime Zero spreads disease, we can spread the vaccine.'

'But I still don't see how we're going to be able to make enough of it,' moaned Jim Balke. He was clearly worried how his two large but by no means infinite production facilities at the north of the ViroVector campus were going to produce what was needed.

'But, Jim, that's the whole point,' said Kathy. 'What we have to do is create an infectious vector that distributes itself – a contagious cure, if you like. Crime Zero is spreading via the population. To have any chance of combating it we must make the cure do the same. So the amount we produce won't need to be vast, so long as the vector is both extremely fast and extremely efficient. If the Crime-Zero flu vector is a family saloon, then our vaccine will need to be a Ferrari.'

Kathy paused and checked the notes on the table in front of her. She had to quell a surge of panic when she saw the number of stages they had to cover in order to reach a solution, assuming they could even develop an antidote in the first place. But she forced herself to sound positive. 'Once we have a vaccine and a vector we'll have to splice them together to form a viable vaccine. Once we have that, and Jim's ensured we can scale up production, then we need to get it out there.'

Kathy turned to Tom Allardyce. 'Obviously your people will be helping with the early stages, but your expertise is vital for the weaponization part of the process.'

'Understood,' Allardyce said. 'We're already selecting a cohort of infected volunteers for testing the mass-produced cure. And in conjunction with the British, Israelis and Russians we're working on the logistics of spreading the virus once we have the go-ahead. Obviously it will be dependent on what you guys come up with, but we're already exploring everything from bomblet and warhead design and production to aircraft availability and weather patterns. But rest assured of one thing: if you can come up with the vaccine, then we'll get it out there.'

Kathy nodded, trying to look as confident as he

411

did. That was the damn problem. They had to come up with the cure. She opened the laptop in front of her and began to type in the main action points. 'OK, if the USAMRIID team of Rose and Floyd focus with me on the vaccine, Sharon and Al and Mel can focus on finding a vector. The production issues are with Jim, and Tom has responsibility for the weaponization logistics.' She looked round the room and everyone nodded. 'OK, I propose that we re-meet every six hours to discuss progress and share problems. Anything else?'

'One thing,' said Allardyce. 'What are we going to call this?'

Floyd Harte, a quiet USAMRIID scientist, raised a hesitant arm, like a child in class. 'The way I see it, men all over the world are now effectively on death row. Some have got an earlier execution date than others but they're all going to be dead in three years. What we're trying to do here is get them a reprieve.'

Everyone nodded.

'Well then,' said Kathy, typing her notes of the meeting into her laptop, 'that's what we'll call it: Project Reprieve.'

40

The Fairview Hotel, San Francisco, California.
The same day. 9.17 a.m.

Billy Caruso watched the woman open the swing doors, enter the gloomy hotel lobby and walk across the faded, threadbare carpet towards him. Already he was checking her out. Billy was one of life's spectators and proud of it. In his forty-two years, boy and man, Billy had seen all of life pass through his family's small hotel – the underbelly of life anyway. Nothing shocked him any more, and he prided himself on knowing a person's story just by looking at them.

He divided his clientele in two: those who paid for rooms by the hour – mostly hookers and their johns – and those who stayed longer, often much longer. One guy – said his name was Frank Smith, not that Billy cared – stayed almost a month in room eleven. Then, early last Tuesday morning, Billy had woken to the screeching of tyres followed by three gunshots. Billy knew when to stay out of sight and hadn't called the police or nothing. The next morning he'd shown no surprise when he'd

413

found a large wise guy waiting at the check-in with a bundle of dollars. 'Mr Smith's checked out,' the guy said, handing over the wad. 'His room needs a clean.'

The thing is, Billy had known from the start that 'Mr Smith' was on the lam from the mob. Everything about him pointed that way: the bulging sports bag, the dark glasses, the smell of booze and the shaking hands. But it was when the glasses came off and Billy saw the man's eyes that he'd known the man was living on borrowed time. They were scared eyes, and they looked half dead already.

Watching the woman approach, Billy took another Chiclet from the packet on the scratched check-in desk and began chewing. Billy rarely drank, never took drugs and only took a hooker when his wife was out of town, which was rarer than hearing the Pope fart. Billy got his kicks from watching life, not living it. It was safer.

'So, how can I help you?' he asked with a smile. Like his mama always said: manners don't cost nothing.

'I need a room.'

He studied her closely. She'd dyed her hair a kind of copper colour, but her dark roots showed through underneath. She was tall and skinny, which helped disguise her age. Could be anything from forty to sixty. She carried a fully packed green tote bag in her right hand. She wore a lightweight cardigan over a long floral dress and the obligatory pair of dark glasses. Billy reckoned that at least 80 per cent of his clientele wore dark glasses – which was kind of weird considering how gloomy the lobby was.

'Staying long?' he asked, already guessing the non-committal answer.

'Just a few days.' Her voice sounded shaky.

'Name?'

'Simone Gibson.'

Yeah right, thought Billy, and he was Martin Luther King.

'How you paying?' Again he knew she'd say cash. And, like he'd guessed she would, she reached into her bag and pulled out some notes to give him. Her hands trembled as she handed over the money. She seemed desperate to get to the room. He guessed that if he rolled up one of those cardigan sleeves he would find a network of needle holes. A strung-out junkie. Probably an old pro on the run from her pimp.

Now he had guessed her story Billy lost interest, idly wondering how soon it would take her pimp to find her, or whether she was too old for him to bother.

'Room eleven,' he said, handing over the key, guessing she wouldn't notice the stain on the rug. If she complained he'd just tell her it was ketchup. Popping another Chiclet in his mouth he hoped the next guest would provide more of a challenge. Some people were too damn obvious.

As soon as Madeline Naylor entered room eleven she locked the door behind her and wedged it shut with one of the chairs. Not bothering to unpack, she opened the tote bag and set up her laptop on the rickety desk by the window. She'd stored the car and the stolen black biohazard suit in a lock-up garage.

415

It took her two minutes to plug the laptop into both the power and phone sockets, switch it on and dial up TITANIA's access number. She didn't bother to use her gold-clearance code in case it had been closed down or McCloud's people were monitoring them. Instead she carefully tapped ten keys in the correct order, opening an electronic back door Alice often used to get into TITANIA, giving access to all files. It was doubtful the FBI IT people would ever find this, and even if they did they couldn't use it to trace her.

On the turquoise screen a list of options suddenly appeared. Ghosted into the background, like a watermark, was the ViroVector logo.

Quickly she clicked the search icon at the top of the screen. She had to find the file quickly in case Kerr and the others had managed to get in. She still couldn't believe Alice had done this and not told her about it.

She typed 'Crime Zero antidote' into the search box.

Within seconds a response came back from TITANIA. One file found on secure X drive. Entitled: Crime-Zero-Phase-Three modified anti-sense construct.

Naylor smiled. She could see her face reflected in the turquoise screen. Her fingers danced on the keys as she answered the necessary queries and carried out her command. The urgent task had been done.

Next she called up the ViroVector plans. A map of the site appeared on screen, showing all the above- and below-ground facilities, including the access tunnels.

Clicking the personnel icon she saw a list itemizing everybody on site. A large proportion had the prefix 'visitor' and Naylor guessed that many were agents drafted in to secure the building. Later she could cross-reference some of the names with the FBI personnel database. It would be vital to identify exactly who she was up against. Using the mouse she selected two names on the list: Kathy Kerr and Luke Decker. Kerr flashed red and Decker green. Then she clicked the location icon.

There was a pause as TITANIA checked its door-sensor records, then a red dot flashed in the outer circle of the underground lab facility. As Naylor watched, the dot moved into the centre of the rings as Kerr made her way through the doors towards the Womb. It gave Naylor a sense of power to follow the movements of her prey.

The green dot flashed deep underground, beneath the biolab complex. This dot wasn't moving. Decker was in the biosafety level-four hospital. Watching these two flashing dots crystallized Naylor's mission and the reason why she couldn't flee and sit out the coming years of transition. To protect Crime Zero she had to extinguish both of those dots.

But for now she must rest. She stood and moved across to the bed. It was uncomfortable, but she didn't care. Using the TV remote on the bedside table she switched over to CNN. On the screen a man stood before a crowd of jubilant women waving placards. Most of the women wore T-shirts with slogans such as *Womankind ManUnkind* and *The Fairer Sex is the Only Sex* printed on them.

The male reporter was saying, 'With concern

417

growing that the so-called peace plague has spread beyond Iraq, some factions in the US are actually welcoming the disease, *hoping* it spreads to our shores. So far all documented deaths have been male and some women's groups now see this as a final reckoning for all the centuries of what they term "male tyranny".'

Naylor shook her head. 'Oh, Alice, why did you have to go and do it?' she said. A wave of sadness flowed over her.

As she thought of her friend she watched the women begin to chant. When they put aside their petty allegiances to a particular lover or family member, every woman secretly agreed that men were expendable. Deep down they knew that everything evil in the world came from men; they just didn't want to admit it. 'Ali, everyone would have understood. You would have been a heroine.'

Naylor's eyelids were heavy, but she was at least resolved on a course of action. When she'd rested and made the necessary preparations she would destroy the only remaining threats to Crime Zero. Then the world could start using its energies to build a new future rather than fighting to preserve its diseased past.

41

Kathy Kerr stared at the blank screen, unable to believe her eyes. 'What do you mean it's been deleted?'

Louis Stransky, the tech agent working on TITANIA, gave a pained shrug. 'Like I said, Kathy. We've got gold clearance. TITANIA'S ours now. But the file's gone. There was one there, though, because Alice Prince made a directory. But it's not there now.'

Kathy's shoulders slumped in front of the screen in the level-one conference room. She'd hardly slept for days, only using the bunk provided in the dome upstairs to snatch an hour or two. Since Monday she, Harte and Patterson had been trying to sequence and understand the instructions carried by Crime Zero. Only once this was done could they define and build a safe vacine. But the more they ran the complex iterations on the Genescope, the more Kathy realized they would need more time, a lot more time.

Secretly she'd been banking on using Alice Prince's vaccine. Knowing her methods, Kathy had thought it would only be a question of finding it. And when Stransky had called her in the Womb to tell her he'd gained control of TITANIA's gold clearance she had been convinced the search was over. But it wasn't. The file had been deleted and Kathy didn't know where else to look for a short cut. The only approach left was to continue the painstaking processes required to build safe anti-sense construct from scratch, all the time knowing that tens of millions of men were dying as the time passed.

'Do we know who deleted it? Or when?'

Stransky shook his head. 'Nope. It was a complete delete, no trace. But it had to have been recent or the empty directory would have been automatically deleted too. If you're thinking about Madeline Naylor, I've cancelled her gold clearance so she shouldn't be able to get in now.'

An urgent beeping suddenly sounded, but Kathy was so lost in thought she barely noticed it.

Stransky said, 'Aren't you going to check that?'

'What?'

'It's your pager.'

Blankly she reached down to the pager attached to her waistband. She peered at the liquid-crystal display and for a moment her mood lifted.

Decker was finally awake.

Biosafety-level-four hospital, ViroVector Solutions, California.
The same day. 2.21 p.m.

He had been buried alive. He was about to be reborn.

In the gloom, through the translucent nightmarish walls, he could see white ghosts staring in at him. The rushing in his ears sounded like his own blood flowing in his veins. The smell of chemicals and disinfectant hung in the air.

He was one of his father's embalmed victims, imprisoned in some transparent underground prison. That was why he felt so much pain; why his whole body ached.

He turned to his left, but found it difficult to move. He was wired up to a series of beeping chrome instruments and monitors. The rushing sound came from an air pipe to the right of his head. He rolled over and was rewarded with excruciating shooting pains down his left side, which rose above the general ache enveloping his whole body. The pain in his chest took his breath away, literally leaving him gasping, like he'd been rescued from drowning.

The pain cleared his head and helped him to focus. He was in a bed enclosed in a plastic bubble. To his left, inserted in the plastic wall, was a pair of reversible gloves. His only contact with the outside world.

The bed was the only one in a small, featureless room. The ghost floated to his left, just out of his peripheral vision. Then it stepped closer to him and smiled through a glass face-plate. It told him in a strange distant voice that he was OK and that he should rest.

But it wasn't a ghost at all; it was a woman in a white biohazard suit. Why was she in a biosuit? And why was he in here?

With a groan he compared this dark, surreal waking to all the times he used to wake in Matty's home. No bright sunlight crept in here. He wondered for a moment if he'd ever see the sun rise again. However hard he listened he couldn't conjure up the sound of his grandfather's violin, only the rasping rhythm of the bed's air pump and the dull beep of the instruments that surrounded him.

Despite this he felt a strange sense of wellbeing. Like water settling in a pond his disturbed mind became clearer. He slowly remembered fragments of what had happened: the airport, Alice Prince, the amulet around her neck and the fall. But there was something else, something more important that his fractured memory was edging towards.

42

White Heat Science Park, Palo Alto, California.
The same day. 2.30 p.m.

The emerald-green rented jeep Cherokee pulled up at the top of the rise overlooking the science park and the adjoining ViroVector campus.

Through her binoculars Madeline Naylor could see there were no media vans camped outside, which was good. Most of the TV stations had assumed that USAMRIID in Maryland and the CDC in Atlanta were the focal points for combating the peace plague, and the authorities hadn't disabused them of that. It annoyed Naylor that Pamela Weiss still hadn't announced Crime Zero's release so that people could start preparing for the inevitable.

The science park next to ViroVector had been cordoned off. Police sat by the main gates and no-one was allowed in or out. So she couldn't go in via the inspection tunnels on the perimeter fences as she'd originally planned, but that didn't bother her. After much preparation she knew what she was going to do.

On the back seat of the jeep two bags contained all she would need. And on the passenger seat next to her was a pile of printouts. A woman's face smiled out from a block of text on the top one. Across the header were the words, *FBI Personnel Database. Highly Confidential.*

Just then a black van drove down the main road. The windows were tinted and there was a strange air-filter device on the roof. She recognized it as one of the specially equipped biohazard vans the FBI used to transport agents through contaminated areas. She watched as it turned into the main gate of the ViroVector campus. It stopped by the main dome and she saw three figures in black Racal bio-suits get out. All were female. According to TITANIA's lists of on-site personnel every FBI ninja on duty around the campus was a female agent. No risks were being taken and they wore full protective clothing all the time – not to protect them from contamination, but to stop them from contaminating any of the male project team inside. This way the female agents didn't have to be confined to campus. They could work in shifts and go back out into the contaminated world.

The arrangement suited Madeline Naylor perfectly.

Biosafety-level-four hospital, ViroVector
Solutions, California.
The same day. 2.35 p.m.

Looking at Luke, Kathy bit back her disappointment and frustration at Alice's deleted file. She was relieved Decker had surfaced from his coma and could only guess how bad he felt.

She wanted to reassure him that it wasn't Alice's amulet that had released the virus. In fact, Kathy wasn't even sure how contagious the version of Crime Zero Decker had been injected with really was. He'd only been put in the slammer as a precaution, so he could be nursed through his coma.

Entering the isolation room, she saw him lying in a plastic-enclosed bed, his head swathed in bandages. He looked so alone lying in the bubble, cut off from human touch. She wished she could reach in and rescue him from his disease as immediately as he'd rescued her at the Sanctuary. In that moment, seeing him completely vulnerable, she realized she didn't want to lose him again.

'Hello, Luke,' she said. 'How are you feeling?'

His smile took her by surprise. She wondered what painkillers he'd been given.

'Oh, I've been better,' he said. His voice sounded weak. She had to strain past the ear mufflers protecting her from the airflow in her suit to hear him. Suddenly he frowned, as if trying to remember something. 'Come closer, Kathy. I'm sure there's something I should tell you.'

'Don't worry about it,' she said. 'It'll come to you.' Sitting down on a chair beside the bed she placed her right glove through one of the reversible gloves in the side of the bubble and held his hand. She felt him grip her tightly through the layers of latex. 'Before you try to tell me anything, there are a few things you should know.'

Slowly she explained how Alice Prince and a stack of luggage had broken his fall. Alice Prince was dead, but he'd escaped with a fractured arm, a row of cracked ribs, concussion and some spectacular bruises. Then she told him about Crime Zero; that it was now spreading uncontrollably around the world; that it was just a question of time before the body count started.

As he lay there, she told him Alice Prince had infected him with an earlier version of Crime Zero, and that he had been isolated in case he was contagious and infected the core team working on a vaccine at ViroVector. She reassured him that at his age the lethal stage shouldn't kick in for a year. And by then they might have found a vaccine.

'What about Madeline Naylor?' he whispered.

She shook her head. 'We don't know where she is, but McCloud's convinced she'll be caught.'

As she spoke, Decker frowned and let out a sigh of revelation, as if finally understanding or remembering something important.

'I think you do have the vaccine.' he whispered.

'No, Luke, I don't,' she said. Perhaps she shouldn't have tried to tell him so much. Decker had only just come out of a coma. 'We'll get the vaccine, but I haven't got it yet. There was an antidote on TITANIA, but it was deleted.'

'No, no, it's not on the computer.'

Kathy frowned, not understanding. 'Well where is it then?'

Decker gave her a puzzled smile, disentangled his good hand from hers and pointed to himself. 'I think it's in here,' he said.

It was so clear to Decker now as he looked at the shock on Kathy's face.

Before Kathy could even ask him to explain, and despite his stricken breathing, he told her about his meeting with Alice Prince at the airport.

'She gave me the vaccine, Kathy. She told me so. It was in the amulet. Somehow she realized who she was hurting. She wanted me to say sorry to Weiss and ensure her godson was OK.'

Kathy looked stunned when Decker finished his halting story. He could tell she didn't want to let herself believe it in case it wasn't true. 'But how do you know she wasn't lying?'

'I just know, Kathy. Why would she? She was about to die.'

'But it looks remarkably like a version of Crime Zero. And your genes have already begun changing: your serotonin levels are up and your testosterone and catecholamine levels are being modified.' Then Kathy seemed to think of something. 'But if it was an antidote construct it would work in an opposite way to Crime Zero. And perhaps your early symptoms are—'

'Kathy,' interrupted Decker, 'I don't know what the hell you're talking about. You're the expert. Why don't you just infect me with Crime Zero Phase Three and see what happens? If I've already got the virus then who cares, and if I've got the antidote we might learn something.'

Kathy didn't respond at first.

'C'mon, Kathy, I feel useless in here and this is something I can do to help. So just do me a favour. Give me the goddamn bug and let me contribute to the war effort.'

Calcutta, India.
The same day. 3.11 p.m.

The two Indian boys swimming at the Tollygunge Club were separated by two years of age. The eldest brother, Babu Anand, was fourteen. He had been the youngest post-pubescent male on BA186 from Heathrow. He coughed frequently as he swam.

Four days after infection the Crime Zero virus had unloaded its DNA into the cells lining his lungs and respiratory passages. It had moved to the cells in his testes and the hypothalamus in his brain. Each of these target sites was now an amplification zone, reproducing more and more of the virus's DNA.

His younger brother had also been infected, but he hadn't yet reached puberty. The virus was benevolent. He would be corrected and spared.

But as far as Crime Zero was concerned the older brother was a man, only distinguished from other men by the fatally long telomeres of youth. His life was about to be over before it had begun.

43

Smart Suite, ViroVector Solutions, California. Saturday, 15 November 2008. 2.18 p.m.

Kathy Kerr held up the test tube in her right hand and all twelve pairs of eyes in the Smart Suite stared at it, including those of the US president. There were still two huge issues to resolve, but nevertheless Kathy found it amazing that this inch high sample of cloudy liquid in her hand could contain the salvation of mankind.

'How does it work?' asked the president from the White House. Pamela Weiss's face looked out of one of four separate screens on the screen wall in the Smart Suite. Todd Sullivan, her chief of staff, sat with her. Jack Bloom of the National Security Agency's Doomsday Committee and General Linus Cleaver, the chairman of the Joint Chiefs of Staff, looked out from two other screens, and Director McCloud from a fourth. All were in Washington.

In the Smart Suite itself the rest of the core team sat round the long conference table. The only absentee was Luke Decker.

'The vaccine works on two levels,' said Kathy.

'First it cancels out the harmful DNA instructions being sent by Crime Zero, then it inserts new instructions.' She turned to the screen-wall. 'TITANIA, show the hologram.' Immediately a multicoloured spiral of DNA appeared, rotating above the holo-pad at the end of the table. The rungs that made up the spiral staircase suddenly split and each side of the double helix broke away like a zipper opening. These then linked with another, shorter piece of DNA, with opposing nucleotide bases, to form two spirals. 'As cells divide, the DNA inside the chromosomes splits and re-forms like you see here. Each side of the rungs, or nucleotide pairs, can only bond in a certain way. By using a matching antisense section in the vaccine it tracks down and binds to the sequence of genetic material Crime Zero has changed, cancelling it out.' Again the DNA hologram began to split, but this time a new section of DNA floated in and bonded itself to the unzipping sequence, effectively neutralizing it. 'Once this has been achieved a second section is introduced to re-calibrate the gene expressions back to safe levels.'

'Excellent, but how do we know it works?' asked Bloom. His usually pale face was chalk-white and his eyes were sunken in puffy, dark sockets. Kathy could only guess what he and his team had been doing to plan for Armageddon since their last meeting. 'Have you tested the vaccine yet?' he asked.

She paused before explaining how Decker had received it from Alice Prince, emphasizing that saving Pamela Weiss's family, particularly Alice's godson, had been a key motivator. The president nodded at this, but if she was moved by Alice's gesture she didn't show it. 'When Luke came round he told me what had happened. And, to test whether he did indeed have the vaccine in his blood, he asked me to infect him with Crime Zero Phase Three; so I did.'

'And what happened?' asked the president.

'See for yourself.' Walking to the main door of the Smart Suite Kathy opened it, letting Decker enter and take the seat next to her. His left arm was in plaster and he had a slight limp, but the bandage on his head had been removed. 'Luke is unaffected by Crime Zero,' said Kathy. 'Just as you saw on the hologram, the virus is cancelled out because the vaccine in his blood identifies and repairs any cells affected by Crime Zero.'

There was a sudden spontaneous round of applause around the room. Even Jack Bloom smiled.

'So what now?' asked Pamela when the commotion died down. She looked like someone who had just received good news but knew that there was more bad news wrapped up inside it. 'I assume that little drop of stuff isn't going to save the world?'

Kathy nodded. 'You're right. But before we tackle how we get the vaccine into the population you should be aware of a small twist, which explains why we thought Luke had originally been infected with Crime Zero.' She cleared her throat. Decker knew what she was going to say next and she knew he was pissed off about it. 'This vaccine was developed by Alice Prince, and she's given it an interesting side effect. The vaccine cures men of the lethal effects of Crime Zero, but it also gives

431

them what amounts to a treatment of Project Conscience. Men and boys aren't returned to how they were before being infected. Instead the vaccine modifies their genomes to stay within certain tolerances in a virtually identical way to my FDA-approved Conscience serum – except it affects their germ cells. In essence, all males will become recombinant organisms. They will contain foreign DNA.'

'Meaning what exactly?' asked Todd Sullivan.

Decker answered him. His voice was calm, but Kathy could hear the underlying strain in every word. 'Meaning that you can't save men without changing them for ever. Men, boys and their children will no longer be as naturally violent or aggressive as they once were. In short, men will never be the same again. *I* will never be the same again.'

There was silence for some moments before Pamela Weiss asked, 'How do you feel, Luke?'

'I feel OK, I think. Believe you me I still feel anger and aggression – especially about this. But apparently I'm now instinctively more likely to chose less-violent options. Only time will tell what that means.'

Pamela Weiss turned back to Kathy. 'And what's the alternative?'

Kathy exchanged a quick look with Bibb, Allardyce and the others. 'We've discussed this,' said Kathy, 'and we reckon that, with luck, we could probably create a new antisense construct within a few months – but there's no guarantee it wouldn't have other, possibly worse, side effects.'

'And by then, of course,' said Allardyce, 'we'll

already have lost hundreds of millions of men. Whatever we do people are going to start dying in the next couple of days. This compromise is the only way to save a majority of male lives.'

'And', said Kathy, holding up the test tube, 'the serum we got from Luke is designed to be injected into the patient. Even if we agreed to go with it and accept the side effects it would take us years to produce and distribute enough to inject every infected individual in the world.' She turned to Jim Balke, who was nodding vehemently.

'So', continued Kathy, 'the only way round this problem is not to rely on injections but to insert the antisense DNA vaccine into a genetically engineered viral vector that's spread and caught in the same way as the disease. And that's what Sharon's team has been working on.'

Kathy turned to Sharon Bibb and retook her seat. The twins, Bibb and Kathy had been up most of the night discussing the options. They'd all ended up coming to the same conclusion. Assuming they went with the imperfect vaccine they still quickly needed to find a vector that was highly infectious and was not only airborne but robust enough to survive for long periods in the air. The one vector they all came back to seemed perfect in every way, except for two major drawbacks. The first could be overcome with genetic engineering, but the second was more serious. Their only hope was that Pamela Weiss might know a way round it.

Sharon Bibb stood and brushed back her black hair. Like all of them she looked pale and tired, but there was an underlying strength in her voice. 'In essence,' said Bibb, 'we need to use a vector even more infectious, rapid and robust than the influenza vector used by Crime Zero. This would allow Tom's people, in conjunction with other world airforces, to distribute relatively small amounts of bomblets over major population centres using known weather systems. We could also use the same airport air-purifier tunnels Prince and Naylor used to spread Crime Zero.'

'So, have you found it, yet?' asked General Cleaver. 'This wonder- vector for Reprieve?'

'We think so, but there are two problems with it. Firstly it's lethal − to both males and females. We need to ensure we remove all the virus's harmful genes before replacing them with the therapeutic DNA vaccine. Otherwise we could end up not only failing to save men but endangering women too.'

'OK, let's assume you stop the cure killing the patient,' said Bloom. 'What's the other problem?'

Bibb cleared her throat. 'The virus we need to spread the cure is smallpox, but according to international law it was made extinct back in June 1999. We at the CDC and the Russians at Koltsovo had the only remaining stocks, but now they've all been destroyed.' Bibb paused and looked meaningfully at the president. 'Apparently.'

'What do you mean, "Apparently"?' asked Weiss. 'As far as I'm aware we destroyed all our stocks.'

'We did,' confirmed Bloom. He spoke as if expressing a fact, not an opinion. It was clear he knew things that even the president was protected from. 'The question is: did the Russians destroy theirs? Their biological-warfare programme was always more aggressive than ours and they were

434

frequently caught breaking the Biological Warfare and Toxin Convention of '72 – both by us and by the British.'

President Weiss paused for a moment and then frowned in concentration. 'Let's get this straight. I've got a meeting with the UN Security Council scheduled later and I want to make sure I know what our options are. Basically, in order to stand any chance at all of saving the male population, we're going to have to use an antidote that will genetically alter them for ever – whether they like it or not?'

Kathy nodded, as did Bibb beside her.

'And even if we do go with this imperfect antidote,' continued Weiss, 'the only way to ensure it gets through the population fast enough to save anybody is by getting hold of the smallpox virus, so that you can engineer it to become an infectious carrier of the cure?'

'Right,' confirmed Bibb.

Weiss let out a deep breath. 'OK, I need to speak to the Russian president.'

Allardyce nodded. 'We've already taken the liberty of locating President Tabchov. We've explained that you need to speak to him regarding the crisis.' The fifth screen on the wall dividing the Smart Suite from TITANIA's Cold Room promptly fizzed into life and a heavily jowled face stared out at them.

'President Tabchov, this is President Weiss,' said Pamela Weiss. 'You know the urgency of the situation and there's little time for pleasantries. We need your help with a pressing matter.' Briefly Weiss outlined what had been discussed. She spoke clearly and with a firm grasp of the issues. The Russian premier listened silently, and when Pamela Weiss finished his broad face broke into a half-smile.

'So you wish to ask whether the Russians destroyed their stocks of smallpox as agreed? Or whether we lied?'

'I wouldn't put it so bluntly,' said Weiss with a similar smile. 'Let's just say that any remaining stocks of the smallpox virus need to be located for the benefit of all mankind. Any help in locating those stocks would be to our mutual advantage.'

For a moment the huge face froze on the screen, showing no emotion or expression of any kind. Then it flickered into life again and Tabchov turned to his left. There followed a lengthy heated debate in Russian with an off-screen adviser before the president turned back to face them. Kathy could feel her heart racing, hoping. It seemed contradictory that they were relying on a dreaded disease dating from the Middle Ages to help combat the most technically advanced genetically engineered virus ever created.

'I am sorry,' he said with a slow shake of his head. 'But, despite your obvious prejudices, we did indeed destroy our stocks.' Kathy could feel a palpable slump in the room's morale. 'However,' said Tabchov, raising a large hand, 'a number of our best scientists defected from our virological research programme in the late Nineties. Many were not entirely scrupulous and went for money. We suspect that some took more than their expertise with them.' Tabchov turned again to his unseen adviser, as if to confirm something. 'There

436

is one such person who may have what you seek.' He paused then and the heavy slabs of his face shifted to form a sad smile of acknowledgement. 'What we *all* now seek.'

Sutter Street, San Francisco, California. Sunday, 16 November 2008. 3 a.m.

Lana Bauer always slept naked. She'd done so ever since she was a child. And now she slept like a baby in her apartment on Sutter Street. For the first time in weeks she had the whole weekend to herself. Last night, she'd gone out for a few drinks and actually got drunk.

As she slept she dreamed of her job. It had been even more tiring than usual recently. It was only her third major assignment and it was weird; she didn't know exactly what was going on at the place, but it was important – she knew that much.

The window by her bed was open and the night air blew the curtains into the room. The gentle movement had become background noise, so when the figure on the fire escape outside pulled the window open a few inches more and climbed into the room Lana Bauer barely stirred.

She didn't even wake when a hand was placed over her mouth. Only the click of the gun pierced her unconscious dreams.

She opened her eyes and was alert in an instant. A gun barrel pointed at her right eye and a hand was clamped over her mouth. Above her a tall figure looked down from the darkness.

'I need to ask you some questions,' the figure said. 'I suggest you answer them.'

Two hours later Lana Bauer was dead, a bullet buried in the frontal lobe of her brain.

44

Al Manak baby-milk factory, Baghdad, Iraq. The same day. Four hours later.

The world had turned upside down. Civilians were protecting themselves from their own infected soldiers. Enemies were becoming allies and now plagues of death were offering elixirs of life. But Yevgenia Krotova did not complain as she marched down the long dark corridors of the Al Manak baby-milk factory in northern Baghdad, the cover for the largest of Iraq's seven biological-warfare laboratories.

The recent death of the Iraqi president from the peace plague meant a reprieve from execution for Yevgenia and her family, for failing to cure the disease. But she still feared for their safety. Deaths in Iraq were already estimated in the high tens of thousands, with many more – particularly infected soldiers – dying in the isolated and hastily constructed concentration camps in the desert. The measures were brutal but necessary, and it now appeared that some kind of containment had been achieved.

Yet now the Americans had contacted the new Rais, offering money and help to rebuild his shattered country, specifically seeking access to Yevgenia Krotova's treasures to combat an airborne strain of the disease roaming the world beyond Iraq's quarantined borders. They had warned that a death toll of biblical proportions was only days away, but with her help they could vaccinate the world, including Iraq, against this mystery scourge.

Descending into the hidden labs beneath the factory, the irony that the key to stopping this apocalypse lay with her and the lethal work she had been conducting over the last ten years was not lost on Yevgenia.

After showering and donning her protective suit, she went down into the gloomy maze of concrete storage tunnels where her arsenal of pathogens was kept. Opening a six-inch-thick steel door, disguised to deter UNSCOM inspectors, she walked down another corridor, passing a large room with dented steel walls: the underground testing site for explosive biological warheads. Continuing on to the end of the corridor she came to another steel door. Unlocking this, she found herself in a room surrounded by racks of glass vials. Going to the far wall, she reached up to the top shelf and lifted a rack onto the steel worktable in the centre of the room. Here she examined four vials – her four horsemen of the apocalypse.

The first was Ebola. The second was a toughened, more lasting strain, devised to yield a 100-per-cent death rate. The third was the doomsday virus that had encouraged the last Iraqi president to invade Kuwait and defy the Americans. It was a chimera: a blend of Ebola and other viruses that made it airborne. This chimera had only been possible because of the contents of the fourth vial – a virus so rare it was virtually unique. It was this that had made the Iraqis pay Yevgenia so much blood-money to get her here. And now it seemed as if God, and not the devil, had been looking over her shoulder when she'd smuggled it out of Russia. Holding up the vial she studied the toughened strain of smallpox, marvelling at how this medieval scourge of mankind might become its saviour.

Isolation ward four, Ballygunge hospital, Calcutta, India. The same day. 11.28 p.m.

By day seven Crime Zero had fully established itself in the cells of Babu Anand's hypothalamus and testes.

Because of the fourteen-year-old's youth, the first stage of the virus was short-lived. The telomeres on his chromosomes and the SRY gene on his Y chromosome immediately triggered the final and fatal stage.

The surge of androgens was so fast and high that weeping pustules broke out on his face within hours. His hair began falling out in clumps and his voice deepened.

Rushed to hospital he convulsed in his bed, manifesting physical symptoms of acute anxiety as vast levels of adrenalin began to course through his system. The other brain fuels, dopamine and norepinephrine, which stimulated cerebral activity, also kicked in, rocketing to intolerable levels. Simultaneously the influx of the inhibitor serotonin was now so high that his blood was saturated with monamine oxidase.

His brain was frying in an electrical thunderstorm brought about by massive and conflicting neural traffic, trying to contend with peaking aggressive stimuli while experiencing steel-clawed emotional inhibition. Revving on full power while braking at the same time, his inflamed brain began to rupture as it attempted the impossible task of accommodating these opposing forces.

Hallucinations, terror and guilt dominated what was left of his disintegrating mind.

As his brain imploded, crushing itself, his blood pressure shot up in a shock response known as Cushing's syndrome. This heralded his imminent death. His brain had to have blood to survive, and as the swelling from the inflammation closed off vital arteries the pressure rose further. His body drove its blood pressure higher to meet the rise in brain pressure, in order to force blood into the brain. The resulting terminal spike in blood pressure triggered a series of haemorrhages throughout his body and finally his brain. A haemorrhagic nosebleed marked the point of death.

His final minutes did not go unnoticed by the authorities. Within an hour of his admission to hospital the Indian government's senior medical officers had registered his mystery symptoms, along with the results of various tests. And before

Babu Anand's body was cold an encrypted message was being sent to all the leaders of the world.

Crime Zero Phase Three had claimed its first victim. And it was only the beginning.

45

'Take a look, Luke. It's beautiful,' said Kathy Kerr. In the darkened Womb the electron microscope bathed her helmet and visor in a green aura.

Taking Kathy's place, gazing down into the sub-microscopic cellular landscape, Decker couldn't see any beauty in the virus. The Conscience vector Kathy had showed him earlier looked like a shimmering halo, and Crime Zero was a coiled noose, whereas the Project Reprieve vector looked like a deformed half-moon.

According to Kathy the complex viral vector he was looking at was a hybrid, containing DNA from the antidote in his body and from the smallpox vector they'd received from Iraq. It had been lovingly crafted and was potentially the DNA vaccine with the power to save mankind. But it still wasn't beautiful.

Within an hour of the conversation between the president and the Russian premier, Iraq had been contacted. The new Rais was more reasonable than the last, and because of the crisis in his country he had been more malleable. But he had still been highly suspicious of the Americans' motives, initially refusing to admit they had any stocks of smallpox in the country. Eventually, after Pamela Weiss had promised to help fund the rebuilding of Iraq's infrastructure and cure the plague devastating his country, they came to an agreement.

The real revelation, however, hadn't been the discovery that they did indeed have smallpox stocks, which was a relief in itself, but that Yevgenia Krotova had developed a toughened strain, which she sent them. It was so perfect for their uses that Kathy warned them how if they paused to consider the implications of someone with Krotova's skill helping Iraq's biological-warfare programme no-one would sleep easy again.

The Schlossberg twins had laid much of the groundwork over the last week, and when the engineered virus arrived, Kathy, Sharon Bibb and their teams had been able to shortcut the splicing process, merging the antisense sequence with the smallpox envelope genes. They were now satisfied that all the necessary genetic characteristics were in place and that each of the inserted sections should express their instructions when reaching their target cells. Jim Balke had run off a batch of weapons-grade viral droplets in the pilot bio-reactor, and this was what Decker was looking at now.

'I think we can do it,' said Kathy beside him. Her tired face was aglow with excitement behind her faceplate. 'We've got to test that it's safe and that it works. But, if it does, then we could stop Crime Zero. This is good, Luke. Don't you think?'

'Yeah, of course. It's great.' But he still felt uncomfortable. For the last few days he'd been trying to understand the implications of this 'cure'. He still felt angry that his genes had been changed. He didn't enjoy possessing Axelman's genes, but they were *his*, and he was just coming to terms with them. Now genetics had robbed him of his right to grapple with his own past.

'What's wrong, Luke?' Kathy said, watching him carefully.

'I don't know. You're right; this is the best, the *only*, option. But I can't help feeling it's wrong somehow.'

'How can it be wrong? Assuming this thing works, we'll save all men.'

'That's the point. You won't. At least not men as they were. Men as we know them will still die. I can't help thinking that the survivors will be different people – perhaps better, perhaps worse – but *different* in some way. I'll be different. Perhaps I already am?' He wanted Kathy to argue with him, so that he could get these concerns out of his system. But she said nothing; she just stood there and nodded, as if to acknowledge the point he was making.

'Don't you see,' he went on, 'despite what Alice Prince and Madeline Naylor believe, men serve a purpose. Yes, men are more aggressive than women, and they commit the majority of violent crimes, and they want to dominate rather than negotiate. And yes, they seek sensation and take risks. But it's precisely this drive and aggression that makes them challenge the oceans, the galaxies and everything from religion to unjust rulers. For good or ill, men, *not women*, have been the agents of change and civilization; not exclusively, but for the most part. Project Conscience on hardened criminals is one thing, but taming the spirit of every present and future male is something else entirely. The implications for the future could be disastrous.'

'Surely not as disastrous as what will happen if we do nothing?' said Kathy

'Of course,' he conceded. 'But it still sucks.'

Kathy smiled. 'Look, I know this is a compromise. But I'll tell you one thing, Luke, I'd rather have you here with a few genes changed than dead. And there's something else to consider: this change, whether it's Conscience or the more drastic Crime Zero, will affect civilization more than any other initiative in our history. But it *wasn't* conceived or implemented by men. Perhaps, in a perverse way, this proves that women have more drive than men credit them with? Who knows? Far from being doomed, perhaps humanity will benefit from having both genders share the driving seat for a change.'

Decker shrugged. 'I hope you're right.'

Kathy hoped she was right too. A week had passed since Crime Zero had gone live, and people would soon start dying, and they'd continue to die in increasing numbers, unless the vaccine was released – side effects or no side effects.

Suddenly the door to the Womb hissed open and Kathy saw two blue Chemturion biohazard suits

447

enter. She recognized the wearers as Sharon Bibb and Major General Tom Allardyce.

Allardyce was rubbing his gloved hands together, as excited as Kathy imagined a military type ever got. 'It's all set,' he said. 'We've got twenty infected male volunteers – all military personnel. All have agreed to be exposed to the Reprieve smallpox vaccine. Each has been fitted with a gene-sequence and blood-test wristband. The predictive gene scans and blood readings should tell us if they're in the clear by tomorrow morning. We're already recruiting female subjects, and once we know it works on men we'll test it on them – to ensure it's safe. So, by tomorrow night, assuming all the tests are positive, we might, no, *should*, have a vaccine to deliver.

'Strategic production sites have been set up here, in the UK, Russia, China, Iraq, Brazil and Australia. They are waiting for the go-ahead from our tests and then each will receive a transfer file, giving the full genetic sequence and production spec for the vaccine. In turn, they will supply squadrons of military and commercial aircraft from most major nations, who will bombard every significant population centre on earth with the viral vector. By analysing global weather patterns to harness the airflow effects they have on microclimates we'll be able to target the airborne spread. And this assault will be supplemented by the use of bacteriophage air-purifier tunnels at every major airport. Over the next week we'll blanket bomb the world. Crime Zero will have no place to hide.'

'So you'll only release the samples and gene

sequence of the vaccine once you're sure it's safe and effective?' asked Decker.

'You bet,' said Allardyce. 'For all we know the vaccine could be useless, or worse, lethal. So we're keeping it under strict control until we know it's OK.' He walked over to a white box in the corner of the Womb by the Genescope. It had no monitor, only a series of lights, a large red button and a key-pad on one side. It looked like it had been recently installed. 'This is an SDU, a secure data unit. It's not linked to TITANIA or to any other network until a six-letter code is keyed in and the red button is depressed. Then, and only then, the data stored on its drive will be sent down secure lines to the designated production sites. Until that happens it's effectively a bullet-proof, hacker-proof strongbox for data.

'As well as the data, all the samples, including those produced by Jim Balke in the biosafety-level-four pilot plant area, are now here in the safe or with the test subjects down in the slammer. Effectively every piece of data and material relating to the vaccine now resides here in the central core of the lab complex.'

'In that case,' said Decker with a wry grin, 'if the vaccine works, let's hope nothing happens to this place.'

Allardyce smiled behind his visor. 'I wouldn't worry about that. This is one of the most secure places on earth.'

Kathy was more concerned about timing. 'Can't we test the vaccine faster? You said you had to wait to test it on men before testing it on women. Why?'

Sharon Bibb answered, 'Female volunteers are

449

less easy to find, and frankly we don't want to risk women's lives until we know Reprieve works on men. Crime Zero won't harm women, but Reprieve could, especially if we haven't properly attenuated the smallpox vector Krotova gave us.'

Kathy frowned at this. 'But every minute could be crucial. There are almost 300 million teenage men in the world. The youngest of these will die a week after infection. That means that any time now our youngest males are going to start dropping like flies. We've got to test women now. Each hour represents hundreds of thousands of lives.'

'Hang on a minute,' said Allardyce. 'Wait until we get an OK from the men. If Reprieve doesn't work, or worse, if it kills them, then there's no point in putting women at risk.'

Suddenly the computer by Alice Prince's safe began to beep.

'What the hell's that?' growled Allardyce, turning to view the monitor.

'It's a message,' said Bibb, as Kathy watched the short, terse report come up on screen.

'Shit,' said Decker softly as he read the text.

On the screen was a picture of a young Indian boy. According to the classified report he was the first recorded casualty of Crime Zero and he'd died a little over an hour ago. Time had run out. The death toll had begun.

Kathy made a decision.

46

ViroVector Solutions, California.
Monday, 17 November 2008. 2.12 a.m.

No-one challenged the tall FBI ninja in the black biohazard suit. At the main gate, where her suit militated against using the DNA sensor, she knew the correct personal access codes to punch into the ancillary keypad. Once inside the campus she gave her personal call sign and she knew all the passwords when challenged by central security via her headset.

It was gone two in the morning and the campus was dead. The ninja with the badge marked *Special Agent Lana Bauer* knew from her headset where most of the other agents were and how to avoid them. Hardly anyone passed her as she made her way to the silent dome. And those who did ignored her.

Madeline Naylor felt no fear as she paused outside the dome and adjusted her grip on her bag, only a cold sense of purpose. Ahead of her a scientist in a white coat left the doors of the dome open for some fresh air. He made no move to approach or acknowledge her. It was as if her suit depersonalized her, made her invisible. She'd found Lana Bauer's address in her FBI personnel files. She lived alone and in San Francisco and her apartment had been easy to find. Before she'd died, Bauer had told her all she needed to know about the on-site security, including all the codes and guard movements.

Between one and six in the morning the place was deserted, with people sleeping in the departments in the upper part of the dome. TITANIA was relied on to alert the guards who patrolled the grounds if there was an intruder, but Bauer had said that no intruders were really expected.

Naylor hadn't wanted to kill her, but she'd had no option. Anything else was too risky. She put two bullets in her head, then wrapped her body in a rug and rolled it under her bed. Bauer would be found soon enough, but after tonight it wouldn't matter.

Madeline Naylor thought again of Luke Decker and Kathy Kerr. Alice had told her she was going to give the vaccine to Decker, and Naylor knew Kerr had the knowledge to exploit it. Between them they were dangerous.

Naylor couldn't see how Kathy could stop Crime Zero at a global level, but she might be able to create a vaccine that would seriously limit its impact. And unless Crime Zero was total it was pointless. If some malignant cells remained – however few they were – then in time the cancer would return.

Biosafety-level-four hospital, ViroVector Solutions, California.
The same day. 2.25 a.m.

Kathy Kerr checked the clock on the instruments by her bed. She hadn't slept a wink. Her decision may have been a terrible error.

Since no-one could do anything until the test results on the twenty men had come in, the core team had taken the opportunity to get some sleep in the dome. When they'd gone, she'd stolen back to the Womb and taken a sample of the Reprieve vaccine. Leaving a note by the Genescope explaining what she'd done, she'd come down here to one of the isolation rooms.

She had inhaled the Reprieve smallpox vaccine four hours ago and had been lying in her bubble ever since. Once she learned that the first victim of Crime Zero had died she knew she had to act – to test the vaccine on herself. Because if she was OK, and it worked on the men, they would save time and hundreds of thousands of extra lives. She hadn't told the others what she'd planned because they would try to prevent her. Back then she'd been so sure it was the right thing to do and had felt so confident Reprieve would work.

Now she wasn't at all sure.

She checked the chrome bracelet on her left wrist. A small sensor with a needle on its inner edge monitored her blood and DNA. The bracelet had a liquid-crystal display, with two small windows about the size of a digital watch face. One LCD window would show the status of her blood and the other her genome. Currently both were blank. In two or three more hours the screen would flash with information, telling her if she was OK or if there were complications. Those complications could be immediately lethal or have long-term genetic mutations that would affect her later in life – however brief that life might be.

She knew that elsewhere in the slammer some twenty men were also being tested. But she felt no real kinship with them. They were infected, effectively dying, so taking the Reprieve vaccine was a last resort. She, on the other hand, was under no threat. And she knew only too well the terrible complications that could arise if the genetic vaccine went AWOL and played havoc with her DNA. What she was doing was right, she was sure of it, but the thought of contracting a mutant strain of smallpox, or some awful hybrid of it and Crime Zero, chilled her blood. She felt the urge to scratch her face just at the thought of smallpox bubbling under her skin.

Until this moment she'd had little time to think of anything but fighting the disease. Every waking moment had been focused on that aim and any chance to sleep had been taken without any real thought. But now sleep wouldn't come and her mind was free to reflect on matters beyond the virus. For the first time since this began she felt overwhelmed by the enormity of what had happened – by what *was* happening.

She found it hard to believe that fewer than three weeks had elapsed since Madeline Naylor had tried to lock her away in the Sanctuary. If she died, who would tell her family in England what had happened? Would it matter anyway if Crime Zero ravaged the planet? And what would she do if she survived and the Reprieve vaccine worked? Her dream of Conscience would have been realized in a way far more ambitious and absolute than she'd ever dreamed of or wanted. What would she do next?

By asking herself these questions and dwelling on the future she managed to keep at bay her fear of the present. But only just.

Then she saw the door to her isolation room open and a tall figure in a biohazard suit slip inside. Squinting in the half-light she peered through her creased plastic bubble at the approaching figure. It seemed to pause for a moment, and Kathy craned to see the person's face, but in the shadowy reflective glow she couldn't see into the visor. She tensed when the figure reached for the plastic wall of her bubble. Then, when the helmet turned, she saw the face.

'I thought you'd be doing something stupid like this,' said Decker.

Kathy didn't know what to say.

'Anyway,' Decker said, sitting down on the chair beside her bubble. 'Since you've gone and done it I thought you could do with some company. I know what it's like being stuck in there. It certainly isn't a barrel of laughs.'

47

Decontamination Room, ViroVector Solutions,
California.
The same day. Two hours later.

Sharon Bibb felt exhausted as she pulled on her
blue biohazard suit in the decon room between the
biohazard-level-three laboratories and level four.
The room consisted of a row of lockers, showers
and toilets, and a rack of biohazard suits. There
were two basins at one end, with a row of bleach
bottles and various virus-killing chemicals lining
the wall. It was four thirty in the morning and
everywhere was quiet. After her earlier meeting
with Allardyce, Kathy Kerr and Luke Decker, she
had gone up into the main dome to grab a bite to
eat and a few hours' sleep in the makeshift sleeping quarters set up in the dome.

She'd agreed with Allardyce that at five o'clock
this morning she would check on the twenty male
subjects. Assuming the results were good she
would alert the major general. After presenting
their results to the core team and acquiring

permission from the president, they could then key in the code to the secure data unit and send the protected gene sequence and specifications of the Reprieve vector to the various production sites around the world. Only Allardyce, Kathy Kerr and she knew the code.

She yawned twice. God, she hadn't been this tired since handling the Ebola outbreak in Congo back in '99. She hadn't seen her husband or two kids back in Atlanta for almost two weeks. Just the thought of losing her husband to Crime Zero brought on a rush of panic. The Reprieve vaccine would work. It *must* work.

Instinctively and carefully checking her suit for any tears, she paused in front of the door that led to the central hot zone of the complex, containing the biosafety-level-four labs and the Womb, and the elevator going down to the biosafety-level-four hospital and morgue.

She only became aware of someone else being in the decon room with her after she'd keyed in the six-character password and presented her eye to be scanned through the face-plate of her helmet. With mufflers on her ears to protect her from the suit's rushing air supply she only just heard the rustle behind her. But before she could turn the door began to open in front of her and she felt something hard push into her back.

'Carry on and don't turn round,' hissed a cold female voice behind her. 'I saw you key in the code, so I only need one of your eyes to get the rest of the way. I can either come with you as your guest or you can refuse to co-operate, in which case I'll take out your eye and get into the

Womb alone. The choice is yours.'

Sharon Bibb was too shocked to say anything, and before she could even frame a response she'd been pushed through the door into the glass corridor beyond. Wildly she looked through the glass partitions into the level-four laboratories, but she was alone. Everyone else was up in the dome asleep.

'Go on,' said the voice behind her as they passed the elevators to the slammer and the submarine below, and she was pushed towards the door at the end of corridor.

A wave of relief flowed through Madeline Naylor. She was so close now. The biohazard symbol and the large *Biosafety Level Five* emblazoned on the glass door of the Womb seemed to beckon her on.

After getting into ViroVector, Naylor had patiently made her way to the centre of the biolab complex, using the radio to avoid any other agents. It seemed as if the agents had been placed at all the key points on the perimeter but few, if any, were in the lab complex itself at this time of night – probably to avoid getting in the scientists' way. However, the difficult part was still to come; she had to gain access to the central hot zone of the complex where the Womb was. She didn't have access codes for that and would need retina identification.

Using her knowledge of the labs from the numerous times she had accompanied Alice Prince to the Womb, she made her way through the less-secure outer rings of the complex. As she stole her way from biosafety level one to three, each lab had been a deserted white library of chrome and glass, with only the hum of the apparatus and air-conditioners to disturb the silence. Eventually she had reached the decon room, the gateway to the hot zone, and waited patiently behind the row of lockers for someone to arrive and take her in.

Dr Sharon Bibb – her name was written on the front of her suit – had been that person.

'Go on,' Naylor said, pushing her towards the door of the Womb. 'Open it. I'm right behind you.'

Bibb paused for a moment and Naylor could tell the shock was wearing off and the scientist was thinking of self-preservation.

'Do it now,' she hissed, pushing her gun firmly into Bibb's side, so as not to give her time to think.

With steady fingers Bibb punched the code onto the keypad by the door, then stood still while the laser scanned her retina. As the door slid open Naylor checked her watch. People would start to wake in the next hour or so. She would have to hurry if she wanted to plant the explosive and escape before detonating it. Carrying the tote bag in her left hand she felt the reassuring weight of the device inside; it was small and simple, but would be enough to rupture one of the reinforced glass walls. TITANIA should then go into close-down mode, sealing the hot zone with airtight thermo-resistant sutured panels, containing the level-four and level-five labs, as well as the hospital and mortuary. Then, unless an override code was keyed in from outside, TITANIA would release a shower of viral-killing bleaches and chemicals into the contained area, followed by an ultraviolet light show and finally a firestorm of 3,000 degrees to

459

destroy any living organism in the hot zone. No human, plague or vaccine would survive.

When the door to the Womb fully opened, Naylor pushed Bibb through and followed her in. The first thing she noticed was the recently installed secure data unit. She'd used them often enough in the Bureau. They were only ever used to store data that was too sensitive or valuable to risk being lost or illegally accessed. Copies were rarely made of files in an SDU. It could only mean that whatever progress Kathy Kerr had made on a vaccine was in that box. It was isolated here.

'Now,' she said, dropping her bag on the floor and pressing her gun into Bibb's visor, 'tell me how much progress you've made, and tell me where I can find Kathy Kerr.'

Then she saw the note by the Genescope. It was from Kathy, and it answered all her questions.

Luke Decker woke with a start. At first he didn't know where he was, the glass was so close to his face, and the rushing noise was so loud in his ears. Then he realized he was in a biohazard suit and had fallen asleep in the chair next to Kathy's bubble.

He turned to the digital clock by the bed. 4:47. Quickly he turned to Kathy. She was lying in a ball, her dark hair splayed over the pillow, her mouth half open. He tried to see the bracelet round her wrist but it was obscured under the covers.

'Kathy,' he said. 'Wake up!'

Her eyes opened and she looked panicked for a second.

'How are you feeling? How's the bracelet?'

Her eyes widened and she was suddenly fully

460

awake. She whipped her hand out from under the covers, exposing her bracelet. Both LCD windows, the blood and genome indicators, were green.

'What does it mean?' he asked, suddenly nervous.

Kathy looked at him, a look of disbelief on her face; then she smiled. 'I'm in the clear. I don't know if Reprieve actually works, but it's safe. Green means that the odds of it causing any harm are so low as to be statistically insignificant.'

'In that case,' he said, picking up her discarded biohazard suit and passing it to her. 'Let's get the hell out of here.'

48

Kathy could barely contain a sense of impending triumph as she and Luke travelled in the elevator to the lab complex above. Both wore white hospital biohazard suits. Minutes ago they had rushed to the main ward in the slammer and checked the male test subjects. All were asleep, but their gene readings were showing huge improvements.

Kathy was beginning to believe they could prevent the impending biological cataclysm. She looked at Decker, thinking of how he had come to sit with her last night, and she felt an overwhelming sense of partnership. Together they'd uncovered Crime Zero and fought against all the odds to foil it. And now they were close, so close, to stopping it.

As the elevator doors opened, Decker stepped out and turned left towards the biosafety-level-five door of the Womb. Through the angled glass Kathy could make out part of the interior. The sight of the blue Chemturion biosuit leaning over one of the work surfaces made her quicken her step. 'Look, Sharon's up. Let's give her the good news. Then we'll alert Tom and the others.'

She keyed in the code to the Womb and allowed her eye to be scanned. When the door hissed quietly open she slipped inside, with Decker following close behind.

Kathy didn't understand the strange way Sharon Bibb was leaning against the Genescope at first, so she moved nearer. She saw the bullet through Sharon Bibb's helmet and realized she was dead at virtually the same time as she saw the black FBI biohazard suit. The figure was turned away from her, crouching over what looked like a square steel box in front of the glass-fronted refrigerator, which contained many of the world's most virulent and lethal viruses, including Ebola and Marburg.

Stunned, Kathy froze as the black helmet turned towards her. And though Madeline Naylor's dark eyes looked surprised when she saw her, the one-time FBI director was smiling.

It took Luke Decker a few seconds to take in the situation. Nine yards ahead of him Madeline Naylor crouched over what looked like a small bomb. Four yards behind Naylor, in the no man's land between them, was her bag. And on it was her gun.

Kathy stood to his right. The secure data unit, which contained all the Reprieve vaccine data that now urgently needed to be dispatched, was on his left. But he didn't know the code. Only Kathy did.

He could tell Naylor had weighed up the situation too. She seemed torn between finishing priming the bomb and reaching for her gun.

Kathy looked straight at the SDU, obviously realizing it was vital to send out the data or all would be lost.

For a long breathless moment no-one moved. They just stared at each other.

Then Decker turned to Kathy and, as he dashed for the gun, he shouted to her, 'Send the data. Now!'

Suddenly all three of them were moving as fast as their clumsy suits would allow across the white-tiled floor.

He collided with Naylor as they both lunged for the gun, pushing the bag across the tiles and sending them both clattering to the floor.

Decker groaned as his bruised body hit the floor and his broken arm smashed against Naylor's helmet. Directly in front of him he could see Naylor staring at him with venomous hatred, and to his right he could see the bomb. The black box had a digital display showing the number 9:01 in red digits, presumably a countdown in minutes.

Naylor was now looking beyond him at Kathy, who was standing over the secure data unit, keying the send code into the keypad. Scrabbling to her feet, Naylor kicked his broken arm and Decker heard a bone crack. For a second he could do nothing but writhe in the white heat of agony. Naylor lunged at Kathy, pushing her away from the SDU before she could press the large red send button, which would deliver the transfer files to the production sites around the world.

Gritting his teeth, Decker grabbed the bomb with his good hand, but it was a sealed device with a one-way switch. He was no bomb expert, but even his basic explosives training told him that this was a simple device, designed for ease of use. Once the timer was set the sealed device would go off at the designated time and nothing could stop it. The only way to avoid the explosion was to get the hell out of the way.

Then he saw Madeline's Glock under the safe. It must have been catapulted along the ground when they collided. Pushing his good arm under the safe he tried to reach for it, but his fingertips only managed to push it further away. He changed his angle and gained another inch; just enough to pull it out. Then he heard the sound of glass smashing behind him, and when he turned and aimed at Naylor he realized it wasn't going to be that easy.

Madeline Naylor closed her hands round Kerr's helmet and felt the rage eat into her, twisting her entrails, tightening her chest.

Sharon Bibb wouldn't tell her much before she died, but Kathy's note had explained enough. Naylor had been delighted Kathy was in the hospital suite because then the bomb explosion would kill her. All the data in the SDU and the samples of the vaccine would be destroyed too. And when the bomb prompted TITANIA to close everything down and purge the hot core of the complex, all electronic and organic trace of the vaccine would be destroyed, along with Dr Kerr. It was an ideal solution.

But then Decker and Kerr had entered the Womb.

Decker was injured, so pushing him away hadn't been difficult, but Kathy had almost keyed in the send codes to transmit the vaccine files. It was vital the files didn't get out and that everything was destroyed. So she'd made a decision and

465

leaped at Kathy, pushing her away from the SDU.

Kathy struggled hard, but Naylor smashed the back of Kathy's helmet through the glass door of one of the refrigerators, dazing her and sending row upon row of vials crashing to the ground, releasing every major virus from ebola to marburg to hanta. Madeline held Kathy face-down in a head-lock, her face as close to the virus-drenched floor as her visor allowed.

But now Decker had her gun.

'Put it down, Decker,' she yelled, 'or I'll rip her helmet off. This place is so hot she'll die in minutes.'

'We could all die in minutes,' said Decker with irritating calm. He stood, aiming the gun at her. 'Six minutes now, according to your bomb. Kathy, are you OK?'

But Kathy said nothing. Obviously concussed, Kathy's body felt heavy when Naylor lifted it in front of her as a shield.

Suddenly, through the glass walls, she saw three people in blue biohazard suits rushing down the corridor, through the level-four laboratory to the Womb. Naylor thought through the options, then realized she had no choice. She would die. But before she did she'd ensure this place was destroyed and Crime Zero was protected. Pulling Kathy closer to her she lunged for the lock by the door. There was a hissing noise as two deadlocks slid into place. Now the Womb could only be opened from the inside.

'Decker', she said, 'if you make any move towards the SDU I'll kill her.'

* * *

466

Kathy's silence wasn't helping Decker at all. for a start he wasn't sure whether she'd had time to key the entire code into the SDU – and he didn't even know what the code was. He could only stare at the large red button, knowing that if he pressed it without the full code nothing would happen. And if he moved towards it, Madeline would undoubtedly kill Kathy. Decker's only hope was that she would come round before the bomb went off in five minutes.

Outside he could see Allardyce and the Schlossberg twins pawing the glass, helplessly looking in. If only he could hear them, Allardyce could give him the code.

'I thought you were against violent crime, Naylor,' he said. 'And yet you've already killed more people than most of the murderers I've hunted down. And if you get your way with Crime Zero you'll be responsible for more murders than all men combined – living and dead. My whole gender won't have been as effective at killing as you. Does that make sense? One woman – the head of the great law-enforcing FBI – murdering every adult member of the opposite sex simply because she's against murder?'

'How would you understand?' hissed Naylor. 'Your father raped and killed young girls. Of course you don't see the necessity of purging your own kind.'

Kathy seemed to stir, and through her face-plate Decker could see her eyes trying to focus. If he pressed the red button he *might* save almost two and a half billion men. But he would *definitely* kill Kathy. He had to wait for her to confirm the code.

'Of course I see the need to hunt down and destroy the evil amongst us,' he said to Naylor. 'I've done it all my working life. But a violent criminal is anyone who has committed a violent crime, not simply a man. A violent criminal is someone like you.'

Naylor was visibly rattled, making her loosen her grip on Kathy and focus on him.

He raised his voice now, almost shouting, continually glancing at Kathy as he spoke. 'The real irony is that *you* are the violent scum you're so against. You should purge yourself rather than anyone else.'

Naylor gave him a venomous smile. 'It doesn't matter what you think now. In a few minutes this place, and everything in it, will be destroyed. Crime Zero will prevail. My only regret is that I won't be able to experience the benefits. But that's a small price to pay to know that all your meddling has been in vain.'

Suddenly Kathy spoke. 'The code's in,' she said. 'Press the button.'

For a second Decker looked at her, then at Naylor.

'If you make one move towards it I'll kill her,' Naylor said.

The deal had changed. Pressing the button would save the lives of millions, *billions* of men. It would also kill Kathy. Logically the choice was simple, but this had gone way beyond logic. In that instant he realized how much she meant to him, and what he was about to lose. But he also knew there was no choice.

Outside the Womb a crowd of scientists had

468

gathered, frozen by the scene in front of them.

'How strong's the glass in here?' he asked.

'Very,' said Kathy.

Before Naylor had a chance to react, he moved his good arm, took aim at the red metal button on the SDU and fired. For a moment Naylor's concentration was broken and Kathy managed to tear herself from Naylor's grip. She lunged for the door. Naylor threw herself at Decker, her eyes narrow with rage, her voice shrill like a wounded beast. 'No!' she screamed. 'No!'

He only had time to see the green light go on beneath the keypad, telling him the data had been sent, before Naylor was upon him. She tore at him as though possessed, pushing him to the floor and knocking the gun from his hand. Behind her he could hear Kathy press the release button on the door's dead bolts and call to him.

'Luke! Luke!'

'Go,' he shouted, 'leave me!'

Pushing Naylor back with his strong arm he raised himself to his knees. To his left he saw the small bomb. A minute remained on the timer's countdown. In anger he reached for it, clutching the black box in his gloved hand, and then, as Madeline Naylor came for him again, he brought it crashing down on her face-plate, smashing the hardened plexiglas. Rising to his feet he could hear her screams mingle with the hiss of air escaping from her helmet. Kathy was beside him now, pulling him towards the door.

'Come on,' she shouted. 'I'm not leaving without you.'

But behind him he could see Naylor staggering

to her feet, her demented eyes already red from the contaminated air. In her right hand she held a shard from her face-plate, which she wielded like a knife. He had to reach the door, but he knew that just one rupture in his suit from her blade would mean death. Kathy had the door to the Womb open, and only seconds remained on the bomb. Making one final surge he pushed forward, sweeping Kathy ahead of him, through the doorway and into the corridor beyond. Allardyce and the others were there, pulling them out and away. Turning back for a split second he saw Naylor make a final lunge at him, her eyes ablaze with hatred, missing by inches as the door sprang shut, crushing her outstretched arm.

Madeline could not believe it. Sitting on the floor of the Womb she wheezed in the foul, contaminated air and stared at her crushed arm. She didn't care that she had only seconds to live before the bomb detonated.

This wasn't how it was supposed to be. Her vision of Crime Zero was ruined. Many men would die – millions perhaps – *but not all of them*.

In her mind, if just one adult male survived Crime Zero then the purity of her vision was tarnished. Eradicating all men was a great deed that would ensure the survival of the species. But to kill some was little more than a sordid act of murder.

She was suddenly racked with remorse. Not because she had killed so many men, but because she had killed so few.

And as she heard the bomb's detonation switch

470

click, she cried out in pain and frustration, realizing she had changed nothing.

But even as her body was ripped apart by the explosion and TITANIA sealed off the hot zone, purging it of all life with chemicals and heat, Madeline Naylor was wrong.

She had changed everything.

As he catapulted himself out of the Womb, Decker was dragged by Allardyce down the corridor towards the door leading out of the hot zone, to the decon room and safety. The steel door seemed to take an age to open and even longer to close again. But standing beside Kathy and the others in the decon room, he heard and felt the explosion rip through the centre of the complex and saw TITANIA instantly bring heavy black screens down over the door through which they had just come, sealing in the hot zone before purging it from within.

Decker's last image as Kathy began to spray bleach on his suit in the decon showers was of Naylor's eyes staring at him. He would remember the hatred he saw there for the rest of his life.

49

Pentagon War Room, Virginia.
Sunday, 23 November 2008. 11.06 a.m.

The vast chamber of the Pentagon War Room dwarfed the Smart Suite at ViroVector. The floor was filled with lines of computers, at which uniformed men and women sat processing information. The vast front wall, which seemed to curve like the horizon, was over fifty-feet high and twice as wide and it was tiled with screens. The central one was ten feet wide by eight feet tall and showed a projection of the world.

The other, smaller screens had legends beneath them indicating the location. Many showed United States Airforce airfields in the States and abroad. There was some footage from the news networks around the world, but the rest showed the airforces of other nations, including Britain, France, Israel and even Iraq, all focusing on one shared mission.

Since the Reprieve vaccine had been dispatched six days ago to all the production sites across the world, all subsequent test and production trials had been successful. Under Major General Allardyce's stewardship the necessary bomblets were produced to the correct specification. And, pending approval, a global armada of aircraft was assembled to distribute the vaccine.

Three days previously, at a UN meeting in New York, Pamela Weiss had outlined the risks and benefits of the planned vaccine to all the world leaders. She had also announced the latest death toll from the airborne Crime Zero. Globally it was already in the millions – a generation of young men just out of puberty had died. No country had been spared.

There was some debate about the long-term implications of the side effects, but all agreed that the benefits far outweighed the risks. For the first time in the history of the United Nations every country, without exception, regardless of politics, religion or historical enmity, had signed the resolution. Following the proposal, agreement was reached in a record fourteen minutes.

No precise figure was placed on the global armada, but it was confidently estimated to exceed half a million commercial and military aircraft. It was the largest bombing mission the world had ever seen, and many optimists predicted it would be the last.

As the first bomblets were dropped, the map on the vast central screen erupted with tiny red pin-pricks. London and Paris glowed red, followed by most of mainland Europe. The United States and Canada were soon the same, as was South America and the vast tracts of Africa and Asia. The dots were small on these larger, less populated lands, concentrating on the major cities. But the dots grew and distorted in line with the prevailing winds, spreading the vaccine far and wide. Soon the dots merged into each other, creating almost blanket coverage.

As Kathy Kerr stood with Luke Decker at the back of the chamber in the raised viewing area she shook her head in disbelief.

Nothing would be the same again. Just as the spreading red represented salvation it also represented a revolution – or perhaps a self-inflicted evolution.

Man had changed irrevocably, had been forced to evolve, in effect creating a new species. *Homo sapiens* was dead. A new man was being born.

'What will the future bring, Kathy?' Decker asked, staring at the screen.

She took his hand and smiled at him. 'I don't know, but I hope it's good.'

He squeezed her hand in his. 'God! So do I. So do I.'

EPILOGUE

San Francisco, California.
Wednesday, 23 November 2108.

The man was old, but the house was older. He lay down the violin and moved his chair closer to the open windows that overlooked the bay. The celebrations were starting in earnest now. The sky was a riot of fireworks which lit up the night. The children had probably already joined the crowds down by the bridge. He could have gone too, but he preferred to stay here and look up into the sky.

He turned and wheeled the telescope by his side to a better angle. Looking through the glass, the multicoloured explosions were almost blinding in their intensity. It seemed strange to celebrate the Pax Centennia – the hundred years of peace – with explosions. There had even been talk of digging up the ancient armaments and building huge bonfires – beacons of peace.

With stiff legs he stood up from his chair and walked to the ancient piano. Of all the photographs, one stood out. It showed a smiling couple holding a baby in their arms. An old church loomed in the background and a striking, familiar-looking woman stood beside them. The picture made him smile with pride. Not many people could claim to have had a US president at their christening. He studied the picture and wondered what they would have made of the last hundred years – his hundred years.

There had been much talk this year, on the centenary, of The Change. Not so much of the costs – eighteen million young men had died; the equivalent of three times the number of Jews who died in the Holocaust. That was ancient history now. Instead, many World Council members made presentations evaluating its benefits. Most were happy to have enjoyed an unprecedented period of global peace and prosperity. However, some lamented that technological progress wasn't what it used to be without the catalyst of war, that Blake had been right when he'd said there could be no progress without conflict.

His father, Luke, used to tell him stories of a different world, of hunting down men so evil he could only imagine them. But he also used to talk of adventure and courage and the honourable desire to fight for what was right. Even his mother, Kathy, often used to speak of the *need* at times to fight for what you believed in.

He moved back to the telescope and pointed it to the heavens, past the puny human pyrotechnics to the majestic planets beyond. He focused on Venus and then the nearest star, Proxima Centauri, a mere twenty-four million million miles away. He imagined what someone there would see if they aimed their telescopes at earth. A medium-sized planet, orbiting an average star in the outer suburbs of an ordinary spiral galaxy, itself one of a million million galaxies.

A shadow passed over Proxima Centauri and his old shoulders trembled. Suddenly he saw the universe as no more than a vast world: the galaxies, its continents; the planets, its countries.

In his mind's eye he looked at earth from space again. He saw a lone planet, rich in resources. A peaceful, decent planet that had risen above the base need for aggression.

He saw a planet which no longer knew how to defend itself.

THE END

THE MIRACLE STRAIN
by Michael Cordy

'*Jurassic Park* meets the quest for the Holy Grail meets *Raiders of the Lost Ark*'
Mail on Sunday

A heart-pounding international thriller of retribution and redemption. One man battles for the life of his daughter in the face of seemingly unbeatable odds. But to save her he must first reach for the ultimate knowledge . . .

Doctor Tom Carter, surgeon, geneticist, husband, father, needs a miracle. As the inventor of a revolutionary machine, the Genescope, he has the power to read a person's genes, predicting the onset of disease . . . their lifespan . . . their future.

But at the moment of his greatest triumph, the Nobel Prize for Medicine, Carter's world is shattered by the assassination of his wife. He knows that the killer's bullets can only have been meant for him. In the aftermath of her death, a scan reveals that his daughter Holly has an incurable brain disorder and less than a year to live. Even the most advanced cnventional science cannot save her. Something more radical is required.

A secret brotherhood, two thousand years old, may have the answer. They need his new technology to complete their own sacred quest. In return they offer Carter the chance to look beyond the genes of man . . . and into the genes of God.

0 552 14578 5

SHADOW DANCER
by Tom Bradby

'Taut, purposeful and above all else human . . . a compelling story of love and torn loyalties . . . Exceptional'
Daily Telegraph

Colette McVeigh: widow . . . mother . . . terrorist. A woman who has lived the Republican cause for all of her 29 years. A woman whose brothers are both heavily involved at senior levels in the IRA, whose husband was killed by the British security forces. A woman who is now an informer for MI5.

Apprehended by the police in an aborted bombing attempt in London, Colette is given two choices: talk and see her children again or stay silent and spend the rest of her life watching them grow up from behind the bars of a prison cell.

Unwillingly she is led to betray her past by her young MI5 handler, David Ryan, who always knew where his loyalties lay. But when he follows Colette across the Irish Sea to Belfast, the values are quickly sacrificed on the pyre of the province's history. And, as he watches Colette put herself in increasing danger to keep her side of the bargain, he realises that his professional integrity is irrevocably and fatally compromised . . .

'A remarkable first novel . . . Bradby handles the tension with skill to produce a gripping tale'
The Times

'The best book on the northern conflict since *Harry's Game* . . . An excellent read on any level'
Irish Independent

0 552 14586 6

A SELECTED LIST OF FINE WRITING
AVAILABLE FROM CORGI BOOKS

14168 2	JIGSAW	*Campbell Armstrong*	£5.99
14169 0	HEAT	*Campbell Armstrong*	£5.99
14496 7	SILENCER	*Campbell Armstrong*	£5.99
14497 5	BLACKOUT	*Campbell Armstrong*	£5.99
14645 5	KINGDOM OF THE BLIND	*Alan Blackwood*	£5.99
14646 3	PLAGUE OF ANGELS	*Alan Blackwood*	£5.99
14586 6	SHADOW DANCER	*Tom Bradby*	£5.99
14578 5	THE MIRACLE STRAIN	*Michael Cordy*	£5.99
14654 4	THE HORSE WHISPERER	*Nicholas Evans*	£5.99
14495 9	THE LOOP	*Nicholas Evans*	£5.99
13275 9	THE NEGOTIATOR	*Frederick Forsyth*	£5.99
13823 1	THE DECEIVER	*Frederick Forsyth*	£5.99
12140 1	NO COMEBACKS	*Frederick Forsyth*	£5.99
13990 4	THE FIST OF GOD	*Frederick Forsyth*	£5.99
13991 2	ICON	*Frederick Forsyth*	£5.99
13678 6	THE EVENING NEWS	*Arthur Hailey*	£5.99
14376 6	DETECTIVE	*Arthur Hailey*	£5.99
13691 3	WHEELS	*Arthur Hailey*	£5.99
13699 9	HOTEL	*Arthur Hailey*	£5.99
13697 2	AIRPORT	*Arthur Hailey*	£5.99
14717 6	GO	*Simon Lewis*	£5.99
14591 2	REMOTE CONTROL	*Andy McNab*	£5.99
54535 X	KILLING GROUND	*Gerald Seymour*	£5.99
14605 6	THE WAITING TIME	*Gerald Seymour*	£5.99
14682 X	A LINE IN THE SAND	*Gerald Seymour*	£5.99
14723 0	FIELD OF BLOOD	*Gerald Seymour*	£5.99
14722 2	HARRY'S GAME	*Gerald Seymour*	£5.99
14391 X	A SIMPLE PLAN	*Scott Smith*	£5.99
10565 1	TRINITY	*Leon Uris*	£6.99
14047 3	UNHOLY ALLIANCE	*David Yallop*	£5.99